Betrayed

"Do you know a Christine Adelle Lowell Jackson?"

The name Jackson meant nothing; the name Lowell meant everything. Even after all this time, Christine Lowell inspired memories that Gray had fought long and by whole measure to eradicate. He'd known that he was playing with fire—a lowly gardener didn't fool around with the lofty daughter of his rich employer— but, from the moment she'd seduced him, he'd been lost, as lost as a sinner on the streets of Heaven.

They had spent one hot summer as lovers, exchanging fierce kisses, their bodies struggling in the heat of passion to say what they either would not or could not give verbal expression to. For all his silence, however, Gray had understood only too well the warm feeling that swelled within his heart. He'd stupidly thought the same feeling swelled within Christine's.

What had really stunned him, frightened him, was just how quickly that warmth had turned into something cold and hard and unforgiving.

NIGHT MOVES

Sandra Canfield

Bantam Books
New York   Toronto   London   Sydney   Auckland

Night Moves

A Bantam Book / June 1996

All rights reserved.

Copyright © 1996 by Sandra Canfield.

Cover art copyright © 1996 by Gabriel Molano.

For information address: Bantam Books.

ISBN 0-553-57433-7

Published simultaneously in the United States and Canada

Bantam Books are published by Bantam Books, a division of Bantam Doubleday Dell Publishing Group, Inc. Its trademark, consisting of the words "Bantam Books" and the portrayal of a rooster, is Registered in U.S. Patent and Trademark Office and in other countries. Marca Registrada. Bantam Books, 1540 Broadway, New York, New York 10036.

PRINTED IN THE UNITED STATES OF AMERICA

OPM   0   9   8   7   6   5   4   3   2   1

NIGHT MOVES

Chapter 1

Gray Bannon, his hands buried deep in manure-rich soil, heard someone approaching. Footfalls, clean and crisp, called out on the concrete walkway of the greenhouse. Gray frowned. It was barely seven o'clock on a Friday morning. Most of Atlanta's population was still en route to work, many too sleepy or insensitive to see the subtle shades of green on this spring-filled May morning. So, what had brought this caller out so early?

A *swish* told Gray that the individual had passed by, perhaps even tangled with, one of the many fan-shaped fronds of a palmetto palm. Another second or two, another turn or two, and the man—he was fairly certain it was a man because of the rhythm of the footsteps—would come into view.

Gray pushed from the balls of his sneakered feet, stood, and waited. With each *click-click-click* of the visitor's heels, an odd, disturbing cadence began to build. Disturbing because there was a fatalistic quality to it, a premonition that seemed, like the sword of Damocles, to hang precariously in the air.

Shaking his head, Gray gave a small smile. Lord, he was going to have to give up those late-night horror movies. Plus the cold pizza and warm beer.

No sooner had Gray concluded this than a man, with dark hair and features, wearing a suit and sunglasses, appeared at the table of ivies and ferns. From there, he wended his way past the pink-blossomed weigela, cornered his way past the dramatically veined caladiums, dodged a newly arrived shipment of petunias, their velvet flowers ranging from white to rose to purple, and stopped directly in front of Gray. From instinct, Gray swiped his hands down the front of his jeans, dislodging some of the dirt, but none of the smell.

"Gray Bannon?" the man asked in a voice underlaid with authority, and an East Coast accent.

Gray thought he'd been right about that disturbing feeling. It definitely had no foundation. Aside from the fact that the man looked totally out of place in this sultry, hothouse setting—a fine sheen of sweat had already broken out across his brow—he in no way looked sinister.

"Yeah, I'm Gray Bannon," Gray answered. "What can I do for you?"

"Mr. Bannon, I'm Agent Terrence Carrelli." As the man spoke, he whipped out identification in such a practiced way that it was obvious he'd performed just this introduction hundreds of times.

Agent? What kind of agent? Hoping to answer this, Gray glanced at the proffered credentials. This only led to more confusion as he read the words *Federal Bureau of Investigation*. The FBI? What did the FBI want with him?

"What's this about"—Gray looked again at the man's name—"Agent Carrelli?"

After repocketing the identification, Terrence Carrelli removed his sunglasses, perhaps in a gesture intended to evoke intimacy. However, what the apologetic something in the man's eyes managed to do was rekindle the fatalistic feeling Gray had experienced earlier, a feeling justified by the words that followed.

"I'm sorry to have to be the bearer of bad news."

Gray tensed for the unknown "bad news," although he couldn't even begin to imagine what it might be. His was a simple life of hard work and scattered pleasures, centered around the small nursery and landscape company he'd started ten years before. There was not even family to lend to his vulnerability.

"Your daughter has been kidnapped."

Gray took in the statement, let it settle, then gave a sigh of relief. "Look, there's, uh, been some mistake. I don't have a daughter."

An expression flickered across the agent's face, strongly suggesting that Gray wasn't going to like what he heard next. And, sure enough, he didn't.

"Do you know a Christine Adelle Lowell Jackson?"

The name Jackson meant nothing; the name Lowell meant everything. Even after all this time, Christine Lowell inspired memories that he'd fought long and by whole measure to eradicate. He'd known that he was playing with fire—a lowly gardener didn't fool around with the lofty daughter of his rich employer—but, from the moment she'd seduced him, he'd been lost, as lost as a sinner on the streets of Heaven. They had spent one hot summer as lovers, exchanging fierce kisses, their bodies struggling in the heat of passion to say what they either would not or could not give verbal expression to. For all his silence, however, Gray had understood only too well the warm feeling that swelled within his heart. He'd stupidly thought the same feeling swelled within Christine's. What had really stunned him, frightened him, was just how quickly that warmth had turned into something cold and hard and unforgiving.

"Yeah, I know her," Gray said.

The agent now looked downright uncomfortable, as though he preferred to be anywhere but where he was, as though he preferred most any other tidings to those he must deliver.

"I've been authorized to tell you that you do, indeed, have a daughter. She's nine years old, her name's Amanda, and she was kidnapped yesterday afternoon."

Gray stared at the man as though he'd spoken in a foreign language, one Gray didn't understand.

Terrence Carrelli allowed a few seconds' pause before continuing on. "Mrs. Jackson wanted you to know this, but she wanted me to impress upon you that you were free to do what you chose."

"Meaning?" Gray wondered if he sounded as bewildered as he felt. Yes, that's what he was, bewildered, and numb. Other feelings would come, probably all too soon, but for now he was blessed with an emotional inertia.

"I interpreted that to mean that should you choose not to become involved, she would understand. However, should you wish to return to Natchez, she wanted me to tell you that you would be welcome at Rosemead."

Under other circumstances, Gray might have had a good laugh. Him welcome at Rosemead? Ten years ago he'd been run out of town on a rail, with the warning that he was never to return. The warning had come on the heels of a beating that, by all rules and regulations, should have killed him. It hadn't. But it had left scars, both physical and emotional. Neither had healed prettily.

"In fact, sir," the agent added, "the family's private plane is at the airport. If you'd like, you can accompany me back."

"You tell the family to take their private plane and shove it up their asses," Gray said. "And you can tell *Mrs. Jackson* . . ." He halted, then said, "On second thought, don't tell Mrs. Jackson anything."

Terrence Carrelli nodded. "Yes, sir."

"Why is she telling me this now?" Gray heard himself asking.

"You'd have to ask her that." Silence, followed by, "I'm sorry. This is a lousy way to learn that you're a father."

The sympathetic tone of the man's voice was oddly comforting, and Gray decided on the spot that Agent Carrelli was not only a good agent, but probably a decent human being. As he thought this, he watched as the FBI agent replaced his sunglasses, then started back down the path he'd only minutes before negotiated.

"Is the child going to be all right?" Gray called out. He was well aware that he'd said *the* child, not *his* child, but he couldn't yet think of this child in a personal way.

Agent Carrelli turned. Gray was certain that he saw a grimness in the man's mouth, a grimness echoed in his next words. "I really couldn't say."

Gray appreciated the honesty of the response. It had taken courage not to dodge the ugly truth, and courage was something that Gray admired. Still, like all else he'd recently heard, the bleak, blatant response would sink only so far in and no further. And so, Gray simply stood, rooted to the spot, until the agent disappeared from view. Gray followed his fading footsteps, still crisp and clean, but now possessed of a finality. Soon they paled altogether, leaving the peaceful silence to approach once more.

So normal was the silence that Gray actually entertained the notion that perhaps he'd only imagined the scene that had just played itself out. Suddenly, though, his legs grew weak and wobbly. He had no choice but to ease onto the brick ledge of a nearby aquatic garden. There he sat, beside a pool inside which a fat, lazy goldfish swam in and out among the reeds and grasses and the large-leafed water lilies. A fountain gurgled, a bird, white-winged and watchful, warbled from a trellis overburdened with the claret blossoms of a climbing rose. Gray neither saw the fish, nor heard the fountain or bird. He was too concerned with feeling nothing. He'd just been told that he had a daughter, and yet he felt nothing. The reality of a child simply wouldn't compute.

Are you sure you're protected?

Yes. Gray had heard Christine answer, amid sighs and pants of pleasure. *I wouldn't care, though, if I did get pregnant. I want to have your baby.*

No, no! Gray had protested, and yet he could remember how alluring that thought had been. A baby would make them a family, something that he could but barely remember having. There'd be a ring on Christine's finger, a little white vine-covered cottage somewhere, and he'd help to bathe, and change, and feed their child. He'd even get up in the night and rock it when it cried. He'd sing soft lullabies the way he remembered his mother singing them to him. Even then, as seductive as the fantasy had been, he'd known that there would never be a ring on Christine's finger, no white vine-covered cottage, no child.

But there had been a child.

No ring.

No cottage.

But a child.

She's nine years old and her name's Amanda.

"Amanda . . ." Gray whispered, trying on the word for size. It didn't fit, and so he repeated it, as though doing so would give substance and shape to something still too formless to be anything more than mind shadows. It did.

Abruptly, an invisible fist punched Gray hard—once, twice, thrice—in the solar plexus, splintering the shock like a shattered mirror. At the same time, the invisible fist knocked the breath from him, emptying his lungs of oxygen and replacing it with a piercing pain.

He had a daughter.

Sweet Jesus, he had a daughter! he thought as he raked his dirty fingers through his hair. An honest-to-God daughter. What did she look like? Was she anything like him? What did nine-year-old girls think, feel, do? And what were the repercussions of having a child in his life? Now, after all these years of a safe, solitary existence?

How did he feel about this child he once would have welcomed with open arms? Nothing. Gray still felt nothing. Wasn't he supposed to feel something? Shouldn't there be some paternal bonding? Surely, though, that could come only with time.

Time.

That was the one thing that might well be denied him, for Agent Carrelli had made it plain that he couldn't guarantee the child's safety. Quite possibly, Gray had been denied the child, not only in the past, but for all time to come. Quite possibly, he might never know this child personally. And he had the child's mother to thank for that. Anger and fear—he thought of every horror story he'd ever heard in regard to a kidnapping—fought for equal footing, but, ultimately, anger led by a step.

Damn Christine!

Damn her for making him think that she had really cared!

Damn her for making him believe that she had been different from the rest of her family!

While it might be too late for a great many things, it was not too late for one. It was not too late to confront Christine. He would have an answer as to why she'd kept this child from him, even if he had to fight his way through all of Natchez and half of hell!

Christine, a stuffed and very worn rabbit clutched to her chest, stared out a window of the formal living room of Rosemead. In front of her stretched a sea of emerald-green lawn, its every slender blade of grass lavished with care, its every rosebush, of which there were many, resplendent from the same precise attention. It was not at lawn or gardens that Christine peered, however, but rather at the elm-lined drive that began at the white wooden gate barely visible from where she stood. She knew the winding path that drive took, as it passed a copse of magnolia trees, then the rose gardens, and the enormous live oak that grew so near the mansion, finally curving into a semicircle in front of the grand gallery.

Yes, she knew that drive, with its every twist and turn, not only because it had been recorded in her heart by years of living at Rosemead, but also because she had looked at little else since the evening before. She had kept the tiresome vigil—the calves of her legs cramped with fatigue—throughout the long, dark night, hoping, praying, to see the headlights of a car that might herald the return of her missing daughter. Now, by the early afternoon light of this seemingly endless day, she watched for the same sign. Though she considered herself a strong woman, she could not bring herself to use, to think, the word *kidnapped,* although everyone around her had said it with a shocking frequency. No, she preferred the word *missing,* for it allowed her to pretend that Amanda had merely been mislaid and that some kind soul would find her and return her eventually. Even so, pretense would carry her only so far, which left nightmarish questions to claw at unguarded moments.

Was Amanda hungry? Thirsty? Was she scared? Did she understand what was happening to her? Had she been mistreated?

This last question caused Christine to break out in a cold sweat. Closing her eyes, she hugged the rabbit closer, needing to feel the warmth of something, of anything, against her. She forced herself to take a deep, cleansing breath, knowing that she had to keep her wits about her. For Amanda's sake, if not for her own.

The house was filled with people, many of them strangers wandering from room to room, but little conversation made its way to her ears, for everyone spoke softly, as though there had been a death.

Was Amanda dead?

How odd that she could use the stark word *dead,* but not the word *kidnapped.* She desperately wanted whoever had taken Mandy to call, as promised in the single note they'd received. She wanted to beg—she was prepared to cast all pride aside—for the safe return of her daughter. Even so, she'd been strong enough not to ask the FBI for meaningless reassurances.

No, Christine thought, Mandy wasn't dead. She would know if her child, her baby, were dead. From the moment Mandy had been born, there had been a special bond between them, one she had shared with only one other person during the whole of her thirty-two years, and she had sacrificed that person so cruelly, so unconscionably. Her only consolation was that she had hurt herself far more than she ever could have hurt him.

She had tried hard not to overly question Agent Carrelli about his meeting with Gray. Even so, she had come away with the feeling that, aside from Gray's anticipated astonishment, Agent Carrelli was reluctant to disclose details. She'd concluded that he was trying to spare her feelings, which meant only one thing: Gray was angry, evinced by the fact that he hadn't returned to Natchez on the plane with the agent. And there had been no indication that he intended to return at all.

"Here, drink this," came a voice at her side.

Christine opened her eyes to find her friend Nikki offering her a mug of a steaming something.

"You have to keep your strength up." Nikki, her eyes a vibrant shade of green, her blond hair bobbed about her oval face, smiled. "If I have to take this soup back, Esther's going to whip both our butts."

Christine couldn't manage a smile, but she did take the mug. Nikki was right. She had to keep her strength up. And there was no brooking Esther Hawkins, who at fifty-four had spent thirty-five service-filled years at Rosemead. For a long time, Christine pretended that Esther was her mother. For a longer time, she'd wished Esther had been. Before that there had been the adolescent fantasy that her mother had been a Gypsy who'd sold her into the Lowell clan, a fantasy supported by her wild black hair and bold gray eyes, neither of which was shared by any other family member.

"Drink," Nikki ordered.

Christine brought the mug to her lips and sipped. The robust taste of homemade tomato soup rushed across her tongue. Despite herself—how long had it been since she'd had anything to eat or drink?—Christine acknowledged that it tasted good. So good that guilt instantly consumed her. She looked at her friend.

"What if Mandy's hungry?" she asked. "What if she's scared and calling for me? What if they've hurt her? Dear God, Nikki, what if they've hurt—"

"Stop it! You can't afford to entertain those kinds of questions. They'll kill you. And we can't think beyond getting past just this moment. We're going to take it one second at a time. Okay?"

Christine heard the switch from the pronoun *you* to *we*. That, more than anything else, symbolized her relationship to Nikki. They had become friends the summer both had struggled to turn a turbulent sixteen. From that moment on, she and Nikki Janowitz had been bosom buddies, a friendship that had spanned the years, seeing both of them through college and troubled marriages, and, finally, Nikki's divorce.

Slipping her arm about Christine's shoulders, Nikki guided her toward a nearby chair. "You sit down and rest."

Christine balked. "No, I—"

"I'll keep the vigil," Nikki said. "I'll tell you the second I see anyone coming down the drive."

Christine acquiesced, slipping into the softness of the overstuffed chair. Relinquishing the mug to a companion table, though she held firmly to the rabbit, she laid her head back. In the background, she could

hear the muffled voices of the FBI agents. Although
the FBI was in touch with local law officials, it had
been decided to keep Amanda's abduction as quiet as
possible, on only a need-to-know basis, for the safety
of the child, to prohibit weirdos from coming out of
the woodwork, to keep in-coming telephone calls to a
minimum. The telephone had been tapped and Christine was advised to answer it when it rang. So far, the
calls had been few and of no consequence. Until now,
she had managed to handle her impatience with some
degree of dignity, but she had no idea how long that
dignity would last.

Deliberately channeling her thoughts elsewhere,
Christine brought her gaze to rest on her friend, who,
true to her word, was standing watch at the window.
"Are you disappointed in me?" Her deception regarding
Amanda's parentage extended not only to Gray and her
husband alike, but to everyone in her circle.

Nikki glanced over at her. "No," she said without
hesitation. "Only in myself. I should have guessed. All
the signs were there. I just didn't put them together."

"No one suspected."

"I wasn't just anyone. I knew what you and Gray
had was the real thing, and I do admit I thought it
strange that you married Peyton so quickly. That
should have been my first clue."

It was difficult for Christine to be reminded of what
she and Gray had once had. Not that she'd forgotten,
or ever would. No, she'd remembered every time
Peyton had kissed her, every time he'd made love to
her, every time she'd pretended to make love to him.

"As for you and Peyton," Nikki continued, "I knew
you two had your problems, but I guess I thought all
married couples did. My own marriage was hardly
idyllic."

"As I said, no one knew," Christine responded.

She wondered what her deceased parents would have thought about her revelation. They would have been mortified, shamed, disgraced. Public opinion, maintaining their place in society, was all that mattered to the couple. She had never been close to either of them and for years had called both by their given names. She and her father had managed to extend, if not a whole branch, at least a few olive twigs toward each other, but Christine didn't delude herself. Much of her father's peace efforts were rooted in pragmatism. As his health had begun to fail, he'd been forced to rely upon his daughter, especially regarding business. She'd always been a major stockholder and, as such, had sat on the board of directors of Lowell Enterprises, but more and more she had assumed the responsibility of running the company. At her father's death, she'd discovered that she'd been named president of the company, while her brother, Claiborne, had been made vice president.

The irony of it wasn't lost on Christine. Claiborne wanted the presidency, while she had it and didn't want it. As for her announcement concerning the fact that Gray was Amanda's father, he'd been horrified. The blue blood of the Lowells had been tainted with a blue-collar virus.

"Have you heard from Sandy?" Nikki broke into her thoughts.

Sandy Killian was Amanda's nanny and always picked her up after school and stayed with her until Christine came home in the evenings, now from Lowell Enterprises, but earlier from the antique shop she and Nikki co-owned, and which Nikki single-handedly ran now. Because she'd been a few minutes late the day before, Sandy blamed herself for what had happened. So much so that, ultimately, she'd had to be sedated.

"No, but the doctor said that it would take a while for the drug to wear off." Christine sighed. "I know they want to talk to her again, but I don't think she knows anything more than she's already told them."

Silence, then Nikki softly asked, "Still no word from Peyton?"

Christine shook her head. After her confession that he wasn't the father of the child he'd raised as his, Peyton Jackson had been incredulous, crushed. Had he been any other man, he would have stormed out in a heated rage. Instead, he had simply walked out of the house without saying a single word. Which had made her feel all that much worse. The truth was that Peyton had been both a good husband and a good father. His only mistake had been that he wasn't Gray.

"He'll be back," Christine said. "Peyton always does the noble thing." The self-deprecating tone of her voice couldn't conceal her opinion that she lacked Peyton's nobility.

"Don't be so hard on yourself," Nikki said. "We all make mistakes."

"Some of us make bigger ones than others."

"Why tell the truth now?" Nikki asked. "Why didn't you just leave everything the way it was?"

"Funny, according to Agent Carrelli, that's what Gray asked."

"So, what are you going to tell Gray when he shows up?"

"*If* he shows up."

"Do you want him to?"

Christine jerked up from the chair. "What I want is for this nightmare to end. Dear God, why doesn't someone call!"

She was well aware that she had no idea how to answer. Neither did she have the slightest idea why she'd told the truth. She'd told herself the grim circumstances demanded it, yet how did she explain the fact that the need had been there before the demand?

An hour later, Christine got her wish. Someone did call. A woman wondering if anyone at that address could collect for the heart fund. Christine politely declined, then took her place back at the window. She counted leaves on the trees, the gathering clouds in the once-clear sky, and wondered where her daughter was. At a little before four o'clock, Sandy Killian called saying that she was on her way over.

Ten minutes later, the telephone rang again. This time Christine was not so eager to confront disappointment, and so she let it ring until all eyes in the room were focused on her. Slowly, she crossed the carpet and, on a signal from one of the agents, picked up the receiver.

"Hello?"

She listened to the man's soft voice, as he stated his mission with clarity. With each word, Christine's hand tightened about the receiver until her knuckles gleamed white. Finally, without a word, she hung up. Everyone watched, waited, and when she offered up nothing, Agent Carrelli, who'd monitored the call, spoke for her.

"Someone wanted to clean the carpet." There was no mistaking the empathy in his voice.

One of the agents swore.

As for herself, Christine merely made her way back toward the window and to the bunny she'd left perched in a corner of the chair. As she reached for the toy, with what she realized was a shaking hand, the doorbell in the distant foyer rang. Sandy, Christine thought idly. Moments passed before she heard Nikki call her name.

Christine turned.

She saw him at once. He stood in the doorway, strong and tall and with a self-possession that had always characterized him. Discounting worldly possessions, few or many, Gray Bannon owned himself, so completely that she had no choice but to envy him. She had done so years before; she did so now. She likewise had had no choice over the years but to wonder how those years had changed him. In the shadows of the doorway, he looked older, perhaps bolder, but very much as she'd remembered him. That fact comforted her.

And then he stepped forward.

Like a magnet, the scar on his cheek drew her attention. It puckered the flesh in an almost perfectly straight line that had its beginning at the left corner of his mouth, traveled the contour of his jaw, and disappeared into the hairline just beneath his ear. She had assumed he would have a scar. But she had also assumed that it had faded over the years.

The sight of it sickened her. How could one human being be that cruel to another? She fought, with every ounce of strength she had, the urge to cross to him and trace the marred skin with her fingertips, as if by doing so she might erase the injury and all that had led to its being there.

I'm so sorry, something whispered deep inside her. *For the scar and for so much more.*

She raised her eyes to his, hoping to say with them what fragile words could not. She never got the chance. Instead, she got caught in the cold blast of his own silent conversation, and her heart froze. She had expected his anger. She had never forgiven herself for her actions, the first cowardly and leading so irrevocably to the reprehensible second, so why should he? She had not, however, expected hate.

She wondered how she could have been so incredibly naïve.

Chapter 2

"Why did you keep her from me?"

With each mile, the question had become more pressing until Gray now heard himself blurting it out. Angrily. Part of his anger had to do with the fact that he felt as though he'd stepped back into the past. She had changed so little. Her black hair, unfettered and falling in waves about her shoulders, coupled with the silver-colored eyes that he'd thought he'd forgotten, reminded him of the Gypsy heritage she'd so proudly claimed. The dark hair had always suggested a wildness, while the contrasting fair eyes seemed uncannily capable of seeing straight through to one's soul, especially his. Above it all, just for a second, he could have sworn he smelled the redolence of rose, a scent he'd always associated with her. But the fragrance ebbed, as did his journey into the past. She might look the same, but she wasn't.

In answer to his question, Christine said, "Perhaps we would have more privacy in the library."

She walked toward Gray, past him, and after handing Nikki, whom Gray recognized, a stuffed animal, Christine paused at the door, waiting, like all Lowells, for her wishes to be met. Her haughtiness rankled Gray, even as her suggestion forced him to realize that the room was far from empty. A number of law-enforcement types, local and federal, including Agent Carrelli, were staring at him. Christine was right. What he had to say had to be said privately.

Gray followed Christine's lead, across an ebony marble floor which shone as brightly as the cut-crystal chandelier overhead and which threw back his footsteps as though he were inside a mausoleum. All the while, he noted that Christine had a grace and poise, a composure, that she had lacked ten years before. What had happened to the wonderfully rambunctious child he'd once known, the one who could trip over her own feet, who could outrace the wind, who was always poised at the edge of a giggle? What had happened to the daring and uninhibited young woman that child became? They entered the library, filled with family portraits and smelling of polished wood, polished leather, and, above all, polished manners, and Christine closed the door behind them. Without a word, she walked toward the bank of windows, where she stood with her back toward Gray.

Gray waited, then waited some more. At length, his patience wearing thin, he repeated, "Well? Why did you keep her from me?"

Christine turned, and Gray saw the direction of her gaze. Good, he thought. Let her look at the scar and be reminded of the ugly past. And of the ugly part she'd played in it.

Slowly, Christine's gaze raised to his. "I thought it was the best thing to do."

The simplistic answer surprised Gray, and he gave a short laugh. "*You* thought it was the best thing to do? Well now, isn't that just like a Lowell not to trouble yourself with what someone else might think."

Christine said nothing. But Gray was spoiling for a fight, and he wasn't about to be denied one.

"Let me get this straight. What you're saying is that you didn't give a tinker's damn what the child's father thought." He gave her no time to respond before adding, "I was good enough to fuck, but not good enough to be acknowledged as the father of your child. Is that about the size of it, *Mrs. Jackson*?"

Christine's cheeks burned instantly, as if she'd been slapped across the face. But she remained silent.

Gray had specifically used the vulgarity, hoping to shock her. The moment he'd said the word, though, he wished he hadn't. While it had clearly hurt her, it also profaned every memory he had of that summer, memories that, even under the circumstances, he felt the need to safeguard. That he did baffled him, and so he pressed.

"*Slumming* is the word you and your friends used, I believe."

"What?" Christine managed to ask. Of all the things in the world she'd expected Gray to say, this might well have been the last.

"Slumming. You know, the act whereby you fancy ladies and gents get your pleasure making it with someone socially beneath you."

"Where did you hear that?"

"Are you telling me that you and your friends never discussed slumming?"

No, she couldn't tell him that. Some of the young women in her group, more acquaintances than friends, had been smitten with Gray and had spoken of what fun it would be to make it with the broad-shouldered, thin-hipped gardener. That he was unapproachably silent and mysteriously aloof only added to his mystique. That he was the gardener and, therefore, verboten, was the greatest aphrodisiac, of course. It stung Christine to realize that he thought her no better than those shallow women.

"No, I didn't think you could deny that. What did you do? Share all the sordid details with them?"

"Don't—"

"Did you tell them every time we did it? Did you tell them how hot you could get me? Did you tell them what it felt like to spread your well-bred thighs for me?"

"Don't—"

"I'll bet you laughed when you told them how easy it was to make me believe that you cared."

"Don't—"

"Don't what? Don't ask questions you don't want to answer? Don't remind you that you led me on, that you lied to me, that you never had any intention of leaving with me? Well, it just so happens, Mrs. Jackson, that I deserve answers to my questions. Wouldn't you say that a man denied a daughter had earned the right to some answers?"

"Don't—"

"Wouldn't you say that when a man's daughter is raised by another man, the real father has a right to some answers?"

Christine struggled to hang on to her composure. She had never heard Gray speak so crudely, and the things he suggested were so preposterous, so injurious, that she could only stare at him in utter bewilderment.

If Christine fought to hang on to her composure, Gray let his fall apart completely. Charging forward until only a desk separated them, he cried, "Dammit, I want some answers!"

He stood so near that Christine could see the narrowing of his eyes, the way his shoulders leaned forward, as though he were more than ready to lunge at her. She'd never heard his voice raised before. Was this the same voice that had spoken so gently, so sensuously, to her?

With the greatest of difficulty, she spoke calmly. "Yes, you deserve some answers. But not until you're in a frame of mind to really hear them. And just for the record, Peyton has been a good father to Amanda."

Gray's breath escaped in a hiss. Then he said, "Just for the record, *I* would have made a good father too."

A silence fell between them. Despite himself, Gray thought of that fantasy he'd had so long ago—the ring on Christine's finger, the vine-covered cottage, a baby tucked in his arms as he rocked and sang, rocked and sang. Yes, he would have been a good father.

Christine's thoughts ran in a similar vein. She thought of Gray's being by her side when Amanda was born, of him placing the child at her breast and watching it suckle, of changing diapers, and taking turns rocking her when she'd cried. She thought of first steps and first words and a home, their home, somewhere far away from Rosemead.

At last, Christine asked, "Why did you come back, Gray?"

He didn't want her using his name, not in that soft, pleading voice that had once urged him to do such sensual things to her, and so he answered harshly. "You have something that belongs to me."

"A child or a pound of my flesh?" Before he could respond, she said, "Are you aware that you haven't once asked about Amanda? You haven't once asked if we've learned anything more about her whereabouts."

Gray hadn't been aware of that fact, and he wasn't certain what his failure to do so meant. He chose not to try to explain it, even to himself.

But Christine wasn't about to let him off the hook so easily. "I repeat, did you come back for a child or for a pound of my flesh?"

Gray gave the question a few seconds' worth of thought, then said, "Both."

Regret riddled Christine's sigh. "You really hate me, don't you?"

This time, Gray didn't hesitate. "Yes, I really hate you."

His candor cut deep, a fact he could see clearly. He wondered why she would care in the least what he thought of her.

Tilting her chin as though to lift herself above his poor opinion of her, she said, "If I might be so bold as to make a suggestion—"

A tap on the door rang out.

Halting, Christine looked toward the sound and said, "Come in."

Agent Carrelli stuck his head inside. "Excuse me. Sandy Killian is here. I thought the two of you might like to be present when we spoke with her again."

"Thank you," Christine responded. "We'll be right there."

When the door closed, Gray asked, "Who's Sandy Killian?"

"Amanda's nanny. She picks Amanda up after school and stays with her until I get home. Sandy was the first to realize that Amanda was . . ." She paused before adding, "Missing."

It seemed an odd choice of words, but Gray didn't

point that out. He was pondering whether Christine's work involved some socially acceptable charity. That's what it had meant for her mother.

"As I was about to suggest," Christine continued, "I think it would be a good idea if we put aside our differences for the present. Nothing matters except getting my child back."

"*Our* child," Gray corrected. "Amanda is our child."

Christine didn't bother to tell him that she was hardly likely to forget now what she hadn't been able to forget for over nine years.

Sandy Killian's sedation might have worn off, but not her guilt, which surfaced repeatedly as she once more related the events of the previous afternoon.

Her terrifying story was actually very straightforward. Amanda, who attended a private school, got out at 2:50 P.M. Since it took less than ten minutes to drive from Rosemead to the school, Sandy always left at 2:40. Except for the afternoon of the kidnapping. Time had gotten away from her and she'd left at 2:50, although she didn't consider the additional ten minutes a problem. She had coached Amanda about what to do should she ever be late: the little girl was to wait inside the building. Sandy had parked the car and headed toward the school, still thinking that all was well. En route, however, she had run into Heather Tryde, a schoolmate and friend of Amanda's, who had told her that Amanda had already left . . . with a man wearing a uniform and a badge.

Here Sandy broke into tears once more. Snuffling into a tissue that Christine handed her, she said, "I shouldn't have been late."

"Why were you?"

Gray's question was delivered in a curious rather than an accusatory tone. At his inquiry, all eyes turned his way. His arms folded across his chest, he stood on the periphery of the group gathered in the living room, a group that consisted of Sandy Killian, Christine, and five law-enforcement officers—one from the local police department, one from the county sheriff's department, and three FBI agents. Among the latter, there was Terrence Carrelli, an older man named Phil Birmingham, who had a walrus mustache which he constantly fingered, and a younger man with a football player's bulky build and the seemingly appropriate name of Hamm Clancy. Everyone had accepted Gray's presence with a naturalness that suggested they had been briefed on his relationship to Amanda. Nikki Janowitz had disappeared discreetly into the kitchen.

Sandy, tall and willowy and with hair the color of butterscotch, looked directly at Gray. If the dark circles under her hazel eyes were any indication, she was, as Gray had gathered, taking the kidnapping hard indeed.

"Time just got away from me," Sandy answered Gray. "I was making Mandy's costume for a school play. Her class is putting on *Snow White* next week and Mandy is the witch. I had made her hat, but it didn't look right. It was lopsided. I'd scrapped it and started over, and I was trying to get it finished so she could try it on after I picked her up." Tears flowed anew. "I should have been watching the clock more closely, but I wasn't. I was in a hurry and . . . I'm so sorry."

Christine slipped her arm around Sandy's shoulders. "No one's blaming you."

Phil Birmingham said, "I talked to Heather Tryde and she insists that the man was wearing a uniform, but she couldn't tell me anything about the color. She seemed more impressed with the badge."

"Of course," Agent Carrelli said, "both the uniform and the badge were probably as bogus as the day is long. Most children would accept anyone with any kind of uniform or badge as an authority figure."

"I can't believe that Amanda would go with someone just because of a uniform or badge," Christine said. "I've told her repeatedly never to go with a stranger."

"Obviously, then, there's the possibility that she knew the man," Gray said.

Again, Agent Carrelli spoke up. "Anything's a possibility, but"—he glanced back at Christine—"it's been our experience that children, however trained in safety measures, sometimes forget everything they've been cautioned against. Not only that, we don't know what he might have told her. What if he'd told her that you'd been hurt, say in an accident, and that he would take her to you? Don't you think she might go under those circumstances?"

That she might have been, even unwittingly, the instrument by which her daughter had met foul play saddened and sickened Christine. Unable to bear the cruel thought, she stood and walked to the window, which was answer enough to Agent Carrelli's question. Crossing her arms about her, she longed for a pair of strong arms to hold her together, to bind emotions that threatened to splinter. That she'd once known such a strong pair of arms made her longing all the greater.

With an apology for going over material they'd already covered, Hamm Clancy redetermined that Sandy Killian, after realizing that Amanda had left with the uniformed man, called Christine from her cellular phone, and that, in turn, Christine called the police, thinking, hoping, that they knew something about an

officer meeting Amanda. The police knew nothing
and understood immediately the gravity of the situa-
tion. At that point, they instructed Christine to return
to Rosemead, which she did sometime around 3:30 to
3:45. The ransom note, contained within an unpost-
marked envelope, was discovered later by the housekeeper as she went through the daily mail.

Christine shuddered. Up until the discovery of the
ransom note, she'd held out the hope that there was a
logical explanation for the afternoon's occurrence.
Someone would step forward, Amanda in tow, and everyone would have a good laugh that all had jumped
to such malevolent conclusions. The note had extinguished that hope.

"How did the letter get in the box?" Gray asked.

Agent Hamm Clancy answered. "The mail carrier
delivered the mail between two o'clock and two-thirty.
Sometime after that, someone put the letter in the
box. It's located on the outside of the gate. Anyone
could have driven by and shoved it in."

"What about fingerprints?" Gray again.

"None, except for the housekeeper's," Agent
Carrelli said. "The police did a preliminary search for
prints, then, on the chance that the more sophisticated
equipment at Quantico could pick up something, we
sent the note there, but nothing turned up. It was as
clean as a whistle."

"What did the note say?" Gray asked.

"The usual," Carrelli answered. "In letters crudely
cut from a magazine, it demanded two million dollars
in unmarked bills. The note indicated that they, he,
she—whoever—would call later."

"But no one has." Gray stated the obvious.

"No," Carrelli said. "I'm certain, however, that the
delay is all part of the game. Make the family wait a

while, let their nerves get good and frayed, and they'll comply with any demands."

"My nerves are already good and frayed," Christine said.

"I know." Carrelli's voice was filled with compassion.

Phil Birmingham said, "Mrs. Jackson, yesterday we discussed the possibility of your father, of Lowell Enterprises, having made a business enemy."

"I'll tell you again what I told you yesterday," Christine said. "Of course my father made business enemies. In fact, he seemed to have a talent for that, but in all fairness to him, you don't get where he was without making a few enemies. On the other hand, I can't believe anyone would take a grudge this far."

"Records show that within the last five years, Lowell Enterprises bought and sold any number of companies," Agent Carrelli said.

"We sold, bought, combined companies when the need arose. The company has business dealings throughout the South, primarily in cotton. We have a lot of timber-related holdings too."

Agent Carrelli persisted. "Doesn't all this buying and selling disrupt lives?"

Christine sighed. "At the risk of making my father sound insensitive, he didn't consider the disruption of lives his responsibility. His only concern was running a productive business, keeping the figures in the black." She paused, then added, "Having worked with my father those three years before his death, I can honestly say that his being able to wear blinders was an advantage."

As Gray listened, it became clear that Merritt was out of the picture. At Christine's reference to her father's death, everything fell into place. What, if any,

was Christine's role in the company now? Merritt
Lowell had a warrior mentality, which meant that he
readily, callously, accepted the fact that casualties occurred on the battlefield of business. All that mattered
was winning the battle, and the war. Had his daughter
taken up where he'd left off?

"So, Mercantile Tech and Hoogland Timber were
the last transactions carried out by your father?" Agent
Birmingham asked.

"Yes," Christine said. "In fact, I carried them out
for him. Eighteen months ago, we sold Mercantile
Tech and bought Hoogland Timber for a small sum
that was actually more than it was worth. It had been
losing money for five years. If Hal Hoogland hadn't
been a friend of my father's, we never would have
bought the company." Christine paused, then added,
"But suppose the worst. Suppose someone associated
with either transaction wasn't pleased. Why wait eighteen months to kidnap Amanda in retaliation?"

No one could argue with this logic.

"By the way," Hamm Clancy said, "I checked for
any arrest record on this Ernie Shaw. He has none.
And he wasn't at home this morning when I went over
to talk to him. The place looked locked up tight."

"Wait a minute," Gray said. "Who's Ernie Shaw?"

Christine glanced over at Gray. "He's the owner of
Deep South Petroleum Products. They supplied bulk
fuel—diesel fuel, gasoline, lubricants—for our equipment. I had just recently fired his company. Accounts
payable showed that we were paying almost double
what we had been, but the field hands were complaining about machinery running dry too quickly. I don't
think he was filling up the tanks. He was most likely
shortchanging us, selling the excess fuel on the side,
and charging us the full price."

Agent Birmingham thumbed his mustache. "And even though you said that your brother was in charge of all the equipment, you were the one who discovered what was going on by going over the accounts payable."

"That's correct," was all Christine said.

The reference to Claiborne Lowell knotted Gray's stomach. There was unfinished business between the two of them that he'd see settled before all this was over. "Could we get back to this Ernie Shaw? Is he a suspect simply because he was fired?"

"Because he threatened Mrs. Jackson," Hamm Clancy said.

Gray's eyebrow rose. "Threatened her?"

Christine explained. "I came home early one afternoon with a headache and went upstairs to lie down. I heard the doorbell, heard someone talking loudly, heard someone start up the stairs. I got up and stopped Ernie Shaw at the landing. He swore that he'd been unjustly fired, that he had delivered exactly what he'd been paid to deliver, and that he wasn't going to let me get away with this. By then, I wasn't paying all that much attention. Amanda had just come home."

"When we entered the house, we walked in on this fight," Sandy said. "It frightened Amanda. She hates hollering and shouting. I rushed her into the kitchen for cookies and milk."

"Did she see him?" Carrelli asked the nanny. "Did he see her?"

"She saw his back, but I don't think he ever saw her."

Gray filed away the fact that this child called Amanda didn't like arguments. It was the first bit of personal knowledge he had about her. It was the first thing that gave her any real definition, the first thing that caused her to emerge, ever so slightly, from the shadows.

"So, this Ernie Shaw looks promising?" Gray asked.

"Not according to Mrs. Jackson," Agent Carrelli said.

Gray looked over at Christine. "I don't get it. The man made a threat."

Christine sighed. "You have to know Ernie Shaw. He's a simple man."

"You'd be surprised how few PhD's we arrest for kidnapping," Agent Carrelli interjected.

"He was smart enough to steal from you," Gray pointed out to Christine.

"But not smart enough not to get caught."

"And you still know of no one who might have a grudge against your husband? Say, no business associate?" Phil Birmingham asked.

"No," Christine said. "But, as I told you yesterday, I really know very little about Peyton's business."

"One last thing," Hamm Clancy said. "I understand you've had problems with the theft of your equipment."

"Nothing beyond normal. Theft of commercial equipment is big business and, regrettably, part and parcel of this industry. I can't believe that equipment theft has anything to do with Amanda's kidnapping."

The issue of equipment theft seemed put to rest. However, it was decided that Terrence Carrelli would check once more on Ernie Shaw and, that goal in mind, the agent left immediately.

It was nearing the midway point of six o'clock. Outside, more clouds had assembled, to Christine's grave disliking, while inside the mansion shadows had begun to fall. Sandy Killian left, but reluctantly and with the promise that, should the kidnapper be in touch, she be notified. Peyton Jackson didn't return, and speculation began as to Claiborne Lowell's whereabouts. The lawmen huddled together quietly, while Christine continued to peer out the window.

"I didn't think Merritt Lowell was mortal enough to die."

In the coppery dusk that had crept across the room, Christine could see only the hollowed planes and whetted angles of Gray's face. She'd heard no sarcasm in his voice, merely disbelief that her father had gone the way of all flesh.

"Cancer has a way of making everyone mortal."

"How long has he been dead?"

"About six months."

"And Adelle didn't want to be bothered with running the business?" A confirmation wouldn't surprise Gray. Christine's mother had never bothered with the business.

"She died four years ago of a massive stroke. On the heels of that, we learned that Merritt had cancer. Like him or not, he fought valiantly."

"And so the empire fell to you," Gray said.

"By default."

"Is it like father, like daughter?"

"That sounds like an accusation."

Was it? Gray wondered, but said, "Not necessarily. I'm just curious."

Christine smiled. "I have the feeling that no matter how I respond, you'll believe what you want to believe."

Something in the stoop of her shoulders spoke to him, and, inexplicably, he wanted to ease the pain his question had caused. Strangely, hurting her was the same as hurting himself. "Maybe you're right. Maybe I would. Whatever, now isn't the time for any of this. Besides, I'm interested only in the child."

Gray should have walked away then, but didn't. He couldn't. Not when she was so near, he could almost feel her shoulder brushing his.

He said, "You were right about something else too. I never once asked about Amanda. But you've had years to accept the fact that you have a daughter. I've had only hours. She's real to you in a way she isn't yet to me. I don't even know what she looks like."

"Would you like to see a photograph of her?"

"Yeah."

Christine stepped from the window and across the room to a grand piano, whose top was covered by elegantly framed photographs. She selected one and started back toward Gray. Once again by his side, she bent to turn on a lamp. Light swallowed the darkness, illuminating Christine's face. There he saw fatigue and fear and something much more. He saw the past.

In a split second, a thousand memories came charging toward him, memories that he'd fought to keep at bay. Now, he remembered his first realization that the awkward child with the mismatched features had grown into a beautiful woman. He could see her hair, kissed by the sun, flowing about her shoulders. He could see her eyes, a luminous gray that could steal a man's breath and leave him pleased with the loss. He'd thought then that someday some man would lose himself completely in their depths; he just hadn't known he'd be that man. And then, with a shocking rapidity, he saw her standing before him in the hothouse—the same sun-heated hair, her thief-gray eyes now filled with need, her voice sexy and seductive. This was the one memory he avoided like the plague, for that day he had learned a truth that would haunt him for the whole of his life.

"This is the most recent photograph," Christine said. "It was taken a couple of months ago."

Gray took the photograph, and the moment he viewed it, all other thoughts, all memories, fled from his mind. He was too busy feeling, although the truth was that he wasn't quite certain what he felt. A sense of unreality, without question. He had fathered this child and yet she didn't seem a part of him, perhaps because she looked nothing like him. Familiar stranger. She looked like, and felt like, a familiar stranger. Perhaps in an attempt to make the unreal more real, he drew his fingertip across the image of this child—across hair as black as a raven's wing, across a smile that lay somewhere between sweet and devilish, across eyes that, like another pair of gray eyes, seemed to see right through him.

"She looks like you." Gray didn't know anything else to say as he stood in stunned awe.

"Yes," Christine answered, wondering if he'd have the slightest interest in knowing how her prayers had vacillated all the while she'd been pregnant, vacillated between hoping that this child wouldn't look like him and hoping that she would. In the first prayer lay her safety, in the second lay her heart. Part of her would have risked anything to have a reminder of what she'd lost.

No, she decided, Gray would care nothing about her suffering, and so she repeated simply, "Yes, she looks like me."

Chapter 3

From the doorway of the spotless claret-red and copper kitchen, Gray watched Esther Hawkins preparing sandwiches. The first time he'd seen the housekeeper, some twenty years ago, she'd been standing in pretty much the same spot. Merritt Lowell had just hired him, a seventeen-year-old with little to his name except the reputation for being able to make any plant grow, and had sent him to the house for something to eat before beginning work. Everyone in town knew that he was poorer than Job's turkey, and that he didn't always get three square meals a day.

He'd been on his own since he was fourteen, when his dad, out of the blue, had died of a massive coronary. That traumatic event had left him to fend for himself, taking every odd job he could find and filling in the spare hours with enough school to get passing marks. In the beginning, a do-good social worker had placed him in a foster home, but he'd run away and returned to the shanty he and his dad had lived in. From that point on, they hadn't much messed with him, nor he with anyone. He'd hated the pity he'd seen in the townsfolk's eyes, and the way they'd whispered behind his back, mostly about his mother. His father had refused to speak about her, except once when he'd said that she just hadn't been cut out for the responsibilities of motherhood. All Gray could remember was a soft voice that sang lullabies, a soft voice that had disappeared from his life about the time he was five years old. Because of that, he'd been particularly susceptible to Esther's mothering, oftentimes pretending, always wishing, that she was his mother.

"Hey, lady, don't you ever get out of this kitchen?"

The housekeeper glanced up. Surprisingly, or perhaps not surprisingly, Esther hadn't changed much. No doubt in her mid-fifties, she appeared to have valiantly met the years and to have emerged victorious. Her sable-colored hair, always arranged atop her head in a precise knot, bore not a trace of gray, while her blue eyes, located beneath a sweep of thick, naturally curled lashes, still sparkled. He'd referred to her as a lady, and that she was, from the gentility of her movements to the gentleness of her voice and spirit. Even so, she had a directness—no mincing of her words—that had caught more than one person off guard.

"You took your sweet time getting in here," Esther said, proving that she could, indeed, be candid. As she spoke, she skirted the wooden work block and stepped toward Gray.

The closer she moved toward him, the more Gray was forced to alter his first impression. Dark circles indicated a lack of sleep, and deep creases of concern lined her forehead. Her blue eyes had recently been filled with tears. Clearly, the kidnapping had taken its toll.

Without hesitation, without apology, Esther embraced Gray, giving him a fierce hug, which he, without hesitation, without apology, returned. In fact, he needed this hug. Badly. He sensed that Esther did, as well, and so the two of them, once fellow employees of Merritt Lowell, and good friends, simply clung to each other.

In time, she held him at arms' length, studied him, then announced, "It's good to see you, although I wish it could have been under different circumstances."

"Yeah, so do I." Pause, then, "I still can't believe that it's true, that I have a daughter or that she's been kidnapped. I mean, none of this seems even remotely real."

Esther pulled away from Gray and walked back to the wooden block. "No, it doesn't."

As he had any number of times over the years, Gray followed and climbed atop a stool. "Yesterday my life was so simple. Today . . . I'll be lucky ever to make the pieces fit together again."

The housekeeper resumed the preparation of sandwiches. Tuna, from the smell that wafted in the air. "And we do like for our pieces to fit, don't we? Not that we ever manage to make them do so, but we keep trying."

If Esther had a direct way of speaking, she also had a way of making it sound as if she had some grand understanding of human beings, both their strengths and their weaknesses. This seemingly innate wisdom had always fascinated Gray.

"Did you have any idea that the child was mine?"

"No. Looking back, I should have, but I didn't. Christine's pregnancy was difficult from beginning to end, but then pregnancies can be that way. I think now that Christine's had to have been complicated by what had to be the emotional strain she was under."

Gray laughed—harshly. But before he could utter a word about what he thought of that "emotional strain," Esther said, "Here," and pushed a sandwich and a mug of coffee toward him. When Gray hesitated, she added, "Don't be so stubborn."

Reluctantly—he was fond of his stubbornness—Gray picked up the mug and took a sip of the coffee. It reminded him of just how long it had been since he'd had anything in his stomach. He'd driven straight through lunchtime, stopping only to gas up the van and make the necessary visits to a rest room.

A comfortable silence fell between Gray and the housekeeper, one she finally broke with, "You look good."

"Sure I do."

She didn't pretend not to understand. "Nonsense. The scar makes you look rugged. A woman likes her man rugged."

"Is Peyton rugged? Or is Christine's type different?"

Despite himself, Gray was curious about this man who was so crazy about Christine, this man to whom she'd been so happily wed, this man who'd raised another man's child as his own. "I assume he's prominent. Anyone with a name like Peyton has to be prominent."

"He's prominent. He's also a nice man, and he's crazy about Christine."

"He's not from Natchez, is he?" Had he been, Gray would have recognized the name. In a town of under twenty thousand people, everyone knew everyone, or everyone had at least heard of everyone.

"No, he's from Vicksburg, although he settled here after his marriage to Christine. They had a lovely home outside of town, but when Merritt became so ill, they sold it and moved into Rosemead. He's an investment broker. He and Jim Lytle have a very successful brokerage."

"How did Christine meet this paragon of virtue?"

Esther's look said that the remark was beneath him. His return look said that he didn't care one whit. "His family knew the Lowell family."

"Ah, the joining of one wealthy scion to another."

"Well, of course, it was that, wasn't it? However, it doesn't change the fact that he's been a good husband to Christine and, perhaps this isn't what you want to hear, but he's been a good father to Amanda."

"I'm not quite certain what I want to hear, but I'll tell you what I told Christine. *I* would have made a good father too."

Esther smiled. "Yes, you would have made a good father. You know, I knew about what was going on between you two long before Claiborne took the matter into his own hands. You took such reckless chances. If her parents hadn't been so involved in their own lives, you would have been found out long before you were."

Gray didn't want to be reminded of the reckless chances he and Christine had taken, of the way they'd sneaked here and there, stealing kisses and a whole lot more. Mostly, though, he didn't want to be reminded of the way she'd stolen his heart, of the careless fashion in which he'd surrendered it.

"She hasn't changed," he said.

"No, she hasn't." Gray barely had time to consider the remark when she added, "But you have. You've grown bitter, cynical."

The accusation, right on target, stung. "I had reason to grow bitter and cynical."

"We all have choices."

"Right. And so did Christine. She chose to keep a child from its real father and to deceive another man into thinking it was his."

"I'm not excusing what she did."

"Well, that's damned nice to hear!" On a sigh, he said, "I'm sorry, Esther. I have no right to take this out on you."

"My shoulders are wide," she said.

As though she sensed that he needed time to regain his composure, she busied herself with the task of placing sandwiches on a silver tray. Gray let his mind run free, allowed his thoughts to tumble over one another, and settled on the irony of what he'd just learned. It was doubly ironic, because he had just told himself that he didn't care two hoots about her personal life.

"You know, she always hated Rosemead. She always hated Lowell Enterprises, and yet she now lives in the house and runs the company."

"A woman of lesser intelligence, lesser fortitude, could not have done what she did. She literally jumped in and learned the business overnight."

"I'm sure sainthood awaits her," Gray mumbled.

"Like I said, you've grown bitter, cynical." Esther paused, staring at him, studying him. She smiled. "Amanda's a great deal like you. I don't know why I never noticed it before."

Gray didn't feel comfortable being too eager to hear how this child was like him and so he merely said, "She looks like her mother."

"Yes, but like you, she can make things grow. She and I have a garden. We have the best tomatoes in town. And great herbs—parsley, sage, dill, oregano, and thyme." Esther nodded toward the uneaten sandwich. "She's also stubborn like you. In order to make a point, she wouldn't have eaten the sandwich either."

"I don't want anything from the Lowells."

"Pride is an expensive commodity, Gray Bannon."

"Pride is one of the few things I own."

"Funny thing about pride. It's often difficult to tell if you own it, or it owns you."

Gray thought of this parting comment often over the next hour.

The *Natchez Rose* rode the rippling Mississippi River with an indifferent determination. Inside the three-tiered riverboat, packed to capacity on this Friday night, Claiborne Lowell rambled about, past slot machines and table games and any number of women who eyed him. But then, why shouldn't they? He was tanned and good-looking. The first time he'd noticed a thinning of the hair on his crown, a regrettable family trait, he'd had the best hair transplant that money could buy. Of course his being heir to both a powerful name and sizable fortune added immeasurably to his appeal.

What no one knew was that his two biggest advantages—the name and money—were also his two biggest disadvantages. He'd learned early on that he couldn't measure up to his father—there was only one Merritt Lowell, thank you very much—and so he'd just thrown in the towel and stopped trying. He'd thought that with good ole Pop buried six feet under that he'd finally assume his rightful place, but, oh no, good ole Pop had had other ideas.

Claiborne greedily sucked in the sights and sounds and smells of the rousing chaos that reigned around him. Slot machines, their colored neon glowing, chattered their invitations, while people, a hungry clutch of humanity, hummed a continuous song. Claiborne could smell perfume and perspiration and a certain desperation. He was familiar with that desperation, a gnawing need to turn loss into gain, to numb his mind, like a narcotic, to the troubling thoughts that all too often filled it. Right now, those troubling thoughts centered around the kidnapping. He'd had to get away from what was happening at Rosemead. It was suffocating him, but then Rosemead itself had a way of doing that. He could take it in only small doses. He couldn't take Christine at all. What in God's name had his father been thinking about, giving the presidency to her, leaving him the paltry scraps of the vice presidency? How humiliating!

A woman whooped, obviously in delight at a win, and Claiborne's fingers began to itch. Yes, forget about Rosemead, forget about Christine, forget about Amanda. And forget that son of a bitch Gray Bannon. Who would have thought that he was really Amanda's father? Though the truth was that Christine had never had a lick of sense when it came to the gardener. It was one thing, however, to spread her legs for him, another to allow him to father a child. He wished Pop could see Christine now, and how she'd defiled the Lowell name. But he'd make Christine pay, and good, for her stupidity and for sucking up to their father. This thought warmed him.

"Good evening, Mr. C.," the man running the craps table said.

" 'Evening, Dale."

"Joining us, sir?"

"Why not? Let's see how charitable Lady Luck intends to be tonight."

She obviously intended to be friendly. On his first try, Claiborne rolled an eleven. On his second roll, he came up with another winning number, and continued to do so on his third, fourth, and fifth tries. The sixth time out, with another winning number brandished across the green baize table, a round of applause broke out.

"You're hot tonight, Mr. C.," the croupier said.

Yes, he was, Claiborne thought, taking stock of his chips, which totaled an impressive sum.

"Roll again, Clay," a man beside him said.

Claiborne recognized the man as one of the town's doctors, a general practitioner with blue eyes and a receding hairline. Everyone liked him, even if everyone thought him a bit of a sap. It was common knowledge, no doubt even to the doc, that his wife had a roving eye, and that her body often followed it.

"Hey, Doc," Claiborne said, although his gaze never made it past the breasts of the woman beside him. When men gathered, and testosterone governed, the conversation always came down to one question: Were Dr. Sanders's wife's breasts real or implants? There were those, based on a touchy-feely authority, who swore they were the real McCoy, others, on the same sensual strength, who vowed that they were as real as rhinestones.

"I don't know," Claiborne said, "maybe I ought to quit while I'm ahead."

"Oh, go on," Miriam Sanders said, leaning forward until just a hint more cleavage showed. "I promise to bring you good luck."

Claiborne grinned. "Well, now, how can I resist such an offer?"

Bets were made among the onlookers, some supporting Claiborne's victory, others certain of his defeat. In the end, Claiborne couldn't refuse a bit of drama. He staked everything on one roll of the dice. His heart began to pound as he piled his chips high.

"Last call for bets," the croupier declared, then passed the dice to Claiborne. He scooped them up.

"Go for it, Clay," Dr. Sanders urged.

More encouragement followed, some of it dispensed by total strangers. Miriam Sanders offered her own support as she discreetly moved to stand between her husband and Claiborne. She made certain that her body grazed Claiborne's.

Claiborne shook the dice, then, uncurling his fingers, he sent the cubes flying down the table. He watched as they scrambled end over end over end.

No thoughts of Rosemead or Amanda.

No thoughts of Christine.

No thoughts of how his father had humiliated him.

Just adrenaline pumping a million miles a minute.

And then it was over.

The groans told it all.

A smiling Claiborne viewed the losing toss with a curious satisfaction.

"Easy come, easy go," he said.

Amid the condolences—one would have thought someone had died—Claiborne threaded his way back through the crowd and up the sweeping stairway that led to the second floor. It took only a few minutes to lose another fifty dollars—two tries in the twenty-five-dollar slot machine. From there, he headed his Gucci loafers in the direction of the bar and, once seated, he ordered something strong and tall. He was halfway through the potent drink when Miriam Sanders appeared. He wondered what had taken her so long.

"Mind if I join you?" she asked.

In response, Claiborne said, "Where's your husband?"

She slipped onto the stool next to his, carefully orchestrating the meeting of two thighs. "Making his acquaintance with Jack. Blackjack, that is. He'll be at the tables for a while."

This addendum wasn't lost on Claiborne, but he wasn't certain how he felt about taking her up on the offer that was bound to be forthcoming. He hated performing on command, yet sex could be an entertaining enough diversion.

"A Blushing Lady," she said to the bartender, ordering the drink for which the floating casino was renowned.

It was an interesting choice, Claiborne reasoned, for the woman beside him was certainly no lady, blushing or otherwise, as her subsequent behavior proved. She brushed, touched, teased. Her lips pouted, her fingers plowed enticingly through her long blond hair, while careful choreography plumped her breasts. Still, Claiborne didn't take the bait.

Finally, obviously exhausted and sensing failure, she said, "So, what's going on at Rosemead?"

"What do you mean?" He forced casualness into his voice.

"I've heard from any number of people that there's a lot of traffic up there."

"There's always a lot of traffic at Rosemead."

"Rumor says there's more than usual, that the local police and the county police are practically living there. I even heard that the FBI was up there."

"The FBI?" Claiborne snorted. "Hardly. As for the police, they sometimes stop by. Especially if they want a donation to one thing or another."

Miriam Sanders persisted. "Amanda wasn't at school today. At least that's what Mark said. And everyone says Christine didn't go into Lowell Enterprises, and Nikki didn't show up at the antique shop. Rumor says the shop was closed."

Claiborne knew that Mark Sanders was Amanda's classmate. He knew, too, that only Amanda's teacher and the school principal had been told what had happened.

"Amanda has some kind of bug. Christine stayed home with her and, as for Nikki, you're going to have to ask her where she spent the day."

"Mark said that Heather Tryde said that Amanda was missing, that some men came to talk to her about Amanda, and that she heard her mother use the word *kidnap*."

Claiborne laughed. "Trust me, I think I'd know if my niece had been kidnapped." He slid from the stool, pulled out his wallet, and laid down enough money to cover both drinks. "How about the two of us getting out of here?"

Miriam brightened, forgetting Amanda just as Claiborne had hoped she would. "I *did* promise to bring you luck, didn't I?"

Claiborne grinned. "You did. And I know just how you can do that." He leaned forward to whisper something sumptuously scandalous, something deliciously dirty.

Miriam smiled her approval.

"I'll meet you in the parking lot," Claiborne said. "No need setting tongues to wagging."

Claiborne gave the woman a substantial lead, then meandered through the casino and its ever-swelling crowd and, finally, out into the parking lot. Behind him blinked the bright lights of the riverboat and before him burned those of Natchez-Under-The-Hill, the first site of the town, the one-time rowdy setting of gambling, drinking, and brothels. A fine mist had begun to fall, leaving Claiborne to feel as though he'd stepped beneath a slow shower. At the sight of Miriam slipping from the shadows, he decided that maybe a little quickie was exactly what he needed to quell his troubled thoughts.

They decided on Doc Sanders's Cadillac—a Porsche was no place to screw—which Claiborne drove to a nearby residential area. There, he cut the lights and brazenly pulled into a private driveway. Before he could even shut off the engine, Miriam had unbuttoned her designer blouse and had freed from a lacy bra two breasts the size of melons. Both hands plunged beneath her matching designer skirt, and she wriggled out of a scrap of silk that some manufacturer had the nerve to call panties. She then reached for the zipper of Claiborne's slacks.

He grabbed her hand. "Whoa! Whoa!" he said, trying to keep the irritation from his voice. He hated it when a woman tried to take control of sex, of any part of his life.

"C'mon, baby, we haven't got all night."

"We've got plenty of time," he drawled.

For the next twenty minutes, he taunted and teased and tortured her, kissing and almost kissing, stroking, stroking, stopping short of giving her what she wanted, what she begged for.

"You son of a bitch!" she yelled finally.

With that, he buried himself deeply, hurtfully, inside her, riding her, riding her, riding her. At the same time, he buried his face in her breasts, breasts which were as real as a plastic surgeon could make them. Their cries mingled inside the car.

By marked contrast, the drive back was quiet. Once Claiborne had reparked the Cadillac, he looked over at Miriam Sanders. She'd managed to put herself back into a somewhat presentable order.

"You son of a bitch," she repeated, without even a hint of a smile.

"And don't you forget it," Claiborne said, throwing wide the car door and getting out. He slammed the door behind him.

No, he thought, it would *not* be wise for any woman to forget that he was a son of a bitch.

Especially not his sister.

Chapter 4

The rain, which had begun as a mist, now peppered roof and windowpanes. Christine, stuffed rabbit in hand, stood peering through the deluge. Occasionally, thunder boomed, while lightning electrified the sky, once illuminating the policeman who'd been assigned to stand watch in the yard, his job principally to guard the mailbox.

For her daughter to be missing in the rain was almost more than Christine could bear. Amanda should be here, cozy in blanket and gown, having to be coaxed to do her homework. She should be snacking on cookies and sneaking a listen to Mariah Carey's or Janet Jackson's latest CD. Or worried about the fragile tomato plants that she and Esther had recently planted in carefully tended soil.

Soil.

The image came suddenly, of a shallow grave, the soil clotted and cool and chock-full of leaves and twigs and creepy-crawly things. And beneath this soil lay a still small body, dressed in a black and green plaid jumper, with eyes eerily open, a hand outstretched, a leg bent at an unnatural and painful angle. No, the angle was no longer painful, and that was the cruelest reality of all. That, and the fact that this was a child who would never know hearth and home again. A child who would never know the love of a parent again.

When was the last time she'd told Amanda that she loved her? Thursday morning? Wednesday night? Lord, Christine thought, raking her fingers through her hair, she couldn't remember. Why couldn't she remember something this important? She must have made a sound because Nikki, seated nearby, glanced over at her.

"Are you all right?"

"I can't remember when I last told Amanda that I love her."

"It doesn't matter. She knows you love her, and that will get her through."

"But I can't remember. Did I tell her Thursday morning? I always tell her, but I can't remember if I did Thursday."

At the building urgency in Christine's voice, Nikki glanced over at Gray, who was silently watching, then back at her friend. "It doesn't matter, Christine. She knows."

"She knows," Christine repeated, as though there were power in the words.

"Yes, she knows." Pause, then, "Why don't you go upstairs and lie down—"

"No!"

"Christine, you need some rest—"

"Not now," Christine insisted, adding, "But why don't you go rest."

Nikki rose. "I'm going to go freshen up, but I'll be

right back." Nikki smiled slightly. "Are you going to be all right while I'm gone?"

Christine smiled and held up the ravaged rabbit. "I have Thumper."

In the silence that followed Nikki's departure, Christine wondered if Gray would even remember the stuffed rabbit. Since the scene in the library, he had kept his distance, disappearing once to speak with Esther. He'd refused food, as though it were a point of honor to accept nothing that could even remotely be labeled the property of a Lowell. He had returned more than once, however, to Amanda's photograph. Occasionally, he spoke to the FBI agents, inquiring once as to why Agent Carrelli hadn't returned. She'd begun to wonder the same thing. And where was Peyton? She had expected him back long before now. Checking her watch, she saw that it was only eight-thirty. Dear God, would this night never end?

"Tell me about her."

The command came unexpectedly, but what surprised Christine most was the tone in which it was delivered. No accusations. Just a softness to match his eyes, his expression, as he stared at the photograph.

"What do you want to know?"

Gray glanced toward her. "Anything, everything."

Gray could tell that his request had surprised Christine, but then he'd surprised himself. Just as he'd surprised himself by returning repeatedly to the photograph of the child. Something had drawn him time and again, something charging him to check one more time the dark hair and fair eyes and devilishly sweet expression, as if in one more time lay a deeper understanding of this child he'd sired. Curiously, addictively, with each look came the need for one more look, for one more bit of information to add to the piteously small amount that he possessed, information that he now heard himself recapping.

"All I know is that she looks like you, and that she likes gardening. Plus she hates fighting."

A memory rushed at Christine, one of her shouting harsh words at Peyton, demanding that he shout back. But, of course, he hadn't, because Peyton didn't shout. Ever. It went against the principles of good breeding. Even when he was frustrated, angry—he had to be frustrated and angry at a wife who simply couldn't give him the things he rightfully demanded—he never raised his voice. Only she did, a fact she wasn't particularly proud of, but what was one to do when emotions were strung as tight as a new drum? And what did you tell a daughter who'd begun to ask too many questions? Why was she angry with Daddy? Why didn't Daddy come home at night? Why did he sleep in the other bedroom? Finally, unable to hold the charade, and, more importantly herself, together any longer, Christine had sought a divorce. In retrospect, she regretted not having done so sooner.

"I don't know where to begin," Christine said, returning to Gray's request, desperate to find just those words that would make this man love their child as much as she did. Christine knew how any such choice, however cleverly made, flew in the face of logic, for if Gray were ever to love his daughter, it would take time, with both its simplicity and its complexity. Finally, she said, "She's . . . she's a typical nine-year-old."

"And what's that?"

"A child one minute, an adult the next. One minute she's playing with toys, the next she's talking about boys. Oh, nothing serious. At this age, boys and girls mostly tease and taunt one another. Actually, I think she's too interested in softball to care much about boys."

Gray frowned. Funny, he hadn't imagined this child in anything but fancy dresses, with fluttery ribbons in her well-kept hair. He certainly hadn't envisioned her with dirt-streaked cheeks and sliding into home, though perhaps he should have. Her mother had been a tomboy. Not that she looked it now with her expensive blouse and tailored slacks, both a shade just shy of a pale pink rose. On the other hand, Gray saw a ghost of that former tomboy as Christine spiritedly spoke of her daughter's impressive sports credentials, of catching fast balls and curve balls, of tagging runners out in record time, of batting one homer after another. Christine also seemed relaxed in a way she hadn't been since he'd arrived. He could almost hear a young Christine's laughter, the laughter he'd grown uncommonly fond of. Gray brought himself up short. It had been another man who had heard that laughter through the years.

"Apparently, she more than looks like you," Gray said. "I seem to remember that you were interested in softball, as well."

Each stared at the other. What they both remembered was a young Christine who'd begged Gray to teach her how to throw a curve ball. They remembered, too, one softball game that had changed the course of their relationship. It was Christine who looked away first.

"Yes, well," Christine said, "I was never as good as Mandy. Of course, she doesn't think softball all the time. She loves to play with video games and with her Barbie dolls. She's active in the Girl Scouts, and she also likes sleeping over at friends' houses and having them sleep over."

Visions danced in Gray's head, visions of a child

playing endless video games, of a child's room filled with Barbie dolls, of a child going door-to-door to sell Girl Scout cookies. There were other visions, too—of the houses of Amanda's friends, all of which Gray would wager looked very much like the Lowell mansion.

". . . pierced ears."

This grabbed Gray's attention. "Pierced ears?"

"Getting her ears pierced is the ruling passion of Amanda's life these days. Some of her friends have pierced theirs, and, peer pressure being what it is, she wants to pierce hers."

"Isn't nine a little young?" Gray asked, not realizing just how much like a father he sounded.

"I told her we'd talk again when she turns ten," Christine said, then, obviously realizing what she was saying, she sighed. "Funny, now that she's missing, the piercing of her ears doesn't seem at all important."

Missing? There was that word again, as if she were deliberately avoiding the word *kidnapping*. And Esther was right. Christine wasn't budging from the window. How long had she stood right where she was, waiting for her daughter to return, for that surely was what she was doing?

"Why did you name her Amanda?"

"I named her after my grandmother—Amanda Adelle. She was spunky, gutsy, something I hoped this child would be."

"And is she spunky?"

Christine didn't even have to consider this. "Yes, Mandy has her share of courage, spirit, good ole grit."

"You call her Mandy?"

"I swore no one would, but, of course, it was inevitable. In fact, I'm probably the worst offender."

"What's her favorite food?"

"Pizza. With pepperoni and mushrooms."

"What's her favorite color?"

"Blue."

"What's her favorite movie?"

"Whatever the latest Disney film is. No, probably *Beauty and the Beast*."

"Who's her best friend?"

Christine paused, then answered, "In all likelihood, Wendy Solomon. She has a number of good friends, including Heather Tryde, but I'd say that Wendy is her best friend."

Gray recognized the Solomon name as another with clout in the small town. Although his business was successful, there was no way Gray could compete with the Lowell wealth, nor could anyone confuse his house, however nice, with Rosemead. Yeah, he could just see a lot of fancy-smancy kids spending the night at his house. More to the point, he couldn't see them at all, because no fancy-smancy parent would allow his kid to sleep over in such common surroundings. Furthermore, and this hurt the worst, he could just see Amanda wanting her friends to sleep over. He couldn't admit any of this—it was too sharp a blow to his pride—and so he struck out in another direction.

"What grade is she in?"

"Fourth. At Saint Mathias."

Christine tilted her chin, as though expecting to have to defend her choice of a private school.

"Is she a good student?"

He could tell that his question had taken Christine off guard. But then, she'd been readying herself to justify her choice of a private school. Then again, maybe it hadn't been the question at all, but rather how eagerly he'd asked it. Or how paternal it had sounded, even to Gray's own ears. Truth be told, and this surprised him, he didn't want the child to be the indifferent student he'd been.

"Yes, she is," Christine answered. "Her grades are always well above average to exceptional. Her teachers are particularly impressed with her writing. She's very creative. She's always inventing the most elaborate stories, always telling the wildest tales, which she swears are true."

"Like her mother?" Gray asked, remembering the outrageous stories Christine often told.

"Yes and no. She's had no need for an imaginary friend. I saw that she got the attention I didn't. I'm really a very good mother."

Christine waited for Gray to make some snide remark, but he didn't. And that flustered her perhaps more than if he had, for she was left to wonder what he was thinking.

Finally, Christine continued. "Mandy also loves to read, particularly stories about animals. We've read all of James Herriot's works and all the classics like *Black Beauty* and *The Yearling* . . . anything about animals. She owns a tank of fish, a hamster, a bird, and I've promised her a dog soon. The one she had for several years died last year."

Gray remembered that Christine, too, loved animals, but had been denied them because her mother didn't want them in the house. The only pet she'd been allowed was a pony.

Hi, my name's Christine, and I have a new pony.

Gray heard the words as clearly as he'd heard them in the rose garden all those years ago. Christine had been twelve, little older than their daughter, and filled with delight over her new pony.

"And does Amanda"—the name still spilled awkwardly from his tongue—"have a pony?"

"Yes, she has a pony. Her grandfather bought it for her."

"Of course."

Christine refused to take the bait. Moreover, she had the nerve to resort to logic. "Would you feel better about any of this if Mandy didn't have a pony?"

Gray sighed. "Of course not." He paused, then said, "I'm sorry. That was uncalled for."

His apology took Christine by surprise. Maybe it did him as well. They stared at each other for what seemed like an eternity. Finally, she said, "It's okay."

Gray considered a moment. "I'm going to try hard to put the past to rest for now. All we should be thinking about is Amanda."

When he stepped forward to stand beside Christine, assuming the vigil along with her, each worked equally hard at ignoring the other's presence—no remembering the floral scent of the sweltering hothouse, no remembering sweat and secrets, no remembering the private dark smell of sex. No, each thought, it was far better to recall where these things had led them. To a place called nowhere, where dreams survived only a summer, where heartaches lasted a lifetime, where a nine-year-old child was missing in the rain.

Lightning streaked and thunder shuddered, awakening Sandy Killian from a bad dream. Actually, it was *the* dream. For seemingly the whole of her life—the beginning was shrouded somewhere in her memory—it had been the same. Darkness. The sound of endless even-falling footsteps. The sudden pounding of her heart. The slow, silent—mustn't let anyone hear!—opening of her bedroom door. The wedge of light that always preceeded *him*. And then, his image filled the doorway. Shoulders too broad, a waist too thick, lips too wet, hands too rough. From that point on, the dream was never explicit, as if it knew only too well that she couldn't handle the particulars. She always awoke a captive of the frightening feeling of being smothered.

Throwing back the sheet, Sandy sat on the side of the bed, swallowing great gulps of air. Sweat soaked her cotton gown, leaving her to feel slightly chilled despite the warmth of the room. She knew better than to try to walk yet, for the dream always left her weak. Weak and feeling out of control. God, how she hated feeling out of control! And so she waited. Sitting in the dark. Always in the dark, for she was afraid that the light would reveal that it had been no dream. Little by little, her heart eased its rabid rhythm. Little by little, her battered breath returned to normal.

At last, she reached for the lamp, turned it on, and, when light flooded the room, she glanced down at the carpet, following it all the way to the door. Nothing. No footprints. She sighed with relief. Then looked at the bedside clock. A little after nine o'clock. She'd been so weary that she'd tumbled into bed after returning home from Rosemead. That weariness had only been exacerbated by the remnants of the sedative the doctor had given her. Now, standing on legs that felt stronger but by no means sturdy, she drew the gown over her head and dropped it to the floor in a moist heap. Naked, she crossed into the bathroom, and the shower. Minutes later, as she tugged a clean gown, one of several perfectly folded and perfectly stacked in the dresser drawer, over her head, she caught her reflection in the oval mirror. Damp strands of hair were glued to her forehead, while her eyes shone with the aftershock of fear. Her eyelids were puffy from crying.

Tears.

She wasn't certain that she'd ever cried so many.

Even now, thoughts of Amanda haunted her. Dear, sweet Amanda.

Unwilling to dwell on the child, Sandy finished pulling the gown down over her full, firm breasts and slim hips, both the result of rigorous exercise and religious dieting. She headed for the kitchen and a mug of hot tea. Her mother's panacea for all of life's ills. As always, thoughts of her mother set her awash on uncertain seas, and she pushed those thoughts away. For a long time, she'd hoped to resolve her feelings for her mother, but had come to doubt that she ever would. So be it.

The tea, hot and sweet, acted as a stimulant, and she began to feel better. Stronger. Surer. Less a slave of the dream. She drank the tea to its very last drop, then, as always, she took the dirty mug to the sink, applied a sudsy detergent, swiped around a dish cloth, then rinsed and dried and placed the mug back in the cabinet. She aligned it in an orderly row with the other mugs.

Order.

Control.

The first led to the second, the second to a life where no one could hurt you. She controlled her own destiny now. Of that, she was most certain.

On the outskirts of town, by the same light of the storm, the man watched the mouse. Brownish-gray, the color of earth and ash, the small creature thrust its nose into the air in search of the smell of danger. The man stepped farther back into the fallow shadows of the kitchen, willing his human scent to follow. Emboldened by hunger, the mouse ventured forward, scooting over the cracked linoleum tile, edging around the corner of the cheap wooden cabinet on which sat a small-screened television, past the piles of magazines and papers, following the outline of the outdated refrigerator. The tiny beast hesitated, sent its twitching nose on a last hunt, then, with its ears pinned back and its long tail pointed straight behind him, he scurried forward. Toward the chunk of golden-yellow cheese. Toward the metal jaws of death. Suddenly, the mouse stopped. Cold. On a dime. In the silence, in the stillness, thunder rolled. The the mouse turned and fled, once more disappearing behind the thin strip of paneling.

The man eased from the shadows, disappointed, but by no means defeated. He was a patient man. In truth, patience might well be his strong suit, but then patience was always the strong suit of someone traveling the pathway of revenge. And he'd been following that trail for a while now. Stepping forward, the man studied the photograph posted to the refrigerator door. A memento of a happier time. In the photo stood three men, the one in the middle smiling hugely and hugging, unashamedly, the young man to his right. Yes, happier times. Times when his life didn't seem out of control.

But he was taking that control back. He glanced toward the back bedroom of the rented house. A slow smile spread across his face. He reached for the uniform that lay across the kitchen chair, then, before leaving the room, he glanced once more at where the mouse had disappeared. His smile grew. If truth be told, he respected the animal's survival instincts. He himself possessed them. He only hoped that Christine Lowell Jackson did as well. It would greatly sweeten the taste of victory.

Chapter 5

Headlights suddenly appeared from out of the damp night, headlights that slowly made their way up the drive of Rosemead.

"Probably Terry returning," Hamm Clancy said.

But it wasn't Agent Carrelli.

Claiborne Lowell surveyed the living room, letting his gaze come to rest on Gray. Gray's stomach tightened, while a rash of memories rushed at him. He recalled being held down and beaten to within an inch of his life, managing to pull his pocketknife only to have it wrenched from him, feeling the searing pain of blade cutting flesh, being told to get out of town and to stay out, then waiting, waiting for Christine to return, and realizing with a heavy heart that she wouldn't.

"Well, well," Claiborne drawled, "the proverbial bad penny."

"Claiborne," Christine pleaded. "Not here. Not now."

"Wrong, sister dear, here and now," Claiborne said, never taking his eyes from Gray. "I think that Mr. Bannon and I need to have a talk. Man to man."

"Claiborne, this is none of your business."

"Wrong, again, sister dear. When you slept with this white trash, you made him my business."

The room went utterly still, and Gray could see the color draining from Christine's face. Inexplicably, he felt protective.

"Your brother's right. He and I do need to have a talk. Man to man. But I think we need to have it privately."

Without a word, Claiborne walked from the room and started for the library. Without a word, Gray followed.

Portraits of Lowell men, roughly a dozen generations in all, including Merritt Lowell, stared down, critically, at Gray from the paneled walls of the library. With few exceptions, each bore a marked similarity— robust builds that defied the passage of time, faces with craggy, irregular features that blended alchemically into handsome, and hair, a color neither brown nor blond, that was wont to fall out prematurely at the crown. Their eyes, of varying dark shades, were possessed of one singularity: the ability to pierce with greater accuracy than any stiletto.

At first glance, Claiborne, now seated behind the wide desk, bore a marked resemblance to his predecessors. At second glance, the robust build seemed to be headed to seed too early, the handsomeness a little contrived, while the dark eyes appeared dull and jaded, as if they'd seen just a bit too much. Gray first thought that maybe the Lowell line was petering out, but then decided that Claiborne had simply misused what he'd been given.

Gray had often wondered how he would react to seeing Claiborne again, but he hadn't expected such strong feelings, some of them contradictory. Of course, there was anger, anger enough to spare, to provoke a need to beat the crap out of this man. But, ironically, he felt pity too. Claiborne compared most unfavorably with his strong, dynamic father, a comparison that Claiborne had had to live with every day of his life. So while it was true enough that Gray wanted to beat the crap out of Claiborne, pity demanded that he display the restraint that Claiborne had so lacked.

Claiborne looked over at Gray, who slouched in the leather visitor's chair in an attitude of disrespect. Claiborne's look seemed to say that Gray's all-too-casual appearance—dirty jeans, worn tennis shoes—was no more than he expected, yet overwhelmingly distasteful.

Finally, Claiborne said, "I really think that you should leave town. Just get in your car and go."

Gray laughed—mirthlessly. "Anyone ever tell you that you sound like a broken record?"

Claiborne, undaunted by the comment, replied, "I think that I can persuade you to my way of thinking."

With that, Claiborne opened a drawer of the desk, took out a checkbook, and began to write, arrogantly, offensively, just as his father would have done. Gray said not a single word. He just watched and waited and wondered what the going price of a man's paternal rights was. In short order, the sound of a check being ripped from its companions shattered the silence. Then, in a pitiful display of power, where none really existed, Claiborne shoved the check across the desk. Gray made no move to collect it. He merely let his dark gaze merge with Claiborne's.

"As I said," Claiborne repeated, leaning back in the chair, "I think this will speak to you. Loud and clear."

Gray leaned forward. "You might want to pay close attention to this, because I'm going to say it only once." He paused for dramatic effect. "Neither you, nor Lowell Enterprises as a whole, has enough money to get me to leave town." He paused again, then added, "Not everyone can be bought, Claiborne."

Claiborne's voice hardened as he said, "Christine should never have brought you back into her life. Slumming was one thing, even getting pregnant I can understand—those things happen—but bringing you back after all this time is reckless."

The mention of slumming inflamed Gray.

"What you mean is that Christine should never have brought me back into *your* life. What's wrong, Claiborne, don't know how you're going to explain me to your fancy friends?"

"It's not explaining you to *my* friends that concerns me. It's dear, sweet Amanda who worries me. How is she going to hold her head up when all of her friends discover how tainted her lineage is?"

The comment slithered past Gray's defenses, making him wonder for the first time what this child would feel upon learning the truth. He had just begun to consider the ramifications of her being ashamed of him when he realized what Claiborne was doing.

"Cut the crap. You've never been concerned about anyone but yourself."

"And I suppose you weren't thinking of yourself when you crawled between my sister's thighs?"

The very words on this man's lips were tantamount to blasphemy. How dare he speak so basely of what he and Christine had shared? He felt that protective urge again, to somehow shelter her from the ugliness of the words.

"Leave your sister out of this."

"Leave town," Claiborne repeated.

"Make me." Gray knew how pathetically adolescent the dare sounded, but couldn't deny that the words felt good on his lips.

"I don't think that will be necessary. I think you'll see reason." He purposely allowed his gaze to wander the length of Gray's scar, his face filled with pride at his handiwork. "I made you see reason before."

Gray slumped farther into his chair, giving a laugh. The man had tried bribery, now he would try intimidation. "That's not exactly the way I remember it. I remember you being such a gutless wonder that you had to have half a dozen of your friends help you."

The rebuke hit the mark. Claiborne's eyes narrowed. "Like I said, you were white trash then, you're white trash now. Your daddy could barely make a living, and your mamma wouldn't even hang around."

Gray refused to stoop to this man's level. "You always were slime," he said. "I disliked your father, but at least there was something there to respect." At the look that spread across Claiborne's face, Gray knew that he had been right. Claiborne had suffered from standing in his father's shadow. It was his weakness, his Achilles heel. "What a disappointment you must have been to him."

Claiborne turned livid. "Get out of town while you can."

Gray pulled slowly to his feet, took the couple of steps to the desk, and placing his palms on the perfectly grained wood, leaned forward. This close to the man, Gray smelled the unmistakable odor of semen.

Disgust rumbled through him. The man's niece had been kidnapped and he was out screwing.

"Don't you ever threaten me again," Gray drawled. "Don't you ever touch me again, because if you do, I might just forget that I'm a helluva lot nicer guy than you. To tell you the truth, I'm just looking for a good excuse to rip off your shrunken balls and stuff them down your throat. And I won't have to have half the town holding you down to do it."

"Get out!" Claiborne snarled.

Gray straightened. "Before it's over, everyone in this town is going to know that the child is mine. In fact, I think I'll check with a lawyer and learn what my paternal rights are."

"No lawyer in Natchez will touch you as a client."

"Then it's lucky for me that there are lawyers outside of Natchez." Gray started for the door, but stopped, turned, and added, "You're right, the child does have a great deal to overcome, but if she can overcome the knowledge that she has Lowell blood flowing in her veins, she can overcome the knowledge that she has mine."

"You son of a bitch!" Claiborne shouted.

Gray flung open the door of the library, and Claiborne Lowell's obscenity followed him to the foyer. There Gray ran into the man who'd just entered the house, the man heading for the living room.

"I'm sor—" Gray began, but stopped abruptly when he realized who the man was. The two men, in a ritual as old as time, sized each other up. It was difficult—no, impossible—to tell what lay behind the man's impassive façade. On the other hand, Gray felt as though he could be read as easily as an open book, and what the words on the pages of that book fairly shouted was that Christine had played him for a bigger fool than he'd ever imagined.

Suddenly, the walls of Rosemead, and the past, closed in on him, and as he hurried for the front door, he thought that surely he would suffocate if he didn't get away, from this house, from Christine's lies and deceit.

Everyone said that they were a stunning couple, and Christine supposed they were. In truth, Peyton would have complemented anyone. With a tanned and healthy California-blond appearance, despite the fact that his association with the state was only recreational in nature, he had a substantial build and a pair of pale blue eyes that at times appeared almost transparent and ghostly. Aside from his physical attributes, he possessed an energy, a vitality, a savoir faire that would have made him a perfect mate even without the significant sums of generations of money salted away in the bank.

Yes, any woman would have considered Peyton handsome, but he meant more to Christine than that. She considered him her savior, for that was precisely what he'd been—unwittingly, unknowingly, and to her shame. To her even greater shame—which, of course, symbolized her marriage, didn't it?—it was not this savior who occupied her thoughts, not this man who'd barged into Rosemead and demanded to speak with her in much the same way another had earlier that evening, but rather the man who'd just exited the house. She knew precisely what Gray was thinking. She'd seen it in his dark eyes, and the accusation was far from pretty. In fact, it had been downright ugly. At best, Gray believed that she'd conveniently turned to Peyton when she'd found herself in need of a husband.

At worst, he believed that she'd been seeing Peyton in earnest, courting the acceptable suitor while having her fun with the unacceptable hired help. Yes, that would more likely fit his slumming theory.

No, you can't go out with him!

Christine heard Gray's agonized plea from years before. She remembered the warm, tight feeling that spread across her chest at the realization that he was jealous. They had been lovers, repeatedly and with a passion he couldn't have faked if he'd tried, but he'd hidden his emotions from her. Perhaps even from himself. But in one unguarded, and precious, comment, he'd revealed his feelings. Even so, they—she—had had to be practical.

I haven't been out with anyone since we . . . I haven't been out with anyone all summer. Mother's wondering why.

Actually, her mother had done a great deal more than wonder. She had insisted, as only Elizabeth Adelle Lowell could, that Christine accept one of the many requests for a date that the more-than-suitable son of Rutherford and Mimi Jackson had made. Peyton had tried, unsuccessfully, for the better part of a year to ensnare her attention, by word, by deed, by anything he thought would work, but while Christine thought him pleasant enough, he just didn't stir her. At least not in the way Gray did, but then, even at that tender age, she'd suspected that no man would ever be Gray's match.

My going with him is the perfect cover, she'd said, being careful to say no more, for at the heart of the issue was the delicate matter of Gray's social unsuitability. She had no real prognosis for the relationship, except to believe in some vague and innocent way that love would win out. But until it did, she'd be pragmatic, sensible, and so she'd said, "It's only a party. There'll be lots of people there."

"I won't be."

"No," she said, splaying her hand across his face. The feel of the stubble shadowing his cheek was sensual, a wonderfully wicked abrasion of her skin. "Tell me I can go."

"You don't need my approval."

"Tell me I can go, or I swear I won't."

Gray's eyes, Gray's voice, both softened and hardened. "Go. But don't let him touch you. You belong to me!"

The point seemed unarguable then and later that night when Gray sneaked into her bedroom. It was the one and only time they'd made love there. He half ripped their clothing off—there was none of his usual gentle foreplay—then impaled her beneath him in a single and savage thrust. His lips ravaged hers, leaving them swollen and aching, his fingers tangled themselves, hurtfully, in her hair, while his body pumped his seed into her. Afterward, his breath ragged, he merely held her. So tightly that he compromised her breathing. She hoped that he'd declare his love for her, something he'd never done, but he didn't, and she contented herself with the knowledge that his body had said what his lips had not.

"I betrayed you."

Peyton's voice surprised Christine, for surrounded by the specters of the past, she had easily forgot that she wasn't alone. If his presence startled her, his comment did so doubly.

"How have *you* betrayed *me*?"

Peyton had taken a seat in the upholstered chair and now leaned his head against the wing back. He looked tired, yet he in no way looked rumpled, but then

Peyton didn't rumple. She'd never seen him look less than immaculate, not in the morning, not at noon, not in the evening, not even at midnight when his body would roll from hers and back into his space on the far side of the bed. Even now, although Amanda was missing, although he possessed the knowledge that Amanda wasn't his child, Peyton appeared crisp, as though awaiting a military inspection.

"I shouldn't have walked out on you the way I did."

Christine knew that at the root of good breeding lay the ability to mask one's feelings—it was the credo by which Peyton lived—but this was taking good breeding a bit too far.

"You walked out because I had just told you that the child you thought was yours was another man's. I'd say that I betrayed you, wouldn't you?"

Peyton leaned forward in the chair, grasping one hand in another. Christine's gaze dropped to those clenched hands. He often did this in times of restlessness. Otherwise, on those occasions when life became too much and his composure slipped, he had a tendency to shred anything—magazines, newspapers, napkins—into thin strips, each of which he tied, square in the middle, with a precise knot.

"That's just it. I've spent the day going over everything, studying it backward and forward, forward and backward, and I'm not certain it's important who betrayed whom." He leaned even farther forward in the chair. "Just hear me out before you say anything."

Christine found this last petition ominous. She worried that she wasn't going to like what she was about to hear. Then again, maybe it was his sudden animation that worried her; he was as animated as a kid on Christmas morning.

"Okay, so Amanda isn't mine. At least not biologically. But she's been mine in every way that counts. I've been a father to her. She's been a daughter to me. I was there when she was born. I was the first to hold her. I taught her to ride a bicycle. I put Band-Aids on scraped knees when she fell off the bicycle. Surely you can understand that I can't just stop loving her."

"Of course I understand that," Christine said. "Nor will Amanda stop loving you. Ever."

"No, no!" Peyton said, lights appearing in his pale blue eyes. "You don't understand! Listen to me. Who knows that I'm not Amanda's real father?" Peyton answered his own question. "Your brother, your best friend, Esther, the FBI, a few of the local police. We all could keep this our secret. Amanda doesn't have to be told. We could continue as a family. After this kidnapping is resolved, she's going to need stability. She's going to need a mother and a father. She's going to need us, Christine. And maybe therapy. We could all get therapy. That's what I mean when I say it's not important who betrayed whom. I betrayed you too, Christine. I obviously wasn't a good husband. I could learn how to be. I swear I could."

Christine couldn't believe what she was hearing. That he couldn't see that their divorce and Amanda's parentage were totally unrelated troubled her. As did his dishonest proposal to keep Gray's relationship to Amanda a secret, for it mirrored her own deception. How clearly one could see another's misjudgment; how clearly it sharpened and defined her own egregious error.

"What about Gray?" she asked.

"What about him?"

"He knows that Amanda is his daughter."

"Right, I know," Peyton said, "but surely we could count on him to be reasonable."

Reasonable? Christine wanted to tell Peyton that they could count on Gray for a great many things, but not on his being reasonable. Not concerning this subject.

"If all else fails, we could offer him money," Peyton added.

"Not everyone can be bought."

"Nonsense. Everyone has a price. Some are just higher than others. Trust me, with a man like him, we can strike a deal."

Again, Christine doubted her hearing. If Peyton had any knowledge of Gray, he would have surmised that Gray couldn't be bought. But this wasn't even the issue; Christine struggled to find the words to express her thoughts.

"Peyton, our divorce is almost final."

"I know, but you can drop the proceedings. Just tell them we've reconciled. It's happened before; it'll happen again."

Frustration flooded Christine. Why couldn't he see the obvious? Why was he going to make her spell it out, thereby hurting him even further?

"I want a divorce."

"No," he responded categorically, patronizingly, "what you want is for things to be different between us, and they're going to be. I promise."

There was that light in his eyes again. This time it had moved past animation and into a kind of zealousness. He was clearly deaf to what she was saying.

Irritation now mingled with frustration. "No, Peyton, I want a divorce."

"Well, I don't. I never did."

"I'm genuinely sorry about that, but it doesn't change the fact that I do want a divorce. What's happened to Amanda or you not being her real father has nothing to do with it." Her voice softened. "I care for you, but not as a husband. I care for you as a good friend."

Peyton appeared unable, or unwilling, to understand. He merely stared at her as though she'd just sprouted another head. Finally, he shook his head.

"My God, Christine, do you know what I'm offering you?"

Yes, Christine thought, he was offering her emotional charity. His proposal to take her back, to raise another man's child as his own, was overly fair and overly generous, and it made her uncomfortable, for it was totally inappropriate. Under the circumstances, he should despise her.

When she didn't answer, Peyton said, his voice ragged, "You want him back, don't you?"

Christine avoided answering the question by responding, "I think that Amanda, as any child does, has a right to know her real father."

Just as Christine had avoided the question, Peyton avoided the answer. "No, you want him back." Peyton gave a harsh laugh. "You've always wanted him. It's been the three of us in bed all these years." Peyton leaped from the chair, crossed to Christine, and placed his hand on her shoulder. "I know you love him. You've always loved him—in retrospect, it's the only thing that makes any sense—but it doesn't matter. I'd prefer you love me, but if you don't, I can live with that. I just want you and me and Amanda to be a family." He looked at her pleadingly. "If you'd give yourself half a chance, you might actually fall in love with me."

The uncomfortable feeling that had taken root earlier now grew within Christine. It was one thing to suggest overlooking her deception and raising another man's child as his own, but quite another to grant her the right to love another man as long as she continued with her marriage. This proposal went far beyond inappropriate.

Again, Christine chose her words carefully, seeking by their content to make him understand that she'd never love him. "You deserve better than second place."

For a fraction of a second—later she'd wonder if she'd seen anything at all—Christine saw a hardening in Peyton's eyes. She was certain, beyond a doubt, that the hand on her shoulder tightened, painfully, just prior to releasing her.

"And you deserve something better than what this man can offer you."

Without another word, Peyton walked away from her and out of the room. Christine followed him to the foyer and watched as he climbed the spiral staircase. A dozen thoughts raced through her mind, chief among them that Peyton had, indeed, placed his finger on the pulse of their failed marriage, that she *had* never stopped loving Gray, and never would. But she was no fool. Gray had no intention of offering her any kind of future. Earlier, she'd wondered why she'd admitted the fact that Gray was Amanda's father. She now knew. She wanted to try to make him understand why she'd done what she had . . . and perhaps gain some measure, if only meager, of forgiveness in the bargain. That was all she could expect.

Thoughts of Gray turned Christine's attention toward the front door. Gray was, of course, believing the worst about her.

The deeply carpeted steps stood firm beneath Peyton's footing, a curious paradox to the fact that his world was suddenly crumbling about him. He could not believe that Christine had refused to halt the divorce, that she had refused, and so thoroughly, the generosity of his offer. She was not the injured party. He was. And yet, he had promised to forgive and forget . . . if only they could be a family again.

I care for you, but not as a husband. I care for you as a good friend.

He had wanted to shout at her that he didn't want her friendship, that he wanted her to love him as fiercely, as devoutly, as he loved her, but failing that, he would settle for what she could give him. He had wanted to rant and rave about how she had driven him crazy with her aloofness all those years ago, making him want her all the more each time she'd turned down his offer of a date. Did she know how he'd lain awake at night, pretending he was holding her, kissing her, making love to her? Did she have any idea how happy he'd been when she'd finally allowed him the intimacy he so craved? Or how delirious he'd been when she'd told him she was expecting his child? Did she have any idea how happy he'd been the day she'd become his wife? Or how sad he'd been to realize that she would never be his, except in name?

No. She knew none of this, for it wasn't within his capability to tell her. No more than it was within his capability to shout, to rant, to rave. Control. One had to control one's emotions. It was the civilized thing to do. Besides, losing control had always frightened him, making him feel alone and small and trapped. Losing control stripped one of power, baring one to the circling vultures of life, those beings who preyed on anyone who looked even remotely weak.

Ah, but Christine, he thought, his breath balled in

his chest, all that I have done has been for you. And now you would reward me by wanting your old lover back. For a fleeting instant, love and hate mingled together, making it impossible to separate one from the other—love with its brightness, its purity; hate with its darkness, its putrid dross.

Peyton's breath quickened.

His heart pounded.

His hands trembled.

No, no, don't feel! Not love. Not hate. Nothing.

At the top of the stairs, he turned left and headed for the nearest bathroom. Gilt and more gilt, all inlaid in virginal white, greeted him, along with a garish light that faded his tan and blanched his blond hair. Locking the door behind him, he stepped forward, collected numerous sheets of bathroom tissue, and spent the next few minutes meticulously shredding them into equal pieces, all of which he tied into precise knots. He then flushed the whole of them down the commode . . . with hands strong and steady and no longer shaky.

Chapter 6

Raindrops spattered Gray, drenching his clothes and his hair as he sprinted to his nearby van. It was his only sanctuary, the only place that was his amid this inhospitable, even hostile, setting. Wrenching open the door, he slid in behind the steering wheel. He allowed the sweet familiarity to assail him, the worn seats that knew every contour of his body, the coffee mug that always sat in the console beside the seat, the earthy, peaceful smell of peat and loam and manure. Oh, God, he thought, what he wouldn't give to be back in Atlanta, ignorant of all that was going on here. But there would never be any going back to that blessed blissfulness.

Was he serious about consulting a lawyer to see what his parental rights were? Yes, he was. And for a couple of reasons. He had begun to feel a bond with ... Mandy—this name seemed less formidable than Amanda. The bond was still hazy, but it was taking shape. Little by little, the child had begun to stake a claim on him that, while still fragile, was nonetheless very real. His second reason was less noble. He wanted to make certain that Christine understood she wouldn't be able to walk all over him.

As Gray watched the rain come down, he thought of Mandy's tomato plants, which most assuredly were taking a beating in this weather. He thought of their limp bodies being battered, the soil being washed away from the young and still vulnerable roots. He sighed, thinking that maybe Esther would rescue the plants. He was certain that Christine wouldn't dirty her hands with the task.

Christine.

The man with whom he'd collided.

This guy has asked me to a party. I think that I should go.

Even after all this time, the words felt like a stake being driven through his heart. Because they'd come so unexpectedly. He and Christine had been such ardent lovers, it had never crossed his mind that she'd even want to go out with someone else. Of course, she had protested that she didn't really want to, that her mother was pressuring her to accept this invitation. Looking back, at best, her protestation was suspicious. At worst, it was a downright lie. How was he to know that she hadn't been seeing Peyton Jackson—then a nameless entity—all along?

And yet . . .

He remembered so vividly that July night. As though drawn back in time, Gray glanced through the driving rain and up at the mansion with its gracefully columned gallery, its russet brick walls and green shutters, the front door that welcomed everyone, except him, with the wide arms of Southern hospitality. He noted the white waist-high railing that surrounded the

small, second-story balcony, the mammoth live oak
tree that grew so near the house. The sight of both
balcony and tree unleashed a torrent of maddening
memories. On a grumble of thunder, he recalled how
he'd waited in the shadows, his heart so consumed by
feelings he'd never had before, he felt near to bursting.
He recognized the demon feeling named jealousy. He
even recognized the softer feeling, though instinctively,
intuitively, he knew that it was best not to give it a
name.

The demon feeling grew when the sports car strut-
ted to a stop in front of Rosemead. The top of the car
was down, giving an unimpeded view of its occupants.
Christine's hair, which she'd piled atop her head,
looked invitingly mussed, though curiously the driver
of the car appeared untouched. There, in the bright
lights, Gray had his first glimpse of the man he'd seen
again tonight, a handsome, fair-haired man who would
have made Adonis envious. Gray hated him on the
spot.

He also hated the way he touched Christine as he
assisted her from the car. He took her hand, then oh
so subtly slid his arm about her waist as he walked her
to the door. Gray's heart stopped, then rushed forward,
pumping the demon feeling to every part of his body.

Would he kiss her?

Would she allow him to kiss her?

Gray waited for the scene to play out, perhaps for
madness to engulf him, for if this stranger kissed
Christine, he would surely go crazy. A lunacy from
which he'd never recover. He heard trickles of laughter, snippets of conversation. The man moved closer to
Christine. Gray's heart stopped beating, while his
breath caught in his throat. The man leaned toward
Christine and brushed a kiss upon her cheek. It was a

simple, chaste kiss, but Gray knew that the man wanted more. Male to male, he sensed it, smelled it, like animal lust upon the hot, humid air.

Suddenly, painfully, Gray was seized by a need. No, by an obsession. Christine belonged to him and, as such, he had not only the privilege, but also the un-contested right, to claim her. It was his duty to im-print himself on her, to erase any trace of the man who'd just been touching her, of the man who'd kissed her chastely, but had wanted to kiss her passionately. Gray's obsession made him daringly reckless.

To this day, what happened next seemed more dream than reality. After the sports car disappeared from the drive, Gray slipped from the shadows, looked for something to throw at the window from which a light now shone, but found nothing in the yard his own hands had manicured meticulously. No stone, no downed piece of wood, nothing! Dammit, surely there was something somewhere! But there wasn't and he verged on despair when, suddenly, he remembered the knife in his pocket. He fished it out and pitched it, as gently as possible, at the second-story window. *Thunk!* For a second, he thought he'd broken the glass, but when the draperies parted and a puzzled Christine ap-peared, he realized that the windowpane remained in-tact. He breathed a sigh of relief, watching as Christine peered downward. She saw him immediately, standing bold and brazen on the lawn. Opening the window, she leaned out and called to him.

"What are you doing here?"

The question filled the night. Gray breathed it in, indulging himself in the delight he heard in Christine's voice. She was surprised to see him, even fearful that his presence would be detected, but she couldn't hide the pure pleasure she felt. In that moment, he would have climbed the highest mountain, swum the deepest sea, done anything, right or wrong, careless or cautious, to get to her.

The tree, its branches rambling toward the railed balcony, was his only hope of reaching her. With a strength and skill he hadn't known he possessed, he shinnied from one toehold to another, then grabbed hold of the first substantial branch he came to. From there, he grappled for another, sending a barrage of bark and leaves raining downward. In short order, he found a branch that would place him near the balcony. Moving now more on prayer than skill, Gray clung, balanced, and, finally, lunged. He caught the railing with his bare hands and, gritting his teeth against the burden of his weight, heaved himself upward. Breathless and damp with perspiration, he scaled the railing and, as though he had every right, he slipped through the open window and into her bedroom.

"You're crazy," she said, a smile at her lips.

"Yeah," he replied, thinking that maybe he had gone a little—perhaps even a lot—crazy at the sight of her with another man. How else could he explain the fact that he was standing in her bedroom? How else could he explain the fact that he was encircling her waist and roughly drawing her to him? How else could he explain the fact that his lips were slamming into hers?

Obsession.

Possession.

A fever that burned brightly within him. From the moment he touched her, from the moment his lips ground into hers, the fever was like a contagion gone wild. It was a contagion Christine happily absorbed. She needed to be possessed as badly as he needed to possess her.

He tore at her clothes, sending a button of her sundress tumbling under the dresser. In seconds, thin straps had cleared her tanned shoulders and her arms, leaving the fabric bunched at her waist. Eagerly, she snatched at his clothing, causing his shirt to fall open, and the snap of his jeans to give way. Her hands rushed across his warm, damp skin, trailing through the dark hair that matted his chest, then, with a brazenness and a boldness he adored, she slid her eager fingers past the vee of his open jeans and sought the swell of him. He was hard and hot and snarled sensuously at her touch. At the same instant, he wrenched his mouth from hers, stared deeply into her hazy eyes, and bared her breasts from the lacy confines of the strapless bra. At any other time, he might have appreciated the delicate firmness of her breasts, their dark crowns, the way they responded to him without even being touched, but now he knew only need, a need far greater than the physical act of intercourse.

During the journey to the bed, he hiked her dress upward and drew the scrap of lace from between her legs. As for his own clothes, he managed to consign his shirt to the carpet, but he never quite made his way out of his jeans. A tug here, a shove there, and he found himself lying atop her. With no foreplay, no subtlety, no sensual diplomacy, he rammed himself into her, impaling her with the firm, full length of him.

Her body buckled and she gasped, her fingers grasping for and digging into his bare shoulders. He loved the way she clung to him, so greedily, so needily, the way her eyes were melting under the heat of their passion. He'd intended to drive himself into her repeatedly, to ride her until they were both crazed with the need for completion, but after only a few thrusts into the warm wetness of her, he felt the tumultuous end rushing toward him.

No, no, no! he pleaded.

Yes, yes, yes! his body insisted.

His body won, and he began to pour himself into her. He heard a loud guttural sound begin in his throat and felt Christine's hand slip across his mouth. Her palm, sweet bondage that it was, tasted warm and salty and sexy. Exhausted, exhilarated, he collapsed, his body sprawled atop hers, his lips emitting small, broken breaths at her ear.

"You . . . belong . . . to . . . me," he growled.

"Yes," she answered.

The single word, spoken without hesitation, without reservation, and with such sincerity, obliterated all doubt and wiped the slate clean of the nagging memories of her with another man. That, and the fact that they spent the rest of the night making love. No experience had ever been so sensual. Perhaps it was the risk, the thrill of taking her right there in her bedroom, with her parents only doors away. Perhaps it was the power-endowing act of taking her amid all the rarefied glory that was Rosemead, of thumbing his nose at such ostentatious wealth. Perhaps it was the new level of intimacy they achieved that night.

Intimacy?

No, it had been more than mere intimacy. Much more. The softness of her caress, the whisper of her kiss, the unreserved giving of her body to him, his to her, the sounds that had flowed from her mouth to his ear had given birth to feelings best described as spiritual. Sometime in the middle of the night, he, who had so few beliefs, had found himself believing in a new religion. The religion was called Christine. The dark, desperate kisses that came as dawn lightened the sky made him a worshiper.

Before the summer was out, he'd discovered that his goddess had feet of clay. Tonight he'd discovered more. Christine had possibly been a liar and a cheat, possibly a manipulator extraordinaire. He wanted to be consumed by bitterness, but the truth was that beyond bitterness, beyond hatred, lay hurt. As much as he wanted to deny it, what he'd seen tonight, realized tonight, hurt him. After all this time, it still hurt. It made no sense, but there it was. Was that hurt what lay behind his wanting to consult a lawyer? Did he just want to hurt Christine in return?

Gray was contemplating this question when he saw the headlights of a car appear on the driveway. Even in the inclement weather, he recognized the unmarked car of Agent Carrelli. In due time, the automobile stopped in front of the porch.

Gray threw wide the van door. "Did you find Ernie Shaw?" he asked the second Agent Carrelli opened his car door.

Obviously surprised to see Gray standing out in the rain, Agent Carrelli, still seated behind the steering wheel, nonetheless said, "Yeah, but I didn't learn much." Then, "Get in and I'll fill you in."

Gray dashed around the hood of the car and slid in beside the FBI agent. Porch lights glowed, illuminating the interior of the car.

"Do you always wander around in the rain?" the agent inquired.

Gray glanced back at Rosemead. "It was either get out of there or serve time for murder."

"Of whom?"

"Mr. and Mrs. Jackson and charming Claiborne Lowell. Pick one or all."

Agent Carrelli nodded. "They are a bit much." Then, obviously thinking that, perhaps, he shouldn't have been so frank, he added, "Like I said, I didn't learn a whole lot from Ernie Shaw."

"Nothing? You were gone so long that I was hoping you'd run across something."

"Ernie Shaw wasn't at home again, but I decided to wait around and see what happened. After two hours, he showed up, that was around eight forty-five, a take-out pizza in hand, obviously ready to settle in for the night. He said he'd been in Jackson."

Gray wasn't quite ready to accept the fact that the agent had nothing to report. "What about being fired? What about his threat?"

"He candidly admitted that he was upset about being fired, and he swore that he hadn't cheated on his deliveries."

"You believe him?"

The agent shrugged. "I don't know."

"What about the threat?"

"Again, he candidly admitted making it, but said that he'd just been blowing off steam. He said that, as it turned out, his losing the Lowell account had been a big plus. Said he'd been trying to decide for a while whether or not to sell the business. He said that even with the Lowell account, it was getting harder and harder to operate in the black. Then there was all the government hassle, the DOT, EPA, all that endless paperwork. Bottom line, he was tired of the struggle, had an ulcer, and had just been diagnosed with high blood pressure. He said that without the Lowell account, however, the business wouldn't be worth as much. He also didn't expect to make much on the sale, because he had a couple of heavy-duty loans to pay off, loans he'd taken out to keep the business afloat. Long story short, there was a company in Jackson interested in acquiring Deep South Petroleum. I checked out the name he gave me and, sure enough, a Mr. Hardin is thinking about merging his company with Shaw's. No definite decision has been reached, however."

"Did you tell him that Amanda had been kidnapped?"

The agent shook his head. "No, I merely told him that certain threats had been made concerning the child, and that we were checking out everyone who might have any grievance against the family. Of course, he denied making any such threats against the child."

"Of course."

"I did ask him if I could look around his house, just to see what his reaction would be."

"And?"

"He seemed perfectly at ease allowing me to. Of course, if he hadn't given me his permission, I would have had to have a search warrant."

"I take it you found nothing suspicious?"

"Nothing. The house was messy—dishes on the kitchen cabinet, the bed unmade, lots of magazines piled around—but nothing to indicate that anyone had been, or was being, held hostage there. No, just him and the mice."

"Mice?"

"Yeah. He said he had mice in the attic. If you ask me, he had them everywhere. I saw half a dozen traps." Pause, then, "I take it there's been nothing new here."

"Nothing. Unless it came through in the last fifteen to twenty minutes."

"I was able to corroborate that Sandy Killian did, indeed, call Mrs. Jackson from her cellular phone at"—Agent Carrelli reached inside the breast pocket of his suit and pulled out a notebook, which he flipped open—"three-thirteen. Of course, we had already verified that Mrs. Jackson had called the police, then, just as she indicated, she called her husband. Following that, she placed a call to Sandy Killian, again with the cellular phone."

Gray frowned. "Are you saying that Sandy Killian or Christine had something to do with the kidnapping?"

"No, no. What I'm saying is that we check everything. With phone records, it takes a while unless the telephone is tapped. At this stage of the game, everyone is suspect. That includes all family and friends, along with everyone else." Then, with a frankness that was unnerving, he added, "I even had your whereabouts yesterday checked out."

Gray gave a laugh that was partly amused and largely incredulous. "You can't be serious. How could I kidnap a child I didn't even know I had?"

"We have only your word that you didn't know." Before Gray could comment further, the agent said, "In the end I rely heavily on gut instinct, and my gut instinct says that you didn't have anything to do with the kidnapping."

"Thanks," Gray said, a little testily, then added, "I'm sorry. I know you're only doing your job." Pause, then, "So, is your gut instinct pointing you in anyone's direction?"

"I'm afraid not, but it's still early. However, I'm inclined to believe Mrs. Jackson regarding Ernie Shaw's simplicity."

"By your own admission, you arrest few PhD's for kidnapping. Plus, the guy was smart enough to run a business."

"True on both scores, but as far as the business goes, it apparently wasn't overly successful."

"Right," Gray said, but something more, something about ulcers, nagged at him, something he couldn't define.

Neither spoke for a bit. In the silence could be heard the first slackening of the rain. It had gone from storm to shower. In the heightened visibility, a BMW and a Porsche could be seen parked just beyond the front door.

"Whose cars?" the agent asked.

"I don't know which belongs to whom, but both Claiborne Lowell and Peyton Jackson showed up."

"When?"

"Just recently."

"That's interesting. I wonder where they've been all day."

"What do you mean?"

"Both have been out of pocket. We checked Claiborne Lowell's office and his house, several times, actually, but he wasn't at either place."

"If you ask me, he's been with a woman."

"His niece is kidnapped and he's out screwing?"

"Mr. Sensitivity," Gray said. "What about Peyton Jackson?"

"I stopped by his office and his apartment this morning on the way back from the airport, but he wasn't at either location. I called several times during the day, but he never answered."

The words *his apartment* had grabbed Gray's attention. "What do you mean, his apartment? I thought he lived here at Rosemead."

"No, only his wife and his daugh— Sorry, only his wife and the child." A pause, followed by, "He and his wife are separated, and apparently have been for some time. As I understand it, the divorce is very near to being granted."

Separated. Divorce. What had happened between Christine and the paragon of virtue whom she'd married? Whatever it was, it had nothing to do with Peyton having learned the true paternity of the child he'd thought of as his, loved as his. That knowledge had come only recently, after the separation. Again, he wondered what could have gone wrong. It was only when he heard Terrence Carrelli's response that Gray realized he'd given voice to the question.

"Who can say what goes wrong between a husband and a wife?"

Something in the man's voice tugged at Gray, and he said, "I take it you're divorced."

"No, no," the agent hastened to say. "I was thinking about a friend of mine, a colleague. Only in his case, I know why his marriage failed. The FBI is a hell of a mistress, one most women won't put up with for very long. Even in lasting marriages, the agents travel so much that they miss all the important events in their kids' lives." He sighed. "I'm not fooling myself. I'm married to my job—for better or worse."

Gray wasn't certain that one precluded the other, but it was what Terrence Carrelli thought that mattered. Besides, he had enough to worry about without taking on someone else's problems.

Seconds passed before the FBI agent nodded toward Rosemead, saying, "I'd better let them know what I found out about Ernie Shaw. Or, more to the point, what I didn't."

As though on cue, both men threw open their respective doors, exited the car, and started for the house.

*   *   *

"Why didn't you tell me you were getting a divorce?"

Like so much of what he'd said since first arriving, Gray's question took Christine entirely by surprise. Indeed, his very approach had taken her by surprise. After hearing Agent Carrelli's report on Ernie Shaw and Claiborne's and Nikki's departures, she had returned to her post at the window. Without the company of the stuffed rabbit, which she'd sent upstairs to Mandy's bedroom before she ended up destroying the frail toy, or maybe before Gray recognized it and asked questions she didn't want to answer. She had been engaged in observing Peyton slipping from the room, taking with him a pile of knotted strips of silver gum wrapper, when Gray spoke to her.

She glanced up into a pair of brown eyes that seemed uncommonly interested in a reply, a reply to another question she was uncommonly interested in avoiding. She noted, too, the stubble of beard which was, by her wristwatch, almost six hours beyond being a five o'clock shadow.

"Who told you?" she asked.

She'd hedged on her answer. But Gray was willing to indulge her, providing he ultimately got the answer he wanted.

"Agent Carrelli," he said.

Christine looked stunned.

"He mentioned that he'd gone by your husband's apartment. When I commented that I thought you all lived here, he said that you two are separated, that he thought the divorce would be granted soon."

"Yes, soon," she said simply.

It didn't surprise him that she was offering no additional information, and so he pressed. "That's it?"

"I didn't tell you about the divorce because I didn't think that it was any of your business. More to the point, I didn't think you cared one whit about my personal life. In fact, you've indicated just the opposite."

She'd avoided the question—again. "The divorce I care about."

"Why?" she asked, turning the tables.

Earlier, he'd asked himself this very same question. Why was he prying into something that wasn't his business? On reflection, he'd decided that anything that concerned the child concerned him. This he told Christine and hoped that she believed it better than he did.

The fact that he'd referred to his daughter so impersonally hurt her. "You know, you've called her *the* child, you've referred to her as *she,* you've used her given name, you even once called her *our* daughter—of course, you wanted to remind me that I had no single ownership—but you've never referred to Amanda as *your* daughter. Can't you even try to say: 'Amanda is *my* daughter'?"

"What the hell does that mean?" Gray asked, realizing belatedly that his voice had carried and had ensnared the attention of several people in the room. When he looked their way, they quickly found other things with which to occupy themselves. Lowering his voice, Gray repeated, "What does that mean?"

"Just that it would be so easy to punish me through Amanda. It would be so easy to make her pay for my sin." As soon as the words were out, Christine worried that maybe she'd been too frank, and perhaps dead wrong to boot.

Gray, on the other hand, wondered if Christine

might be right. He did want Christine to pay for her sin, and pay for it dearly, but surely he wouldn't use Amanda as a means toward that punishment. Of course not. No, his inability to acknowledge the child as his own was rooted in a simple fact.

"I've been a parent for less than twenty-four hours," he said.

Christine said nothing, but she looked unconvinced.

"So, when is the divorce final?" Gray asked, quickly lobbing the ball back into her court.

"Several weeks. More or less."

"And how's Mandy handling it?"

"The way you'd expect any child to."

"I take it she didn't want the breakup."

"No, she didn't," Christine answered, adding, truthfully, "She and Peyton are close. They really are, Gray."

Don't say my name! he thought, but said, "Why?"

"I told you. Because I didn't think you'd be interested—"

"No. Why are you two getting a divorce?"

It was the question she'd most dreaded, the question she hadn't wanted asked at all. She turned away, because she didn't want to be tempted into telling him that she was divorcing her husband because he wasn't Gray. His kisses hadn't thrilled her; his touch hadn't heated her. It was not his name that she'd silently chanted into the stillness of the night, not his face that had bittersweetly haunted her every dream. Then again, maybe she turned away simply because it was too painful to look at Gray.

Finally, she said, "Irreconcilable differences."

Gray had no idea what set off his anger. Maybe it was the way she'd avoided his question, maybe it was the way she'd turned her back on him and looked the picture of composure. Maybe, just maybe, it was the way her hair, lush and full, fell about her shoulders. Or perhaps it was nothing more than the mounting tension that came from waiting, a tension that was eating them whole—a little at a time. Whatever the reason, he wanted to reach out, to place a hand on her shoulder, and to haul her around to face him. He didn't, however, because he didn't want to take the risk of touching her again.

"Tell me something," Gray said, "were you seeing good ole Peyton while you were seeing me?"

"You knew I was."

"No, no, what I thought was that we were using him as a cover." Pause. "Were you seeing him for real?" Another pause, then, "Were you sleeping with him?"

The last question proved as effective as physical contact in turning Christine around. God, she hadn't expected that one! An awful emptiness, a chill, bypassed bone and went straight to her soul. But enough of her tattered pride remained to demand that she not grace his question with an answer.

"Is that a yes?" Gray asked.

"Believe what you will," she said.

"No, I want you to tell me what to believe."

"I'm not going to do that, Gray."

Don't use my name!

"Then I'll tell you what I believe. I believe you played both ends against the middle. I believe you're like every other Lowell who ever lived in this house. I believe all you know how to do is use people and toss them aside. Isn't that right, Christine?"

Christine said nothing.

"Dammit! Answer me!"

Gray's voice thundered through the room, once more drawing everyone's attention. Even Peyton, looking duly shocked, hesitated in the act of reentering the room. Everyone waited. And into the stillness came the sudden, jarring ringing of the telephone. Everyone stood stock-still, as though the ringing of the telephone had no relevance, as though they had not waited and prayed for just this moment.

"Mrs. Jackson?" Agent Carrelli called.

As though being roused from a spell, Christine pulled her gaze away from Gray and walked—hurried—toward the telephone. Gray checked his watch. It was three minutes after midnight.

At Terry Carrelli's nod, Christine picked up the receiver. At the same time, machines began to both record, and trace, the call.

"Hello?"

"Mamma . . ."

Joy, complete and sweet, consumed Christine. Alongside the joy, however, ran a painful need. "Amanda, are you all right?"

". . . I want to come home, but . . ."

"Has anyone hurt you?"

". . . I can't until you do what he says . . ."

"Amanda, answer me, darling. Are you all right? Has anyone hurt you?"

"You have to give him the money, Mamma. Then I can come home."

Frustration seized Christine. Why wouldn't Amanda answer her? "Where are you? Tell me where you are."

"He'll instruct you later where to bring it . . ."

Christine sensed that her daughter was about to end the call. Panic raced through her and she tightened her hold on the telephone. "Amanda, don't hang up. Listen to Mamma, tell me where you are."

"Please, Mamma . . ."

The line went dead.

"No, Amanda! Don't hang up! Amanda!" she cried out.

"Mrs. Jackson?" Agent Carrelli said.

Bewildered by the phone call, Christine glanced over at him.

Agent Carrelli hesitated, as though he dreaded saying what he must. Finally, apologetically, he said, "It was a recording."

Because she understood all too well the implications couched in the agent's statement, Christine said, "No."

"I'm sorry," Terry Carrelli said, gently prying the telephone from Christine's hand.

Gray watched as Christine sank into the sofa and buried her face in her hands. Gray could find no adequate words of comfort. He was hardly indifferent to her pain; it was a pain he shared.

Hanging up the telephone, Terry Carrelli glanced over at Hamm Clancy. "Call in the trace."

The trace was capable of pinpointing the exact number within minutes if it were a local call. Beyond that, it could record only that it was an out-of-town call, and what that town or city was. It could not specifically identify the number.

Clancy, his wide jaws occasionally taking a chew of his gum, nodded. Shortly, after speaking with the telephone company, he announced, "A public phone here in Natchez. Want me to go check it?"

"Yeah," Terry Carrelli said. "But I doubt you'll find anything."

The address of the public telephone in hand, Hamm Clancy departed.

"That's good, isn't it?" Peyton asked. "I mean, that means that Amanda's here in Natchez."

"Unfortunately," Phil Birmingham said, his forefinger and thumb absently smoothing down his mustache, "all it means is that the recording was played here. The child could be anywhere."

Christine raised her head, addressing the issue that everyone in the room was avoiding. "She's alive. I feel it."

No one argued the point.

Gray watched as Christine slept on the sofa. Esther had insisted that she lie down, although Christine had fought against the idea, just as she'd fought against the sleep that had finally overtaken her. Gray wished that he, too, could doze off. Everyone had waited so impatiently for a call, and now, under the circumstances, he thought that everyone wished the call hadn't come. It had worsened everyone's anxiety, and they were no closer to finding Mandy than they'd been before. The child had referred to the kidnapper as he—masculine, singular—but perhaps that meant nothing since it was almost a certainty that what she'd said had been scripted for her. Even Christine had been forced to admit that a nine-year-old wouldn't be likely to use the word *instruct*. It could be the obvious: an attempt to mislead them into thinking that there was only one kidnapper, a man, when, in truth, a woman and/or more than one kidnapper was involved.

Restless, Gray stood and walked toward Agent Carrelli. Over the last couple of hours, Gray had listened to the tape any number of times. At his approach, Carrelli handed him the earphones and, after Gray had seated himself, the agent turned on the tape. Gray listened to the telephone call, impressed with the strength of the child's voice under what had to be the most frightful of circumstances. Christine was right. This child did have spunk and grit, and damned if he didn't feel a sense of pride. The young voice, full of spirit and life and just a little bit of arrogance, reminded him of another young voice. Drawing his hand across his bristly cheek, Gray tried to keep that other voice at bay, to keep it hidden away in the past. It would not stay so neatly tucked away, however. In retrospect, he supposed he'd known the first time he'd heard that voice that his life would never be the same.

Chapter 7

"Hi, my name's Christine, and I have a new pony."

Seventeen-year-old Gray, who'd spent the morning spraying the roses—the previous gardener had been far too tolerant of pesky insects—glanced up to find a child standing beside him. He immediately recognized her as the daughter of his employer. In the week he'd worked at Rosemead, he'd seen her any number of times, although this was the first occasion he'd had to see her up close. Proximity confirmed what he'd suspected: that she was at that gawky, pre-adolescent, nothing-seemed-to-fit-together stage of life.

Somewhere around ten to twelve years old, she had a long, narrow face with a patrician nose that almost dared to be too prominent. Cheekbones rode high, while her chin, dramatically pointed to a triangular apex, rode low. Her onyx-black hair, escaping in corkscrew curls that coiled about her face and neck, and were presently damp from perspiration, had been coaxed into a single braid that swung from shoulder to shoulder when she walked or ran. And she ran often, with a zest and zealousness that was downright tiring to watch, with a fevered hurriedness suggesting that she barely had time to get from one place to another. Gray suspected that all this exercise was to blame for her string-bean slenderness. The pounds simply couldn't cling to such animation.

"His name's Beauregard," she continued. "Bold Beauregard. That's fifteen letters. You can't have more than sixteen, including the space." Pause. "Daddy says that Beauregard's a stalwart Southern name, but I'm not sure what *stalwart* means. Are you?"

Gray made no response, but none seemed necessary.

"Mrs. Anniston, she was my teacher last year, said that vocabulary's important, that it sets the uncommon apart from the common." Christine frowned. "She talked funny like that. Anyway, she gave us a list every week. Hard words. But she never gave us *stalwart*."

Still, Gray maintained his silence, although he thought how like a teacher at a posh private school to want to keep the uncommon apart from the common.

"Beauregard came from a black-type mare, and he was sired by a son of Bold Ruler. That's a very, very, very famous horse. He's two years old." Christine added quickly, "Not Bold Ruler. Beauregard." She kicked at a clump of earth with the toe of her tennis shoe and said, "He's a colt. A colt is a boy horse, and a filly is a girl. Daddy paid an absolute fortune for him." Finally, her exasperation obvious, the child said, "Did the cat get your tongue?" With a deadly earnestness, she asked, "Can cats really get your tongue?"

Gray grunted a reply that was impossible to interpret. Nothing personal, but he wished the kid would get lost. He had work to do, and he wanted to prove to Merritt Lowell that he hadn't exercised poor judgment in hiring him. No one had ever placed this kind of faith in him, and he didn't want to disappoint the only man who had. With that goal in mind—impressing a man who appeared larger than life—Gray finished one bed of roses and moved on to another. Uninvited, Christine tagged along, past buttery yellow blossoms, edged in cherry-red and exuding a strong, spicy fragrance, past pale pink petals, past those of purest white, past the velvety deep-red rose called Mister Lincoln. There were some twenty beds in all, each bordered in upended brick and each containing a dozen or so bushes.

"I don't think so," she said. "Mary Alice had a cat, and he never got her tongue. I would have known if he had because she wouldn't have been able to talk." Then, with the suddenness of a lightning strike, she changed the subject. "Why are you spraying the roses?"

Gray mumbled something about pesky insects, emphasis on the word *pesky*.

"Mamma says that fresh flowers in the house are a mark of good breeding and gentility." Pause. "But I'm not certain what *gentility* means. Are you?"

No reply was forthcoming from Gray.

At last, her indignation showing, young Christine hiked both hands to her lean hips and proclaimed, "I do believe you're being rude."

Her accusatory tone, her provoked posture, caught his attention. He stopped what he was doing, looked at the child, and noticed for the first time how very ordinary she looked. With her frayed denim cut-off shorts and her worn shirt, she could have been anyone's daughter. On the other hand, there was nothing

ordinary about her eyes. A dim gray that appeared almost translucent silver, they shone, literally shone, as
though they were alight with fire, the fire of indignation. Beneath the fire, however, he could see plain old
hurt. Two thoughts crossed Gray's mind: she'd earned
the right to be hurt—he'd treated her like crap—and
someday, some man was going to lose himself completely in those gray depths.

"You know," he said, "you're right. I *am* being
rude."

"Why?"

"I guess I'm just not used to having someone to talk
to." His answer surprised him. He could have said that
he was busy with work; he might even have said
that his talking to her wasn't all that good an idea. All
of which was the truth, but obviously the truth went
even deeper. The truth was that with only four walls
to talk to, none of which ever talked back, he'd grown
weary of the exercise. With work and high school—
thank God, he'd graduated that spring!—he didn't
even have the usual friends.

"Why not?"

He shrugged. "I work a lot. It's hard to make friends
when you work all the time."

"Mary Alice is my friend," Christine announced.
"We talk all the time. For simply hours."

"That's nice."

Changing the subject, she said, "What's your
name?"

"Gray."

She frowned. "Like the color?"

"Yeah."

"I don't know anybody named Gray."

"Well, now you do."

She thought about this, then smiled. "Yeah, now I

do." She reached down, picked up a chip of a brick, and sailed it high and wild in the air, asking as she did so, "Do you know how to throw a curve ball?"

The question took Gray off guard. "Yeah, I guess so."

"So does Claiborne—he's my brother—but he won't teach me how." She made a face, as though she'd just smelled something highly offensive. "He's a real snot."

Even though Gray had been at Rosemead only a short while, he suspected that Christine spoke the truth. Young Claiborne Lowell, probably no more than a couple of years older than his sister, but big for his age, had condescension down to a fine art. Their paths had crossed several times, and each time the young heir to the throne had made certain that Gray understood his subservient position. Beneath his haughtiness, however, Gray had sensed that the young boy was unhappy.

As though to prove her point, she said, "He told me to stay away from you. That you're from the wrong side of the tracks. That our kind doesn't have anything to do with your kind. That it's unseemly. Whatever *that*"—she rolled her eyes grandly—"means."

Gray knew only too well what *unseemly* meant. That uncommon versus common thing again. What Claiborne had said, via his sister, was the truth, but still it hurt Gray to hear it. He and his dad had been low men on the Natchez totem pole, but his dad had taught him one valuable thing before his death and that was how to work hard. He'd bet money that it was a lesson Claiborne Lowell would never learn.

The comment served as a barbed reminder of why he shouldn't be talking with this child. When he spoke, his voice flirted once more with rudeness. "Yeah, well, your brother's right."

"Why doesn't our kind have anything to do with your kind?"

"Because my kind gobbles up little girls like you."

"No, you don't."

"Yes, I do. I had bacon and eggs and two little rich girls for breakfast."

This made Christine laugh, and the sound was unexpectedly pleasant to Gray's ears. He told himself that it was only because he wasn't accustomed to laughter. It hadn't exactly been a staple ingredient of his life. Oddly, his reaction caused him to cling all the more tightly to his renewed rudeness.

"So, will you teach me to throw a curve ball?"

"Nope, I've got work to do." He then added, "If your brother won't show you, get your father to."

"He doesn't have time to show me anything. He's never here. Mamma's never here either. That's why they buy me things. Like Beauregard. They think things will make up for not spending time with me." She sighed, and with the perceptiveness of someone far older, she said, "But, of course, things never do."

Gray didn't reply. This time it wasn't out of rudeness, however. He simply didn't know what to say.

She talked a while longer, then dashed away, disappearing as quickly as she'd appeared. She left behind an unexpectedly loud silence.

In the summer, all of the South is drunk with the potent liquor of heat, each day staggering in nothing short of a stupefying haze into a long, slightly cooler night when it sleeps off some of its drunkenness. But then another dawn dots the sky and a new binge begins, leading irrevocably to another torrid intoxication. June, well-imbibed in the sweltering spirits, tottered into July, with Gray often working overtime until perspiration soaked his body, his hair—he often wore a handkerchief around it to keep it out of his eyes—and his clothes. He was pleased with his efforts, however. The gardens of Rosemead looked good, a fact even Merritt Lowell commented on on one of the few occasions he was home to do so.

Increasingly, Gray had realized that Christine was right: her parents *were* never home. Merritt Lowell spent endless hours at his office and on work-related trips, while Adelle Lowell flitted around like a social butterfly, attending one charity function after another, which the newspaper chronicled as though it had nothing better to report. Like his parents, Claiborne spent little time at home, no doubt hanging out with friends. All of this translated into Christine's being alone. Although he didn't investigate too closely the reason for it, he resented the child's solitariness. For a reason that was purely selfish, Gray equally resented the Lowells' behavior for his own sake. He had convinced himself that the Lowell family must be nigh on to perfect, maybe he'd even seen Merritt Lowell as something of a father figure, and it ticked him off that they weren't. With all that money, and having each other, they had an obligation to be happy.

But Christine wasn't. Clearly. She darted here and there, doing things that might outrun her loneliness. She practically lived with Beauregard, and when she wasn't with the colt, she often dropped by the gardens. He had mixed feelings about her seeking him out. He knew without question that her family wouldn't approve, but then was there any real harm in their exchanging a brief conversation? After he'd found out that she was playing on a softball team, he sometimes allowed himself to be conned into throwing her a few curve balls. She often complained about the dance lessons and the piano lessons that her parents insisted she take, activities they assured her she would one day thank them for.

Mostly, however, Christine bent his ear about Mary Alice. She was always going somewhere exciting with her parents—river rafting, camping out, Disney World. Furthermore, Mary Alice didn't have to take dance or piano lessons. It was evident that Christine envied her friend. Increasingly, Gray began to look forward to Christine's visits—her soft voice, her unbridled laughter, her impetuous nature, which in five minutes might have her telling an outrageous knock-knock joke, chasing a butterfly, and skipping rope. The fact that he did look forward to her visits troubled him. But not nearly as much as what he came to suspect.

"Mary Alice is getting a dog," Christine announced one day in the second week of July.

"Is she?" Gray asked as he cut the basketful of roses that the housekeeper had requested.

"Uh-huh. At first her mother said that a grand house was no place for a smelly old dog, not with priceless antiques scattered everywhere, but then she changed her mind. Mary Alice is ve-e-ry"—she turned the word into three syllables—"happy."

The adult phraseology—more to the point, Gray could hear the words being crisply churned out by Adelle Lowell—set him to wondering.

"What kind of dog?" he asked.

"A German shepherd. She's going to name him Champ. Is that a good name for a dog?"

"Yeah, that's a good name." He handed her the bas-

ket and said, "Here, String Bean, make yourself use-
ful."

"Don't call me String Bean," she said, as was the
custom in the name-game they played.

Normally, he'd call her a few more playful names, all
of which she'd rail against until the giggling set in, but
this time he cut several long-stemmed white roses, laid
them in the basket, and asked nonchalantly, "What's
old Mary Alice up to? I mean, besides getting a dog?"

"Oh, a zillion things."

"Like what?"

"Like picnics and movies and baking cookies and
going to the Gulf. Her parents take her everywhere.
They love her soooo much."

Later, when he delivered the flowers to Esther, Gray
asked, as casually as he knew how, "Does Christine
have a friend named Mary Alice?"

The housekeeper, who'd taken a shine to Gray, and
he to her, replied, "I don't think so. She has a couple
of friends who come over occasionally, but Mary Alice
isn't one of them. Why do you ask?"

The answer didn't surprise him. He told himself that
it was no big deal, that, from the beginning of time,
kids had had imaginary friends, and yet he saw this as
slightly different. Mary Alice was more than a companion to a lonely girl. She was Christine herself, a
Christine with loving parents, with parents who gave
of themselves, of their time. She had shared her fantasy
with him, and he felt strangely honor bound to keep
her secret.

"I guess I was mistaken," Gray said, leaving it at
that.

Two days later, a breathless Christine rushed to his
side.

"Hey, Princess Run Too Fast, slow down."

"I'm . . . going to . . . pitch . . . in the game . . . Saturday," she sputtered, her excitement causing each word to bubble over. Furthermore, she hadn't even protested his teasing around with her name.

"Are you now?"

She nodded. "It's our . . . last game. For the championship. And Mamma . . . and Daddy . . . are coming."

"They are?" Gray replied, going along with her but in all honesty thinking that it was just another of her fantasies. When he again questioned the housekeeper, he was surprised to learn that Christine had spoken the truth. Her parents really were going to the game. But he had a tough time imagining them taking time out from their busy schedules to attend such an event. All he could see were two people impatiently counting the minutes, one from beneath the big brim of a hat that protected a porcelain complexion from the sun, the other fearful that he was missing out on some big deal. And, unless he was mistaken, Esther couldn't picture the scene either.

In the end, he and Esther had been right. The Lowells hadn't taken time out from their busy schedules. When he'd found out that they'd left for New York the very morning of the game, a business trip that just couldn't wait, he sought Christine out. He found her in the stable, stroking the muzzle of Beauregard and cooing endearments. She was cavalier about the change in plans, too cavalier for a mere twelve-year-old. Gray knew that her indifference was an act. Soon her chin began to quiver, quickly followed by tears pooling in her eyes. Her shoulders heaved. Her breath caught. The tears fell in earnest. She eased down into the fresh-smelling hay, and there she sat. This was no dainty bout of crying, no half-spirited sobbing, but rather a full-out purging of wounded feelings. Gray didn't know what to do, although he felt she'd earned the right to cry. In the end, he simply eased down beside her, covered her hand with his—hers was lost in the vastness of his—and watched her teardrops splatter against his skin. At last, the crying faded to a sniffle, the sniffle to a worn whimper, and then silence.

"They're not my real parents, you know," she said after a while. The announcement was made so flatly, so matter-of-factly, that Gray could almost believe it. Especially since she was so very different from the rest of the family—in looks, in manners, in attitude.

"I had no idea," he replied with the sincerity that the fantasy demanded

"My mother is a beautiful Gypsy. She wears gold hoop earrings and dances in the moonlight. She sold me for a million dollars."

"That's a lot of money."

"I know, but she's very sorry she did." Pause. "She's coming back for me one day. When she does, I'm going with her."

With this statement, spoken with great emphasis, Christine divorced herself from her parents. From that day forward, she called both by their given names.

Some powerful force, one that couldn't be denied or ignored, drew Gray to the softball game that afternoon. As was his habit, he sat apart from everyone else, most of whom consisted of cheering parents. Christine stood on the pitcher's mound, tall, proud, defiant. Her every pitch was perfect, flawless, as though she were determined to make her parents sorry that they'd missed this fine occasion. Teammates, and the crowd, began to chant her name. Christine! Christine! Caught up in the moment, Gray, too, called her name. Whether coincidence or the possibility that she heard his voice among the many—he preferred this latter, but wasn't comfortable preferring it—she turned toward the bleachers and searched him out. He knew the instant she found him. Their eyes held, and Gray sensed a bond, strong and sure, lace them together. Discreetly, he gave her an encouraging thumbs-up. Discreetly, she acknowledged it, then turned her attention back to the game. At game's end—Christine's team won the championship, largely because of her efforts—Gray slipped quietly from the scene and returned to the silent, and miserably lonely, shack he called home.

Gray had kept her secret concerning Mary Alice, but that day the two of them conspired to share another secret. The sharing lent an intimacy, a sacredness, to the act. Christine seemed to understand that others might misinterpret his reason for attending the game, if they ever learned that he'd come to see her. After all, they were from two different sides of the track. Furthermore, Gray knew what young Christine did not know, and that was that their relationship would be frowned upon simply because of the difference in their ages. He was, after all, five years her senior and verged on manhood, while she stood, innocently, on the brink of adolescence. And yet, what he felt for her was chaste and pure. In a way too complicated to explain, even to himself, she became the family he'd lost, while he believed that in her mind, and heart, he became the family she'd renounced.

Christine's Gypsy mother never showed up, although Christine's belief that she would never wavered. At least for a long while. She had a slew of excuses for why this ephemeral figure, this model of motherhood—never mind that she'd once sold her daughter—hadn't arrived to claim her child. One reason was that she'd been delayed by whatever natural disaster had recently occurred—tornado, flood, fire, earthquake. Then there were the ever-popular explanations that she'd been detained to spy for the government, that she'd developed amnesia, always temporary, of course, for how else could she come for Christine if the past were permanently wiped from her mind? As age made her braver, Christine entertained the notion that her Gypsy-mother had fallen ill, perhaps even died, because of the wretched remorse she felt over abandoning her daughter.

Sometime around her fourteenth year, Christine forsook her Gypsy parentage for a fantasy closer to home. For a reason that was never quite clear, Christine decided that the housekeeper was really her mother, although she never bothered to explain why the woman had given her daughter away and then gone to work in the very household to which she'd given her. Of course, that was the beauty of fantasies. They didn't need to be logical and were often downright contradictory. Gray thought this choice of mothers far more appropriate, for, if truth be told, he himself, though nearing the age of nineteen, had elevated Esther to a maternal position. She always had a ready ear and was willing to give wise counsel. She also liked him and disapproved of the way the Lowell children, particularly Christine, were being raised, although loyalty forbade her from saying so.

In her fantasies, Christine never bothered to create a father figure. Gray wondered if he himself came to fill that position, at least to some extent. Certainly, she sought his advice and devoured his praise. It was to him she ran with her joys and sorrows. And, in many respects, he felt paternal toward her. He surely felt pride in her accomplishments and felt both physically and emotionally protective toward her. Perhaps he even felt a little possessive, for he knew that she shared her life with him in a way she shared it with no one else. To preserve their secret relationship, she chose her visits with care, which was to say that she came to the garden, to him, when none of her family was at home. Considering her all-too-absent family, however, her visits were frequent. Throughout the years, she expressed her feelings—hurt and happiness, pain and pleasure—with an honesty that he admired.

It was a relationship, a friendship, that would last until the summer of Christine's sixteenth year.

Earlier that year, he'd turned twenty-one and had been slightly disappointed to discover that he felt no differently now that he was legally a man. He told himself that was because he'd been shouldering a man's responsibilities for so long. He still worked long hours at Rosemead and, although he had few illusions regarding the kind of man Merritt Lowell was, he found that he still reveled in his employer's praise. Merritt Lowell was a powerful man, and powerful men had the ability to make others want to please them. As for Claiborne Lowell, there was no pleasing him in any form or fashion, and so Gray simply stayed out of the young man's way.

Over the years, despite all the long hours he worked, Gray had managed to eke out a slender social life. He dated occasionally, but the few relationships he had all died on the vine without ever really ripening into anything serious. And with no regrets on his part.

He worked, he slept, he worked and slept again, and that pretty much summed up his life.

That summer, Millie Renato, a waitress at the local diner, where Gray sometimes stopped off for supper—the blue-plate special went for $1.99, including peach clobber, buttered cornbread, and iced tea—began to show some quiet interest in him. She lingered a little longer than was necessary at his booth, slipped in an extra serving of dessert, even took to asking chatty questions about how his day had gone and what it was like over at fancy Rosemead. He liked her, mainly because she was his social equal, with not one single air to put on. While no raving beauty, she did have huge doe-brown eyes and the tiniest waist he'd ever seen. She also had a nice little smile that came quickly and sincerely. Out of the clear blue one evening, she asked him out on a date. He accepted.

Over the next month, they dated every so often. Usually, they would get pizza and beer and go back to her small apartment, where they'd listen to music and talk. At nineteen, she'd graduated high school and was working her way through secretarial school. She was full of plans for the future. On the other hand, Gray was conscious of a future only insofar as the word applied to the next day at Rosemead. He didn't know whether that was good or bad.

From the beginning, Millie was more sure than he where she wanted their relationship to go. For starters, she wanted to go to bed with him. Not that she ever said as much, but a man could always tell when a woman was his for the taking. When kisses were deep, when tongues were innovative, when eyes turned cloudy and misty, a man could write whatever sexual ticket he wanted. He'd written a few such tickets over the years. But Gray didn't take Millie Renato to bed,

because he cared for her. He believed that she deserved
more than a brief encounter, and, while he would
have liked to find someone to fall in love with—he
was tired of being alone—he knew that someone
wasn't going to be Millie. He simply didn't love her.
At least not as he understood the word.

Then came that one summer day, with the sun baking its way ever deeper into his copper-colored skin,
skin so dark that he wouldn't have been surprised if
the layers could have been peeled away. Sweat soaked
his clothes and dripped from his headband to make
tracks through his dirty face. He was thirsty. Incredibly
thirsty. He'd spent the better part of the day in the
hothouse, a grueling ordeal on such a horrendously
humid day. The only thing left to do was to collect the
roses Adelle Lowell had requested for the small gathering she was hosting that evening at Rosemead. It was
the third party that week.

"You stink."

So intent had he been on cutting the usual basket of
roses, calling it a day, and grabbing a cold beer, that
Gray hadn't even been aware of Christine's approach.
He looked up at her, running the back of the hand
holding the shears across his wet face.

"Geez, Fancy Pants, is that one of the fancy words
they're teaching you at that fancy school?"

Christine laughed, a sound that he'd grown more
than fond of. Whenever Christine laughed, it just felt
good to be alive. He handed her the basket the way
he'd done dozens of times over the years in the kind of
wordless communication they'd developed. Silently, he
moved from rosebush to rosebush, clipping the
choicest blossoms and passing them to Christine. At
his side, the basket handle secured in the crook of her
elbow, she took each rose, being careful of the thorns,

and laid it alongside the others. Occasionally, she'd sniff one of the more fragrant flowers.

"So, what's shakin' at the big house?" Gray asked.

"Just the usual. Merritt's gobbling up some unsuspecting conglomerate, Claiborne's raising hell with friends, and Adelle's getting her hair done for the party tonight." She reached for two more roses, one a golden yellow, another velvety pink, then added, "Actually, Adelle's in a bit of a quandary." Christine grinned, saying cheekily, "See, they *are* teaching me fancy words at that fancy school."

Gray never quite grew accustomed to hearing Christine refer to her parents by their first names, never quite got over the sad unnaturalness of that, but he accepted her decision to do so.

"I'm glad to know that Daddy's hard-earned money is being so well spent," Gray responded, then said, "What's Mamma in a quandary about?"

"Well," Christine began as though the answer might be a lengthy one. "It seems that the couple the party is for—Mr. and Mrs. Janowitz, Leo and Stella—have just moved here from Savannah. He's made a fortune in real estate, but has to slow down for health reasons. Something wrong with his ticker, I think. Anyway, Adelle is worried that he might have more money than we do."

"Oh, my God," Gray said with the utmost earnestness.

Christine giggled. "You obviously don't understand how serious this is. Adelle's been the queen bee for a long while now. She wouldn't want to give her position away to this Stella person."

"And what makes her think they have more money?"

"Leo Janowitz sold several Savannah malls for a 'perfectly sinful sum of money.' "

"The dog," Gray said, handing Christine yet another rose.

Christine laughed again. To Gray, it sounded like the lovely notes of a song.

"I told Adelle that it was easy enough to find out if they had more money," Christine said. "I told her all she had to do was take Stella Janowitz aside and ask her . . . to which Adelle replied that I was being impertinent."

"Wow, another big word."

"I told you that the teachers are doing their jobs." Silence fell, and several more roses were clipped by Gray's gentle hands. Finally, she said, "I'm going to be poor someday."

"I don't recommend that."

"Why not? You're happy."

Gray thought about how he'd once believed that the Lowells must be the happiest people on earth. He'd soon discovered that wasn't true, however. In contrast, he'd settled comfortably into his own simple life, taking pleasure in working hard and having a roof over his head and a regular supply of food in his belly. Over the years, he'd even made a few repairs to the old house which he and his dad had shared. Nothing grand, just new windowpanes to replace those that were cracked, a bit of shiny linoleum here and there, a spot of paint to erase the ravages of time. Although he periodically considered moving, he never did. Primarily because the house was filled with so many memories. Good memories. Like his dad's laughter. Like the vague remembrance of a softly sung lullaby.

"Yes, I *am* happy," he replied finally. "But you've

missed the point. Money, or its lack, isn't the basis of happiness."

"I'll take my chances with being poor." Without skipping a beat, she said, "They, Leo and Stella, have a daughter my age. Nikki. We'll be at school together this fall."

"That's nice," Gray said, thinking that Christine could use a friend. She still spent far too much time alone, time that either he or Beauregard all too often filled. It troubled him, too, that she didn't appear all that interested in dating. The boys she knew were all such drebs, she'd say, not that he was exactly sure what a dreb was.

"She's coming tonight."

"That's good. The two of you can get into mischief together." With this, he handed her another rose, this one a pale lavender, whose fragrance was the headiest in the garden.

"I hope she isn't a dreb," she said, reaching for the flower and adding, "All I need is for her to have thick-lensed glasses and a pound of wire on her teeth and— Damn!"

Gray whirled around. The rose lay at Christine's feet, while she herself was intent upon checking the index finger of her right hand. "A thorn got me. I think part of it broke off."

"Christ, Christine, I've told you to be careful of the thorns."

"Hey, it's no big deal. I'll just pull it out."

But she couldn't, a fact established after several tries, even though she could feel the tip sticking just above the skin line.

"Here," Gray said, reaching for her hand in all innocence. In the next few seconds, however, that innocence was to die a quick and painful death.

He studied her finger, brushed the pad of his thumb across the thorn—Christine winced—and determined that it did, indeed, jut from the skin. He, too, tried to use his fingernails as makeshift tweezers, but with the same lack of success that Christine had met with. As though it were the most natural thing in the world, he brought her finger to his mouth. He sucked, then gently teethed. Once. Twice. Her skin tasted sweat-salty, the single drop of her blood sweet. It was an odd, intriguing contrast. He sucked again, this time dislodging the thorn. He spat it out, then looked up. It was then it happened. Funny, he would later muse, how quickly, how unexpectedly, how thoroughly a man could be brought to his knees. One moment his life was order and organization, the next utter chaos.

So many things could be blamed: the way the sun glinted in her Gypsy-wild hair, making it sparkle like diamonds cast upon black velvet; the way the heat had added rougelike color to her cheeks and pearllike per-spiration to her brow; the way her eyes had faded to a mercurial, nearly transparent gray. When had she be-come such a beauty? And why hadn't he noticed be-fore? Had he become so accustomed to seeing her as a child that he'd been blinded to the change?

Whatever the reason, desire, plain and simple and completely out of place, crawled through him. It suf-fused him, leaving him hot and heavy and wanting something that no twenty-one-year-old man should want from a sixteen-year-old child/woman. It also confused him. How could this be happening? For one crazy heartbeat, he thought he saw the same confu-sion, the same need, in Christine's eyes. But he imme-diately saw his error. No, he wasn't seeing confusion and need. That had been mere wishful thinking. What he was seeing was naked fear. As though she'd been stung by a venomous snake, Christine pulled her hand from his. At the same time, she took a step backward, then another. She dropped the basket, strewing roses at her feet, turned, and ran for the house.

"Christine!" he called after her, but she kept running, toward the house and away from him, leaving behind only the forbidden scent of rose.

He felt he was the lowest form of life that had ever oozed from the primordial slime. Hell, he *was* the slime! Christine wasn't even a legally consenting adult. His transgression went far beyond the law, however. He had betrayed a friendship, a trust; he'd broken faith with the only family he had. My God, she'd been like a sister to him! And he a brother to her! He made her laugh with his teasing; he listened to her when no one else would take the time; he protected her as best he could from life's heartaches. So who had been protecting her from him? More than anything, he was sick at heart at the realization that she now feared him.

That night, he'd gone to the diner and consumed one too many beers. Afterward, he'd bedded Millie, hoping she could ease his shame, hoping she could replace images of a raven-haired child/woman. She could do neither. In the end, he vowed he'd talk to Christine, plead with her to let things be as they had been. He never got the chance, because she never came back to see him. Six long, and lonely, years would pass before they spoke of that night. Six long, and lonely, years would pass before he understood the source of her fear.

Chapter 8

As Gray was reminiscing about the past, Nikki Janowitz was inserting the key into the lock of her small house. Upon entering, she turned on the light and was overcome by the silence that always rushed at her when she came home. Its emptiness, its hollowness, surrounded her like a sullen sea, as she moved from living room to bedroom.

She had brought only a few pieces of furniture from her old life, a sofa and chair and lamp for the living room, a four-chair table for the kitchen (a small stove and refrigerator were provided), a bed, dresser, and nightstand for the bedroom.

Without glancing in the direction of the sleigh bed, she passed through the bedroom and headed for the connecting bathroom. She sought out the mirror of the medicine cabinet, peered through its aged spots, and confirmed what she knew. She looked tired, worn, weary beyond words. Her bobbed hair needed the attention of a comb, while her eyes ached from wearing contacts too long. She removed the contacts, replacing them with a pair of gold-framed granny glasses that looked far too old for her thirty-one years. Heck, she *felt* old.

She and Ron had spent their marriage bickering, almost from the moment they'd exchanged their vows. They had been the classic case of opposites attracting, but having nothing thereafter to hold them together. He'd been an outdoorsman, liking sports and hunting, while she loathed anything that necessitated keeping a score or working up a sweat, and she certainly saw no need to kill innocent animals. He was an extrovert, needing the company of others, while she preferred quiet evenings alone with him. They argued about money (he spent too much), about having a family (he thought a couple was crazy to bring a kid up in this gone-to-hell world), about anything, everything. It was she who'd filed for divorce and, ironically, she who'd had the harder time adjusting to the divorce. Bad though the marriage had been, there had been someone in her life. Bad though the arguments had been, they had filled the silence.

As if thinking the failed marriage had sullied her, Nikki stripped off her clothing and slid beneath the warm spray of a shower. Minutes later, with a towel knotted above her breasts, she padded back into the bedroom directly to the closet. She slid back the mirrored door and studied her wardrobe. She'd just grab something quickly and then rush back to Rosemead. She'd just— Her eyes caught the corner of the mirror and she saw him.

He lay stretched out on the bed, his hands stacked beneath his head, one leg crossed over the other at the ankle. He had a long, lanky, loose-limbed build that women liked. That and his dark hair, which fell to his shoulders. More than anything, however, women liked the aura of danger and mystery that drifted about him. Six months before, he'd shown up in Natchez, ostensibly on business, which he never clearly stated. He traveled a lot, always returning to Natchez, to a small apartment he'd rented downtown. Nikki was no longer certain she believed his story about having business in Natchez. More than likely, he was a man who sailed on the wind of opportunity. She didn't doubt, however, that he was, indeed, dangerous, simply because for him there was no such thing as right or wrong. There was only what he wanted.

Nikki turned, her eyes meeting his, and she shuddered anew at their scary shade of fire. Here was a man whose passion lay deeply hidden and richly preserved. "So, tell me, can we add breaking and entering to your long list of vices?"

"Ah, baby, that's cold," he said, unfolding himself from the bed and lumbering toward her. He placed a crooked index finger beneath her chin, tilted her head, and brushed a slow kiss across her lips. In contrast to his heated eyes, his lips were corpse cold.

The kiss in no way moved Nikki, although she was certain that Jacob Purdy would have never believed that. The truth was that, even when they were lovers, he didn't move her. She'd simply used him to fill her long, lonely nights.

"Back door," he said. "Picked the lock in ten seconds flat."

"Congratulations," Nikki said, adding, "What do you want, Jacob?"

"That's cold, Nikki."

No, cold was what she got when she thought about this man. He'd begun to scare her. She'd asked him to stop coming over, but he did pretty much what he chose, showing up when she'd least expect it.

"What do you want?" she repeated.

"I just came by to tell you good-bye."

Nikki could hardly believe her ears and certainly not her good luck. "Where are you going?"

"Greener pastures and all that."

The vague answer suited Nikki fine. He could be on his way to hell for all she cared. "When are you leaving?"

Jacob shrugged his bony shoulders. "A few days. I'm not real sure." He grinned. "So, you going to miss me?"

"Sure."

"We had some good times, huh?"

"Yeah, sure."

"C'mon, babe. You're talking like you don't like me," he said seductively, as he fingered the towel anchored above her breasts. It came unfastened and fell to the floor, leaving her naked. His hand began to trail between her breasts, headed downward toward a thatch of blond curls. "You used to like me. You used to like this. Remember?"

She did remember and wondered now how she could have tolerated his touch. His harsh touch, his rough touch, but then she supposed his harshness, his roughness, had been part of his appeal. Against all logic, a part of her blamed herself for the failure of her marriage, for the death of her dream of a family. God only knew that her mother had told her often enough that in marriage it was the woman who made all the concessions.

Stopping his hand at mid-belly, Nikki said simply, "No."

Jacob shrugged, as though the denial was her loss. "Not even a good-bye kiss for luck?"

"No," she repeated, picking up the towel and redraping it about her.

"Well, I guess I'm out of here," he said, walking to the bedroom door. "See ya in another lifetime, babe."

Not if she could help it, Nikki thought as she listened to his footsteps disappear. And then, there was silence. Relieved, she turned toward the closet and drew out a pair of slacks and a blouse, both in somber black. She walked to the dresser and pulled out her underwear. It was as she held the lacy garments in her hand that the thought occurred to her. Jacob hadn't asked a thing about Rosemead. Considering the rumors sneaking around town, rumors he'd assuredly heard, it seemed odd that he'd said nothing. In the past, almost from the moment he'd arrived in town, he'd been unusually interested in Rosemead, but then everyone in Natchez watched Rosemead out of the corner of his envious eye. It was almost as if . . . The thought was so ludicrous that Nikki dismissed it. Or rather she tried to. The thought kept coming back. Again and again. Until she could no longer ignore it. Had he not asked about what was going on at Rosemead because he knew what was going on? Was that why he was leaving town? Two million dollars would buy a lot of green pastures.

Was she really serious?

No, of course not.

Still, she couldn't deny the fact that Jacob Purdy was a dangerous man, and that he'd always been unnaturally interested in Rosemead.

Although *The Natchez Democrat* never once came right out and said that Amanda Jackson had been kidnapped—how could it do that without proper substantiation?—it did insinuate and speculate and theorize about it. Proving the power of the hinted, if not printed, word, telephone calls to Rosemead began at daybreak, as soon as the newspapers first made their appearances on lawns and drives and breakfast tables.

At first, Christine was instructed to inform the callers that an error had been made, that Amanda was tucked safely away at Rosemead. It soon became apparent that an error, indeed, had been made, and that it had been made by those who'd told Christine to deny the charges. For every call that ended with Christine's disavowing the kidnapping, two more calls took its place, calls requiring further repudiation. By mid-morning, it was clear the kidnapper would be lucky to get through if he tried to phone. Something had to be done.

Once Agent Carrelli suggested a press conference, reversing the earlier policy of denying of the kidnapping, Christine eagerly agreed. She wanted, had wanted from the beginning, the chance to appeal to whoever had taken her daughter. As tactfully as was possible under such delicate circumstances, the agent proposed that Christine and Peyton appear together as everyone would expect. Gray understood the wisdom of the proposal, but still felt its sting.

"May I have a word with you?" Peyton asked a couple of minutes after Agent Carrelli had made his suggestion.

Gray took in the man before him. The immaculately dressed, clean-shaven man, whose every hair seemed to know its place. In contrast, he himself looked like something the dogs wouldn't have even bothered dragging home. His dirt-spotted jeans were wrinkled from the restless night, while his hair knew only the erratic combing of his fingers. Worse yet, stubble had turned to whiskers. He looked like someone no person in his right mind would want to deal with.

Gray's response was a simple, "Yeah."

With a flick of his Rolex–adorned wrist, Peyton indicated the front door. "Perhaps we could speak with some privacy outside."

It seemed more statement than question, verified when Peyton Jackson stepped forward without benefit of an answer, under the assumption that Gray would follow. Once Peyton had opened the front door, he stood back and allowed Gray to precede him onto the grand gallery. The golden sun made Gray think about the tomato plants.

Peyton spoke, never once taking his eyes from the sparkling lawn spread out before him. "I wish a great many things. I wish Amanda had never been kidnapped. I wish I had never learned that I wasn't her real father." He hesitated, as though searching for the right words. "I know, at least I think I can imagine, how galling Agent Carrelli's suggestion of a press conference must be. That is, a conference in which I pose as Amanda's father, although, of course, only a few people will know I'm posing."

At this point, Peyton Jackson fixed Gray with the bluest pair of eyes that Gray had ever seen. They shone with a vividness, a beauty, that seemed otherworldly.

"Will you allow me this one last time to pose as her father?"

From the beginning, Gray had been uncertain where the conversation was headed. Of a sudden, it had veered into a most surprising direction.

Frowning, Gray said, "I didn't know that I had a choice."

"Actually, you do. Christine has indicated that she won't agree to my presence unless you give your consent."

"Has she?" Gray said, simply because he didn't know what else to say. He'd seen Christine in conversation with her husband and Agent Carrelli following the agent's proposal, but it had never crossed his mind that she might have said this.

"Yes," Peyton said, adding hastily, "I implore you. Please, please, can't we shelve the issue of Amanda's parentage until her safe return?"

The proposal, uttered again, didn't sting any less, but it made sense, and so Gray said, "Yeah."

Peyton replied, "Thank you. Thank you very much."

Thinking that Peyton had spoken what was on his mind, smarting from the decision he'd had no choice but to make, Gray turned toward the door and the house.

"May I have just a moment more of your time?" Peyton asked.

Gray swiveled on the heels of his tennis shoes, his gaze merging with the gaze of the man before him. Peyton Jackson looked uncomfortable, a fact proved by his hesitation. Finally, he spoke.

"Christine has made it clear that she intends to tell Amanda that you're her father. Frankly, I asked Christine not to tell her. I even went so far as to suggest that for the right amount of money, we might convince you to walk out of Amanda's life without ever complicating it with the truth. Christine quickly told me that you aren't a man who can be bought off. Whether you are or not, and I'm inclined to think you're not, the suggestion was"—he scoured his vocabulary and settled on a word most appropriate for a Southern gentleman—"dishonorable. My only defense is that it was a suggestion made by a desperate man."

Peyton Jackson's voice didn't sound at all desperate. In fact, it sounded calm and controlled. And yet, two fidgety hands sought out the pockets of his pants. Perhaps the man wasn't as calm as he appeared.

"I've been with Amanda for nine years, believing her all the while to be my daughter. I love her. Surely you can understand that I can't just stop caring for her. Emotions aren't like tap water—feelings can't be turned off with the twist of a faucet. Nor would I expect Amanda to stop caring for me. Surely there can be room in her life for the two of us. Many children accommodate both a father and a stepfather in their lives, and while this is different, of course, the principle remains the same." Pause, then, "I'm a proud man. I'm not accustomed to begging, but, if that's what it takes, I'm quite prepared to do so. I'm begging you to allow me to remain part of Amanda's life. If nothing else, let me remain long enough to make the transition from me to you as painless as possible."

With this, Peyton fell silent. Gray knew that a reply was expected of him, but the words would not form. In theory, Gray had known all along that Christine had wronged Peyton Jackson as much as she'd wronged him, but until now he'd been unable to see beyond his own pain, his own anger. He now saw that Peyton Jackson was hurting. Terribly. While he didn't feel compelled to like the man, he nonetheless felt a bond with him that he hadn't expected to feel. Perhaps he even respected him for his display of honesty under such trying circumstances.

"I don't know what to say," Gray finally replied, with equal honesty. "I'm not thinking too clearly these days." Pause, then, "I do know that out of everyone involved in this mess, the person I least want to see hurt is the child."

"I'll settle for that," Peyton replied, then totally surprised Gray again by adding, "I suppose Christine did what she thought she had to do."

"You're being charitable."

"I love her," Peyton said simply, unabashedly.

Gray remembered the time when he'd loved Christine, too, although he'd been careful not to use that word. It seemed too . . . binding. Peyton Jackson had been right about one thing: you didn't turn off emotion like tap water. What he didn't seem to understand, however, was how quickly the flow of emotion could go from the scalding heat of love to the iceberg cold of something baser.

Something drove Gray from the house. He told himself that it was his rattled nerves, nerves aggravated by worry, sleeplessness, past memories that wouldn't go away, and the impending press conference. When he saw the vegetable and herb garden, however, he instantly knew that the search for this small plot of ground was what had drawn him.

The relentless rain had pounded all but the occasional plant into the coffee-dark, compost-rich soil. The herbs were all but lost. A little TLC, however, might save the tomato plants, some thirty in number and neatly arranged in three rows. Mandy, Esther, the present gardener—someone—had mounded up the soil so that the heavy rain had drained off into the nearby troughlike spaces. Good, Gray thought, the roots wouldn't stay waterlogged.

Immediately, Gray fell to his first-aid efforts. Gently, he reached for the first fallen plant. He straightened it, then drew the soil about it, packing it firmly at the base of the slender stalk. To Gray's relief, the plant remained erect. He began to right yet another downed creature. The rays of the hot sun struck the damp earth, drawing from it a sweltering steam that rose upward. This, too, was good, Gray thought, for already the moisture was evaporating from the soil. So caught up was he in his task that he didn't hear the approaching footsteps.

"Will they survive?"

Gray's gaze collided with Christine's. She had startled him. Moreover, she'd interrupted his desperately needed solitude.

In answer, he said, "The herbs, probably not. The tomato plants, probably. They have youth on their side."

When Peyton had returned to the living room alone, Christine had wondered what had transpired between the two men. Even more, she'd wondered about Gray's whereabouts. That he'd cared enough about their daughter to seek out and save her garden moved her. Perhaps foolishly. His action, she allowed, might mean less to him than it did to her.

Foolish, too, though she couldn't help herself, was the way the blue shadow of his beard begged her to reach out and feel, not like in the dreams she'd held on to, but in the here-and-now reality, while his piercing brown eyes sent her heart searching again for what might have been, had she not been stupid enough to throw it all away.

"Let me help you," Christine said, feeling the need to busy her hands.

"You're going to ruin your clothes."

Christine made no reply. She simply sought another row and, facing Gray, eased onto her knees. In the beginning, she looked over at him to see exactly what he was doing, then copied his ministrations.

"Pack the soil tighter," he said once, reaching over to do precisely that, although he was careful not to touch her.

He said no more, and neither did she. Both were aware of many things—the burning sun, the moistening of bodies and brows, the calming, a comforting effect of straightening a plant, tamping down the earth, and moving on to another. Straighten . . . tamp down . . . move on . . . straighten . . . tamp down . . . move on . . . Soon, the activity began to take on a symbolic meaning. In rescuing the plants, were they not in a fashion doing what they could to rescue their daughter? Would not the life of one better guarantee the life of the other?

"She has youth on her side," Christine said.

Gray glanced up. It was odd, he thought, that she should make the comment, for he'd been entertaining a similar notion. In salvaging the garden, he was salvaging the child's world. He was safeguarding it for her return, as though its existence attested to hers. Images entered his mind, of a child tending the garden. Did her small hands feel this soil with the same joy and peace of soul as his? And would he ever feel her hand slip into his? Would she ever accept him into her life?

Frustration chewed at the edges of his calmness, caused by any number of things: last night's phone call, Christine's appearance in the garden, her present state. Mud streaked her pink silk blouse and pure linen pants, while her shoes, no doubt costing a queen's ransom, were equally soiled. All in all, with her smudged cheek and sweat-dampened hair, she, too, looked every bit the reprobate—and utterly beautiful.

"We've done what we can," he said abruptly, and rose.

Christine came to her feet, then, while surveying what they had done, said, "The press conference is set for two o'clock. Representatives from *The Natchez*

Democrat will be there, and some television reporters from Jackson. Maybe even someone from the local radio stations."

The lineup of participants didn't surprise Gray, especially the television reporters from Jackson. Since Natchez had only cablevision, live coverage was always handled from outside. "I won't be there. I'm going into town."

Although Christine had expected this announcement, at least the part about his not being present for the interview, it nonetheless disappointed her, a fact she strove to hide. She had no right demanding anything of Gray. "Fine. However, should you need anything, I could send Esther into town to pick it up for you."

"I'll do my own picking up."

"Fine," Christine repeated.

He stared. She stared.

Finally, she said, "Well, I should go get changed."

He watched as she turned and headed for the house. She had taken only a dozen or so steps when she turned back.

"Thank you," she said.

"For what?"

"For giving Peyton permission to appear as Amanda's father during the interview."

"I did it for Mandy."

"For whomever or whatever, thank you."

Gray watched as she made her way back toward Rosemead.

The Christine he'd once known would have gotten both self and clothes muddy. The Christine he now believed her to be, the one molded in the Lowell image, would never have done so, he'd thought. But he'd been wrong.

And if he'd been wrong about this, what else might he have been wrong about?

Chapter 9

Gray traveled the streets of Natchez with an easy familiarity. Some things never changed, he mused. The basic downtown area was a blend of commercial and residential and, in both cases, some buildings thrived while others suffered. The town boasted more than its share of antique shops, a drugstore with an old-time soda fountain, a movie theater which had been boarded up in the sixties and never reopened. Mansions, like Stanton Hall and Cherokee and the House on Ellicott Hill, dotted the downtown area, all of which would have thrown wide their doors for the Spring Pilgrimage. Other mansions, like Dunleith and Auburn and Rosemead, were situated on streets leading into the town proper. Any number of the older ordinary homes were undergoing reconstruction, probably under the watchful eye of the historical preservation society. Not so watchful were the eyes of the occasional horse that drew a fringe-topped buggy of tourists along the tree-lined streets. This harnessed animal looked neither right not left; it just clomped a slow but steady pace, as though it would not rest until it had finished its appointed rounds.

Gray was just as focused on his mission, which was to find some clean clothes and toilet articles. This he did at a bargain store, where he wondered if, because of his mud-stained and disheveled appearance, he'd be asked to leave. Discounting a few stares, no one said anything and so, after completing his shopping, he climbed back into the van. From there he drove to a fast-food restaurant and bought two hamburgers, fries, and a milkshake. He then drove around in search of a reasonably priced motel. He found one out on Highway 61 and rented a room. Room 132 was simple enough to find, and Gray was able to park the van directly in front of it.

His first order of business once inside was to place a call to Atlanta. Mildred Jefferson, the oldest and longest-employed of his help, answered. He asked how things were going at the nursery and was assured that all was well. He'd told Mildred only that he had personal business in Natchez. She hadn't pressed then, nor did she now. She merely asked if he had any idea when he'd be returning. He told her no, to which she replied that he wasn't to worry about a thing, that they could manage in his stead.

He wasn't to worry about a thing.

If only she knew how impossible that was . . .

The interview aired as planned.

Gray had had no intention of watching, but, come two o'clock, he was drawn to the television. The interview began on time, with the usual, "We interrupt the normally scheduled programming with this special news event." Christine, wearing an apricot-colored suit, stood in front of a bank of microphones. A solicitous Peyton stood by her side, occasionally bending down and whispering something in her ear. Gray strained to hear, as though he might actually make out the words if he worked at it hard enough. When he realized what he was doing, he cursed himself for his stupidity.

To give the devil his due, Peyton spoke with passion about "his daughter," pleading with whoever held her to return her. Christine spoke with even greater passion. She spoke first to the kidnapper, then to the child, imploring her to continue to be brave. Despite himself, Gray was moved, especially by the tears that threatened to fall. She didn't cry, however, and this composed Christine he recognized from their confrontation last night. So she had, indeed, changed, which both troubled and didn't trouble him.

Then Peyton slipped a comforting arm about Christine and led her away from the fast-talking reporters. At the sight Gray grew inexplicably restless. And inexplicably angry.

At the beginning of the interview, Sandy Killian shut off the vacuum cleaner and seated herself on the sofa's edge. Without fail, she vacuumed two times a day, morning and evening. She hated footprints on the carpet. They nudged at painful memories that were never quite recalled, never quite forgotten. Out of habit, she put her hand to her pounding head. A headache always followed *the* dream. Doctors called it a migraine; she called it the black headache, for it always took her to some lost, lightless place deep inside her, a place she had to claw her way out of.

She watched, and listened, as first Peyton, then Christine, begged for the release of their daughter. Except Mandy wasn't Peyton's daughter. How surprising. How unexpected. How like the rich to have their little secrets. Of course, everyone had secrets, didn't they? Because everyone had a past, and the past was little more than layered secrets.

Suddenly, from out of nowhere came the sickly sweet smell of carnations. Red carnations. At five years old, Sandy was barely able to see over the top of the pew, but she'd seen the big wooden box, covered with the flowers, as she'd entered the small country church. She didn't know why, but the box scared her.

"Your father has gone to heaven," her mother had told her earlier, but Sandy was uncertain just where that was. Somewhere in the sky—that's what they'd implied all those times she'd been to Sunday School— but no one was more definite. Was it in the clouds, above the clouds, or high up where the birds flew? And did people who'd gone to heaven ever fall back down, like rain or snow? And how long did God keep you in heaven before sending you home?

"Stop fidgeting," the woman beside her whispered. The woman, who walked with a limp and smelled bad, frightened Sandy even more than the big box. Or maybe she was frightened because she'd been separated from her mother, who sat on the pew in front of hers. Crying. Several times, she'd tried to scoot off the hard bench and go to her, but the woman beside her had stopped her. "Leave your mother to her grief."

Whatever that was.

When the bad-smelling woman began crying too, and reached into her handbag for a tissue, Sandy chose that moment to slide off the pew and start for her mother. A hand clamped around her arm and yanked her back.

But this time, Sandy wasn't going back. She grabbed hold of the arm of the pew and screamed, "I want Mommy!"

"Shh, shh," a soft voice cooed, and then she was being pulled into her mother's arms. "I won't leave you, darling," she could hear her mother promising.

And she hadn't. She'd cared for children in her home instead of searching for work that would have taken her away from her child. Her mother had kept her promise.

And then *he,* a pillar of their small community, had come along, vowing to care for them both, vowing to make their hard lives easier. That he'd done, but he'd also started coming to Sandy's room, always leaving money for the touches, for the kisses, for everything else. Always leaving behind his footprints in the deep-piled carpet. Footprints that she'd always scuffed out, as though doing so would erase all that had happened between them.

Secret.

Their little secret, he'd said.

And she had kept it, because of her shame—it must have been her fault!—and because she could never find the words for what he did. As she grew older, she wondered how her mother could not know. In fact, she grew more certain that she must have known. Had she been sacrificed for financial security, love, social standing? Whether her mother knew or not, she should have, because mothers were supposed to protect their children. She still loved her, but a part of her hated her too. That part that remained uncertain of just how much her mother had overlooked.

On her seventeenth birthday, she'd left that house,

his house, and never returned. By then, she'd become aware of her power and had worked a sweet little deal with him. For a sizable sum of money, she'd keep their little secret just that—secret. She'd realized then the wondrous link between power and money, how both could be used to control people and life, a fact that Merritt Lowell had understood completely. He'd been the consummate controller, and he'd been ruthless when he'd had to be, both traits she admired. He'd lived life on his own terms. No one had screwed with him. No one screwed with the Lowell family. Except right now, someone *was* screwing with the family, someone was controlling them.

Amanda.

Sweet Amanda.

She deserved none of what was happening to her.

But then, wasn't it always the children who paid?

The man, sitting backward in a chair, his arms folded across the top rung, watched the interview on the small television. How perfect. All that angst. All that pain. Christine Lowell Jackson must be beside herself. Although he did hate to see the others so torn up, but then he'd heard from a reliable source that Peyton Jackson wasn't even the kid's real father. Figure that. Then there was the kid. He was sorry, real sorry, that it was always the innocent who ended up paying. But, hey, he didn't make the rules.

At the tinny squeaking sound, the man diverted his eyes from the television and to the grayish-brown mouse. He'd been so caught up in the interview that he hadn't noticed the rodent slipping out of his den, no more than the animal seemed to have noticed him. The creature, ignoring the droning, soporific sound of the television, hoisted its head high and sniffed the air. He either sensed nothing or hunger tugged him beyond the bounds of safety. Without hesitation, the mouse made a beeline for the baited trap, passing so close to the man's booted foot that he could have stomped it to death. But he didn't. He wanted the animal to die because of his own hunger. Just as he wanted to make Lowell Enterprises pay for its insatiable appetite.

As suddenly as before, the mouse stopped and scurried back to its hole. The man smiled. Good. The game was still afoot. The mouse was turning out to be a worthy opponent. Patience, the man told himself. Patience. He'd have the mouse yet. Just as he was going to have Christine Lowell Jackson. It was a promise he'd made.

Looking back, Christine realized that she hadn't known quite what to expect from the live interview. A part of her cautioned against expecting anything, while another part of her foolishly imagined that Mandy's abductor would see the interview, particularly her struggle to keep tears from falling, and feel such remorse that he'd release her daughter.

All too soon it became apparent, however, that whoever was responsible for Amanda's disappearance either hadn't seen the interview or hadn't been moved by it. Christine tried to take solace from the fact that she'd done all she could. She'd gotten her chance to plead for her daughter's safe return, and had done so as passionately as she'd known how. What more could she do? When she'd posed this very question to Nikki, who'd seemed oddly distracted since her return the evening before, Nikki had assured her that there was nothing more to be done but wait. Had it made any sense, Christine might have believed that her friend had been referring to something other than Amanda's disappearance.

As for Peyton, he'd returned to Rosemead with her, where his cloying presence, his stifling attentiveness, smothered her. Sandy Killian, ever contrite, called, pleading a migraine and promising to return to Rosemead when the pain lifted.

Where was Gray?

Next to where her daughter was, it was the single most important question on Christine's mind. He'd gone into town, shopping, but that had been four hours ago. No doubt he had personal business to attend to, perhaps even a woman to call and bring up to date. Surely there was a woman in his life, although she knew that he'd never married. She'd made it her business to know this. More than once, she'd wondered why he'd taken no wife.

At five-thirty-two she saw Gray's van pull into the drive, and she couldn't help but feel relieved. She'd longed to have him at her side during the interview, and when Peyton had placed his arm about her, she'd pretended that the comforting warmth belonged to another.

In minutes, Gray was entering the room. He had changed clothes and shaved. She was sorry that he'd shaved; it made the scar visible once more. The perfect reminder of what her love had cost him.

Their eyes met, and, for a moment, she thought that he was as glad to see her as she was to see him. Then, as the evening wore on, he seemed as restless as she, pacing about the room, chair to desk, desk to chair, with an occasional excursion to Amanda's photograph, the window, even Agent Carrelli, with whom he'd ex-

change a few words. From time to time, she found him
looking at her. At around eight-thirty, Esther served
sandwiches and coffee. As he had once before, Gray
stubbornly refused what was offered him.

Christine's gaze momentarily melded with Gray's.
It's only a sandwich, she said in an unspoken voice.
Gray's gaze said nothing. It, like the room, like the
telephone, was achingly silent.

"Would you like another sandwich? Or more coffee?"

Terry Carrelli had just checked his watch—11:37—
when he heard the soft voice at his side. He glanced
up into Nikki's pretty green eyes, which presently
peered through the clear lenses of gold-framed glasses.

"No to the sandwich. A definite yes to the coffee."
Terry smiled. "If it weren't for coffee, the Federal Bureau of Investigation would cease to exist."

Thinking what a nice smile he had, Nikki set the
silver tray on a small table and filled a gold-rimmed
china cup.

Terry took it. "We're not used to this kind of fancy
treatment. We usually get Styrofoam."

It was Nikki who smiled this time. "I seriously
doubt that Styrofoam has ever been allowed in this
house. Certainly not when Adelle Lowell was alive."

Pretty eyes, pretty smile, Terry thought, covertly
taking in all of her within the black blouse and slacks.
Conclusion? She was pretty everywhere, with an elegance that suggested that she, too, had money. In comparison, he was a working stiff who probably looked
like a slob. He'd discarded his rain-damp suit jacket,
which lay draped over the back of a nearby straight-
backed chair. His tie looked like a snake too lazy to

coil, while his once freshly starched shirt, unfastened at the neck, the sleeves rolled up, showed an abundance of wrinkles. He reached for the jacket and tie with one hand, while he precariously balanced the cup and saucer with the other.

"Here, sit down," Terry said.

"I, uh, wouldn't want to interrupt anything."

Terry made a harumping sound. "Unfortunately, you're interrupting nothing."

When he nodded toward the chair, Nikki sat down. A silence ensued, a silence during which Nikki, as unobtrusively as possible, studied the man before her. He was handsome, and in a way that most appealed to a woman, which was to say that he had no idea how handsome he was. He was particularly attractive now that he was disheveled. She liked that rumpled look, the way coils of black hair peeked from his rolled-up sleeves, the way his black hair, beginning to slightly recede from his forehead, wouldn't quite lie down in back, probably because it had gotten wet. She also liked his sunglasses, not that he presently wore them, but he'd been wearing them the first time she'd seen him. They made him appear mysterious. And his gun, which he wore in a shoulder holster . . . well, it made him seem downright sexy. It—

"Does the gun bother you?"

Unaware of her fixed gaze, Nikki felt flustered. "What?" she said. Perhaps a little breathlessly?

"The gun? Does it bother you? It does some people."

"Oh, no, no," she said, wondering if she looked as flushed as she felt. "Do you use it often?" *Great, Nikki! What an inane question!*

"I suppose it depends on your definition of *often*. It's drawn far more than it's fired."

"That's good, huh?"

"Yeah, that's very good."

As was the way he was feeling in this woman's company. Which surprised Terry a little. He dated, as often as his schedule permitted, but he rarely felt this good with a woman. Certainly not so soon after meeting her. Often not even after spending the night with her. And the man in him had to admit that she was sexy. *Whoa, whoa, Carrelli! You never, never get involved with anyone on a case.* Not, of course, that he was involved, because he wasn't. Thinking someone was sexy wasn't involved. Nor was thinking that someone has incredible green eyes, or . . . *Oh, hell,* he thought, scrambling for a way out of these thoughts.

"How's Mrs. Jackson doing?" he asked. Desperately?

"Far better than I'd be doing," Nikki answered. "Is the waiting always this hard?"

"Always. These bastards enjoy making you wait."

Nikki hesitated, not wanting to seem too eager. "You spoke in the plural. Do you think there's more than one person involved?"

"I was speaking of kidnappers in general."

"Oh." Another pause, during which she strove to sound casual, conversational. "What about this case in particular?"

"There's really no way of knowing. The child referred to the kidnapper in the singular, but who knows?"

"Do kidnappers usually work alone?"

He shrugged. "Some do. Some don't."

"I see," Nikki said, thinking it best to give the subject a rest, and so she introduced another. "Tomorrow's Mother's Day."

"Oh, no. I hadn't realized."

"I hope Christine doesn't remember."

"You have any children?" Terry asked, surprising himself with the question.

"No," she answered.

"But married, right?" he asked, now downright stunning himself.

"No, I'm divorced," she said. "What about you?"

"I'm single."

"Never been married?" That a man this handsome hadn't been caught and dragged to the altar surprised her.

"No," he said. "It's hard to have a normal family life in my line of work."

"The travel?"

"Yeah, it's hard on a wife and kids."

Silence. Another sip of coffee. Nikki stood. "Well, I better get back to Christine."

"Thanks for the coffee."

Nikki smiled another pretty smile. "Sure." She'd taken only a step, however, when she turned back. "Agent Carrelli?"

"Terry," he said. "Call me Terry." This was another deviation from his usual behavior, but surely a guy ought to be friendly.

"Only if you'll call me Nikki."

"Fair enough." Pause, then, "What did you want to ask me?"

"Will you catch whoever's responsible for the kidnapping?"

The answer seemed inordinately important to her, but then, as Christine Jackson's friend, it would be, wouldn't it? He wanted to tell her that positively, without any doubt, he'd make the guilty suffer, but it seemed to him that suffering was more often the lot of the innocent.

Still, although he could make no assurances, he wanted to give her something to hold on to.

"With any luck," he said.

"You should eat something."

Gray turned toward Esther.

"I ate while I was out."

She nodded toward his clean clothes. "And got a motel room."

Gray ginned slightly. "Yeah."

Esther's look said that she had no idea what she was going to do with him.

Gray's grin slipped away. "Why didn't you tell me that they're getting a divorce?"

She didn't answer immediately, then said, "I didn't tell you because it wasn't my place to."

"No, I suppose it wasn't," he conceded. "When I asked her why, she said irreconcilable differences."

"What do you want me to say, Gray?" Esther said, cutting to the chase.

He sent his fingers tunneling through his hair. "I don't know. I swear to God, I don't."

"And I don't know what to tell you. She was always a private person." Esther smiled, sadly, ironically. "You were the only one she ever allowed to get close to her."

"Yeah, well."

"To be honest, the divorce took me a little by surprise." Esther paused, as though remembering when she'd first learned of it. "The only thing I know for certain is that the divorce was her idea. Peyton has fought it tooth and nail, and if she'd have him back, I think he'd go at a run."

The idea of Christine and Peyton getting back together sat uncomfortably with him, as did something Esther had said the day before. "Yesterday, when I said that Christine hadn't changed, that she'd been deceptive ten years ago and that she was deceptive now, you said no, that she hadn't changed. What did you mean?"

"That you're going to have to figure out for yourself."

With that cryptic remark, Esther left him and bustled off toward the kitchen.

Figure it out? Gray almost laughed. Didn't she know how exhausted he was with trying to figure things out?

Over the years, he had repeatedly wondered why Christine had not kept her promise to go away with him. She had arrived on the heels of the beating and had pleaded with him to go to the hospital. When he'd refused, she'd bandaged him as best she could, then had returned home to pack her suitcase. They would run away, make a life for themselves, far, far from Rosemead. But she hadn't kept her promise. He'd waited for three days, fearing Claiborne's, and his friends', return, fearing a visit from her father, certain that she would come when she had the chance. He'd invented excuse after excuse, even going so far as to entertain the notion that her father had locked her up, for surely she would have returned otherwise. Finally, he had to concede that his were the thoughts of a desperate man.

All he had to do now was cross the room and ask her why she hadn't come to him. But he didn't, because he was afraid of what he'd hear. Afraid that he just hadn't been good enough for her and, even now, he didn't think that he could bear to hear her say the words.

Chapter 10

The telephone rang at 1:46 A.M.

Christine, who'd begun to regret that people were complying with their don't-call request—at least for a brief moment she could have lived in hope—whirled away from the window toward the shrill sound. Relief rushed through her, for at this stage of the waiting game, she preferred bad news to none.

As she stepped forward all eyes followed her every move. Briefly, her gaze brushed Gray's. Still, she could read nothing there, and she envied his talent to look so in control. Once she'd reached the telephone, she looked over at Agent Carrelli.

"Ready?" he asked.

Christine nodded, reached for the receiver, and prayed. "Hello?"

"Turn left on Homochitto and go to the first stop sign," the whispery voice commanded. "Send one of those clever FBI agents. I have a little something for you."

Click. The buzzing of the dial tone in Christine's ear. It happened so quickly that she might have disbelieved its having happened at all had not Phil Birmingham said, "I'll bet money it's another pay phone."

"Probably," Agent Carrelli agreed. "Play it back."

The whispery voice filled the room. At its conclusion, one murmur bled into another. Gray said nothing.

"More game-playing," Terry Carrelli said, looking over at Hamm Clancy. "Go get this 'little something.' And be careful."

Clancy nodded and started from the house. Christine walked back to the window, from where she saw the red taillights of the agent's unmarked car as it pulled along the drive. Rosemead faced Homochitto, and she knew the car would take a left at the gate, then disappear from view. Mentally, she traced the route the agent would follow. The first stop sign was no more than two or three blocks away. It couldn't take more than ten minutes to go and return. But what would he return with? Christine fought back a wave of panic.

Hang on! Hang on for Mandy!

Closing her eyes, Christine heard the playing of the tape again, this time muted. Strangely, its low volume made it sound all the more threatening, all the more sinister. It was impossible to tell if the voice was masculine or feminine, and that, too, lent a malignancy to the raspy words. The recording ended. Peyton spoke, sounding inordinately upset. Gray stood alone, as though he needed no one. In the far distance, she heard the confirmation that the call had, indeed, come from a pay phone here in Natchez. Agent Birmingham left to check it out, but Christine knew what everyone in the room feared—that he'd find nothing to further the case.

"Are you all right?" Nikki asked.

"No, I'm scared," Christine said.

Christine sensed the car before she saw it. Headlights jumped into view as the vehicle turned into the drive and headed for the mansion. Her heart sprinted forward. At the same time, her breathing became shallow.

Hang on! Hang on!

Within minutes, Agent Clancy entered the room. He wore rubber gloves, the kind surgeons wear. Christine understood their necessity—no contamination of fingerprints—and yet the sterile sight of them unnerved her. Perhaps because they so dramatically drew attention to the package held in the agent's right hand.

"It's specifically for Mrs. Jackson," Clancy said. "It was leaning against the stop sign."

Christine stepped forward. Agent Clancy set the package on the edge of the glass coffee table—every eye in the room followed it—and peeled off the gloves. He handed them to Christine. She tugged them on. First the left, then the right, her heart hammering in tandem with the act.

Sensing that she should be seated, Christine eased to the sofa. She hesitated, then reached for the package. Wrapped in plain brown mailing paper and tied with string, it was quite ordinary-looking, and that very ordinariness suggested a profaneness. Across the top, in cut-out letters, it read: Happy Mother's Day.

Nikki cursed.

Christine's heart turned over in her chest. Mother's Day. She'd forgotten, but Sunday—today—was Mother's Day. They had planned a picnic. Fried chicken.

Potato salad. And Amanda would have given her some small school-made gift—an irregularly shaped spoon rest, a lace-and-ribbon bookmark, a picture with blue skies and green pastures and grazing horses. This would be followed by a gigantic hug and a heartfelt "I love you." Christine closed her eyes against the painfulness of these thoughts.

Hang on! Hang on! But she knew she had so little left to hang on with.

Seconds passed, then Agent Carrelli's softly spoken, "Mrs. Jackson? The package."

Christine opened her eyes. "Yes, of course," she said, turning her attention to the parcel. For the first time, she realized how weightless it was, and it crossed her mind that maybe there was nothing in the package, after all. Perhaps this was all a cruel joke, and yet, she couldn't bring herself to believe this. Her hands had begun to tremble and, because of that, she fumbled with the string which ran both the length and width of the package and ended in a center knot. From out of nowhere came a pocket knife, a familiar knife, that delivered two quick slits. Christine glanced up. She toyed with trying to say thank you, but doubted that she could get the words past her paperdry throat.

It took but seconds to shed the string and paper. Another second and she'd pulled the lid from the box. The neatly folded tissue paper rustled as she did so.

Christine hesitated.

"What's that smell?" Nikki asked.

Christine, too, wondered what the ammonialike stench was. She'd smelled it before, but couldn't place it. Neither could she bring herself to pull aside the tissue. Dear God, she was afraid. Afraid of what she'd find. Yet that very fear urged her on. She had to know the worst, for in knowing it, she would know her enemy. With a courage she never dreamed she possessed, she plunged her fingers into the tissue and parted its thin sheaves.

Pink.

Lace.

A part of Christine, that part that defends and protects, denied what she was seeing, while another part, the part that knows the truth despite one's best efforts to deny it, acknowledged the fact that the package contained Amanda's panties. Pink panties with the pretty lace. Panties that reeked of urine.

A numbness crawled through Christine. For a moment, she felt as if lights had blinked in her head, a quick darkening that faded to a woozy feeling. Even so, she could hear, though at a distance, Nikki's startled gasp and Peyton's shocked "Oh, my God!" Several other voices mixed together, and she wondered if Gray's was among them. She even heard an inner voice telling her that she'd underestimated her enemy. Whoever had her daughter, whoever sent these urine-soaked panties, was cruel, ruthless.

Perhaps in an attempt to escape this cruelty, this ruthlessness, perhaps simply to free herself from the pain of viewing her daughter's underwear, Christine stood. The box and its contents fell to the floor. She didn't notice, although she was aware of another dimming of those lights in her head.

Move.

Just move.

Anywhere.

Out of habit, Christine headed for the window, discarding first one glove, then another, en route.

The night spread out before her, an uncertain sea of stars and cloud-stricken moon. Prayers. Now was the time for prayers. Please, God, deliver Amanda from this person. Please anoint me with the strength to hang on for just a little longer. Please, God, keep the ugly thoughts at bay. But the thoughts proved all-powerful. Christine could feel her daughter's humiliation at having soiled her panties. She could see some shadowy someone taking that intimate article from her. And if her panties were here, what was Amanda wearing? Nothing. Sweet, God, nothing!

She stepped from the window, now in flight from the frightful thoughts. She was headed . . . She didn't know where she was headed.

Move.

Just move.

Anywhere.

She saw the staircase stretching before her, but it was growing dim, dim, dimmer. Her legs grew weak and watery. She thought she heard someone call her name—Gray?—but then the world turned black. The last thing she saw was the floor rushing up to meet her. The last thing she thought was that she'd held on as long as she could.

Gray knelt beside Christine's fallen body and shouted, "Call a doctor!"

Nothing.

Stillness.

Everyone frozen in place.

Looking back over his shoulder, he hollered, "Dammit, someone call a doctor!"

Esther took the command that no one seemed capable of understanding. To Nikki, she said, "Call Dr. Hearst next door. His number's in the directory in the library." At this, Nikki rallied and rushed from the room. To Gray, Esther said, as she began to ascend the staircase, "Bring her upstairs."

Gray gently lifted Christine into his arms. She was dead weight, and her head lolled forward, causing her cheek to nuzzle his shoulder. One arm lay folded back on his chest, while the other dangled at her side. Lifelessly. Had he not felt her warm breath misting his neck, had he not felt the patter of her heart as it penetrated his body, he might easily have believed she was dead. He had known that she was going to faint, had seen it coming in the weave of her walk, yet when her legs had begun to crumple beneath her, it had stunned him. He'd heard himself call her name, had felt his legs begin to cover the distance between them.

At the top of the stairs, Esther turned right. Gray followed, although he knew well enough that the housekeeper was headed for Christine's bedroom. Once there, he entered, forbidding himself to recall what had happened in this room that fateful day.

"Put her on the bed," Esther said, then slipped out of the bedroom. Gray could hear her moving down the hallway.

Jabbing his bent knee into the mattress, he laid Christine into the midst of the softness. She rolled her head toward him; once, twice, her eyelids fluttered. Easing down beside her, he thought how pale she looked against the scarlet coverlet. In fact, she was so frighteningly pale that he reached for her wrist, intending to check her pulse, but he stopped short of making contact. He contented himself with her steady breathing, with the sturdy rise and fall of her chest.

Esther reentered the room, carrying a small brown bottle, which she uncapped and passed beneath Christine's nose. The smelling salts wafted upward. Christine did not respond. With the second pass of the smelling salts, Christine whimpered, and her head turned away from Gray. He could see her fighting consciousness, and he couldn't honestly blame her.

Suddenly, with a vengeance, consciousness returned to Christine. Her abrupt awakening left her with an addled brain. Where was she? Posy-patterned drapes? They looked familiar. Was this her bedroom? Yes, she was in her bedroom. Lying on her bed. But why? She vaguely remembered—no, maybe not remembered, but sensed—being carried up the stairs by someone, someone with strong arms, someone who then gently laid her on the bed. Who was that someone? Who—

Christine jerked her head toward Gray. Yes, it was Gray. She'd known that at some deep level. But why was Gray looking so grim, so worried? Reality reared its ugly head. She remembered. Every horrible thing—her missing daughter, the arrival of the package, the crinkly tissue paper, the sickening smell, the pink lace panties. Fear, total and absolute, consumed her, followed by a wash of tears. She would have given anything to reach for Gray, to nestle in his arms, to borrow some of his strength.

Gray saw both the fear and the tears. He'd resented her composure, her cool poise and reserve, from the moment he'd set foot in Rosemead and had wanted to see it slip, but now that it had, now that he saw so clearly her misery, he cursed himself for his thoughts.

When she tried to sit up, Gray said, "Lie still. You fainted."

Christine ignored him. "I have to get up."

"Lie still!" Gray repeated, slipping from the bed.

At the tap on the door, Gray turned. Nikki stood in the doorway, looking as though she belonged in the bed alongside Christine. She, too, was ashen, and her cheeks appeared to have instantly, and unkindly, been hollowed out. "The doctor's at the hospital on an emergency. Something about a patient with a heart attack."

"I don't need a doctor," Christine said. "I just fainted."

"You need a doctor," Gray insisted.

"I just fainted," Christine repeated. "A doctor will only want to give me a sedative, and that I won't take. I can't. The kidnapper might call at any time. I've got to stay alert."

Nikki and Esther looked toward Gray, as though he were the final authority. Why? He had no jurisdiction in Christine's life.

Then, her maternal instincts budding, Esther said, "Well, you're going to get some rest. And I'll have no argument about that."

"I agree," Nikki said, stepping into the room and sitting on the side of the bed. "You're running on empty."

"She can't rest in this suit," Esther said, ultimately shooing both Nikki and Gray out into the hall.

Once there, Gray and Nikki appeared reluctant to move too far away, so Nikki leaned against one wall, Gray the other. Silence eddied around them.

Finally, Gray said what he'd earlier thought. "You look like hell."

Nikki replied with, "So do you."

"Yeah, I guess I do."

More silence, then Nikki said, "Everyone looks like hell. I thought Peyton was going to pass out too." Pause, then, "God, Gray, what do you think the panties mean?"

"I'm trying not to think, period."

Gray sensed that Nikki wanted to talk more about the package, but he didn't—he was still too much the captive of fear and shock—and so she ultimately settled for, "I know all of this has been pretty rough on you."

"Yeah."

He thought of how Christine and Nikki had been friends since that infamous summer, the one that had ended his friendship with a sixteen-year-old Christine. He'd always liked Nikki. She hadn't been like some of the other girls who had traveled in and out of Rosemead in Christine's growing-up years.

Finally, Gray filled the silence with the same question he'd asked Esther. "Did you know that the child was mine?"

"No. Looking back, I should have, though."

Funny, both women had answered the question with a similar response. Perhaps funnier yet, he asked neither woman for an explanation of her comment.

"Don't judge her too harshly," Nikki said.

Shortly thereafter, Esther called them back into the bedroom. Christine, wearing a gun-metal gray gown and a peignoir, was tucked beneath sweet-smelling sheets. After exchanging a few words, Nikki left, then Esther. Before she went she had extinguished every light in both bedroom and bath, except for a nightlight. Even in the dim light, Gray could see the way the satin lingerie molded Christine's form in a way the suit had not.

"Try and get some rest," Gray said awkwardly, taking a step away toward the door.

"No, stay!" Christine begged.

She reached out her hand, as though to grab his wrist, and recalled with perfect clarity how, for one summer, the warmth of his skin against hers was a fire that singed, seared, branded her. She recalled the hothouse, where they had become lovers one June afternoon. She could feel his hands, with their calluses roughly, sexily, caressing her body. But he had touched more than her body. He had touched some essential, some elemental, place within her, and from that moment on, her life had never been the same.

Christine had meant to take his hand, but had stopped herself. Yet Gray's body responded as though she had touched him. He could feel the softness of her skin, its heat, the fire in her fingertips. Her fingertips. They were capable of such gentleness, of such erotic acts. The forbidden memory of that afternoon in the hothouse tapped him on the shoulder. Confused, even scared—he could not recall that memory!—he told himself to get the hell out, to explain to Christine that she needed rest, that *he* needed rest, that he was hardly the appropriate one to stay with her. And he would have done precisely that. Swear to God. Had not she said one word.

"Please."

The word was spoken so plaintively, so sincerely, that she left him no choice. Wordlessly—he didn't trust words—Gray acquiesced by seating himself in a chair adjacent to the bed.

She said, "Just for tonight, couldn't we bury our differences? Just for tonight, couldn't you pretend that you don't hate me?"

Gray wasn't certain that he, that anyone, could dig a hole deep enough to bury their differences. As for pretending that he didn't hate her, he made no promises.

Peyton made no promises to the toilet bowl. Ever since he'd seen, smelled, the urine-soaked panties, his stomach had roiled with nausea. He'd gone immediately to the bathroom, where he'd splashed his face with cool water.

Jesus, why had Amanda's panties been removed?

What was she wearing?

If she'd been molested . . .

His stomach churned again. And this time the image of a violated child was more than he could bear. He gave up the battle, tossing the contents of his stomach into the toilet bowl. For long moments afterward, he sat on the rim of the bathtub, his breath coming in gasps, his brow moist, his sensibilities insulted by the disgusting act. But he did feel better. Flushing the toilet, he stood and stepped to the basin. He cupped a palmful of water and rinsed out his mouth. He then dabbed more cool water onto his face, dried it, and studied himself in the mirror. He looked the way he always did—fashionable, handsome, not a hair out of place. The appearance was comforting. He was going to get through this. That he promised himself. Too much was at stake.

Seconds later, when he left the bathroom, he appeared his usual calm, cool, collected self. Still, he needed some air and so, at the foot of the stairway, he told one of the agents of that need, and headed out of the house. He ended up in his BMW, his head leaning back against the leather seat, wondering where this nightmare was headed.

"I'm scared," Christine said softly.

From his seat in a nearby chair, Gray glanced toward the bed. In the dim light, he could barely make out her profile. He could, however, see the mane of her black hair strewn across the pillow and cascading over the side of the bed. He knew her fear, even before her confession, and he could feel that fear in the eyes she turned toward him, eyes that begged for him to comfort her. All he could offer this very woman who had taught him to hide his emotions was the echoing of her admission.

"I am too."

His answer took Christine by surprise, for, in the faint light, she could see him sprawled—wide-shouldered, cross-legged—in the chair with a kind of negligent arrogance. With an undeniable self-possession. He appeared to need no one, to fear nothing.

"You are?" she asked.

"Of course I am."

"You always seem so fearless."

Gray thought of how, years before, he'd feared for his sanity, feared that he couldn't go on without this woman. But what he answered was, "Only children and fools are fearless."

Christine smiled slightly. "Mandy drives me crazy with her fearlessness. She jumped into the deep end of a swimming pool before she could swim, she tried to ride a horse that hadn't even been broken, and once I caught her ready to jump off the top rung of a ladder. She told me she could fly."

Gray, too, smiled slightly—the first smile she'd seen since his return. "You're right, she sounds fearless. And she evidently does have your vivid imagination."

"Mandy's scared now, though, isn't she?" she asked.

"I'm sure she is."

Christine appreciated the fact that he hadn't lied to her. It gave her the courage to broach the topic she both wanted and did not want to bring up.

"We've underestimated the kidnapper," she said.

"What do you mean?"

"Whoever he is, he's ruthless and mean-spirited. Cruel."

"Don't let that vivid imagination get away from you."

"I'm serious. Lord, Gray, what if we're dealing with a pervert?" There, she'd said the word that had been tormenting her.

And the very word unleashed a torrent of images that turned and twisted in Christine's and Gray's minds. Frightening images. Of a child caged like an animal. Of a child crying, begging for release. Of a child screaming from pain. Or from sexual molestation. Of a child being brutally tortured and killed and buried. Never to be found.

Gray shifted in his chair. "I don't know what we're dealing with." Things weren't adding up to him, and yet he couldn't quite formulate why. "Look, let's not jump to any conclusions. Right now, all we know is that she's been kidnapped by someone whose identity is unknown."

At the mention of the word *kidnapped,* Christine had flinched. "You avoid the word," Gray said.

"What word?"

"*Kidnapped.* You haven't once said it."

No one else had noticed. "I can't make myself say it. I know it doesn't alter reality, but I just can't say the word."

Gray said nothing, yet Christine saw, felt, his torment. "You do feel something for her, don't you?"

"Of course I feel something for her," Gray said, his voice a harsh whisper. "Just don't try to pin me down as to what it is."

Christine wanted to hold out her hand and have Gray place his hand in hers. When joined, they were invincible, two halves united into a whole. They had learned that the afternoon they'd first made love. But

Christine could not ask for his hand. Instead, she asked for the only thing she could.

"Tell me everything's going to be all right," she said. "Lie to me if you have to."

"Everything's going to be all right," he said, feeling protective again. "Now go to sleep."

Christine closed her eyes, but in the self-imposed darkness, visions too horrible to imagine stalked her. In self-defense, she tried to recall past memories. Memories had been the mainstay of her life, the way she'd gotten through the years. She'd learned how to recall the smallest detail of the summer she and Gray had spent as lovers. Of all her memories, those of the hothouse were the most cherished. She had been unprepared for that kind of spiritual bonding, a bonding that had taken second place to any physical union.

Gray sensed Christine's restlessness. Her hand twitched, catching his attention. She had almost touched him a short while before, reminding him of all the deeper ways she had touched him that one afternoon, of how their union, physical and spiritual, had been the first, and only thing, to end his loneliness.

Silently cursing, Gray shot out of the chair and walked to the window. Pulling back the drapes, he stared into the black night. A wedge of a timid moon hid behind gauzy clouds. There had been a time when the night was his friend, his coconspirator, the cover under which he and Christine met and mated, but now the night was an enemy, pressing him to remember what he did not want to. Even the old tree, the one whose branches he'd daringly climbed, demanded that he remember.

"You remember, don't you?" Christine asked softly. The question stunned Gray, although why it should he didn't know. They'd always had the power to read each other's minds. And that very vulnerability had made him an easy mark. "You bet I remember. I remember how you had me believing in a vine-covered cottage when all you were doing was playing your little slumming game."

Slowly, Christine sat up, as though she couldn't take, literally, such an accusation lying down.

"Do you believe that?"

"It's what I was told."

"Who told you that?"

"Well, let's see. The first person was one of your friends who came around wanting some of what you were getting. The second was Claiborne, right before he almost killed me."

"Nikki was my only friend," Christine said defensively, defiantly. "The talk about slumming came from an acquaintance. Probably Jo Beth Kane. As for Claiborne, he never understood a thing about me. And never will." Pause, then, "Everything I did that summer, everything I said that summer, was from the heart."

"Yeah, right. That's why this turned out so happily ever after. Tell me something. Were you saying and doing the same things to Mr. Husband-to-Be?"

"You've already asked me that."

"And you didn't answer it."

"Do you believe that I'm capable of that kind of duplicity?"

"Just tell me the truth," Gray said roughly, in a voice that didn't even sound like his own.

"Don't ask for the truth unless you can take hearing it."

Gray snorted. "So far, I've taken everything you've handed out. The truth might be refreshing."

"So be it," she said. "The truth is that I thought of you as a friend, a lover, but never as someone beneath me. In fact, you were head and shoulders above anyone I knew. That included Peyton. Truth. I dated him only as a ruse. Truth. He never laid a hand on me. Until after I realized that I was pregnant." Silence followed, and when she spoke again, Gray could barely hear her. "Truth. For the next ten years, every time he touched me, I pretended that I was making love to you. You ask why I divorced him. Truth. I finally figured out that he just wasn't you."

Her words gutted Gray's stomach. He'd asked for the truth, said that he could deal with it, but now he wasn't so sure.

"He just couldn't make me feel the way you did," she added.

Instinctively, Gray said, "I don't want to hear any more."

But Christine wanted him to. "I remember that summer, that first time in the hothouse, as though it were yesterday." Pause, "And I think you remember too."

"No," he said. Even as he made the denial, he could feel the hot, humid, breath-stealing stillness of the hothouse.

"I think you do," Christine said, throwing back the covers and slipping from the bed. She wanted, desperately, to place her hand on his cheek. The way she had so very long ago. The way she'd wanted to ever since his return, as though a sweep of her fingertips could obliterate the scar to body and to soul. And in his healing perhaps lay her own.

At the sight of her walking slowly toward him, her gown, her robe, swishing about her, her feet bare, Gray's breath escaped in a sigh. Her hips swayed slightly, like a seductress, yet he knew that her actions weren't calculated. She had always moved with a sexy innocence that no man could resist.

"In fact, I think you remember every detail of that day in the hothouse," she said, still walking toward him.

"Forget that day," he said firmly, but the dank smell of earth and aroused bodies filled his starved senses. As did the smell of a lavender rose.

"I remember the way you kissed me."

No! Gray screamed silently.

"I remember the feel of your hands on my body."

Dammit, no! Had he said that out loud?

"I remember how you felt buried inside me."

The statement was provocative, but no more so than the picture she presented. She had stopped directly in front of him, her eyes mysteriously dark in the faint light, her hair a curtain of black, her voice softer than midnight shadows.

And then she did it.

She reached out a hand toward his cheek. He could almost feel it whispering against his skin. Exploring fingertips. Soft to his bristly beard. Need. And satisfaction. Desire. And fulfillment. Wholeness and—

"Don't!" he cried in a voice that turned out to be nothing more than the stirring of the air.

Christine halted her hand, but it was too late to stop the memories.

Chapter 11

Christine stood in the doorway of the hothouse. Her heart hammered such an erratic rhythm that, for the first time, she questioned the sanity of what she was about to do. Seducing a man with whom she had not exchanged a single word in six years might easily be viewed as crazy. Even Nikki had asked her if she was sure she knew what she was doing.

After the thorn incident, she and Gray had stayed out of each other's way. She'd told herself that she'd forgotten the hungry look in his eyes, but then on her arrival home a week before, their gazes had met and the past had melted away. She thought she saw that same hungry look. She had to know if she'd been right. She had to know if he hungered for her as she hungered for him. She didn't know quite how to define this hunger. Certainly, there was a sexual component to it, but there was something more. Something that had to do with loneliness.

Christine stepped deeper into the hothouse, moving past earthen pots of ruby-red bougainvillea, pink-flowering dwarf azaleas, yellow and purple butterfly irises, and a sea of green made up of shelves of plants for which she had no name. And there were rose cuttings, dozens of them waiting to take root. Smells trailed through the air. The rich loamy fragrance of tilled soil, the astringent aroma of chemicals—fungicides, insecticides, fertilizers. Above all the scents, however, rose that of gardenia and jasmine and honeysuckle, their sweetness wafting densely, intoxicatingly.

She moved onward, past bags of peat and mulch and sphagnum moss, and finally spotted Gray, ministering to what obviously were plants in need of a little TLC. He was good at supplying that. Hadn't he once doled it out in therapeutic portions to a young girl? She watched as his large hands clipped and pruned. Mostly, though, they touched and caressed, and she could have sworn that she heard him speaking low and lovingly. With each movement, she watched the rippling play of shoulder muscles beneath the thin cotton of his T-shirt. The shirt clung to his skin, sopping up the sweat, as did a bandanna tied about his forehead. She took in his slender waist, his taut thighs covered with denim.

Christine stepped forward. "Hi."

Gray whirled. He honest to God thought that he was hallucinating, that he'd somehow conjured up the one person who had been so consistently on his mind for the past week. Okay, for six damned years! There had been a lot of—some—Millie Renatos, but none of them had done more than physically satisfy him for the moment, none had ever eased the dull ache of loneliness that dwelled, but never companionably, within him. All had left him with an unnamable hunger.

None had ever made him feel whole. Nor had anyone, or anything, ever assuaged his guilt. He'd had, and God forgive him he still did have, carnal desires for this woman. How could be continue to defile the trust she'd once placed in him?

"What are you doing here?" he asked roughly.

"I came to see you."

"Yeah, well, you've seen me," he said, lowering his eyes and returning to the plant he'd been working on.

Christine refused to be deterred by both his dismissive tone and his inattention. For a full five minutes, she prowled around, fiddling with a plant here and there, picking up and laying down shears or trowel, but mostly glancing at him out of the corner of her eye. She was pretty sure she saw Gray sneaking a look at her. That was encouraging.

"It's hot in here," Christine said finally, pulling the white silk blouse away from her skin.

Gray noticed the way the fabric stuck to the slopes of her breasts and cursed himself again for the feelings the sight awakened in him. His retort revealed his self-anger. "Hothouses are supposed to be hot."

"I guess so," she replied. "What's wrong with that plant?"

He turned his attention, or what he could muster of it, to a rosebush with a smattering of yellow leaves. "Bugs," he said.

"Ah. Is that what happened to the lavender rosebush? Did it have bugs?"

Gray jerked his head toward Christine. No one had ever asked about the lavender rosebush, which he'd savagely yanked from the soil six years before, as though it, and not he, had been responsible for driving Christine away. As always, the thought of the rosebush reminded him of the single rose that had changed his life. Memories of that rose came hurtling back through time, memories of clipping the blossom, of handing it to Christine, of her soft cry, of her dropping the flower, of his bringing her thorn-riddled finger to his mouth, of the decadent feelings that roamed through him, of the look of fear in her eyes. Mostly, however, he remembered the flower's fragrance. Its strong, sweet perfume permeated his mind until he would have sworn that it swirled about the hothouse. More than sweet, however, the rose had smelled dark—like sin.

"Yeah, it had bugs."

"That's too bad," Christine replied. "It was my favorite."

Suddenly, Gray grew tired of whatever game she, they, were playing. "What are you doing here?" Before she could answer, he said, "I thought you were afraid of me." His voice turned deeply salacious. "And well you should be. I gobble up little girls like you."

That was almost exactly what he'd said years before when she'd told him that Claiborne had told her to stay away from his kind. Then, she'd laughed. Now, she said, "I'm not a little girl. I haven't been for a long time."

Something in the soft and sensual way she spoke, something in the candidness of her comment, caused Gray to take a hard look at her, at the way her ink-black hair scrambled about her shoulders, at the fullness of her breasts, at the slimness of her waist, at the hips that formed sensuous curves in her straight skirt. She was dressed in white—white blouse, white skirt, white sandals—making her look pure and virginal. She might well be, but she'd been right about one thing: She wasn't a little girl. That fact acknowledged, it nonetheless did not change one other: She was off-limits. For any number of very real and very rational reasons.

Christine was in no way surprised to hear that Gray had thought that she was afraid of him. She'd had a long time to deduct as much. Her behavior, fleeing and not returning, could have led to no other logical conclusion. But it was time to set the record straight.

"I was never afraid of you, Gray," she said. "Only of the way you made me feel."

Gray. He loved the way she said his name, kind of breathy, kind of whispery. It was the way she'd always said it, even as a child, as though the two of them were sharing a secret. Gray thought he'd never hear her say it again. Moreover, he thought that he'd never hear her say that she hadn't been afraid of him. This possibility had never crossed his mind, so intent had he been on clinging to the presumption of her fear for him.

Christine saw his confusion and took a step toward him. "I swear that it wasn't you I was afraid of. It was me . . . and the way you made me feel. I'd never felt that way before. It scared me. I know that I was sixteen, but I was incredibly naïve."

Gray thrust his hand in the air, palm out. "Whoa! Whoa!" he said, uncertain if he was trying to stop her forward movement or the flow of words that would cause him to rewrite history. If he'd hoped to stop her advance—or the words—he was sorely disappointed.

"For a while," she said, "I tried to ignore what I'd felt, to belittle it, but it was always in the back of my mind. And so I admitted that I had felt what I'd felt, and I set out to feel that way again. I tried to feel that way with a couple of boys in high school, I really tried, but I never could. I told myself it was because they were just that, boys, and when I got to college, I'd feel that way again, because by then boys would have become men." Another step toward Gray. "But guess what? I still felt nothing, and so I told myself that I'd romanticized what I'd felt with you, that I'd just been young and impressionable, that I didn't feel what I thought I had, and if you were to touch me again, I wouldn't feel the same way. And then," she said, closing the distance between them even more, "I came home and you looked at me . . ." She smiled, sweetly and with a touch of surprise. "All you did was look at me, and the feeling was back."

Without question, Gray felt a sense of relief. He'd imagined himself guilty of frightening her, and now he was given sweet absolution of her denial. And yet, a crime had been committed, the crime of misplaced passion. Their feelings for each other were wrong. Gray knew this even if Christine didn't, and because of that knowledge, he had to protect her. Even from herself.

"Get out of here," Gray said, intending to deliver the imperative harshly, but it was difficult to make a whisper sound harsh.

Christine stepped closer, her words bolder than ever. "Not until you tell me if I make you feel the same way." Pause. "Do I, Gray?"

Gray had no intention of telling her how she made him feel. Assuming he could find the words, which frankly he didn't think he had a chance of doing. Yet, if he continued to peer into her pearl-gray eyes, he couldn't be responsible for what he might try to say, and so he closed his eyes.

The instant he felt her fingertips on his jaw, he knew he was lost, set adrift to drown in a dark sea of desire. When those fingertips trailed from his cheek downward, going against the grain of his whiskers, as though searching out, and luxuriating in, the abrasiveness, he stopped breathing. When the pad of her thumb brushed his lower lip, he pleaded, "Go."

His fractured breathing, his urgent entreaty, told Christine all she needed to know, and she felt that sky-high feeling that comes to all women when they fully understand their feminine power.

"No, I won't go," she said, bringing her free hand to join the first. She palmed his cheeks, loving the way his stubble sensuously scratched her skin She loved the dampness on his face, the hot, wet warmth of his lip. She could easily believe that they stood in some tropical, even primeval, forest. Just the two of them. One man; one woman. A new Adam; a new Eve.

Christine stood so near that Gray could feel the heat of her body, the stammering beat of her heart. Gray opened his eyes. Hers were pewter-gray, darker than he'd ever seen them, and they were half-shielded behind lids heavy with desire. And then, she rose on tiptoes and leaned closer and closer and closer . . .

Gray sensed what was coming, but foolishly asked anyway. "What are you doing?"

"I'm kissing you," she whispered, lightly brushing her lips across his.

The sensation was one of a soft rose petal being drawn across his mouth. He had dreamed of kissing her—dozens, hundreds, thousands of times. In the dark of night, in the bright of day, while in the arms of another woman. Even so, he could not give in to a temptation so dangerous, and because of that, he hardened himself to the kiss.

"Go!" he said, withdrawing her hands from his face and stepping away.

"Why?"

"Because this is wrong."

"Why?"

Gray laughed—curtly. "How many reasons do you want?"

"Three," she said, then smiled at the absurdity of her answer. He didn't.

"You want three reasons," he said, with dead seriousness, "you'll get three reasons. One, we're . . . we're like family."

"But we're not family. We're not related in any way. No blood of mine runs in your veins, no blood of yours runs in mine. What about reason number two?"

"We're friends. At least, we used to be."

"Friends. Ah, yes. Well, haven't you ever heard that friends sometimes become more than friends? That only leaves reason number three."

"Your father would kill me."

Christine's smile widened. "Probably."

"Dammit, Christine, I'm the gardener!"

"So?"

"So, get the hell out of here!"

"All right," she agreed. "If you can honestly tell me that you don't want me."

Didn't want her? Jesus, God Almighty, he'd wanted her for so long that he couldn't remember not wanting her. Even now the thought of having her made him ache. So badly that he whirled from her and growled, "Get out!"

He delivered this imperative with such vehemence, such finality, that it crossed Christine's mind that maybe he was really serious. Maybe the years had diminished any feelings he might once have had for her. Maybe she'd simply read into his words and actions, past and present, what she'd wanted to read. Suddenly, painfully, a thought occurred to her.

"There's someone else, isn't there?"

Her question surprised Gray so completely that he

turned back toward her. Her eyes were wide, her color pale.

Christine gave her own interpretation to his silence. "Oh, Lord, there's someone else." She laughed, half out of embarrassment, half out of the need to keep from crying. "How stupid of me. Of course there's someone in your life."

When she turned, intending to retrace, quickly, the flagstone steps to the hothouse entrance, Gray acted on pure instinct. He grabbed her hand and whirled her around. Later, he would blame the bleakness in her eyes, the way she'd gone from seductress to the desperate child he'd known so long ago, for what he did next. He pulled her into his arms, growling, "There's no one else!"

Christine clung to him hard and fast. Their bodies fit with a precision she didn't question. She had known that he would feel this way, just as she'd known that she would be able to tuck her head beneath his chin, just as she'd known that his back would feel strong, his stomach taut. Standing in the shelter of his body, she allowed his words to calm her. Still, he had not said that he wanted her.

"Please want me," she whispered. "No one's ever really wanted me." As she spoke, she was very much aware of the male body beneath the thin T-shirt—the ridges and planes of his chest, the washboard of his ribs, the pebbly protrusion of male breasts. The shirt smelled of perspiration, a musky fragrance that unexpectedly moved her, causing her to sigh, to moan, to nuzzle her cheek against his chest.

"Not my parents. Not even my Gypsy mother," she said, wanting more than anything to feel more of this man, wanting to make him want her. She nuzzled again . . . and again . . . until the shirt rode up and her cheek connected with skin. His was warm—hot even—with trickles of salty sweat streaming through dark swirls of hair. She rubbed her cheek, catlike, in the dampness.

Her words, particularly those about her make-believe Gypsy mother, burned through Gray, as did her actions. At the moment her body had made contact with his, Gray had moaned. At the nuzzling of her cheek against the fabric of his shirt, Gray groaned. When she placed her cheek against his bare chest, he grabbed her head and dragged her mouth to his. He didn't think. He didn't consider the consequences of what he was doing. There'd be time enough later for the condemnation of his foolhardiness.

He kissed her hard, as though punishing her for all the years he'd wanted to kiss her, but had had to settle for unsatisfying alliances with other women. She met his kiss with the same hunger, the same passion. Then their kisses became softer, deeper, more soulful. Both of them felt a fire burning in body and heart.

"Tell me you want me," Christine whispered against his lips.

Gray eased his mouth from hers and found her eyes. He thought the request odd since his hard body made it all too clear that he wanted her.

"Say the words," she insisted.

She had become that child again, the one who'd learned to live on scraps of attention, mere morsels of love. This was the child who spun fantasies with her imagination. This was the child who had come to him and entrusted him with her dreams, her fears, her feelings. Palming her face in his large hands, his thumbs resting near the corners of her mouth, he whispered, "I want you. I've wanted you for so long, I can't remember not wanting you."

Christine closed her eyes to the simple beauty of his declaration and turned her face until her lips met with his palm. She kissed it. Softly. Reverently. Then kissed the other palm. Slowly, confidently she lowered her own hands to the top button of her silk blouse. She unfastened it, then the second and the third, followed by another, then another. Boldly, she guided his hands downward, into the gaping fabric, onto the swells of her breasts.

"God!" he whispered reverently, with not a hint of blasphemy.

"Make love to me," Christine begged.

Her request was sheer lunacy and, but for the moment, Gray embraced lunacy.

The next few minutes were a melange of sensations for Gray. The feel of lace crushed in his hand. Skin softer than silk. Dark coinlike crowns and sweetly shaped mounds. Ebony hair into which he could tangle his fingers and bury his face. Hot swollen lips ravenously seeking his. Having his mouth guided to tightly beaded nipples. Whimpers. Sighs.

She called his name and her hands yanked the T-shirt over his head. Her mouth paid homage to his bare chest, her tongue tasted the sweat, then brought the piquant taste to his mouth. His hand fumbled with the button of her skirt. He was so hot, so hard, he was sure he was going to explode. Where, where did you make love in a hothouse?

Christine felt the bag of peat at her back. It was hard. Just like Gray. Everything about him was hard—chest, stomach, callused hands, his ravaging lips—and yet his hardness made her feel soft. His firm hand slid inside her lace panties, eliciting soft sounds from her—a little moan, a throaty groan. As he touched her in private places that seemed his and his alone to touch, she pleaded with him to ease the exquisite ache. Finally, he stripped away her panties and discarded his jeans. And at last she saw that part of him most male. He rose above her, settled between her legs, then hesitated. His sweat dripped from him to her. Her body throbbed, wanting, needing, hungering.

"Gray . . ."

With one last vestige of sanity, he whispered, "I have nothing to protect you with."

"I'm protected," she whispered.

Freed from that burden, he plunged deep inside her, wanting in one fell swoop to ease all the years of needing and hungering. What he got was so much more. Magic. Simple magic. A magic neither could ever explain. He knew that she felt it too, for tears had gathered in her eyes. For both, the wanting, the needing, the hungering was over. Their fractional lives had just been made whole, an inexplicable completion had occurred. At long last, they belonged to one another.

In the aftermath, Gray waited for guilt's arrival. It never came. How could he have thought that something this right could ever be wrong?

Christine jerked awake. For the span of a heartbeat, she thought that it was just any typical morning, with the sun shining brightly outside the window and the birds singing melodiously. All too quickly, however, reality shouldered its way back into her life. At the thought of her daughter, at the thought of the lacy pink panties, Christine's stomach roiled and her heart filled with fear. She'd tried to cope with this nightmare, but she didn't know how much longer she could brave it. Even with a houseful of people, she felt so alone, so incredibly alone. Except for last night . . .

Christine's gaze rushed to the chair beside the bed. It was empty. Disappointment darted through her, although she refused to cling to this negative emotion. Instead, she cleaved to two things she now knew with certainty: One, the memory of that afternoon in the hothouse moved him still, and two, he'd panicked when she'd tried to touch him. Why panic if he felt nothing for her?

Eager to hear if there had been any news regarding her daughter, eager to see Gray, Christine showered and changed into fresh clothes, then left the bedroom and headed for the stairs. She quickly descended to the first floor. At the sight of Gray in the living room, she stopped. He was engaged in conversation with Agent Carrelli, a serious conversation if bent heads and fixed concentration meant anything.

"You're absolutely right," Terry Carrelli said. "There *is* a discrepancy between the ransom note and what the underwear implies."

As if sensing her presence, Gray looked up at her, and Christine started to smile. The smile died at the blankness in Gray's eyes. Had she really thought that one night could erase the past? Yes, she stupidly had.

Saddened, Christine stepped into the room, ready to face what she must.

Terry Carrelli followed Gray's gaze, saw Christine, and said, "Good morning. I understand you got a little sleep."

"A little," she said. "Have you heard any—"

"No," Terry said regretfully. "We had the package and its contents analyzed. As expected, there were traces of human urine on the underwear, even some fingerprints picked up by a new high-tech process of fingerprint identification, but nothing beyond what you'd expect—the child's and yours. I thought perhaps her nanny's might be there, as well, but they weren't."

"She rarely has occasion to handle Mandy's underwear. I lay her clothes out in the morning and take her to school. Sandy picks her up, but only when I'm running late does she help get her bath in the evening. I usually do that."

"I see. By the way, there wasn't any seminal fluid found on the underwear."

At the mention of seminal fluid, Christine's every previous thought vanished in a rush of panic. She heard little of what followed. Something about the agent having come upstairs to discuss this with her last night, then something about Gray having arrived at this conclusion on his own.

"Mind you, I can't give you a guarantee," Terry said, "but I don't think the arrival of the underwear is as menacing as it was meant to appear."

Christine forced herself to listen to the agent.

"Let me make it simple," the agent said. "Most kidnappings are motivated by one of two things: someone wanting money; someone wanting a child. The kidnapper who wants money sends a ransom note; the kidnapper wanting a child sends nothing. This guy— it's almost always a guy—doesn't want to return the child for any amount of money. These children are the ones we find sexually abused . . . if we find them at all."

"But you don't think—"

"The ransom note came right on cue," Terry said. "I think whoever kidnapped your daughter wants money. The underwear was sent to psych you out. Just one more mind game. I've said all along that this is a person who has a real need for control."

Christine allowed herself to feel a cautious optimism, for she wasn't foolish enough to think that all children kidnapped for money were returned unharmed. "What happens next?"

Terry Carrelli sighed. "For all our expertise, your guess is as good as ours, although, if I were the kidnapper, I'd be making my move soon. Generally speaking, the longer a child is held, the greater the risk of someone seeing or hearing something."

Gray was barely listening to the exchange between Christine and the agent. He was too busy watching Nikki, who had come in bearing a tray. Under the guise of collecting the dishes, mostly cups and saucers from the night before, she had moved closer and closer. He could almost believe that she was trying to eavesdrop. The instant that idea occurred, he was forced to dismiss it as absurd. All Nikki had to do was ask Christine what had been said, and Christine would tell her all.

"But at this point, all we can do is wait," Christine said, knowing the agent's answer even before he gave it.

"Regrettably, yes." Looking over at Hamm Clancy, who was motioning for him, Terry added, "Excuse me."

That left Christine and Gray alone, but Gray immediately turned to leave.

"Gray?" Christine called and instinctively reached out for him. She caught him by his shirt sleeve, and he turned back toward her, his unfathomable eyes meeting hers. Wouldn't he say anything, not even a single word? What if he simply, silently, pulled his shirt from her grasp? What would she do then? What could she do?

She didn't find out—perhaps she was spared—because an officer from Lowell Enterprises showed up, with profuse apologies under the circumstances, to obtain her signature on some papers.

Gray watched her lead the gray-haired man into the library. For a long time last night, he had watched Christine sleep. Interestingly, nothing had been said after their shared remembrance of the past. There had been a great many things that he'd wanted to ask, that he should have asked, such as how she could have gotten pregnant if she'd been protected, or how she could have betrayed him if she'd cared for him. The words wouldn't come, especially not this last question. Or maybe he simply hadn't trusted himself to voice those words. He'd felt, still felt, totally consumed by the memory, that forsaken, wonderful memory of completion. For the first time in ten years, he'd remembered, really remembered, what it had once felt like to be whole. He hadn't realized how incomplete he'd been. How lacking. How empty. The realization scared him, for it gave this woman power over him, power he couldn't afford to succumb to.

And yet . . .

Perhaps he'd made more of this than he should, the proverbial something out of nothing. Perhaps the power lay only in the memory of their union, a memory whole and pure and perfect. His gaze had been drawn to her hand, and he told himself to reach out and prove his point, that he would not feel the same completion in the present, but, in the end, he hadn't touched her. And he was downright angry with himself, for not having done so and been finished with it.

Chapter 12

Nikki slipped inside Christine's bedroom and—for the umpteenth time since that morning, and it was now late evening—moved toward the telephone. She picked up the receiver, punched in the number she already knew by heart, and waited.

Ring . . .

Although she'd caught only an occasional word, she'd heard enough of Agent Carrelli and Gray's conversation to conclude that the FBI thought the kidnapper was most likely after money. Ordinarily, such a conclusion would have pleased her. God only knew that she didn't want Mandy in the clutches of some weirdo, but that left her in the unenviable position of . . . Of what?

Ring . . .

Suspecting the identity of the kidnapper? God, she couldn't even believe she was posing that question. And yet, from the very beginning she'd been uncomfortable with Jacob's interest in Rosemead. Was he up to no good?

Ring . . .

Of course, his interest in Rosemead might mean nothing. He'd told her that he was leaving town, going on to greener pastures. Maybe he'd already left. In fact, the more she thought about it, the more inclined she was to believe it.

Ring . . .

After all, what proof did she have of his involvement in the kidnapping? None. Absolutely none. If he didn't answer on the next ring, she was going to call herself the idiot she was and forget about Jacob Purdy. She wouldn't call again.

Ring . . .

There! She was an idiot, she admitted as she hung up the telephone. There was no telling where Jacob was now. She felt better than she had in a long while. She felt . . . free, she thought as she crossed the room, headed for the door. She was glad to have him out of her life. No one would ever know of her affair with him, she assured herself as she opened the door and plowed right into—

Terry Carrelli reached for Nikki's shoulders in an attempt to steady her, at the same time saying, "I'm sorry."

"Oh, my God, you surprised me!"

"I'm sorry," he repeated, his heart fluttering, and he wasn't altogether certain that it was from the start he'd received. It just might have something to do with being so near to this woman. It was those eyes again, the way they stared so honestly into his.

"I, uh, was just making a telephone call," Nikki said, instantly regretting that she'd said anything. He hadn't asked what she was doing. Did her explanation seem odd, suspicious? And did it seem the least bit strange that his hands still clasped her shoulders? Not that she minded. In fact, she rather liked the comforting feeling. And having those dark, compassionate eyes staring into hers.

Suddenly, as though just coming to himself, Terry released her, saying, "I was just getting a little exercise. I'm about to go stir crazy."

Nikki felt relieved. Obviously, he'd thought nothing of her unsolicited explanation for being in Christine's room.

"Yeah," she said. "Everyone's going a little nuts."

"Yeah," he agreed, starting down the stairs, Nikki at his side. "Everyone's restless."

And, indeed, everyone was, Terry thought. The whole house was in upheaval. Mrs. Jackson, her husband, and even Nikki had been up and down the staircase a dozen times. Only Gray Bannon had remained relatively still.

"I don't think any of us can take much more of this," Nikki said. "I'm at my wit's end. I wouldn't tell Christine that. I mean, I put up a brave front for her, but it's hard." She glanced over at him. "I'm scared, you know?"

Nikki's admission of fear moved Terry. She'd laid herself bare, confessing to her vulnerability. Nowadays people felt they had to be invincible. Admitting their fear would be a sign of weakness.

"I know," Terry said, adding, because he thought talking might help, "Are you close to the child?"

Nikki smiled. "Oh, yeah. I'm her godmother. I was there when she was born."

"Tell me about her."

"She's . . . special. She's bright and funny, sensitive, but she can be brutally honest. You always know where you stand with Mandy. She's also capable of great passion. She's going to be one of those people who changes the world."

At the sudden lights that danced in Nikki's eyes, Terry said, "You sound like her mother instead of her godmother."

"She's everything a mother could want in a daughter. I couldn't love her more."

"You like kids, don't you?"

Without hesitation, Nikki said, "Yeah, I do." She then surprised herself by asking, "Do you think the world is such a horrible place to bring a child into?"

"I think the world has always been a horrible place to bring a child into. From prehistoric times to the present, there have been wars, plagues, famines, floods, and there always will be, but through it all children have been born, and many of them have made significant contributions to civilization. Thank goodness that the parents of Plato, and Michelangelo, Shakespeare, Alexander Graham Bell, Madam Curie, and—"

Terry stopped when he realized that Nikki was no longer at his side. Glancing back up the stairway, he found her several steps behind, a smile at her lips.

"Sorry," he said.

"Don't apologize. Passion becomes you." And it did. It had transformed his face into a living work of art. "You love children, don't you?"

"Yes, I do. I'd love to have a houseful of them." He smiled. "I always thought I would, and God knows my mother would like it."

"Then I don't understand why you don't," she said, although she was glad he didn't.

"The job takes its toll."

"No one in the FBI is happily married?" she asked,

negotiating the steps necessary to bring her to his side once more.

" 'No one' isn't accurate, but it's hard for even the most solid marriages. It takes a special woman to cope."

"And you haven't found her yet?"

"No," he said. "The truth is, even outside the bureau many marriages don't last. The divorce rate is alarming. Excuse me for being personal, but yours didn't and neither did the Jackson marriage."

"You're right, but even so, I still believe in the institution."

Terry shrugged and changed the subject. "Tell me why a woman who adores children has none."

"My husband thought it was wrong to bring children into this world. I disagreed, but then we disagreed about most everything. The issue of children was the primary reason we got divorced." She smiled sadly.

"I'm sorry."

By mutual consent, the subject was changed and they chatted their way down the rest of the stairs, then parted company reluctantly. Terry peered back over his shoulder, stealing a glance at Nikki. Leave it to him to be attracted—okay, okay, he was attracted to her!—to a woman who wanted a family. At the same time he thought this, Nikki thought what a tragedy that this man would never have a wife and family. She also suspected that he wasn't a man to easily forgive a transgression.

A telephone rang in Natchez.

After half a dozen rings, the phone was answered.

"For God's sake, when are you going to do it?" the caller yelled.

The voice at the other end replied, calmly, "You can't rush something like this."

"Do it. Tonight!" The caller hung up.

The other individual smiled at the cocky display. Let the caller think he was in control. It was the best way to handle those who never were.

The call came at three minutes to eleven o'clock.

Everyone glanced up.

Terry Carrelli looked over at Christine, who once more stood in front of the window. At the sound of the telephone, she turned, but made no other move. Terry waved her forward. Christine walked through the room without a glance right or left, fervently hoping that this might be the call that would unite her and her daughter.

After admonishing Christine to insist upon talking to Amanda, Agent Carrelli directed her to pick up the receiver. She did so on the fourth ring.

"Hello?" Christine said.

Nothing, then a raspy, weathered whisper. "Grand Village. Leave the money at the hut. If it's all there, your daughter'll be returned." Pause. "Come alone."

Click.

Dial tone.

Followed by Christine's shouted, "Wait!"

The single word told everyone that the call was, indeed, from the kidnapper. They began murmuring excitedly as the taped call was rewound. At the same time, Phil Birmingham was following the normal procedure of having the call traced. Not that anyone thought it would lead to anything other than another public pay phone. And then, the message filled the room for all to hear. After it ended, Terry spoke.

"What's Grand Village?"

"It was the village of the Natchez Indians," Gray answered. "It's an historical landmark."

"Where is it?" the agent asked.

"Out on Jefferson Davis Boulevard," Gray said. "It's a good choice. It's within the city limits, yet isolated."

"Get me a map," Carrelli called out to an agent. Then again questioning Gray, he asked, "You know it, then?"

"Yeah," he answered. "I knew it ten years ago."

"Any changes would only be superficial," Christine said.

"Are we going to deliver the money without confirming that the child's alive?" Hamm Clancy asked.

The bluntness of the question brought everyone up short.

"Of course we are," Peyton said adamantly. "If we don't comply, we'll certainly put her life in jeopardy." Pause. "She's alive . . . and we're going to get her back."

"That's another thing," the same agent said. "All the kidnapper said was that she'd be returned. When? How?"

"I don't know when or how," Peyton said, "but he'll return her."

"You certainly have undying faith in this, or these, individuals," Gray said.

The remark flustered Peyton, but only momentarily. Calmly—always calmly—he replied, "At this point, we have little choice but to have faith in this, or these, individuals. They have Amanda and they're calling the shots. We have to hope that there's some honor among them."

The room erupted into a discussion of just how much honor one was likely to find among individuals who'd kidnap a child. In the middle of the boisterous conversation a voice spoke up, so soft that it was a miracle that it even managed to make itself heard.

"Peyton's right."

All eyes turned toward Christine. Everyone had seemingly forgotten her. That she had hung up the telephone and had stepped back to the window apparently took some by surprise.

"If there's only one chance in a million, we have to take it," she said, her voice, her stance, brooking no opposition.

Finally, Gray said, "She makes the decision."

Christine's eyes found Gray's. He'd avoided her all day. She couldn't forget how he'd not responded to her touch.

"It's a go, then," Agent Carrelli said, adding, "We're not without a plan. We're not going to just let them walk away if we can help it. We'll stake out Grand Village and, if we can do so without endangering the child, we'll try to make an arrest."

"Make an arrest?" Peyton asked, clearly stunned by the agent's suggestion. "Isn't that risky? They made it clear that Christine was to come alone." Then he seemed to realize how negative he sounded. "I want Amanda back as much—more—than anyone, and that's the whole point. I don't want to do anything that might place her in jeopardy."

"Mr. Jackson," Terry said, "I fully understand your concern, but I did say that we'd act only if we could do so without endangering the child." Pause. "Let us do our job."

Peyton sighed, then said, "I'm sorry. You're right, of

course. That's why you were called in. It's just that I want my daught— I want Amanda back."

"I understand," Terry said, looking over at Gray. "Can you go over the map with me?"

Gray nodded.

"We're going to need the money too," Terry said to Hamm Clancy.

As prearranged, Clancy moved off in the direction of the library. In the interim, Phil Birmingham confirmed that the call had, indeed, been made from a pay phone. No one registered the least surprise.

Both the money, carried inside a burgundy-colored suitcase, and the map showed up at the same time. Hamm Clancy placed the suitcase on the floor beside Agent Carrelli.

Opening up the suitcase, the agent began to remove the packets of hundred-dollar bills. They had been bundled a hundred to a packet, and there were two hundred packets. "We're going to plant an electronic device that can be monitored. That way, if the kidnapper gets away, we can follow the car."

Christine's eyes brightened. "Does that mean it could lead us to Amanda?"

"Theoretically, yes," Terry said. "If the device remains undetected."

In due time, the electronic device, about the size of a Bic lighter and fitted into a decoy pack of money, was placed at the bottom of the suitcase and buried beneath a pile of authentic bills.

"Now, here's the game plan," Terry said. "And it's as straightforward as a plan can be. Mrs. Jackson, you're going to do exactly as you were told—"

"No!" Gray roared. "You can't be serious about sending her to make the drop."

"Of course I'm going to make the drop," Christine retorted.

Gray ignored her, appealing instead to Agent Carrelli. "You have no way of knowing what kind of danger she's walking into."

"You're absolutely right," Terry said. "I don't."

"I'm going to make the drop," Christine said.

Again, Gray paid her no attention. "They could take the money, then shoot her dead. Or shoot her dead, and then take the money."

"They're not going to shoot—" Christine began only to be cut off by Peyton.

"They're not going to shoot her."

"How the hell do you know?" Gray asked, then rushed forward, saying, "I can't believe you're letting her do this."

"They specifically asked for her," Peyton pointed out.

"Like I said, I can't believe you're letting her do this."

Gray's comment was insulting, emasculating, and Peyton reacted accordingly, although his voice never rose. "What you believe is irrelevant. And what I believe is that you have your nerve coming back here expressing your opinion on anything."

The comment punctured the civility that the two men had managed to maintain.

Gray's eyes darkened, hardened, as did his voice. "Nerve or not, I wouldn't let my wife risk her life."

"She isn't your wife."

"Yeah, well, she won't be yours much longer, either, will she?"

"Stop it," Christine said, and simultaneously, Terry pleaded, "Gentlemen, please."

Gray and Peyton stared at one another, each defiant, challenging, Gray with fire, Peyton with ice.

At last, Gray said, "I'll make the drop."

"No you won't," Christine said. "I will."

"This isn't a decision for me to make," Terry said, "but I want to go on record as saying that Mr. Jackson has made a valid point. It's Mrs. Jackson they're expecting. If someone else shows up, especially someone they don't know, it could spook them. I'd hate to see us get this far, then screw it up."

Silence, followed by more silence as Gray and Christine wordlessly battled each other.

The turning point came with Terry's sensible statement, which he directed toward Gray. "You can best help by looking over that map."

With great and obvious reluctance, Gray capitulated.

Everyone, FBI agents, city police, and members of the Adams County Sheriff's Department alike, plus Nikki, Christine, and Peyton, gathered around Gray.

"This," he explained as he ran his finger along a line, "is Jefferson David Boulevard, which leads to Highway Sixty-one. Here's the entrance to the village. To the immediate left is a parking lot, to the immediate right is a building that serves as a visitor's center. Now, over here"—Gray pointed to a place to the left of the parking lot—"is a reconstructed house, but it looks like nothing more than a thatched hut."

"How far from the parking lot is the hut?" Hamm Clancy asked.

"I'm guessing," Gray replied, "but I'd say two to three hundred feet. Now the rest of this"—he indicated the remainder of the map—"consists of burial mounds . . . two or three of them . . . and walking trails connecting them. It looks a little like a golf course. Surrounding the village, all back here, and here, about up to here"—he indicated most of the map, the left side and the back, stopping short on the right-hand side—"is forest."

"What's this?" Terry asked, pointing to a thin strip that ran along the left side. The forest followed most of the strip, then stopped, leaving an inch or so of the map clear.

"That's Saint Catherine Creek."

"A creek?" Terry asked.

"Yeah, but in name only," Gray said. "There's a little water in it. Ten years ago, it was filled with grass, bushes, vines, low-growing stuff."

"It's still no creek to speak of," the city policeman, a skinny, skeletal-looking man who answered to the name Bones, said. "After a heavy rain, there's a little to slosh around in. That's about all."

"The forest ends here?" Hamm Clancy asked, pointing to that spot on the map where the forest line stopped.

"Yep," Bones confirmed. "That's a right of way, a back door into the Grand Village. It's grown up with grass, but there's a road along here"—he indicated a line on the map that ran parallel to the creek—"and where the creek runs into the right of way, it's been converted into a drainage ditch. Where it intersects the road, there's a large concrete culvert. To the right of the village is a residential area."

"A residential area?" Hamm Clancy asked.

"Yep. In fact, the entire right side of the village is bordered by houses. I don't think anyone could get through that side without being seen."

"The right of way? Can cars get in there?" Terry asked.

"Oh, yeah," Bones said. "I run parked kids out of there all the time. It's a local lovers' lane."

"Then these are the only two ways into the village?" Terry asked.

"I don't know for certain," Bones said. "The Grand Village is run by the National Park Service. Even though I chase kids out, technically it isn't our jurisdiction." After a pause, he added, "As for other ways in and out, you've got to realize that there's more than a hundred acres here."

"Wow," Terry said. "I didn't realize that you were talking about a plot of land that big."

"Should we notify the park staff?" Phil Birmingham asked. "I'm sure they could give us details on the roads."

"No!" Terry said emphatically. "We don't want to involve anyone else. At least not now. Let's go out and take a look around first. I want to see this right of way." To Hamm Clancy and Phil Birmingham, he said, "You two take one car and Bones and I'll take another."

"I'm going too," Gray said.

"I really don't think—" Terry began.

"I'm going," Gray insisted.

"Then I am too," Peyton announced.

Terry considered, then said, although it was obviously against his better judgment, "All right. But stay out of the way. And I mean it. I won't be responsible for either of you. Mr. Jackson, you ride with Hamm and Phil; Mr. Bannon, come with me and Bones." To the patrolman from the sheriff's department, he said, "You stay here. After the drop is made, someone may call in as to the child's whereabouts. You let us know if, and when, you hear anything."

"Right," the patrolman said.

Terry looked over at Christine. "Are you ready?"

Christine nodded.

"Okay," Agent Carrelli said. "As I said, your job is simple. Drive to the Grand Village, go in the front gate, take the suitcase to the hut, and leave. No heroics. Just leave and come back here to Rosemead." Pause. "You got that?"

"Yes," Christine said.

"How long will it take to drive to the village?" Terry asked.

"Fifteen to twenty minutes," Gray answered.

Terry checked his watch. "I have eleven twenty-two. Let's say it takes twenty minutes, that's eleven forty-two; give us another ten minutes to look around, that's eleven fifty-two." He glanced over at Christine. "Have the suitcase in place by midnight. Okay?"

Christine adjusted her watch. "Okay."

"Let's do it, then." Suitcase in hand, Terry led the way toward the front door.

Once outside, Agent Carrelli walked Christine to her van, placed the suitcase on the passenger seat, then exchanged a few last-minute words with her. She had just slid open the door when something—she could have sworn she heard the calling of her name—spun about her like silvery ropes, slowly turning her around.

Gray stood a distance away, peering over the hood of a car. A dark-eyed shadow within a shadow. She could barely see his face and, consequently, could read nothing written there. For several moments, they just stared at one another. Suddenly, Gray turned, ducked his head, and disappeared inside the car.

Chapter 13

It was going to be over ... it was going to be over ... it was going to be over ...

Christine silently chanted the words as she drove the van down Homochitto Street, then onto John R. Rankin Drive, and finally onto U.S. Highway 61. It was going to be over, and she wanted it to be over—God only knew she couldn't go on much longer like this—but she wanted it over only if she could have a happy ending, only if Mandy was returned unharmed. The thought that she might be harmed still scared her. She felt the kind of fear that dried the mouth, caused the heart to pound, and her breath to come shortly and incompletely. She was ever mindful that the FBI had never promised her daughter's safe return, that the kidnapper had not outlined any specifics of her return. Yes, she was frightened. And not only for Mandy. She was frightened for herself, not knowing what she might be walking into. Not that she wouldn't have

marched into hell for her daughter, but she would have
been afraid all the same.

South of Jeff Davis Hospital, Christine turned onto
Jefferson Davis Boulevard. She checked the watch.
11:35. At 11:48 Christine pulled into the gated driveway of the Grand Village. This was it. Dear God, this
was it! With a trembling hand, she turned off the van
lights, then the engine. Silence surged around her, a silence in which her own fractured breath sounded
loud. She would have been swallowed by the darkness,
save for an outdoor light located near the visitor's center. It offered little comfort, for it created ghostly shadows and night-filled niches in which someone could
hide and watch and wait. Was someone watching her
this very moment? Perhaps the kidnapper? Perhaps a
night watchman? No, there was probably no night
watchman or the kidnapper wouldn't have chosen this
spot for the drop.

Christine checked the watch. 11:49. Only a minute
had passed? She sighed, shifted, wondered how she was
going to scramble past the gate. She'd climb over it if
she had to, she thought. At 11:51—she prided herself
on getting past two whole minutes!—she picked up
the suitcase, as though her departure were imminent.
Could they detect a movement that small? Probably
not. What was Gray doing? Thinking? Feeling?

Even now, she would swear that she'd heard him
calling her name. And no one had ever spoken it quite
as he did, soulfully, sexily, making her forget time and
place. Not once had he used her given name since his
return, however. Nothing else he could have done
would have punished her so thoroughly, so mercilessly.
Maybe she'd just longed so desperately to hear it that
she had just imagined it.

11:52, 11:53, 11:54 came and went. At 11:55—

she'd reasoned that it would take her five minutes to deliver the money—she slid wide the van door. Dragging the suitcase behind her, she stepped from the vehicle. Gravel crunched as she moved forward. A closer inspection of the gate revealed that it was unlocked. The kidnapper must have had access to the gate key.

She pushed the gate, but found it harder to open than she'd expected, and had to shoulder her way past. Once inside the grounds, the lurking shadows appeared more real, more than ready to lunge at her. By sheer force of will, and in order to divest them of their frightening power, she gave ordinary names to the things she saw about her. There was the visitor's center, the parking lot, a picnic table. In the far distance, she could see the beginning of the walk paths and another picnic table.

"Nothing sinister," she reassured herself.

She turned her attention in the direction of the thatched hut. Taking one step, then another, she crossed through the gravel onto the spongy grass, which gave way beneath her feet. In the distance, she could hear night insects practicing their musical scales. Little by little, the light from the visitor's center began to fade. Belatedly, she realized that she should have brought a flashlight. Thankfully, the moon tossed down enough light to partially guide her way. But her eyes were growing accustomed to the darkness. Even now, she could make out what she believed to be the outline of the hut.

Step.

Step.

Yes, she could see the hut in the near distance. In seconds, she had passed a six-legged wooden structure, which she assumed had been used for the drying of grains. Beside it, built on poles, was something whose purpose eluded her. And then she was standing in front of the hut. It loomed before her like some conical creature, its thatched roof reminiscent of a wild head of hair. Behind it were several tall trees, which acted as a doorway into the thick dark woods. The thick dark menacing woods. She just wanted to leave the money and go. But where should she leave it? The caller had simply said at the hut. Noticing that the door to the structure was open, she crouched before it, intending to shove the suitcase inside. She couldn't, however, because of a grate sealing off the entrance. Using the open door to lever herself up—it felt like crude rough stucco—she placed the suitcase right in front of the grate and turned to leave.

It was then that she felt the presence.

Someone was watching her. From the woods. She could feel the heat of someone's penetrating stare. Her heart leapt to her throat and her skin pebbled with fright. The night had grown eerily, mysteriously, quiet.

"Let my daughter go," Christine shouted.

With that, she left, walking at first, then out-and-out running. By the time she slid behind the wheel of the van, she was breathless. Placing her hands upon the wheel, she laid her forehead against them.

"Please, God," she whispered. "Send my daughter back to me."

The black box had been beeping when they'd slid into the car, and it had continued to beep ever since. The principle of the tracking system was simplicity itself: the farther they got from the electronic device, the farther apart the beeps; the closer they got, the closer the beeps. As Terry had negotiated the nearly deserted streets of Natchez, he had maintained a distance that had resulted in frequently spaced electronic chatter. Once Christine had pulled away from them and had headed to the entrance of the Grand Village, the beeps had grown farther apart. At that point, Gray had become restless.

He'd surprised himself by giving voice to his instant concern over her making the drop. And even now, he could still feel her name forming on his tongue, where it lingered with a taste sweeter than nectar. Even now, he still wanted to call out, to warn her to be careful.

Gray looked around him, seeking answers for his actions, his yearnings, in a night that seemed uncommonly dark. The car, its headlights extinguished, had been parked at the end of the residential street. From where he sat, Gray could see the clearing of the right of way, which ran parallel to the drainage ditch. Although he couldn't see the police car, Gray knew that it was parked in the residential area, close, but not noticeably so. Should any vehicle try to exit the Grand Village via the right of way, the two cars would converge and pen it in place.

Much discussion, and some argument, had gone into the decision to take a chance on the spot they had chosen. Phil Birmingham felt, and Peyton agreed, that the village was too vast to concentrate on only one area. There were back roads, and surely they should be covered. In the end, Terry's gut feeling had won out.

"She should be making the drop about now," Terry said.

Gray forced himself not to dwell on all the things that could go wrong, on the danger Christine might be in, on the danger the child might be in, concentrating instead on the clicking of the cicadas, on the continual *beep, beep, beep,* on Peyton's occasional comment. Peyton had ridden over in the other car, but had crawled into the back seat of Terry's vehicle, alongside Bones. There was sweat on Peyton's brow that the warm May night alone couldn't account for, and he kept his fidgety hands clasped together. Peyton Jackson was worried, but then he had reason to be. Christine was still his wife, and Mandy was still the child he'd raised as his own.

"How long should it take her?" Peyton asked.

"I'd guess five to ten minutes," Terry answered.

"Then what?" Peyton asked.

"We wait," Terry said.

And wait they did, the silence interrupted only by *beep . . . beep . . . beep . . .* At some point, someone said that Christine should be on her way back to Rosemead. Gray chose to keep his relief to himself—as did everyone else. From the beginning, a tension had sparked the air. The world seemed to be sitting on the edge of its seat. More than once during this time, Gray observed Terry Carrelli fingering the gun in his shoulder holster.

At first, Gray thought that it was only his imagination that the beeps were growing closer together, but shortly he realized that Terry Carrelli had noted the same increased frequency. Gray glanced in the agent's direction.

"It's possible that it's been picked up by someone on foot," Terry said, "and that someone is headed our way."

"What do we do now?" Peyton asked, his voice calm.

"Wait some more," Bones said. "Give him or her a chance to get back to the car."

"Exactly," Terry Carrelli said. He used what might possibly be the last few minutes to contact the second car and make sure that all was in readiness. It was.

"This is the critical point. We have to hope that the electronic device isn't found."

"How likely is it that it will be?" Gray asked.

"It depends on the savvy, and the thoroughness, of the kidnapper. On our side is the fact that a kidnapper wants to beat as hasty a retreat as possible."

Beep . . . beep . . . beep . . .

Gray's chest felt congested with the tension, and he suspected that everyone else in the car felt the same way. Everyone hung on the monitor's every beep. Both men in the back seat had leaned forward, and Gray would have sworn that he felt Peyton's breath on the nape of his neck.

Beep . . . beep . . . beep . . .

Gray glanced over at Terry. "Are the beeps growing farther apart?"

"Yeah."

"Damn!" Gray said.

A huge sigh escaped Peyton and his eyes closed, he leaned back in the seat.

"Hang tough, Mr. Jackson," Terry said. "It may not be over yet."

Beep . . . beep . . . beep . . .

Gray shifted. Peyton sighed. Terry fingered his gun. Bones swore. All prayed.

It happened in a flash. All of a sudden, the tempo picked up and, within seconds, the beeps tumbled over each other.

"Oh, my God!" Peyton said, at the same time that Terry announced, "Something's headed for us."

The words had hardly slipped past his mouth when a pair of headlights slashed through the night. They lurched and lunged, indicating the swift speed at which the vehicle was traveling and the unevenness of the terrain. Gray clutched at the door handle, anchoring himself for the ride he knew was coming. No sooner had he done so than the agent simultaneously started the engine and turned on the lights of their car. In a burst of speed, the car shot forward. They timed their arrival to cut off the oncoming car, blocking all escape. Headlights battled headlights. At the same time, the second car, Hamm Clancy at the wheel, screeched into place from the opposite direction. In heartbeats, four men exited both cars and took shooting stances.

Not a single shot was ever fired.

At the appearance of the headlights, the driver of the vehicle panicked. Gray watched as the van swerved to the left, and he knew the moment the driver lost control. The van teetered on its two left wheels, tried to right itself but couldn't, then plunged headlong into the drainage ditch. The driver was thrown through the windshield and up against the concrete culvert.

Thoughts raced through Gray as he threw open the door and began to run. Who had been behind the wheel of the van? Was this person dead? If he was, how would they ever find the child? Then, an even more chilling question reared its ugly head. Had the child been in the van? Gray could hear Peyton running behind him. Although Gray was in good physical condition, Peyton passed him, negotiated the incline, slipping and sliding and catching himself with the application of bare hands to rough concrete, and arrived at the bottom just in time to hear Agent Clancy's announcement that the man was dead.

Peyton collapsed, leaning back against the side of the ditch, breathing hard. Gray passed him as he shimmied down the incline and headed for the van, its headlights still glowing. Phil Birmingham had driven one of the cars down to the ditch's edge, and in the area illuminated by those headlights, Gray saw a dented door, a front end that had been crushed, and a windshield smashed into a million pieces, many of which lay scattered about the drainage ditch. Sliding open the back passenger door, he prayed that he wouldn't see a dead or unconscious child.

In the darkened interior of the van, Gray could see little, and he called out for a flashlight. One appeared, and he focused its beam inside the vehicle. What he saw was a mess that had little to do with the accident. Some glass was scattered here and there, but the van was crammed with suitcases, boxes of what appeared to be personal papers, several boxes of food, some of it recently taken from a refrigerator, along with a portable television and a portable microwave. The kidnapper looked like a man on the move. There was no child, however. Thank God. Yet Gray's relief was short-lived. How in hell were they going to find Mandy now?

As Gray passed back by Peyton, who had his head hanging between his knees, he asked, "Are you okay?"

Peyton glanced up, looking as pale as a ghost. "Yes," he said. "Who's the dead guy?"

Terry heard the question and replied, "I haven't a clue." Even as he spoke, he reached for the wallet that Hamm Clancy had just fished out of the man's pants pocket. Terry frowned.

"What is it?" Gray asked.

"According to this, the man is Ernest Alexander Shaw, but it isn't the Ernie Shaw I spoke with."

"What do you mean?" Gray asked, looking down at the man. Whatever he had been in life, now in death he was little more than a mass of cuts, particularly his face, which streamed with blood.

"That Ernie Shaw had black hair, glasses, and a

mustache. This one has brown hair, no glasses, and no mustache. Although," he added, after taking a look at the vehicle, "now that I think about it, that is the same van—a Plymouth Voyager."

Peyton had turned even paler. "Oh, my God, if he's dead, how are we going to find Amanda?"

"Good question," Terry said. "I'm going to start by having another look around his house."

"I thought you'd already looked there," Peyton said.

"Have you got a better idea where to look?" Gray asked.

Peyton's lack of a response indicated that he didn't.

The house, a small white frame with gray shutters, sat on a quiet, dimly lit street on the northern side of town. The yard had been slighted; consequently, willowy weeds had sprung up almost as tall as the iron fence. The bushy shrubs needed pruning, grass grew inside the stone-edged flower beds, threatening to choke out all other life. As Gray followed the agents— Phil Birmingham and Bones had been left at the scene of the accident—toward the house, he sidestepped a huge crack in the sidewalk.

Had someone asked him what he was feeling, Gray wouldn't have been able to find words to express it. A sense of urgency prevailed. Wherever the child was, assuming that she was still alive, her life depended on their finding her. And they had absolutely no leads. She could be anywhere—another city, another state, another country. If they didn't find her soon . . . Gray couldn't even finish the thought. It might yet prove true that he would never see this child.

"Hang in there," Terry said as he and Gray stepped into the house.

"Yeah," Gray said, looking around him.

If the van had been messy, the living room of the house was downright chaotic. Magazines were stacked three and four piles deep, while boxes lined one whole wall. Of these, several were pizza boxes and empty tubs of chicken. Sheets, yellowed from age and bearing more than the occasional hole, covered the furniture. An ashtray rested on the coffee table, its bowl filled with ashes and cigarette butts. The smell of stale smoke, food, neglect, and something more offensive hovered in the air. More than anything else, there was a feeling of emptiness, the feeling a house has when it has been hastily abandoned. This emptiness disturbed Gray, perhaps too painfully reminding him of what it was like to be a child and to be alone.

Suddenly, the sense of urgency returned. He had to find this child. "Amanda!" he cried.

Low-decibeled chatter had been going on around him, agent talking to agent, agents talking to Peyton, Peyton to agents. At Gray's outburst, an abrupt silence descended.

Gray shouted again, "Amanda!"

Nothing.

"We've come to take you home!"

Silence. Deafening. Defeating.

Gray yanked open the door of the closet, and, with the rake of his hand, sent hangers flying. A woolen coat and a raincoat hung toward the back. He pushed them aside, checking beneath them for the body of a child—dead or alive.

Nothing.

He made his way to the bedroom, where he found the same clutter. An unmade bed drew his attention. Falling to his knees, he peered beneath it. Nothing. He then checked the closet, which had been stripped of clothes. Again nothing. His desperation building, he flung open the cedar chest at the end of the bed. Nothing, nothing, nothing! Hands on hips, Gray let out a huge sigh and tried to slow his racing heart. He listened to what was going on around him—someone was in the kitchen, hollering out that the odious smell was coming from several dead mice; someone was in another room, a second bedroom perhaps, tearing it apart; and someone else was in the bathroom, for Gray heard the unmistakable sound of a plastic shower curtain being ripped aside. Then the sound of the toilet flushing. Following that, another silence flooded the house.

"Hey, look what I found!" Hamm Clancy called.

The others hastened into the second bedroom, which had been converted into an office. A desk stood against the back wall, a desk piled high with papers. It was neither the desk nor the papers, however, that ensnared everyone's attention. Instead, all eyes focused on what Hamm Clancy was holding—a black hairpiece, a mustache, and a pair of glasses.

"Well, well," Terry said, stepping forward and taking the hairpiece.

"What do you think?" Gray asked.

"I don't know what to think just yet. Give me a minute."

No one seemed inclined to give him this minute, however.

"Why use a disguise if she didn't know him?" Hamm Clancy asked. "Sandy Killian said that Amanda never saw Ernie Shaw when he came to the house."

"Maybe he didn't want her to be able to recognize him following the kidnapping," Gray said. "Which implies that he intended to let her go after he got the ransom money."

"That sounds logical," Terry said.

"Why didn't he have those"—Gray indicated the articles that Terry was holding—"in the van, then?"

"He obviously intended to come back here and get them," Hamm Clancy said.

"Why come back here if she was being held somewhere else?" Gray said. "Wouldn't he have wanted to get out of town as soon as possible? He was packed to travel. So, wouldn't he have taken them with him in the van? After collecting the money and checking to see that it was all there, why wouldn't he just put on the disguise, go to wherever he was holding the child, and release her?"

Terry said, "You might be overlooking the obvious, and forgive me for pointing it out, but maybe he wasn't going to return her." Pause. "Or maybe he knew that she was already dead."

Peyton had remained silent until this point. "He wouldn't do that. No one could harm Amanda." Realizing how lame this sounded, he eased into a chair, saying, "Oh, Jesus!" He was now so colorless that he appeared near collapse.

"Why the disguise in the beginning if he intended to kill her all along?" Gray asked.

"Maybe the plan changed," Terry said. "Say he intended to let her go, but then she saw him without the disguise, or she became more trouble than he'd thought she was going to be, or he just panicked. Anything could have happened. Maybe he was working with someone else, and that someone else killed her."

Peyton groaned.

In the silence that followed the recitation of this grim scenario, a scratchy sound came from the attic.

"What's that?" Hamm Clancy asked.

"Mice."

Hamm Clancy accepted this without hesitation, rushing forward with, "Well, one thing we know for certain. Amanda isn't here."

Peyton rallied, suddenly looking less pale and stronger, as though he'd gotten a second wind. "I know she's alive. We just have to find her."

Gray, too, had to believe that the child was alive, that Ernie Shaw had intended to return her. Working under that assumption, he couldn't get it out of his head that it was illogical for a man fleeing town to make a trip back to his house to get a disguise that he could have taken with him. Then there were those damned pizza boxes and tubs of chicken, both of which would have been mighty bad on the ulcer Shaw was supposed to have. Gray's heart began to pound. At the same time, the scrambling sound came once more from the attic. Apparently, the house was overridden with mice. But the attic was the only place they hadn't looked in yet.

"We've got to get into the attic," Gray said, his voice filled with energy.

"Why would you want—" Peyton began, but Gray was already running from the room and into the hallway.

"There's usually a passage to the attic through the garage or the hallway." As he spoke, he scanned the ceiling of the slim hallway. At the far end, he saw a short cord dangling. "There it is!" he cried, rushing forward and yanking at the cord. A set of stairs unfolded before him. He held his hand out behind him, saying, "Give me the flashlight."

"It's in the car," Hamm Clancy said.

"Get it," Gray ordered. "And hurry!"

Chapter 14

Unwilling even to wait for the flashlight, Gray took the narrow wooden stairs two at a time. Just a few steps up and he stood waist-high in the attic. The heat was stifling. Even if the child was up here, she could well have suffered a heatstroke by now. Fear caused him to strain to see through the dungeon-like darkness. But he saw nothing.

"Amanda?" he called softly.

Nothing. Not a sound. No, wait. There was something. A humming sound. A mechanical humming sound. A fan?

"Hand me the flashlight!" Gray shouted.

Gray could hear Peyton at the foot of the stairs demanding to know what he saw, demanding to know if the child was there. Gray didn't bother with an answer.

"Here," Hamm Clancy said, and the flashlight was passed upward.

Gray reached behind him for the flashlight and switched it on. He slowly passed the light around the

cavernous room. More boxes jumped into view, as did
an old steamer truck and an old artificial Christmas tree,
missing a number of limbs. A stack of picture frames
leaned lamely against a wooden beam, while a rickety
chair looked as though it had rocked its last. Suddenly,
the light was thrown back at him. He gasped. A mirror.
Dammit, it was only a mirror! Gathering his breath, he
continued scanning the attic—another set of boxes, a
rolled-up rug, a stack of books—

An oscillating fan came into view. It sat upon a
sheet of plywood that offered a solid island amid the
uneven flooring. The air from the fan swept across a
sleeping bag, empty and rumpled. Food—pizza and
chicken—had been stacked everywhere on the plywood, but none of it had been eaten. A container of
water sat nearby. But he could see no sign of the child.

Gray lowered the flashlight, and rested his now
sweaty brow against the back of his hand. He had to
face the fact that she was being held somewhere
else . . . or that she was dead. It was in the middle of
his own defeated sigh that he heard another. Actually,
it was more a whimper. Quickly, he raised his head
and angled the flashlight in the direction of that sound.
There, crouched in a corner was a child. What struck
him most was the fact that the child wasn't cowering.
Her chin was held high and defiant, and for a moment
she looked so much like the young Christine, Gray
wouldn't have sworn that she wasn't.

And attitude wasn't the only reminder of Christine.
He'd known from the photograph that the two were
alike; now he was stunned by just how remarkable that
similarity was. The same eyes, the same hair, the same
face. The kidnapping had taken its toll, however. The
child's eyes were wary, and at present she squinted
them against the glare of the flashlight. Her hair, as

black as her mother's, had been drawn into a ponytail, no doubt once neat and tidy. Now handfuls of hair had fallen free, and dozens of tendrils, wet from sweat, plastered themselves to her face. Her dirty face. Streaked with runnels of perspiration, plump drops of which drooped from her pointed chin. Her white blouse and plaid jumper—her school uniform, Gray concluded—clung to her as though it were a second skin.

At Agent Carrelli's revelation about the child's existence, he had felt nothing. After seeing the photograph of her, after hearing her mother speak of her, something had evolved, but a shadowy something that defied description. Now, a stronger feeling tugged at him. It spread through his chest, creating a pressure, then oozed into his legs, making them just a bit wobbly. The feeling moved upward, settling as a small lump in his throat. He had no name for the foreign feeling.

Though only seconds had passed since he'd flashed the light on the child, it seemed like a thousand forevers. He directed the light away from her eyes, then he moved on up the stairs, taking it slowly so as not to further frighten her. Despite his best intentions, and the child's defiance, she shrank back.

"Mandy," he said, "I'm going to take you to your mother."

Amanda's chin tilted again, and she spoke in a raspy voice that sounded as though it hadn't been much used of late. "I don't believe you. That's what he said . . . but he didn't take me to Mamma."

"No, he didn't," Gray said, feeling a whole new level of rage directed at that son-of-a-bitch Shaw. "I *will* take you to her, though. I promise."

"I don't believe you," the child repeated.

Gray was out of his element. He'd never been

around kids of her generation and had no idea how to talk to one. Maybe you just talked to them like you did to adults. Maybe you just said what you had to say.

"Look, my name's Gray. I'm a friend of your mother's."

"My mother doesn't have a friend named Gray."

"She did a long time ago. Before you were born." Gray paused, searching for anything to say that would convince her of his authenticity. "When I first met your mother, she was just a little older than you are now. She was twelve."

"Did you go to school with her?"

"No. I, uh, I used to work at Rosemead. I was the gardener."

"Did you know my grandfather?"

"Yes, I knew him."

"Do you know my daddy?"

The question pierced Gray like a rusty knife. "Yes," he said, "I know your daddy."

In the silence that followed, he could almost hear the child trying to make a decision. He also heard the voices of Hamm Clancy and Terry Carrelli, whose sole job at present appeared to be keeping Peyton from rushing up the steps. Peyton wasn't happy at being held in check.

Gray tried again to persuade her to come with him. "Do you hear those men? They've been looking for you."

"Who are they?"

"Policemen," Gray said.

"The other man said he was a policeman, but I don't think he was."

"No, he wasn't. He lied to you, Mandy."

"That wasn't nice."

Her outrage disarmed him, causing Gray to smile. "No, that wasn't nice. Lying is never nice."

"And you're not lying to me?"

"No." Then with all sincerity, he added, "I'll never lie to you."

He held out his hand to the child, but still she hesitated. Suddenly, it dawned on him that if she could see him, she'd be more willing to come with him. He angled the light upon himself.

"I'm not much to look at, but I'm not a monster."

As she studied him, Gray wondered what she thought of him. Could she see the scar? Probably not, but if she did, would it frighten her?

"You need a shave."

Gray smiled again. "Yeah, I know. And you need something to eat and a good hot bath. And your mother needs to see that you're all right." He moved closer toward her and held out his hand again. "Come on, Mandy, take a chance on me."

Gray waited. He was so close that he could almost touch her, but he'd promised himself that he wouldn't, that he'd allow her to put her hand in his. He was on the verge of reconsidering this promise when she began to edge her hand toward his, but then, frustratingly, she hesitated.

"C'mon," Gray urged.

His encouragement turned the tide, and Amanda placed her hand in his. Small. Her hand, sweaty and grimy, was so incredibly small and dwarfed by his. Once having decided to trust this stranger, Amanda cast aside both defiance and feistiness and stepped closer. He sensed that she expected something, but wasn't at all sure what that something was. But then, an instinct as old as time kicked in, and he wrapped his arms about the child. Clumsily. Awkwardly.

Amanda reacted by stepping even closer, so close that Gray could feel the sweat from her clothes dampening his own. She draped her arms about his neck and laid her cheek against his shoulder. Vulnerable. She felt so vulnerable. He patted her back, once again clumsily. He brushed back her dirty, smelly hair, murmuring soft assurances to her. Her nearness, her smallness, the way her heartbeat mingled with his, brought a return of the unfamiliar warm feeling.

No, this feeling was one of possessiveness, a feeling different from the one he'd experienced with Christine. Christine had been a possession of the heart. This child was a corporeal possession. She was part of his body, the creation of his seed. She belonged to him in a way that no one ever had and, for a man who'd had no one for such a long time, the feeling was a heady one. She filled his empty arms.

"Bannon!" Terry called.

"Yeah!" Gray said. "We're coming down."

When Gray lifted Amanda in his arms, he felt her bare bottom, and anger—rage—sped through him.

Amanda tightened her arms about him.

"Hang on, sweetheart," Gray said, vaguely surprised by how easily the endearment had flowed from his lips. "I'm going to carry you downstairs and then we'll find your mother."

Negotiating the steep, narrow steps was no mean feat with a child in one hand and a flashlight in the other, but Gray managed. Before he'd even reached the last rung of the attic stairway, Amanda started screaming, "Daddy! Daddy!"

And then she was gone.

Snatched from him by a man with no birth claim to her.

Leaving Gray's arms to ache with the heavy burden of emptiness.

On the Wednesday following the kidnapping, Christine descended the stairway of Rosemead. Everything had, and hadn't, returned to normal. Her child had been recovered, unharmed, but only now was Christine coming to grips with the depth of fear Amanda's kidnapping had evoked.

When they'd called her with the news that Mandy had been found, Christine had been rushed to the hospital, where she and her daughter had wept openly. Although Mandy had been dirty and smelly, she'd touched, kissed, every inch of her. After Mandy had been cleaned up, Christine had touched and kissed every precious inch again. In fact, then and now, she seemed unable to get her fill of her daughter. This need for constant reassurance of her daughter's presence made her uncertain that life would ever be the way it was.

As for everyone else, they appeared to be as relieved as she, but coping better. To his credit, Claiborne seemed genuinely happy over the outcome. Sandy was all smiles, lavishing Mandy with attention; Esther would have, too, had not her duties begged her attention. Nikki was downright beaming. Even Peyton appeared his old self, right down to begging one more time for the three of them to be a family again. In short, everyone but she had returned to their normal lives.

But what of Gray?

She had no idea, for she hadn't seen him since the night of the drop. She had last seen him at the hospital, but he'd left as soon as the doctor had pronounced that

Amanda was all right. What had he thought of Amanda? Christine wondered. Had he felt anything, any fatherly feeling, for her? When questioned, delicately, Mandy had said only that Mamma's friend had found her. Rumor also said that Gray had left town, that he'd returned to Atlanta. But Christine didn't believe for a moment that he'd walk away so easily. When she'd heard that Gray would be present for the wrap-up meeting, which she was currently on her way to attend in Rosemead's living room, she'd felt unnerved. Now at the foot of the stairs, she hesitated, uncertain of what to expect, uncertain of what she had a right to expect.

At Christine's entrance, the men in the room rose to their feet, all except Gray who was already standing in front of the window where she'd spent so many watchful hours. He'd traded work clothes for a pair of crisp khakis and a plain white shirt. Their gazes met, but only briefly, for Terry Carrelli stepped up to Christine and offered his hand.

"Mrs. Jackson," he said.

Christine shook Carrelli's hand, saying to all, "Please be seated."

The men did, all except for Gray. Terry Carrelli sat on a chair that looked too small for his build, while Peyton sat alone on the sofa, one leg crossed neatly over the other.

"Let me begin by saying how pleased I am that this ended so well," Terry said.

"My thanks to you," Christine said, "and all the others, for your help."

"We only did our job."

"Perhaps, but you did it with compassion and sensitivity."

"Thank you. I understand the child is doing well."

Christine smiled. "Quite well. She was a little dehy-drated and very hungry—she had refused, out of stub-bornness, to eat—but she's bouncing back beautifully." Like father, like daughter, Christine thought.

Dr. Allison, who'd been flown in for the consulta-tion, had announced that Amanda had in no way been molested. Dr. Allison had been particularly impressed with Amanda's candor and presence of mind, reporting that the child seemed to understand fully what she was being questioned about and was adamant that she hadn't been touched in any inappropriate way. She said the kidnapper had even made her remove her own panties, then dipped them in her urine. The child had been blindfolded, taken from the attic, and, once in the bathroom, the blindfold had been removed, en-abling the child to take care of her own needs. Peyton had ranted at what he called the barbarism of such an act, but Christine had just been grateful that her daughter's needs had been met.

Terry Carrelli pulled a notebook from the breast pocket of his suit. "I just wanted to bring everyone up to date, fill in a few of the blanks."

"I still can't believe that it was Ernie Shaw," Chris-tine said. "He seemed so . . . simple."

"We went through his records," Terry said, "and they indicate that he wasn't shortchanging Lowell En-terprises. Each month's entry is exactly what it should be."

"How can that be?" Christine asked, her bewilder-ment obvious.

"Surely he wasn't stupid enough to record the fact that he was cheating the company," Peyton pointed out.

"I don't know," Terry said. "All I know is what the records indicated."

"But our accounts payable had practically doubled," Christine insisted. "And the field hands were complaining that the tanks were going dry too soon."

"As I said, I only know what his records indicated," Terry said, adding, for Christine's benefit, "I think that you're just going to have to accept the fact that you may never fully know what happened, or why."

"How did he manage to get the key to the gate?" Gray asked, speaking for the first time.

"Actually, getting the key was easy, as was getting the uniform," Terry said. "It seems that Shaw had a half brother who works at Grand Village. One"—Terry consulted his notes—"Daniel Miller. The two apparently weren't all that close. They'd had a falling out and hadn't been in touch for a good while. Daniel Miller lives near Meadville over in Franklin County. He drives in every day.

"Shortly before the kidnapping, Shaw showed up on Miller's doorstep. Wanting to make amends, he said. I think while he was there, he managed to get the key to the gate. Miller said that he could have done so easily enough, because his key ring was just lying on top of the bureau of his bedroom. Shaw had gone to the bathroom, and he could have slipped into the bedroom unnoticed."

"How did he know which key to take?" Gray asked.

"He didn't," Terry said. "I think that's why he took the entire set."

Gray frowned. "And Daniel Miller never noticed that they were missing?"

"Do you check your keys after you empty your pockets for the night? My guess is you don't. You merely assume that they're where you left them." The agent looked over his notes again, saying, "A man at a hardware store in Meadville made an entire set of keys that night for someone. His records indicate that he made seven, and there are seven keys on Miller's key ring. He couldn't positively identify Shaw, but thought the description could fit."

"How'd he get the keys back unnoticed?" Christine asked.

"He showed up bright and early the next morning, insisting on taking his brother to breakfast. Somehow he slipped them back into the bedroom before the brother realized that they were missing. Miller said that he took a quick shower. My guess is Shaw made his move then. Since he now had the house key, he came back when his brother wasn't there and took a uniform—light brown shirt, dark brown pants. Not a policeman's uniform, but close enough to fool a child."

"And his brother never noticed the uniform was missing?" Gray asked.

"Actually, he did. He has two, one of which he'd recently sent to the cleaners. He's been giving them the devil for not returning it. By the way, we found the uniform in the trash can at the back of his house. And a toy badge, which even to me looked pretty authentic."

"In the trash can outside his own house?" Gray asked incredulously, as though this, and this alone, proved the man's simplicity.

"That's right," Terry concurred.

He then went on to say that Ernie Shaw had told Amanda that her mother had been in an accident, that the child had been kept in the attic for the entire time, and that, in his own way, Ernie Shaw had been nice to her. Terry pointed out that everything, particularly the disguise, indicated that he'd intended to return Amanda, that he'd never meant to harm her, possibly just turn her loose on the street, and flee. He had left the disguise—the hairpiece, the mustache, the glasses; why bother with the uniform when Amanda now knew that he wasn't a policeman?—at the house, where he'd intended to don it again, then release the child. They had gone through everything in the house, but hadn't found the magazines from which letters had been cut out to create the ransom note. They had found, at the Grand Village, the suitcase which had once contained the money. Apparently worried about a tracking device, Ernie Shaw had dumped the contents into a knapsack and tossed the suitcase.

The more Gray listened to what was being said, the more uneasy he grew. The pieces didn't fit as smoothly as he would have liked. By everyone's evaluation, even Terry Carrelli's after meeting with Shaw, the man was simple. He was a follower, not a leader. However, he'd been clever enough to get rid of the suitcase and the magazines, but stupid enough to toss the uniform and badge out the back door. Even if he was leaving town, wouldn't he have wanted to keep his identity a secret still? Why have the authorities looking for him for the rest of his life? Why not just put the uniform in the van, along with everything else? No, the act had been careless, stupid. On the other hand, as the agent had pointed out, one didn't have to be overly bright to pull off a kidnapping. Still the conclusion seemed so simple. Maybe too simple.

"And he was clearly working alone?" Peyton asked.

Terry Carrelli hesitated only slightly before answering, "I have no evidence to suggest otherwise."

At the hesitation, Gray's gaze found the agent's, and for a brief moment, Gray thought he saw the same uneasy feeling in Terry Carrelli's eyes, but then it was gone, leaving him to wonder if he'd seen it after all.

"That's that, then," Peyton said, standing and in so doing effectively drawing the meeting to a close.

Everyone rose. Handshakes passed all around, along with everyone's heartfelt thanks to Terry Carrelli. Again, he insisted that he'd done no more than his job. He and Gray spent a few seconds chatting, and Gray thought it significant that Terry Carrelli expressed no lingering concern. Surely, if he had, he would have mentioned it.

And then Terry Carrelli was gone, stopping only to chat once more with Christine. Gray noted that the agent removed a small envelope from the breast pocket of his suit and handed it to her, saying something as he did so. Christine smiled.

Gray glanced away from Christine's smile and settled his gaze once more on the green sweep of lawn. He'd tried hard not to think about anything, or anyone, over the last couple of days, and he'd managed to meet with some success. Everything was just too much of a jumble, particularly thoughts about the child. Mandy. He kept seeing her standing there in the attic, dirty but defiant. He kept reliving the feelings that had stormed through him, warm feelings of possession that he'd never experienced before. The way she had innately trusted him moved him. He remembered, too, the way her body had fit against his, the satisfaction he'd felt with his arms clasped about her. Mostly, though, he recalled the empty feeling at having her snatched from him by Peyton.

"Gray?"

At the sweet calling of his name, Gray turned, his gaze colliding with Christine's. His feelings for this woman were equally complex. Why had he felt so protective of her? Why couldn't he get her out of his mind? What had happened between them had been over long ago. Hadn't it?

"I wanted to bring you up to date on Mandy."

"Is she really all right?"

"Yes, although Dr. Allison cautioned that sometimes reactions can be delayed."

"What does that mean?"

"That it takes a while for the reality of what happened to sink in. She may be leery of strangers in a way she hadn't been before, may want to stay closer to the house, may have bad dreams, whatever. On the other hand, she may show no reaction at all. Dr. Allison thought Amanda extremely well adjusted."

Gray wanted to ask if the child had mentioned him, but couldn't bring himself to. He turned back toward the window, wondering where the hell all this was going, wondering where in hell he wanted it to go.

Seconds passed, then, "Mandy asked about you."

Gray glanced back at Christine.

"She said that my friend had found her. She wanted to know all about where and when I had known you. I told her, as much as I dared." Christine smiled. "She seemed most impressed that it was you who taught me to throw a curved ball."

Gray wanted to sound unaffected but he knew that hurt was evident in his next comment. "I take it that she hasn't been told that I'm her father."

"No. Dr. Allison thought it best to give her a few days to settle down from the kidnapping. She suggested doing it soon, however, and to be completely honest. She said that children sense honesty, that they respond well to it, that, in general, children adapt well to changes. She thought I should be the one to tell her, and then the three of us should get together. Does that sound all right to you?"

"It sounds like it's already been decided."

Christine gave a weary sigh. "Gray, please don't let your feelings for me cloud your judgment." She paused, then added, "What do you want? To what extent do you want to be a part of her life? What are your plans?"

"I'm still trying to decide," Gray said, but it was a lie. He had already decided to stay in Natchez awhile. And he already had an appointment with a lawyer, for that very afternoon.

Chapter 15

On Thursday, exactly a week to date of the kidnapping, Amanda returned to school. Everyone remarked on her spunk, her resilience, her out-and-out courage. Amanda, however, spoke little of the incident, preferring instead to go on with her life. She spent her energy catching up on her assignments and practicing for the school play, which had been postponed from that Friday to the following Wednesday simply to accommodate her. Both Thursday and Friday afternoons, with Sandy her biggest fan, Amanda had read through her lines—flawlessly and to raves.

On Friday night, Christine told her daughter about Gray being her father. Following Dr. Allison's advice, Christine made it clear that Amanda didn't have to stop caring for the man she'd called father for the whole of her life, nor was she expected to instantly start caring for Gray. Christine simply wanted her daughter to get to know her real father. Amanda said little, making no inquiries as to how all this had come

about. The only thing Amanda asked was if Gray
would live with them. Christine told her no. When
Christine asked her daughter if it would be all right
with her if the three of them got together the next day,
Amanda agreed.

From the moment Gray heard about the picnic, he
was a nervous wreck, eager one moment, searching for
a reason not to go the next. But he knew that he
would go. He had to, he wanted to. He toyed with the
notion of buying the child a present, although he had
no idea what to buy a nine-year-old girl, then decided
against it. If she was to accept him, it would be because of who he was, not because of what he bought
her. Besides, what could he give her that she didn't already have?

Christine had suggested meeting at a spot overlooking the Mississippi River, a spot not generally
known to tourists, nestled among leafy elms and soft
grass. They were to meet at one o'clock Saturday afternoon. Gray fussed around the motel room and finally decided to just go and get it over with. From the
moment he arrived at the small clearing, from the moment he'd seated himself on the pallet, he was struck
by how different the child appeared. Dressed quite ordinarily in jeans and a T-shirt, she looked so sweet and
innocent and pretty. Not at all like the scruffy child
he'd seen in the attic. There, she'd been defiant, but
now she was subdued, not even bothering to make eye
contact much of the time. Gray wondered if it was the
aftershock of the kidnapping or the result of learning
about him.

Finally, he said, "This is weird, huh?"

This got Amanda's attention, and she looked up at
him with silver-shaded eyes. So did Christine. Gray
had sensed that like him, she, too, was holding her

breath, walking on eggshells, waiting for some break in the tension.

"Yes, sir," the child confirmed.

"Did you know that I was afraid to come here to-day?"

"No, sir."

"Well, I was. I was afraid that you were going to get me." He paused, then asked, "Are you going to get me?"

Amanda smiled and shook her head, causing her ponytail to bounce around. Christine smiled too.

"I can't tell you how relieved I am to hear that, and I'm not going to get you, either. I thought that maybe we could just talk a little bit. You know, like friends talk to each other."

"But I don't know you."

"No, you don't, but if we talk, we'll get to know one another. That's how people become friends."

This apparently made sense to Amanda, because she asked, "What should I call you?"

"How about using my name?"

"Gray?"

"Uh-huh."

"Mamma said that I could still call Dad—Peyton—Daddy."

This comment both did, and didn't, hurt. To think of her calling another by a name that was rightfully his hurt, yet he wanted this child's life to remain stable. None of what was happening was her fault.

"Of course you can." He paused, searching for the right words. "This is new to me too. We'll just take everything slowly and see what happens. Okay?"

"Okay."

And one of the things that happened was that Christine produced some fried chicken and potato salad, which everyone dawdled over more than ate, but the conversation, if not lively, did loosen up.

"Why don't you tell him about the school play?" Christine prompted, and Gray watched as the suggestion lit the child's eyes.

"I'm going to be the witch in *Snow White*."

"Are you?" he asked, pretending he'd never heard a word about the play.

"I got the part because I had the scariest laugh."

"Did you, now?"

"Yes," Amanda said. "Heather wanted to be the witch, but her laugh sounded too happy." She paused, then added, "A real witch taught me how to laugh."

Gray thought perhaps that he was being exposed to Amanda's highly imaginative mind. "You know a real witch, do you?"

Amanda nodded. "She lives in this old house and she has a hundred black cats, and they all have these big red eyes that glow in the dark. She has this huge broom, and she taught me how to fly one. It's real easy." Then, in a seque that moved so quickly that it couldn't be clocked, the child said, "I know all my lines. My favorite part is 'Mirror, mirror on the wall, who's the fairest of them all?' Do you know that part?"

Gray hesitated, finally saying, "I don't know. I'm not very familiar with *Snow White*."

"Well, the witch owns this mirror, this really big mirror, and she keeps asking it who the fairest in the land is, and the mirror always says that Snow White is, but the witch wants to be, so she poisons Snow White, but then the prince saves Snow White, and so when the witch asks the mirror again who's the fairest, she thinks it will say her name, but it says Snow White." A quick breath, then, "When I get to that line in the play—it happens twice—I tap the mirror with this ugly stick, and the mirror says that Snow White is the fairest. Mirrors can't really talk. When I tap the mirror, Mr. Dawkins—he's the science teacher—is going to play a recording."

"Ah," Gray said, "that sounds very clever. What about your costume? What's it like?"

"Awesome. It's black and has all these ragged edges. And it almost drags the floor. The hat is black and pointed and has material that falls down my back."

"Wow!" Gray said. "That sounds like some costume."

"It is. Sandy made it for me."

"Did she?"

"Yeah. I mean, yes, sir. She can make anything. She's very smart."

"It sounds like it."

"We have a dress rehearsal Tuesday, with the mirror and the costumes. Mamma's loaning us the mirror, and Sandy's going to help me dress. The play's Wednesday."

It was all Gray could do not to ask if Peyton would be there, but then he didn't really need to ask. Of course the man would be there. Gray wished that he, too, could see the play, this child in her awesome costume, but he didn't think he'd be welcome.

"How about some dessert?" Christine asked, producing a plastic bag of chocolate-chip cookies.

"Mamma and I made these," Amanda said proudly.

"Did you?" he asked, glancing up at Christine, whose look said clearly, See, I told you that I was a good mother.

Although Amanda was still a little reticent, Gray found that he could coax her into talking about her pets, and so, as they ate chocolate-chip cookies, he learned all about her pony, Winchester, her hamster,

Hamlet, her canary, her fish, and the new puppy she hoped to get soon.

"Nipper died," Amanda announced. "Do you think that dogs go to heaven?"

"I think so," Gray said. "What do you think?"

"Me too. At least good dogs do, and Nipper was a good dog."

"Where do you think bad dogs go?" Grey asked.

Amanda lowered her voice. "To that place that Mamma won't let me say."

Gray smiled, then changed the subject to Amanda's plans for the summer.

Christine watched as Gray gently led their daughter in conversation. She hadn't known what to expect of this meeting, had even been dreading it, and in those first few minutes, that dread had been justified. But Gray had stepped in and saved the day. He'd told her that he would have made a good father, and she hadn't doubted that. The truth was, though, that he would have made a great father. A great husband. How could she have been so stupid as to give up the only good thing she'd had up to that point in her life? But Amanda would win him over, he would be a part of their child's life, and consequently, a part of hers. It was a start, one she fervently hoped would lead to their being a true family at last.

Gray sensed Christine watching him, and his eyes found hers. For a moment, those silver eyes stilled his heartbeat. For just a moment, he rewrote history, making the three of them the family they could have been, should have been. Despite all that had happened, a part of him still longed for that lost family, and unless he was mistaken, so did a part of Christine.

The unexpected longing left him shaken, and Gray

said, when the opportunity arose, "I, uh, really should be going."

Christine hid her disappointment, saying instead, "Thanks for coming."

"Thanks for asking me." He looked over at the child. "I enjoyed talking with you, Mandy. Maybe we can do it again sometime."

When Amanda didn't answer, Christine filled in with, "Sure we can."

Gray was disappointed at Amanda's silence, but then he wasn't quite certain what he'd expected. Surely it would take time to build a relationship. He rose to his feet, an action which both Christine and the child repeated. He hesitated only seconds before saying, "Bye."

"Bye," Christine said.

Again, Amanda said nothing.

Again, Gray was disappointed.

Gray started walking toward the van parked on the street. With each step, he felt himself surrounded once more by loneliness.

"Gray!"

At the calling of his name by Amanda, a sound that wrapped itself around Gray's heart, he turned.

"Would you like to come to the play?"

He hesitated, then looked toward Christine, who said, "It was her idea." A pause, then, "You're welcome to come if you'd like."

"I'd like that," Gray answered.

"It's at ten o'clock Wednesday morning," Christine said.

"Fine. See you then."

He turned and walked on toward the van, cautioning himself all the while not to place undue value upon the child's offer. She'd probably asked everyone she knew. Still, she had cared enough to include him in that number, and that small fact filled him with joy.

The telephone rang.

"Hello?"

"Where the hell have you been?"

"None of your business."

"Like hell it isn't!" the caller insisted.

The other man sighed.

"What do you want?"

"It has to be done. Now!"

"The timing is wrong. I told you that before."

"Screw timing. We can't afford to wait any longer."

"We? You're the one with your balls caught in a vise."

"Just do it!" the caller yelled, then slammed down the telephone.

The man let the receiver roll slowly from his long fingers and settle in the cradle. He eased onto the bed, stretched out, and stacked his hands beneath his head. He hadn't seen the mouse in several days, and that troubled him. Was it an omen to get out while he still could? As if he could get out. Too much had already happened. He was in too deep. Besides, there was a debt to be paid.

The face of his father loomed before him, a face with a mile-wide smile, a smile that had disappeared slowly. Maybe that jerk was right. Maybe now was the time. Yeah, he thought, let the games begin. With that, he reached for the telephone and dialed a number.

•   •   •

Claiborne stared at the telephone. Something had to be done about Gray Bannon. So far, few people knew that he was Amanda's father, and he wanted to keep it that way.

He was going to have to do something, and he knew exactly what that something was. He reached for the telephone and dialed a number.

By noon of the following Monday, Christine knew that the day was going to be memorable, and for all the wrong reasons. She had been late dropping Amanda at school, primarily because of Peyton. He'd called repeatedly over the weekend, leaving one message after another, all of which she'd ignored. She just wasn't in the mood to talk to Peyton, whose conversation rarely went beyond the topic of their getting back together. That morning, however, he'd shown up at Rosemead, demanding to talk to Amanda, who later said that all he'd done was question her about Gray, leaving Christine to conclude that Peyton had known about the Saturday picnic. But how?

And then she'd arrived at Lowell Enterprises, where all hell had broken loose. She'd been greeted with the news that half a million dollars worth of brand-new equipment had just disappeared en route from the factory to a textile mill in Charlotte, North Carolina. She had called a meeting, which had had to be postponed because Claiborne couldn't be accounted for. When he had sauntered in finally, she'd pounced on him, they'd argued as usual, and then she'd told him about the equipment. To his credit, he'd immediately set about trying to locate the missing machinery.

At one-thirty-three he poked his head in her office and said, "I've found the eighteen-wheeler on a back road in North Carolina. Or rather, a North Carolina highway patrolman has."

"And?"

He shook his head. "No equipment. No driver."

"What does that mean?"

Claiborne stepped into the office and dropped into a chair. "I don't know. Maybe the driver was on the take. Maybe he's dead somewhere."

"Surely you don't think—"

"I don't know."

By two o'clock, they did know. The driver had been found, bound and gagged, about two miles from the eighteen-wheeler. He also had a whale of a headache, the result of being bashed on the head. He'd seen no one at the rest stop as he'd climbed back into the driver's seat of the rig. One minute he was conscious, the next unconscious. The rig had been found several miles from the rest stop.

As Claiborne rose from the chair and started for the door, Christine called out, "Thanks, Claiborne."

He turned, saying, "I could do the job." He was referring to the position of president, a position she was planning to abdicate. Just as she was planning to move out of Rosemead. "All I need is your recommendation," Claiborne added.

But that she couldn't give. She'd promised her father she wouldn't. Claiborne couldn't hang on to fifty cents, let alone the millions belonging to the corporation. No, Claiborne had some good qualities—he was loyal to the Lowell name, and occasionally she thought that he regretted their not being close as much as she did—but the handling of money and leadership in general weren't among them.

"But you're not going to recommend me, right?" Claiborne said.

"Claiborne—"

A sneer curled his lips. "Of course you're not."

When the telephone call came from St. Mathias School at almost two-thirty, Christine was puzzled. The moment she heard the principal's voice, she became concerned.

"What is it, Mrs. Oliver?"

"I was wondering if you could pick Amanda up today. I think we need to talk."

"About what?"

"I'd rather not go into it over the telephone."

A weight pressed upon Christine's chest. "Is she all right? Nothing's happened to her, has it? She hasn't been kid—"

"No, no, she's right here in my office."

Dire images faded, but concern lingered. "I'll be right down."

"I think that would be a good idea."

Before leaving her office, Christine dialed Sandy's downtown duplex number, got no answer, then tried her car phone. She still got no answer, and so she left word with her secretary to keep trying to reach the nanny. She was to inform Sandy that Christine would be picking Amanda up that afternoon and she should meet them back at Rosemead.

At St. Mathias School, Christine was immediately shown into the principal's office.

Frances Oliver rose, extended her hand, and said, "Mrs. Jackson."

Christine shook the principal's hand, but her attention was on Amanda, seated nearby. She looked pale, and there was something else, something Christine couldn't quite define.

"What happened?" she asked.

Frances Oliver indicated the chair next to Amanda's. "Please sit down."

Christine sat, then repeated, "What happened?"

While the principal was searching for the right words, Amanda answered, "She thinks I lied about the voice."

"What voice?"

"That isn't true, Amanda. I don't think you lied. I just wonder if maybe you weren't letting your imagination run wild."

"I heard the voice," Amanda said respectfully, but firmly.

"What voice?"

"You know how creative you can be."

"What voice?" Christine cried, attracting Mrs. Oliver's attention.

"I'm sorry," the woman said. "Shortly before I called you, Amanda went to the rest room. She claims that, while there, she heard a voice threatening her."

A chill raced down Christine's spine. "What do you mean by threatening her?"

"She couldn't tell whether the voice belonged to a man or a woman. But it whispered that if she talked about the kidnapping, something bad would happen to her."

"Oh, my God," Christine said, looking over at Amanda.

"I heard it, Mamma. I went in, I was using the bathroom, and I heard the door open. I thought it was someone else wanting to use the bathroom. Then I heard the whisper."

Christine now realized that the "something else" her daughter was was indignant. Highly indignant.

"Mrs. Jackson, we searched the entire school and

found no one. We asked every teacher if they'd seen a
stranger. No one had."

"Did you call the police?" Christine asked.

Mrs. Oliver hesitated, then said, "No. I just didn't
think that it was necessary." The principal smiled. "I've
told Amanda before that I think she's going to be a
great writer."

Amanda said nothing.

Christine glanced over at her daughter, took in the
stubbornly set chin and squared shoulders, both of
which reminded her of Gray. Christine then shifted
her attention back to the principal.

"Thank you for calling me," Christine said.

"You're welcome." Mrs. Oliver again seemed to be
searching for the right words. "Amanda's been under
such pressure lately. And understandably. I think she
needs time to recover."

"I'm sure you're right."

Amanda said nothing.

"Amanda, why don't you skip the play rehearsal this
afternoon. You know your lines already."

Again, Amanda said nothing.

As mother and daughter stepped into the hallway,
Christine asked, "Are you all right?"

"Yes, ma'am," Amanda answered, then fell silent
once more. But as soon as they were settled in the van,
Amanda said, "She doesn't believe me. But you do,
don't you?"

"Of course I do, sweetheart." But something Dr.
Allison had said tugged at Christine, something about
delayed stress possibly causing bad dreams. This hadn't
been a bad dream, but did it fall into the same cate-
gory? She preferred that explanation to the frightful
possibility that the incident in the rest room had been
real. Neither she, nor Amanda, needed this horrifying

complication. But then there was the disturbing notion that Ernie Shaw hadn't worked alone, that, in her opinion, he was a follower, not a leader.

At Rosemead, Christine and Amanda were greeted by the worried-looking Sandy.

"What's wrong?" she asked.

Christine turned to her daughter. "Why don't you go on in and change your clothes, sweetheart, and come back for some milk and cookies."

Amanda started up the stairway. Once she was out of earshot, Sandy repeated, "What's wrong?"

Christine told her, but she didn't mention Ernie Shaw and wasn't quite certain why she didn't.

"Oh, my God," Sandy said, so shaken that she eased herself onto the nearest chair. "Do you think that someone really threatened her?"

"I have no idea," Christine answered honestly. "But I told Amanda that I believe her."

"Of course. Oh, Lord, what if it's true?"

When an inquiring Esther was told of the incident, she made only one comment. "The child has always understood the difference between fantasy and reality."

It wasn't what Christine wanted to hear. The urge to talk to Gray was great, but did she dare? Why not? He was, after all, the child's father, and he'd made it clear that he wanted to be a part of her life. Yes, she was going to talk to him. Now.

When Amanda came back downstairs, Christine asked, "Will you be all right here with Sandy? There's something I need to do."

"Yes, ma'am," she said, adding, "Mamma, I *did* hear the voice."

"I know, Amanda," she said, going to her knees before the child and drawing back strands of hair from her forehead. "And I promise you that I won't let anything happen to you again. Okay?"

"Okay."

Christine rose and found Sandy's eyes. "I'll be back early. Don't let her out of your sight."

"Don't worry, I won't."

The drive to the motel where Gray was staying took only minutes, and the whole time Christine prayed that Gray was there. When she saw his van, relief flooded her. Still, she hesitated, garnering her courage, before she could actually knock on his door.

Gray glanced toward the door with a frown on his face. He'd just hung up from talking with a Michael McKenzie—he'd written the name on the pad of paper on the bedside table—a young, hungry attorney in Natchez who hadn't been intimidated by the Lowell name. The knock came again, and this time Gray rose from the bed and stepped toward the door.

"Who is it?" he called.

"Christine," she called back.

Christine? Gray pulled back the latch, opened the door, and there she stood, a vision in black—black suit, black hose, black heels. Her hair, the same lustrous black, sprawled about her shoulders. She looked sophisticated and sexy, but she also looked scared, and this set his heart to racing.

"What is it?"

"I need to talk with you. About Amanda."

He stepped back, allowing her to enter the room. "What about her?"

Christine told him everything that had happened, ending with her notion that everything had just been too pat regarding Ernie Shaw.

"You too?" he asked.

Christine felt enormous relief at realizing that she

wasn't the only one entertaining this doubt. Then confusion sank in again. "I don't know what to believe."

Gray watched as Christine paced, nervously touching this object and that—the edge of the dresser, the back of a chair, the curve of a lamp. She was worried, as perhaps she should be, as he himself was worried. No, he was more than worried. He was angry. If something sinister was happening, it was too much for three people to bear so soon after the previous nightmare.

"How's Mandy handling this?"

A tiny smile curved Christine's lips. "She's outraged that Mrs. Oliver didn't believe her."

"She would be."

Suddenly, Christine's smile disappeared, and her eyes clouded. "What are we going to do?"

We? Gray didn't dare question the pleasure he felt at hearing the word—and that she'd come to him. She could have gone to anyone, but she'd come to him.

"Let's don't rush into anything. The truth is that we just don't have enough to go on yet. We should wait and see what happens."

"But couldn't we be placing her in jeopardy by doing nothing?"

This time, it was Gray who strode about the room, as he considered the question. Christine longed to lose herself in his arms, to have him hold her, to have him whisper that everything was going to be okay. She longed for him to whisper other words too, words of forgiveness, of adoration, of love. Would she ever hear those words from him?

Scolding herself for the wayward thoughts—now was not the time—Christine directed her attention once more to the matter at hand.

"If it wasn't part of her vivid imagination," Gray began, "it was intended as a warning. If whoever it was had wanted to kidnap her again, he or she could have. Easily."

"I hadn't thought of that." By this time, Christine had sat on Gray's bed. Her eyes caught sight of the notepad with the name Michael McKenzie written on it, then moved on to the pile of change, the keys, the pocketknife in the nearby ashtray.

"On the other hand," Gray continued, "I suppose it would be foolish not . . ."

Michael McKenzie?

". . . to take some precautions."

Michael McKenzie?

"I wouldn't let her go anywhere unsupervised."

Michael McKen— Suddenly, Christine recognized the name. And a sick feeling settled in the pit of her stomach.

"You hired a lawyer." She spoke calmly, but she was incredulous.

The accusation, and it was that, came so unexpectedly that Gray stumbled for a response.

The hesitation was damning. "Oh, my God, you hired a lawyer. Claiborne said you would, but I didn't believe it. You're going to try to take her from me, aren't you?"

The idea was so ridiculous that Gray could hardly believe that she was suggesting it.

"I won't let you have her," Christine continued, an edge to her voice. "She's all I have. She's all I'll ever have."

"Listen to me. There's a lot to explain."

But she wasn't listening. She was lost to fear and anger and the pain that came from betrayal. "You came back wanting a pound of my flesh, didn't you? And you won't be happy until you get it."

Gray watched in disbelief as Christine reached for the pocketknife on the bedside table, exposed the blade, and brandished it at him.

"Here," she shouted, "carve out your precious pound of flesh!"

Chapter 16

At the sight of the knife that was responsible for the scar on his face, Gray took a step backward.

"You've wanted to hurt me ever since you came back." Christine heard the wildness in her voice, and questioned if this sound, this savage sound, was coming from her.

"I don't want to hurt you."

"Yes you do! Well, here's your chance. Make me pay for all the villainous things I did to you. Make me pay for not going away with you. Make me pay for keeping your daughter from you."

Gray saw the anger in the glare of her steel-colored, steel-hardened eyes, in the flare of her nostrils. Beneath the anger, however, he saw hurt. He understood how anger and pain fitted together.

"I don't want to hurt you. I don't want you to pay for anything. And I don't want to take her from you."

"Then what do you want?"

"For you to put the knife down, so we can talk."

"No, it's too late for talking. Just take your pound of flesh and leave me and Amanda alone." She placed the knife over her left breast. "How about carving it from my heart? That would be fitting, wouldn't it? I broke your heart, so you can have mine." She smiled wanly. "The only problem is, I'm not sure I have much left. I broke my heart when I broke yours. I have just enough left to love Amanda."

She had told him that she had suffered over the years, that she'd never loved the man she'd married. Well, hadn't he suffered too? And, because of that, her suffering should have pleased Gray. Until recently, it would have. But now ... "Don't—"

"How about from my leg?" she asked, placing the knife against her stocking-clad calf. "Didn't I walk away from you?"

Gray watched as the tip of the blade pierced the silken stocking, creating a gaping hole that quickly turned into a long run.

"Put the knife down."

"How about my eyes?" she asked, shifting the blade of the knife to the corner of one eye, an eye now glazed with tears. "I should have been able to see more clearly what was important."

"For God's sake, put the knife down!"

"I know," she said suddenly, as a single tear coursed down her cheek. "An eye for an eye, a tooth for a tooth, a scar for a scar." She brought the knife to her jaw, to the same location as Gray's scar. "Wouldn't that even the score? That would be your pound of flesh, wouldn't it, Gray?"

"Don't—" He watched as the blade of the knife indented her skin and saw a drop of blood form. His breath stuck in his throat, and he rushed forward and grabbed her wrist. "My God, have you lost your mind?"

"No!" Christine cried, holding fast to the knife.

Gray bound her wrist with his fingers, exerting what had to be a painful pressure, but still she clung to the weapon. At the same time, his weight pushed her back onto the bed. He followed her down and sprawled atop her. She squirmed against him, struggling as though her life depended upon hanging on to the knife, upon fighting the man who was trying to take it from her.

"Leave me alone! Leave us alone!" she shouted.

As she spoke, she jabbed the air with the knife, wildly, recklessly, bringing it only inches from Gray's face. He dodged the steel. Her free hand seemed to be everywhere—pushing against his face, his chest, her fingers digging into the hand trying to free the knife from hers. Finally, pinning her arm with his knee, he wrestled the knife from Christine and threw it across the room. She cried out, and continued to struggle, as though once she'd begun, she couldn't stop.

"Be still!" he hissed.

But she continued to be anything but still, as if the adrenaline would not stop pumping. Her arms flailed, her hands pushed against Gray's chest, a chest pinning her to the bed. She could feel his breath hot against one cheek, then another, as she thrashed about beneath him. One of her shoes had fallen off, her pencil-thin skirt had ridden up. Gray's knee had slid between her legs . . . and she found his arousal.

She stilled so suddenly that it surprised Gray. He heard himself gasping for breath. He stared down at her, her face flushed, her hair a wild tangle. Two buttons of her short jacket had come unfastened, revealing the swell of one breast. He could feel her skirt hiked upward, his knee parting her legs. The silk of her stockings felt so soft, while he felt hard . . .

Hard?

Surely it was only a trick of nature, an exercise in the masculine body's lack of discrimination. Surely any woman pinned thus beneath him would arouse the same response. Yet when she moaned and squirmed beneath him, there might well have been no other woman on the face of the earth. There might well have never been.

On a savage groan, he slammed his mouth into hers, ravaging her lips, her tongue, even as hers ravaged his. They kissed like combatants, like lovers. She tasted sweet—God, so sweet!—making him want more of her. He slid his hand beneath the column of her neck, arched it, and buried his lips in the warmth of her skin. He kissed, teethed, sucked, knowing that he would leave bruises, but unable to stop himself, thinking that maybe, in this primitive way, he wanted to mark her as his. At the same time, his free hand moved to the buttons of her jacket, fumbled, and finally released them from their mooring.

Christine's lips ached from the pressure of his kiss, and she knew that his mouth was currently leaving marks on the side of her neck, but she couldn't have cared less. At the same time, his hand unfastened the buttons of her jacket, then swept inside to touch, not gently, her breasts. He tried to remove the jacket, but couldn't, tried to unfasten the bra, but couldn't, and so he settled for kissing her breasts through their lacy confines. His breath whispered through the flimsy fabric, heating her skin, heating her, making her want what she'd wanted every night for far longer than she could remember.

A new struggle began, this one unhurried, this one

intended to seduce, not to subdue. Fevered kisses gave way to slow, deep, wet kisses. Heated touches to those more gentle and tender. Christine's hands trailed beneath the fabric of his shirt, over his bare skin. His hand slid beneath her skirt, slowly caressing a moan from her parted lips. The taunting passage of her hand down the front of his jeans, drew a tortured groan from him. He removed her single shoe and attempted to take off her pantyhose, but had to have her help. In the end, passion ruled and her skirt and jacket never made it off, his shirt and jeans only partially so.

With each touch, Christine imagined a new beginning for them. Not an easy beginning, for too much had happened between them, but a beginning, one they could build on, add to. Time would be her friend now, bringing him back into her life, slowly but surely, enabling them to deal with anything the future held. There was no way, and this was the sweetest realization of her life, that he could hate her and desire her. He might not have forgiven her, but he didn't hate her.

With each touch, Gray felt himself drawn nearer and nearer to this woman. Each touch was more perfect than the last. It was as it had always been between them. In each lay the completion of the other. In her lay the other half of him. He needed to possess her, to fill her with his essence, for in filling her he would be filled, for in possessing her he would be possessed.

Possessed?

Suddenly, the word frightened him. How could he allow himself to be possessed by someone who'd already played him falsely and for a fool? If she ever betrayed him, he would never survive. He'd barely survived before. And yet, here she was lying beneath him, sweet and supple, her eyes dimmed with desire, her body making promises that her heart might have no intention of keeping. She was even reaching for him, pulling him slowly, slowly, slowly downward.

"I can't do this," Gray said hoarsely, pulling from her, from the bed.

He readjusted his jeans, but didn't even bother fastening them, allowing them instead to fall in a careless vee. He walked toward the motel window, but made no attempt to peer out. Instead, he willed his body to cool down. An icy-cold fear had settled in him, leaving him to wonder what he could have been thinking. Over the years, he'd avoided remembering the first time they'd touched. Since he'd been back, he'd avoided any physical contact with her. He now knew why. She was like an addiction. One touch, one promise of completion, fulfillment, and he was hooked, left to crave more and more.

Years before, the completion had been instantaneous. This afternoon, the completion had been more wonderfully insidious. With each brush of her lips, with each trail of a fingertip, with each graze of her hips against his, she'd forced him to realize how alone he'd been over the years, how empty and barren those years had been. And that scared him.

Christine was so stunned that for long moments, she said, did, nothing. She simply listened to Gray's ragged breathing, to her own erratic heartbeat. Suddenly, she became aware of her partial nakedness, which now seemed an obscenity. Wordlessly, with what dignity she could muster, she repositioned her suit jacket and buttoned it, then pulled down her skirt. She looked around for her pantyhose and found them at the foot of the bed. She hastily put them on, then slipped her feet into her shoes. She tried to straighten her hair, but knew that was a hopeless undertaking. She didn't even try to deal with the hurt and pain crushing her.

Instead, she picked up her handbag and started for the door. There, she hesitated, hoping, praying that Gray would say something, but he didn't and so she slipped quietly from the room.

From his silver BMW, Peyton watched as Christine left the motel room and climbed inside the van. Even from this distance, he could tell what she'd been doing. It was something about the wildness of her hair. He'd never told her—there were a great many things that he'd never told her—but he'd always liked the disorder of her hair after sex. Such chaos in his ultracontrolled world was inexplicably appealing. That chaos now caused his stomach to churn. My God, what did this man have that she found so irresistible? He was nothing, a nobody, yet all he had to do was crook his finger and she came running! It was to him that she gave her kisses, to him that she offered her body.

Peyton fought the pictures swarming through his head, but the pictures proved more powerful. He saw his wife and this nobody sprawled on the tacky bed of the tacky motel room. They were naked, she with lips swollen from his harsh kisses, he cupping, kissing, the soft mounds of her breasts. He would tangle his fingers in her wild hair and force her head downward, bringing her mouth to close over the heat of him to perform an act that she'd never been willing to perform for her husband. And then she'd spread her legs for him, wider and wider.

Hate filled Peyton's heart. No, no, he didn't hate her! He loved her! Didn't she see that his life was coming apart? Didn't she see that he was losing control? No, no, he mustn't lose control. Opening his briefcase, he removed a sheet a paper, tore off a dozen perfectly matched strips, and tied a meticulous knot in the middle of each. That done, he placed the strips in the car's ashtray, then started the motor and drove off.

The pictures had gone.

His breathing had slowed to a steady rhythm.

Christine listened to the chatter of the people filling the small auditorium of St. Mathias School that Wednesday morning. Only minutes before, she'd checked on Amanda, who, with Sandy's help, was getting into her witch costume. Sandy had also applied makeup, turning Amanda from a beautiful child into what should have been a ghastly-looking witch, but, at least in Christine's opinion, the beautiful child still shone through. Christine had been pleased that the day before had been ordinary—no whispered voices from nameless people. It was easy to pretend that the incident never happened, easy to explain it away as only a figment of the imagination of either a fanciful or a traumatized child. Even Amanda seemed to shove the incident from her mind, concentrating instead on the play. Tuesday's dress rehearsal had gone without a hitch, with Sandy again doing the honors of helping her young charge into and out of her costume. Everyone had been relieved that Mr. Dawkins's recording worked, so well that it could be heard throughout the vast room.

The gilt-framed mirror, which now hung on the wall of the auditorium stage, looked great. Nikki had sent it over from the antique shop in time for the dress rehearsal. Because of its enormous size and weight, nearly a hundred pounds, two of the shop's delivery men had been required to mount it. Miss Ingram, the young teacher in charge of the play, had found an innovative way to use the mirror in both primary settings for the play, Snow White's house and the witch's castle, so that the cumbersome piece would not have to be rehung.

"Do you see him?"

Christine glanced over at Nikki. "Who?"

Nikki grinned. "Gray. You know, the guy you've been watching for."

Christine started to deny it, but changed her mind. She *had* been watching for him. She'd told Nikki about Amanda inviting her father, had told her about Amanda's incident at school, but couldn't bring herself to tell even her best friend what had transpired in the motel room. She'd gone to great trouble to hide the passion bruises on her neck—a little makeup and deft placement of her hair had accomplished the concealment she'd desired—while a long-sleeved blouse had hidden the bruises at her wrist. What she couldn't hide, apparently, was her desire to see Gray again. Then there was her physical desire for him. Her appetite now whetted, she spent both nights sensuously tortured by dreams, but with morning came the rude realization that they had been only dreams. And that, except for Amanda, she was alone, and this at a time when Nikki had found someone. Agent Carrelli had left a letter for her, which Nikki had answered. They'd even spoken a couple of times on the telephone.

"There's Peyton," Nikki said. "Did you know that he was coming?"

"Yes," Christine said. "Amanda asked him."

"Does he know about her incident?"

"Yes. He called Monday night to talk to Amanda, and she told him about it. I played it down, saying that we couldn't even be certain that it happened."

Christine followed Peyton's progress as he moved

forward from the back of the room. He looked tired, with deep furrows tunneling through his brow.

"Hi," he said, "I was afraid I was going to be late."

"Actually, you have time to spare." Christine hoped that he wouldn't sit down next to her. She had this crazy notion that maybe Gray would. But, of course, even as she thought this, Peyton took the seat beside her, greeted Nikki, and settled back, crossing one leg neatly over the other.

"How's Amanda?" he asked.

"She's fine. Excited about the play."

"Any more incidents?"

"None, and I doubt there'll be any more."

"I want to know if there is."

"Yes, Peyton."

Several parents stopped by to say hello, including the lawyer handling their divorce. Christine feared that Peyton was going to launch into another plea to end the divorce proceedings, but to her relief he didn't. As the minutes passed, she became certain that he was more than tired. He was deeply worried about something, entwining his fingers so tightly that his knuckles had grown white.

"What's wrong?"

"Nothing."

"What is it, Peyton?"

"I've just had some bad news. Well, possibly some bad news."

Something in his tone hooked her, convinced her that something serious had happened. "What?"

Peyton lowered his voice, so that only Christine could hear. "Jim may have embezzled from the company. *May*," he repeated.

If Peyton had said that aliens had landed on the White House lawn, Christine would have been less

surprised. Jim Lytle had worked for Peyton almost
from the moment Jackson Investments had opened its
doors. The two men were like brothers.

"You can't be serious," she whispered back.

"Roxie's found some things that just don't make
sense."

Christine knew that Peyton's secretary was no fool.
If she suspected something, she must have good reason
to. "But why?" Christine asked, then answered her
own question, "Margaret."

Margaret Lytle, Jim's mother, had had Alzheimer's
for a number of years, and the disease had progressed
until it meant constant care for a woman who was still
too young to qualify for Medicare. The financial burden, Christine knew, was horrendous.

"I don't know anything for certain yet," Peyton said.

Christine was on the verge of a reply when she felt
Nikki elbow her. When Christine glanced over at her
friend, Nikki nodded toward the rear door. Following
her cue, Christine saw Gray step into the auditorium.
At the same exact moment, Nancy Ingram, no taller
than some of her students, stepped onto the stage. In
a few well-chosen words, she welcomed everyone to
the play, then exited the stage, setting the drama into
action. Christine settled in to watch the performance,
promising herself that she would speak with Gray at
intermission.

Gray, carrying a single rose, slipped into a seat in the
very back row as the play was being announced.
Within seconds the play had begun, leaving Gray little
time to consider, as he had a dozen times, what he'd
do if he ran into Christine. Which he was sure to do.
He couldn't get Monday afternoon out of his mind.
He'd spent endless hours going over and over one
question: How could he still desire the woman who

had betrayed him? He'd played all around the edges of the question, and in the end, he was left with the uncontrovertible truth that despite everything, he desired her. And that scared him to the very core of his being. Because it led to another question. What was he to do with that desire?

Pushing these thoughts aside, he concentrated on the play unfolding. There was Snow White. There were the Seven Dwarves. No witch yet. He allowed his gaze to roam. He saw Sandy Killian standing in front of a side door, no doubt waiting for Amanda to make her entrance. Had Peyton come? Stupid—of course, he'd come, and probably because Amanda had invited him. And he was probably sitting with Christine.

At that exact moment Amanda stepped onto the stage, and Gray leaned forward for a better look. Darn, he wished now that he'd sat closer to the stage! Her costume, black and flowing and just as she'd described it, drew instant attention to her, as did the crooked staff she carried. It soon became apparent, however, that she needed nothing to make her the center of attention besides her personality. A warm feeling of pride filled his heart, while a slight smile crept across his lips.

A similar smile curved Christine's lips. Amanda was good, and she looked adorable. Sandy had managed to get all of Amanda's hair beneath the tall, pointed hat, making the child look older than her nine years. She was going to be a gorgeous woman. She hoped that Amanda would find some man like Gray, and that she'd have sense enough to hang on to him. Gray. Where was he seated? What was he thinking? Had what almost happened Monday afternoon crossed his mind? She had thought of little else.

"Mirror, mirror, on the wall," Amanda said, "who's the fairest of them all?"

Amanda tapped the mirror, and the recording filled the auditorium, stating that Snow White was the fairest. Amanda flew into her witch's rage, promising to poison her rival. Suddenly, applause rang out, signaling the end of the first act. All around Christine, people began to talk among themselves, some coming to their feet. Christine also stood.

"Excuse me," she said to Peyton as she passed by him and stepped out into the aisle.

She hadn't seen where Gray had taken a seat, but knowing him as she did, she assumed it would be near the back. No sooner had she thought this than she spotted him at the very back. Sitting all alone. Always alone. He must have seen her approach, for he stood up. Dressed in freshly ironed khakis and a long-sleeved black shirt, with loafers at his feet, he looked good enough to be one of her dreams. He looked good enough to fill her once more with desire, a fact she in no way hid from herself.

As she approached him, Gray watched the gentle sway of her hips beneath the pencil-thin red skirt. It reminded him of another skirt, one that his hand had been beneath. He quickly searched her face for any mark that might have been left by the prick of the knife, and was greatly relieved to find nothing. On the other hand, he noticed that she wore a long-sleeved blouse and that she'd pulled her hair, long and lush, more forward than usual. He wondered how much of a bruise he'd left at her wrist and her neck. He'd had no choice about the first, but the second . . . The rich taste of her sweet skin came back to him.

"Hi," Christine said tentatively.

"Hi," he returned with the same reserve.

"I'm glad you could come. Amanda will be pleased."

"Yeah, well, I promised her that I would."

Christine smiled, nodding toward the rose. "That's nice."

Gray had to glance down at his hand to see what she was talking about. "I, uh, wasn't sure it was appropriate."

"A flower's always appropriate for a lady." She paused, then said, "Red's nice, but lavender's better."

Thoughts raced through both minds and hearts. Christine thought of how he'd desired her and longed desperately to see hunger in his eyes again, but he gave nothing away. Did he even remember her kiss, her caress, the moment that they had almost become one? That completion, that fulfillment, that wholeness she wanted more than anything. As for Gray, he'd thought being around her would be easier, that he wouldn't recall so many vivid details of Monday afternoon—her kiss, her moan, her incredible softness, the way her body had arched invitingly against his, the moment they'd almost become one. Again, he wanted that joining.

Finally, Christine said, "Look, I'm sorry about Monday. I shouldn't have pulled the knife on you. I just went a little crazy about the lawyer."

"I should have told you about him, but there's nothing for you to worry about. I won't take her from you. That was never my intention. Please believe me." At her still uncertain look, he added, "You know you can believe anything I tell you."

Christine smiled. "I know. I guess I was just hoping that we could work it out between us. But do whatever you feel is necessary."

Seeking to change the subject, he said, "Am I just prejudiced, or is Amanda doing the best acting job?"

Christine smiled. "I suspect I'm hardly the one to ask for an objective review."

Gray smiled, ever so slightly, and it took Christine's breath away. "Well," she said when silence loomed, "I think I'll go sit down. The second act should be starting soon." With that, Christine started back down the aisle.

"Wait!" When she turned back toward him, Gray held out the rose, saying, "You want to give this to her?"

"She's your daughter. You give it to her."

Gray watched Christine make her way back down the aisle, thinking that this was going to be harder that he'd originally thought. She was, indeed, like an addiction. Gray was still watching as Christine took her seat, and her soon-to-be-ex-husband cozied about her.

Peyton slid his arm around Christine's shoulders and leaned close to her. His voice was calm, even. "Did you invite him?"

"No. Amanda did."

"Amanda? Why?"

"He *is* her father."

"Her biological father. Nothing more." He leaned closer yet, his dark breath fluttering her hair. "Are you sleeping with him?"

The question stunned Christine, making her wonder if he'd seen her coming out of the motel room, but that would necessitate his following her, and that simply wasn't Peyton's style.

"No, I'm not," she said, "but even if I were, it wouldn't be any of your business."

"You're *my* wife." Peyton's fingers tightened, painfully, on her shoulder. "You'll always be my wife."

He then removed his arm and stared ahead at the stage, where the second act was beginning. His face was calm, his demeanor composed. That calmness, that composure, following what he'd just said was downright unnerving.

The play progressed. Christine tried to pay attention, but found that her mind wandered—to the missing equipment, to Jim Lytle, to the incident at school, to the man beside her, to the man in the back of the room. She had to find a way to make Gray desire her again. Above all, she had to find a way to make him trust her again.

"Mirror, mirror, on the wall, who's the fairest of them all?" she heard Amanda saying and glanced up just in time to see her tap the mirror with the gnarled staff.

Someone screamed, and it took Christine a moment to realize what was happening. The mirror had come loose from the wall and was tumbling downward. Pinning Amanda beneath its harsh weight.

Chapter 17

Christine jumped from her seat, pushed past the people in the same row, and headed toward the stairs that would take her onto the stage. She could feel her feet connecting with the floor, but she seemed to get nowhere. Conversely, everyone else flew past her. Peyton rushed up the steps, close on the heels of Sandy. Several people from behind stage, one of them Mr. Dawkins, hurried forward as well. Out of the corner of her eye, Christine saw Sandy reach Amanda, saw her singlehandedly wrestle the hundred-pound mirror from the fallen child.

When Christine shoved her way through the gathered crowd—"Let her through!" someone cried—she found Sandy on her knees, Amanda's small hand in hers, speaking softly, consolingly, "It's okay, sweetie. It's okay."

Peyton squatted at Sandy's side, making the appropriate cooing noises to the child, patting her hand, stroking her makeup-smeared cheek. Christine, too, went down on her knees by her child's side. At the sight of her mother, Amanda stirred, even tried to sit up.

"No, darling, lie still," Christine cautioned.

"My shoulder hurts, Mamma," Amanda said, her eyes gleaming with tears.

Christine felt helpless again, the same way she'd felt during the kidnapping. "I know, but you must lie still."

"Your mother's right, sweetie," Sandy said, attempting a smile as she wiped the fallen hair from Amanda's forehead.

The conical hat had fallen from the child's head and lay nearby, alongside the gnarled staff, while the fabric of the costume had caught on something—no doubt a screw from the back of the mirror—and had torn a good four to six inches near the waist.

"Excuse me. Excuse, me, please," the male voice said, and Christine glanced up into a face she recognized, the face of Snow White's father, the face of a doctor.

She heaved a sigh of relief. "Bob."

"Thank God," Peyton said.

"Sorry, I was seated at the back of the auditorium," he said, taking Christine's place at Amanda's side.

Christine stepped back, and the next few minutes became a mangled series of sights and sounds and feelings. The doctor asked Amanda where she hurt and teased her about having witch powers, about causing the mirror to fly off the wall. Miss Ingram quieted the other children at the far end of the stage while people talked among themselves in hushed tones. Peyton looked as pale as a ghost as he stood to one side, speaking with Sandy. When Gray slipped up the steps onto the stage, Christine felt relieved just by his presence.

Gray walked over to her, still carrying the rose. "How is she?"

"I don't know. Bob's with her now. He's a doctor."

Gray glanced over at where Amanda lay sprawled on the hard floor, seething that he couldn't just march over to her and treat her like a daughter. He'd told Claiborne that he'd make sure everyone in Natchez knew he was Amanda's father, but he found that he couldn't. He had to take it slowly for the sake of Amanda and Christine.

Gray relinquished his resentful thoughts, saying, "I'm going to have a look at the mirror."

He walked to the mirror, turned it over with what looked like great difficulty, and resting it facedown, squatted before it. For long minutes, he studied what she assumed to be the hanging device. First one side, then the other. The hanging device looked intact. Gray then walked over to the wall where the mirror had been hanging. He studied the hole in the wall, then searched the stage for the nail that had held the mirror in place. When he found what he was searching for, he walked back to the wall, fitted the nail in the hole, then returned to Christine.

"Was it an accident?" she whispered.

"It's impossible to say. The hanging device was fine."

"That doesn't surprise me. I put it in place myself. That wire has been wrapped a dozen or more times. We have to be particularly careful with a piece this large."

Gray frowned. "We?"

"Nikki and I," she said. "The mirror came from the antique shop we own." Before he could reply, she rushed ahead with, "But then, if someone was going to tamper with the mirror, he wouldn't want it to be so obvious, would he? Could you tell if the nail had been loosened?"

"No. Given the weight of that mirror, everyone's going to assume that it hadn't been anchored properly. And that assumption might well be right."

"But what if it wasn't an accident?" Christine said. "How does that fit in with your theory that someone only wanted to warn Amanda not to speak about the kidnapping?"

Gray sighed. "I don't know. I just don't know."

The doctor came searching for Christine and their conversation halted. Gray watched as Christine stepped from his side and toward the doctor. He watched, too, as Peyton rushed forward and took the lead by asking, "How is she?"

"I think your daughter's extremely lucky. I want to take some X rays to rule out any internal injuries, but I'm sure she's going to walk away from this with nothing but a bruised shoulder."

"Thank God!" Peyton cried.

"I'll take her on to the hospital," Christine said.

"Fine," Bob Cullen said. "I'll meet you there."

"You want me to bring the van around?" Sandy asked Christine.

"Please. The keys are in my purse, and my purse is in the seat."

At Sandy's departure, Peyton told Christine, "I'll take my car and meet you at the hospital." He turned a pointed glance at Gray, then walked from the stage, leaving behind something that felt almost like a threat. At least it felt that way to Gray.

"Could you help me get Amanda to the van?" he heard Christine ask him.

"Sure." He passed the rose to her and went over to

kneel before Amanda. "What happened, Little Witch? Did you fall off your broom?"

Amanda smiled. "Yes, sir."

"Well, we're just going to have to take you in for a few repairs." He slid one arm under her knees, the other under her neck, saying, "This might hurt a little bit."

Amanda groaned as Gray lifted her into his arms and stood. Immediately, the crowd on the stage cleared a path, and with Christine taking the lead, the trio headed out of the auditorium. Gray favored the child's left shoulder, but even so she moaned several times. Each time, the sound cut through him.

"Think I don't know what you did?" he teased. At her look of interest, he added, "This is a pretty rotten thing to do to get out of going back to class. When I was a kid, I knew every trick in the book to cut class, but even I never thought of this."

"You cut class?"

"You betcha."

"Didn't you get into trouble?"

"All the time."

As they stepped outside into the mid-morning light, Christine said, "There's the van."

Sandy had pulled the vehicle to the curb, where its engine now idled as she waited. Christine stepped ahead of Gray, slid open the door, and the rose still in her hand, climbed into the seat. Gray gently laid the child in her mother's lap.

"Will you call me when you get back to Rose-mead?" Gray asked, then rushed on to explain, "To let me know how she is."

"You're welcome to go with us."

"There's something I need to do."

"All right."

"All right, you'll call?"

Christine smiled. "I'll call."

Gray watched the van drive away, then got into his own van and drove to the office of his lawyer.

Gray didn't realize how much he'd wanted Christine to call until it was obvious that she wouldn't. He'd offered up one excuse after another all afternoon and into the early evening—maybe she was caring for the child, maybe she'd had to go back to her office, maybe she'd been delayed by supper, baths, telephone calls. At a few minutes shy of ten o'clock, he admitted that she wasn't going to call, and his reaction to that ranged from concern to anger. Then again, maybe he was angry at the fact that Peyton had gone to the hospital, making it clear that he wasn't going to relinquish his paternal rights so easily. Reaching for the telephone directory, he searched for, and found, the telephone number for Rosemead. Surprisingly, Christine herself answered, and on the first ring.

"Why didn't you call?" Gray said, plunging into the crux of the issue.

"I've, uh, been busy."

Her voice sounded strange, filled with hurt, but what about? "I'm certain you have been busy, but you said that you'd call."

"Yes," she said, the word clipped.

What was going on? "What's wrong?"

"Nothing," she said curtly. "Amanda's fine. No internal injuries. The doctor sent her home with a shoulder harness and some pain medication. He suggested a couple of days of bed rest. He said that she'd be better in ten days to two weeks. She's sleeping now."

To Gray's ears, it sounded like a well-practiced response. "What's wrong?" he repeated.

"I've already told you, nothing."

"I don't believe you."

Christine laughed. "So, what else is new?"

A growing sense of frustration claimed Gray. Before he could respond, Christine rushed ahead.

"How could you, Gray? I know I told you that I'd work with you, and your lawyer, but how could you choose to go to your lawyer instead of going with me to take our daughter to the hospital? Why didn't you just tell me that you had a legal appointment, and that it was more important to you?"

Gray was stunned, by the fact that she'd known of his visit, and that it had so greatly upset her. "I didn't have an appointment."

"I saw your van there!"

"Yes, you did. I needed to go by and talk with the lawyer."

"And that was more important than your daughter's welfare?"

"In this rare instance, yes." He paused, then said, "I needed to tell him that his services would no longer be required. That you and I would work things out between us."

For a moment, he heard nothing, then a gush of tears and what he thought were the words, "I'm sorry."

The tears cut at Gray and he lay back on the bed, his eyes closed, his fingers kneading his eyelids. He remembered the tears of a young Christine, who'd cried because her parents had reneged on their promise to attend her softball game. The tears of that young Christine had fallen on the back of his hand. He had comforted the child in the only way he'd known how:

by his presence. He longed to comfort her again, and in the same way.

As for Christine, she folded herself into a chair and continued to weep. She was relieved, but more than that, she was touched by what he'd done. And maybe she was even crying a little bit because he wasn't there to comfort her. She would have given almost anything to have him hold her.

"Don't cry," Gray said, almost desperately. When she didn't stop crying, he rolled to his side, sighed, and pleaded, "Please."

She heard the desperation in his voice and, several sniffs later, brought the tears to a halt. Finally, she said, "I'm sorry. So sorry for everything."

Gray had the feeling that the apology covered more than this recent incident, going way back to ten years before.

"Let's start this conversation over, okay?" Without waiting for a response, he said, "Ring, ring."

Christine's lips twitched into a smile. "Hello?"

"Hello, there. I'm calling to see how Amanda is."

"She's fine. She's asleep." Christine glanced over at her sleeping daughter. "With your rose beside her."

The image was a pleasant one. "It's probably wilted by now."

"A little, but it's still pretty. And it smells wonderful."

Before Gray knew what was happening, the sinfully sweet smell of a rose, a lavender rose, wafted about him. This gave way to other images, these of Christine. He could see her sitting . . . where? In her bedroom? No, in Amanda's. She would spend the night with Amanda. She'd be tucked in a chair, her bare feet beneath her, a box of tissues nearby, her eyes, those silver-shaded eyes that he'd once lost himself so deeply in, now red with recently shed tears. Her hair would be wild. He had no idea what she'd be wearing. He'd seen her in expensive clothes, he'd seen her in cheaper. The truth was that she baffled him. He never quite knew what to expect of her.

And now he brought up one of the things about the new Christine that had surprised him. "I didn't know that you and Nikki owned an antique shop."

"We have for a number of years." She paused, adding, "I love buying and selling antiques."

"I thought you loved running Lowell Enterprises."

"You assumed I did. You found that easier to live with."

It was a statement, and yet at its heart lay a question.

"Yes," Gray said, "I did."

"Actually, I dislike the corporate world very much and can't wait to get out."

"You're giving up your position?"

"Yes, as soon as a suitable replacement is found."

"What about Claiborne?"

"No," she responded simply, then changed the subject. "Thank you for dismissing the lawyer."

"There was no need to keep him. I never meant to hurt you by hiring a lawyer." Gray paused reflectively, then admitted, "I don't know. Maybe I did in the beginning, but as I said before, I never meant to take her from you. I couldn't have even if I'd wanted to. You're too good a mother."

Tears again rushed to Christine's eyes. "Thank you for that much."

"Are you crying again?"

"I'm just not used to your saying nice things to me."

Her words cut like a swiftly drawn sword, because there was truth in what she said. He'd said a lot of hurtful things since he'd been back. "I'm sorry."

"No, none of what happened is your fault. I bear that burden alone."

It suddenly dawned on Christine that not once since his return had he asked why she hadn't kept her promise to him, her promise to go away with him. That might well have been the first thing she would have asked.

Gray sensed that they were moving into deep water, so he said, "I don't want to keep you. I just wanted to see how Amanda was."

"She's going to be out of school for the rest of the week. You're free to stop by and see her anytime."

"Thanks. I'll do that."

Bare and tucked between clean sheets, Gray listened to the night noises. In the distance he heard the occasional rumble of a passing car, a couple entering the adjacent room, someone collecting ice cubes from the nearby ice machine. Nearer, he heard the dripping of the bathroom faucet and the colicky whine of the air conditioner. Nearer yet, in his mind, he heard Christine's soft cries, cries that had knotted his heart.

How could you choose to go to your lawyer's instead of going with me to take your daughter to the hospital?

I'm just not used to your saying nice things to me.

He closed his eyes to the agony of these words, only to find images sweeping across his mind. He could see her silver-shaded eyes, filled with tears that he'd inspired. But he could also see those same eyes laughing, smiling, teasing, taunting. Gray sighed, remembering more. So much more. Like her heated skin, her hungry mouth. Like her eager hands moving over his body. His moving over hers. Her writhing beneath him.

More and more, he was seeing in her the woman she'd once been. She was a little of someone he didn't know, but a lot of someone he did. Someone he had loved.

Christine, still curled in the chair, listened to the sounds filling the room—the hamster treading its mill, the muted ticking of the clock, Amanda's occasional moan.

"Mamma?" called a small groggy voice.

Christine looked at her daughter. "Yes, darling," she said, rising from the chair and stepping to the bed, but the child had already drifted back to sleep.

Christine smiled, then, because she felt lonely, she crawled into bed beside her daughter. The little body snuggled against her. Christine lay cherishing the sweet weight, delighting in the soft breathing filling the silence. As much as she loved holding her child, Christine longed to be held. By Gray.

She felt this ache without the knowledge that a silver BMW hid in the shadows of Rosemead.

The man slipped in and out of the shadows in Sandy's dream. The man, her stepfather, slithered closer, searching for her. She could feel his need, urgent and sensual, and her breathing quickened. He must not find her. And so she began to run, through a black forest of trees and thicket. Thorns caught at her bare feet, making them bleed, but on she ran. Past a shack. An abandoned well. A castle on a hill. If only she could make it to the castle, she'd be safe, protected, cared for.

She hastened up the hill, her feet digging into the

soil. Stones bruised her, the earth clotted between her toes. She was going to make it! She pounded on the castle door, but no one answered, and so she pulled open the heavy wooden door and entered. She bolted the door behind her. Silence. Safe silence. Her breathing began to slow.

Looking around her, she saw a gilt-framed mirror on the wall. Drawn by some inexplicable force, she walked toward it. The mirror lunged from the wall, falling, knocking her small figure to the floor.

Drenched with sweat, Sandy jackknifed to a sitting position. Somewhere in the mirror's fall, she had become Amanda. Amanda crushed beneath the mirror. Sweet Amanda. Why wasn't someone watching out for her? Shouldn't mothers watch out for daughters? She wanted to protect her, Sandy thought, she really did, but there was never a way to protect children.

She slipped from bed and took two aspirins for the black headache.

By Saturday, Amanda was feeling so much better, and was so antsy being confined to bed, that she, with Sandy at her side, was allowed to go to a schoolmate's birthday party. Christine ran by Lowell Enterprises, intending only to sign some checks, but she'd been there only a few minutes when the call came in that several large pieces of equipment were missing from the storage yard of a plant in Savannah.

In a macabre déjà vu, Sandy's call came on the heels of that. Except this time, no voice whispering a threat to Amanda was involved. Instead, according to Sandy, a boy at the birthday party, after listening to one of Amanda's made-up stories, had called her a liar. Although Amanda had maintained her dignity, she was clearly upset. So upset that Sandy decided to take her home. Once in the van, Amanda had stated that nobody believed her about the voice. Sandy ended by saying that they were now back at Rosemead, with Amanda in her room with Esther.

Christine felt like weeping for her child, but instead told Sandy that she would come right home. She then called Gray and asked him to meet her at Rosemead.

By the time he arrived, Amanda had already escaped to the garden and Christine was on the phone with Dr. Allison. He found Esther in the kitchen, who explained what had happened. Then the housekeeper proclaimed, "The whole business with that Dr. Allison is hogwash. And Christine is paying a king's ransom to hear it."

Gray said, "I guess I could assume that you believe the incident with the voice."

"I'll tell you exactly what I told Christine. The child has always known the difference between fantasy and reality. She's creative, imaginative, but she's never confused fantasy and reality before. You go talk to her, then come back here and tell me that she doesn't know the difference."

Gray decided to do exactly that.

Chapter 18

Amanda was kneeling before her tomato plants, but as Gray came closer, he saw that she was only halfheartedly digging around them with her one free hand. Her rounded shoulders made her look dejected, but when she glanced up at him, he saw that defiance still burned in her eyes. Good, he thought, sitting down beside her. Neither spoke. They just let the mid-afternoon sun beat down, warming their backs. A chameleon crawled up the stem of a tomato plant, going from dirt-brown to plant-green.

Finally, Amanda said, "These are magic tomato plants. They were given to me by a fairy princess because I saved her life. The plants will grow a hundred feet tall and will have golden tomatoes. If I make a wish on these tomatoes, any wish, it will come true."

"Is that right?" Gray asked softly.

Amanda glanced up at him with tears in her eyes. "No," the child said, "that isn't right. That's just a silly story. A pretend story. I make them up because they're fun. Sometimes I write them down, sometimes I tell them. I don't know a witch."

"I know, sweetheart," Gray said, unaware of his use of the endearment. "But the voice is real, isn't it?"

"Yes. But no one believes me."

"I do." She eyed him with suspicion, prompting him to add, "Remember when I found you in the attic, and you didn't believe I was a friend of your mother's? Remember I told you that I'd never lie to you? Well, I'm not lying now. I believe you."

Gray realized how strange his conviction was. He didn't know this child, and yet he intuitively knew that she wouldn't lie. Spin stories, yes, but never out-and-out lie.

In a voice that broke Gray's heart, she said, "I'm scared."

He wanted to say that he knew, with certainty, that everything would be all right, but that would have been deceitful, and so he said, "I'm scared, too, Mandy, and I promise to do my best not to let anything happen to you."

"Dad—Peyton said that he wouldn't let anything happen to me either."

"Then you're very lucky to have two daddies looking out for you, aren't you?" Pausing, he said, "Could I ask you some questions about the kidnapping?"

She nodded.

"The man who kidnapped you—did you ever hear him talking to anyone? Someone who was there at the house or someone on the telephone?"

Amanda shook her head. "It was hard to hear in the attic. The fan made a lot of noise."

"Tell me about the man who kidnapped you. What was he like?"

"He was nice." Even she realized the irony of this,

for she said, "He was. He brought me food. But I
didn't eat it," she added quickly as though it were a
point of honor with her.

Gray smiled, understanding only too well. "I know."

"He asked me over and over if I needed anything,
or wanted anything. I told him I wanted to go home."

Gray's smile grew.

"He was sorry that he'd kidnapped me."

This caught Gray's attention. "Why do you say
that?"

"He told me that he was."

Intrigued, Gray asked, "What exactly did he say?"
When the child hesitated, he said, "Think real hard."

"He said . . . he said that he was real sorry that . . .
that . . . he was sorry he'd gotten into this mess."

"That's good. Anything else."

"He was scared."

"What makes you say that?"

"He was nervous."

"One more question. Did you ever see any part of
the house other than the attic or the bathroom?"

She shook her head.

"Did you see anything that you thought was
strange?"

"Like what?"

"I don't know, Mandy," Gray said, shoving his fingers through his hair. "I just don't know."

She thought a moment, then said, "I don't think
so."

Gray had been so wrapped up in the conversation
that he hadn't even noticed Christine's approach. In
truth, she was upon him before he knew what hit him,
sitting down beside him, wearing tight jeans and another long-sleeved blouse. Her hair was again pulled

close to her face. Both blouse and hair meant only one
thing: the bruises still hadn't disappeared.

"Hi, guys," Christine said, then turned her attention
to her daughter. "You okay, sweetie?"

The child shrugged.

"You know, I'll bet Winchester is missing you terribly. It's been several days since you've been out to see
him."

The mention of her horse brightened dimmed spirits, and Amanda decided to pay a visit.

Gray could smell Christine's perfume, a subtle floral
blend that reminded him of the lavender rose. On the
other hand, Christine was keenly aware of Gray's arms,
his chest. She wanted to be held by the first and
cradled against the second. She wanted to be told that
she'd merely fallen asleep and had a bad dream that was
now over.

She glanced over at Gray. "You know what I hate
most about this? Being placed in the untenable position of hoping our daughter has emotional problems."

"Do you believe that?"

"I don't know," she said, then gave a weary-
sounding sigh. "Maybe the truth is I just want so desperately to believe that Dr. Allison is right."

Gray could see her agony and didn't want to add to
it, but he knew that for the child's sake, he must. "I
know you do, but I have to tell you that I think Dr.
Allison is all wet. I think Mandy is telling the truth."

Christine closed her eyes and pulled her hair back
from her neck, allowing a glimpse of the bruise. Gray
couldn't glance away.

When Christine spoke, her voice was full of frustration. "I think I've always known that, but I have to
hang on to the possibility that Dr. Allison is right. Do
you understand?" Before he could answer, she said, her

voice having gone from frustration to the whisper of desperation, "I just can't face it. I'm not over the last nightmare." She paused, adding, "Dr. Allison thinks a change of scenery will help, so I've decided to go on and move out of Rosemead."

"Move out of Rosemead?"

"Yes," she said. "I only moved in because Merritt wanted us to, because he was dying. After Peyton and I separated, I stayed on—it seemed the logical thing to do—but I bought a house here in Natchez. It needed quite a bit of renovation. Fortunately, except for a few small things that can be done after we move in, it's finished."

"I can't imagine you anywhere but Rosemead."

"Why? You know how much I've always disliked it. In fact, I loathe it. Ah," she said as sudden realization dawned, "it's more comfortable thinking that I prefer a grand house, that I've changed, and for the worse."

"What's going to happen to Rosemead?"

"I don't really know. I want to donate it to the historical society, for tours and teas and whatever, but Claiborne's fighting me." She gave a small laugh. "He hates the house even worse than I do, but right now, if I found a way to end world hunger, he'd resist."

"What about Esther?"

"For the present, she's going to stay on, but I think she really wants to retire."

Gray smiled slightly, and the sight made Christine smile too. "I can't think of Esther anywhere else."

"Nor I." Slowly, Christine's smile faded. "Tell me there's the possibility that Dr. Allison is right. Tell me there's the possibility that moving will bring these episodes to an end."

Gray didn't believe it for a moment, and yet he found that he couldn't take away what little hope

Christine had, and so he said, "There's the possibility."
He wanted to enfold her in his arms. For her sake. For
his. Did she not think that he needed comforting too?

"I know this might be an imposition, and if it is,
please say so, but I was wondering if you could help us
move?" Before Gray could answer, she said, "Peyton
offered, but I just don't want to be around him."

Neither did Gray want her around Peyton. And neither did he believe that he was needed for the move.
That's what movers were for. No, it sounded as if
Christine just wanted him around. How did he feel
about that? What was his answer going to be?

"Sure," he said. And felt a tremendous satisfaction at
his recklessness.

Terry stared out the window of his motel room. For
a moment, he had to think hard where he was. Vistas
tended to all run together, to all look alike. Taos, New
Mexico. Yeah, that's where he was, working a case that
had to do with transporting stolen goods—in this case,
guns—from one state to another. He'd had trouble,
though, keeping his mind on his job; it was the first
time that had ever happened. He was usually totally
focused. But thoughts of Nikki just kept intruding.

And now there was Amanda to think about. Nikki
had called him just a few minutes ago and told him
everything that had happened to the child. At his request, she gave him Gray's phone number.

He now walked over to the phone and made the
call. He told Gray to hang tough, that he was checking
into something, which he wouldn't go into, and promised to be back in touch.

Gray hung up, both relieved and moved by the
agent's willingness to get involved once more.

•   •   •

Christine's new house, painted ivory and trimmed in a pale blue-green, sprawled beneath a canopy of live oak branches. It was smaller than its neighbors, one-storied, and possessed a simple elegance. It was not, by any standards, a mansion, a fact that didn't surprise Gray. What surprised him was how easily he'd admitted to himself that being around Christine was what he wanted.

So Gray carted boxes from room to room, emptied boxes, arranged and rearranged furniture, none of which he recognized as having come from Rosemead. He transferred animals from Rosemead to the new location, even helped Christine relocate Winchester to a stable on the outskirts of town. It was clear that Christine was breaking all ties to the house that had never really been her home. At Mandy's request, he converted one of the flower beds into a garden into which her tomato plants could be transplanted, a task they would do together that weekend. At night, Gray was exhausted, leaving him little energy for anything but to contemplate how more than once he had glanced up to find Christine looking his way. Each time, he thought he saw desire in her eyes, and that she saw the same in his.

Come Saturday, as arranged, Gray went to Rosemead and dug up the tomato plants, then headed for the new house. It was while en route that he first noticed the red pickup. He just looked up in the rear-view mirror and there it was. For several blocks, Gray watched it follow the same path as he, and was on the verge of concluding that it was tailing him when, suddenly, it turned off onto a side street. He shook his head. It was obvious that Mandy wasn't the only one with a wild imagination.

As he pulled into the driveway, Gray noted that a couple of workers were doing a few last-minute things to the house. Even before Gray's van had stopped, Amanda, her shoulder still harnessed, bounded out of the house. Behind her ran a huge black Labrador retriever with dark soulful eyes.

"See my new dog!" she cried.

The child's smile lit her face and eyes. She was really quite beautiful, and like every parent, he wondered how in the world he could have been a part of creating something so exquisite, so perfect.

"I certainly do," Gray said, squatting before the black beast and patting its head.

The dog's tail swept back and forth a mile a minute, and it gave a couple of loud, approving barks.

"Shh," Mandy said, adding, "Mamma said that I have to keep her quiet. She said that the neighbors don't want to hear a lot of barking, that we don't want to wear out our welcome—whatever that means."

Gray grinned. "I think the neighbors will understand." By now, the dog had turned all powerful paws and rough tongue. "What's her name?"

"Biddie."

"I like that."

"She's a three-year-old spayed female."

"Ah," Gray said. "I thought you wanted a puppy."

"I did, but when we got to the animal shelter, the man there said that older dogs weren't very adoptable. Everyone wants a puppy. That means that older dogs are"—here she lowered her voice—"put to sleep."

"I see. Well, that was very nice of you," Gray said, thinking that this child had heart. Lots of it. He pushed to his feet. "Are you ready to plant the tomatoes?"

"Yes, sir, and Biddie wants to help."

"Great, we can use another pair of paws."

Amanda giggled.

As it turned out, Biddie was far more interested in wallowing in the freshly tilled earth than she was in planting anything. That and soaking up the warm sun. As though she understood that this child was her savior, the dog was never far from her. As Amanda moved down the rows, awkwardly and basically one-handed, tamping the dirt around the plants, the dog followed her. Gray was touched by the dog's devotion.

". . . the scar?"

Gray glanced up at the child. "What?"

"How did you get the scar?"

Hold him down! Hold him down! I'll teach the son of a bitch to pull a knife on me!

Gray felt pain, but he wasn't certain that it was the physical pain of the knife's cut. It could have been the emotional pain of waiting for three days for the woman he loved to return to him, and the gradual realization that she wasn't going to. He had trusted her, and she had betrayed him.

"Gray?"

"Sorry," he said. "I, uh, got the scar in a fight."

"Fighting isn't good."

She said it with such noble authority that he grinned. "You're right. Fighting isn't good."

They worked on in silence, a silence that Gray felt comfortable with. He'd never liked talking for the sake of talking and, apparently, neither did the child. In that respect, she took after him. He didn't know her well enough to know what other traits they shared. But there would be time enough for that.

Amanda packed the dirt around the last of the tomato plants. She leaned back and said, her voice filled with puzzlement, "I don't understand. If you were my daddy, why didn't you marry Mamma? All the daddies of my friends married their mothers."

It was a simple enough question, one for which Gray had no answer, simple or otherwise. "You'll have to ask your mother."

As though mentioning her had conjured her up, Gray saw Christine push open the back door and start toward them. Her hair was pulled back in a ponytail, which offered a peek at the healing bruise, now green and yellow, on the side of her neck—as always, it drew him—while her face shone with perspiration. Her jeans bore traces of dirt and even paint. She should have looked awful. She didn't.

"There's a telephone call for you, Amanda. Peyton wants to know if you'd like to go horseback riding next Saturday."

Amanda's eyes brightened. "Could I?"

"If you'd like," she said, adding, "Hurry up. He's waiting for you."

The child started for the house, the dog at her heels.

That left only Gray and Christine.

"Thank you for helping Amanda with the garden," she said.

He never looked up from the task of gathering his potting tools. "My pleasure. You might want to turn the garden hose on these plants."

"I'll do that." Pause. "You don't mind if she goes horseback riding with Peyton, do you?"

He did. Like hell! But he said, "We agreed that he should remain a part of her life."

"Just checking." Another pause. "Look, I was wondering if you'd like to come to supper tomorrow night."

Gray glanced up quickly.

"Nothing fancy," she added. "Just my way of saying thank you for helping us move in."

"A verbal thank you would be sufficient."

"I'm asking you to share a meal, Gray. Nothing more."

The "nothing more" was left undefined, yet there was the subtle suggestion of something intimate. Then again, maybe it was just the way she was looking at him, as if she were all hot and bothered. Or maybe it was the way she made him feel, as if he, too, were all hot and bothered. In the end, his response was predicated on one thing: his desire to accept.

"Yes, I'd like to come."

The scream came from out of nowhere, piercing the silence of the late night and Christine's sleep, bringing her fully awake in one heartbeat. She knew that her child was in danger. She rushed from the room, realizing only when she'd careened into a hall wall that she hadn't turned on a light. She kept going, guided now by the dog's furious barking, and the softly glowing night-light in Amanda's room. Stumbling inside, she switched on the light. Amanda sat straight up in bed, her eyes wide with fright as she stared at the back window of the bedroom. The dog, still barking, was staring in the same direction.

"Someone's at the window," Amanda whispered.

Christine's heart jumped into her throat, and for a moment she was frozen in place. Finally, she said softly, "Get out of bed, Amanda, and come with me." To the dog, she said, "Keep barking, Biddie. That's a good girl."

Amanda crawled from bed. Christine put her arms around her slight shoulders, and mother and daughter made their way to the kitchen. Without turning on a light, Christine removed the telephone from the wall and dialed the operator.

When someone answered, Christine said, "Please connect me with"—she gave the name of Gray's motel.

"Ma'am, that number is listed in your directory."

"I'm sure it is, but I don't have time to look it up, and this is an emergency."

"I'm sorry, ma'am—"

"Dammit! Connect me to the motel!"

In seconds the telephone was ringing and a sleepy-sounding night clerk answered. Christine asked for Gray Bannon's room. After what seemed like forever, Gray answered.

"Hello?" his groggy voice said.

"Gray?"

Instantly recognizing the voice, he asked, "What's wrong?"

"Someone's at Amanda's window."

"I'll be right there," he said, hanging up abruptly.

Christine managed to place one more call—to the police—before her legs suddenly turned to Jell-O, and she had to ease down the kitchen wall. She held Amanda close, whispering, as tears filled her eyes, "It's going to be all right. Your daddy's on his way."

The house was dark.

A sinking feeling gathered in the pit of Gray's stomach as he shut off the van engine and the lights. He'd made the trip from the motel to the house in record time, his heart pumping wildly every second of the way, his mind conjuring up the most gruesome of images. He could see the house broken into, Christine unconscious, Mandy gone. Worse, he could see both mother and child lying in a pool of blood. The latter shattered his breath. Throwing wide the van door, he rushed toward the house and rang the doorbell. When there was no answer, the images mushroomed, turning his sinking feeling into panic. He pounded on the door with a doubled-up fist. This was greeted by the loud bark of a dog.

"It's me!" he shouted. "Let me in!"

Gray heard a muted voice speaking to the dog and then a fumbling sound at the lock on the door. Then the door was pulled open, and Gray barely had time to enter the house before Amanda grasped him about the waist and Christine clung to his neck. He picked the child up, cradling her in the crook of his arm, and encircled Christine's waist with the other. She was scared to death. He could feel her fear in every coiled and clenched muscle, and wondered if she could feel his. For long moments, he leaned back against the hall wall, his eyes closed, willing his heartbeat to slow and his fear to dissipate.

Within minutes, two police officers arrived and Christine led them into Amanda's bedroom. Gray carried the child and sat her on the side of the bed. He hadn't realized how tightly she had been clinging to him until she'd released her hold. She explained that she'd awakened to the sound of Biddie growling. The dog was staring at the window, and when Amanda looked, she saw someone there.

Gray, who'd been crouched before the child, pushed to his feet and walked to the window along with the policemen. The lock was checked and found intact.

Turning to Christine, one of the policemen said, "We're going to have a look around outside."

Gray had followed the officers all the way to the foot of the steps before Christine called out. "Gray?" He turned. "Be careful."

Chapter 19

Christine, who'd dashed to her bedroom to get a robe, again stood at the back door waiting for Gray's return. She had just begun to think that he'd been knocked on the head, or worse, when she saw a beam of light cutting through the darkness.

"There they are!" Amanda cried from her mother's side. The dog, its ears alert, stood nearby.

"Did you find anything?" Christine asked as the three men entered.

"No," one policeman said. "There are any number of footprints out there, but then, according to Mr. Bannon, this place has been crawling with workmen."

There was nothing else that could be done that night, the other policeman added. But in the morning they could canvas the neighbors to see if anyone saw anything out of the ordinary.

No! Gray and Christine immediately thought as they looked at each other. Both considered this house a sanctuary for Amanda, and the last thing either

wanted was for the child to have to deal with neigh-
borhood gossip. "That won't be necessary," Christine
told the policemen. "Now that I think about it, I'm
sure Amanda just had a bad dream. Thank you for
your help, though."

The two men looked at her a bit dubiously as they
left. The moment the front door closed behind them,
Amanda spoke up.

"There was someone there," she insisted.

"She's right," Christine told Gray. "There was
someone there. I know exactly when he left. The dog
stopped barking about a minute after I called you."

"I'm certain that there was someone there," Gray
told Christine. "Look, could you ask Nikki to get in
touch with Carrelli and have him call me."

"Sure," Christine said, then looked over at her
daughter. "Crawl back into bed, sweetie."

"No, Mamma—"

"I'll stay with you tonight. Biddie and I both will."

"Can Gray stay?"

Christine's heart skipped a beat, but she said calmly,
"I don't know, sweetie. You'll have to ask him."

Amanda glanced over at Gray, saying, "Will you stay
with me?"

Perhaps it was the picture of vulnerability that she
painted, with her wide, still-frightened eyes, her shoulder harnessed, her bare feet sticking out of a pair
of pajamas which were on their way to being too
small. Perhaps it was the soft, pleading quality of her
voice. Perhaps it was only the spell that every daughter
can cast over a father. Whichever, Gray couldn't deny
her.

"If it's all right with your mother," he responded,
glancing over at Christine. He tried to read what was
in her eyes, but couldn't.

"It's fine," she said. "Could you get her back into bed?"

"Sure," he said.

It took only minutes to phone Nikki and to relay Gray's message. Once done, Christine headed back to the bedroom, but halted at the doorway. The sight of Gray and their daughter moved her. He sat on the side of the bed, speaking softly to Amanda, who lay on crudely fluffed pillows. Gray had draped, again crudely, the sheet at her waist. Lamplight had replaced the overhead light, lending lean shadows to the room, and rendering the black dog, curled beside the bed, almost invisible.

Christine shifted her focus to Gray. For the first time since his arrival that evening, she looked at him. Really looked at him. He had obviously dressed in a hurry, snatching, she supposed, the clothes that lay nearest, which had turned out to be jeans and a plain white T-shirt. He hadn't bothered with socks, but had merely slipped his bare feet into a pair of tennis shoes. She doubted that he'd even finger-combed his hair, which tumbled across his forehead. The stubble of beard that she loved so much shadowed his face, begging her to reach out and touch.

In the fright of the moment, she'd hurled herself into Gray's arms, and she now longed to be in his arms again, especially with fear still roaming her body.

Gray glanced up, and was instantly rocked by the memory of holding her just minutes before. The memory lingered, taunting him. He looked away from the sight of her—of her tousled hair, of the fear in her eyes, a fear that spoke loudly to his protective urge, a fear that reminded him of his own fear, of the mark he'd so passionately put on her neck, the mark that made his fingers itch, his body ache.

Christine stepped into the room. "Nikki said that she'd call him."

Gray started to rise from the bed, but Amanda grabbed his hand, pleading, "No, don't leave me!"

Gray glanced down at the two hands clutching at his. Small though those hands were, they gripped his with a powerful force. Just as her plea gripped his heart.

"Okay, Mandy, I'll stay."

Even so, Amanda continued to hold tightly to Gray's hand.

"Go to sleep, sweetie," Christine said.

"Where's Biddie?" the child asked.

"On the floor," Christine said. "Right beside you."

Amanda peered over the edge of the bed at the dog. Its ears perked up and its tail thumped.

"Can Biddie sleep with me?"

"No. Now, go to sleep," Christine repeated.

"Where's Thumper?" Mandy asked.

Christine looked around for the worn rabbit, hoping that Gray wouldn't recognize it. She found the animal on the floor by the toy box and handed it to Amanda. The child took it and nestled it by her side. She left one hand on the rabbit, while with the other she still held to Gray's hand.

"Go to sleep, little lady," Christine said.

"But what if he comes back?"

"I'll be here," Gray said, his voice earnest and sincere.

Amanda fought sleep as long and as hard as she could, but finally she succumbed to it. Gray sensed that it was overtaking her, for her grip began to lessen slowly, until, at last, her hand relaxed its hold and collapsed onto her stomach. Gray eased slowly from the bed and into a nearby white wicker chair.

Looking over at Christine, who'd taken a seat on the toy box, he said softly, "Go on to bed."

She shook her head. "I'm too keyed up."

"Then lie down beside Amanda and at least rest."

Again, Christine shook her head. For a while, neither spoke. Christine just sat, watching Amanda, wondering if this really could be happening again, or if she was only imagining the whole bizarre thing. No, regrettably she was imagining nothing. No more than Amanda had been.

"I wanted so badly to believe the voice incident had been Amanda's imagination."

"If it's any consolation, I've had second thoughts too."

Christine shifted her attention to Gray. He had leaned back in the wicker chair, his masculinity at odds with the chair's fragility.

"What does all this mean?" she asked. "And why now? After all these days of doing nothing?"

"I don't know. Maybe he just wanted her to know that he knew she had moved."

This was not what Christine had wanted to hear. She folded her arms about her, wishing they belonged to Gray. In his arms, everything seemed more easily borne. She needed him in every way that a woman could need a man—as friend, as protector, as lover. It was impossible to tell where one need began and the other ended. Earlier, while in his arms, she'd felt warm and safe, but she'd also felt the restless, sexual need to satisfy her body's endless ache.

"I'm scared," she whispered.

"I know. Me too."

Amanda chose that moment to moan softly, as though she were being pursued by bad dreams. After that, she seemed only to grow more restless. She tossed, she turned, she whimpered. Christine moved to the child's side, and with a few quiet words calmed her.

From where Gray sat, the scene looked very much like a madonna and child, Christine with her flowing hair, her white cotton gown and robe, and her bare feet, Christine with her sweet words of solace. The scene was a little disturbing, however, since he kept remembering Christine's soft breasts, her small waist, the perfect way she fitted against him. He needed her in ways far more important than sexual, however. He needed her to be his friend. He needed her to console him, to tell him that everything was going to be all right. He hadn't lied when he'd said that he was afraid. When she'd had her arms folded about her, he'd wished that they were enfolding him.

". . . pretty child."

Christine was looking in his direction, awaiting his response. "What?"

"I've often wondered how we could have made such a child."

"I don't know," Gray said, his eyes fully on hers, his voice husky, "I think she had some incredible genes to work with."

His compliment, and it was that, took Christine by surprise. It took a couple of seconds for her to find her voice. "Yes, she did."

Deftly, she had turned the compliment around, and for a moment, an eternity, the two simply stared at each other.

Finally, Christine asked, "Would you like some coffee? I don't think either one of us is going to get much sleep."

"No. I mean, yes to the coffee."

When Christine left for the kitchen, Amanda

whimpered, and Gray looked at her. The bad dream had caught up with her once more. She tossed and turned, sending the stuffed rabbit onto the floor. Gray rose from the chair and crossed to the child, easing down onto the bed beside her.

"Shh, shh," he whispered. "I'm here."

His voice soothed the child and she quieted down, soon falling into a deeper slumber. He reached for the stuffed rabbit, and had just started to place it beside Mandy when something stopped him. The rabbit seemed vaguely familiar. Surely it wasn't *that* rabbit.

A memory flashed so vividly that Gray would have sworn that it was happening that moment. It was a memory of the fair in Jackson, one of the few times that he and Christine had been together in public. He'd been so proud to have her at his side, a pride that had grown as he'd seen the appreciative glances of other males. Acting out the masculine need to show off a bit, he'd won the rabbit tossing baseballs at milk cans. Christine had accepted it as though she'd never been given anything of greater value. He remembered her smile, her kiss of thanks, the way they'd clumsily made love in the back seat of his car on the trip home. They'd found a dirt road that led into a forest posted with No Trespassing signs. They'd laughed and giggled until she'd straddled him, turning the moment sensually serious.

The worn creature in his hand, Gray rose from the bed and started for the kitchen.

Christine loved the sound and the smell of perking coffee. Both always soothed her nerves, and heaven knew that her nerves could stand to be soothed. She wanted Gray to console her, she wanted Gray to make love to her, she wanted Gray to love her. Only minutes before he'd given her a compliment, a compliment that had come straight from the heart. A man like Gray gave no other kind. However, it was a long way from compliment to love.

She turned, intending to collect a couple of cups from the cabinet, but stopped when she saw Gray standing in the doorway. Gray and the rabbit.

That day at the fair came rushing back, inundating her with memories—the piping-hot sun, the sugary smell of spun cotton candy, the heady feeling of being together and not caring that people saw them. She could still see him pitching the baseballs, with a zealousness that suggested the trophy were brilliant diamonds and not a stuffed bunny rabbit. But she'd loved it as if it were diamonds, because it had come from him. And then, there had been the drive home, filled with laughter and loving.

"It was the only thing of her father that I had to give her," Christine said. "The morning I brought her home from the hospital, I put the rabbit in the crib with her. It never left there until she started to crawl." Christine smiled. "She'd grab its ear and drag it along with her. They were inseparable. She wouldn't go to sleep at night without her bun. She couldn't say bunny, just bun."

Gray stepped into the kitchen. "You kept saying that you wanted to have my baby, but, when you did, you let another man raise it."

"Please believe me when I tell you that I didn't know I was pregnant until after you left. I had no idea where you'd gone."

"And if you had?"

"I swear I would have gone to you. By then, I'd realized what a horrible mistake I'd made." It was the perfect place for him to ask why she hadn't returned to him, but he didn't and she again wondered why. "When I realized that I was pregnant, I panicked. Survival, even social survival, is instinctive, and I knew that Peyton . . . cared for me. I let him . . ." She couldn't use the phrase make love, even though she suspected that's what it had meant for Peyton.

The fist of jealousy punched Gray in the stomach. Even after all that had happened, the lies, the betrayal, everything, it hurt to think of her with another man. It didn't make a lick of sense, but he wasn't fool enough to deny that it was true.

"When I told Peyton that I was pregnant, he was thrilled. I was miserable, but he'd never been happier. And Adelle . . . well, Adelle was in her element. She set about planning a grand wedding, pleased as punch that I was marrying Peyton Jackson. Peyton and I never told our parents that I was pregnant, and he never guessed that Amanda wasn't his child."

"No one could count out nine months?" Gray said disbelievingly.

"It was a difficult pregnancy, and Mandy was a couple of weeks early. Everyone was quite willing to believe that she was premature. Looking back, I suppose the doctor suspected, but he never said anything. If he did, he just thought that Peyton and I were having premarital sex."

"What I don't understand is how you got pregnant in the first place if you were using protection, which you told me you were."

"I'd gotten a diaphragm, but I was uncertain how to use it properly. I was naïve, inexperienced. Surely you knew that."

Gray sighed. He hadn't known what to think in regard to her experience. She'd seemed both bold and knowing, tentative and shy. Her use of a contraceptive suggested a certain sexual savvy, although he'd preferred to think that he'd been her first lover. Strangely, flying in the face of fact, he had thought of her as his first.

The enormity of the past settled about them both. Gray glanced down at the rabbit in his hands and said, "I've missed so much."

"Yes," she said, simply, regretfully, staring straight into his silent eyes.

She wanted to just reach out and touch his shadowed cheek, to trace the scar, to have him hold her—because she was scared, for Amanda, scared that she'd never have Gray's forgiveness, scared because she needed him to ease an ache that had had ten years to grow and ferment. Protector, lover, friend.

"Hold me," she whispered.

Her words surprised Gray, simply because he wanted to say exactly the same thing. He wished desperately to touch, once and for all, the bruise at her neck, to be held close—because he was scared, for Amanda, and of the physical need roaming through him. He wanted this woman as comforter, lover, friend, and this want, this need, scared him most of all. And yet . . .

On a low moan, he reached for her, dropping the rabbit to the floor in the process. He held her, she him, both feeling a sense of solace, of succor, that nothing could harm them as long as they stood together. It had always been the two of them pitted against the world, but it had been enough. Slowly, the embrace began to involve more. He became aware of her soft body beneath the layers of fabric, she of the hard muscles of his back beneath the thin T-shirt. Desire nipped at starved senses. Christine nuzzled her

cheek against his stubble, then sent her lips in search of
the scar. She trailed a line of tiny kisses down its
length, as though each was an apology. As she neared
his mouth, she hesitated, fearing that he would turn
away from her kiss, but when he didn't, she pressed
her lips to his. His were warm, sweet, better than remembered dreams.

The kiss overwhelmed Gray, muting the lines between past and present, love and hate. He could almost
believe that it was ten years ago, in the hothouse, she
intent upon seducing him. Her lips had been hot then
too, hot and knowing and innocently carnal. Now, as
then, they elicited a response. Threading his fingers
through her hair, he deepened the kiss, wanting only
to feel. Not to think. Only to scatter kisses to the column of her neck. Only to trace with his lips the bruise
he'd left there. Only to feel her body molding to his.

Christine could feel his arousal, and like a magnet,
it drew her. She slid her hand between them, trailing
it over the fullness of his jeans. Gray's breath caught,
but he managed to whisper against her lips, "W-what
are you doing?"

"Seducing you," she whispered back.

And she proved as good as her word. Over and over,
she drew her hand up and down the length of him.
Once, he placed his hand atop hers, intending to halt
its sensual journey, but discovered that he couldn't.

Having pulled her mouth from his, she watched his
every expression, watched with hazy eyes. "You do
desire me, don't you?" she whispered.

"Yes. God, yes!"

"Then take me," she said desperately. "Make me feel
again."

As she spoke, she started to undo the zipper.

This time, he did stop her, saying, "Not here."

"My bedroom. I'll check on Mandy and be right there."

Gray made his way down the hallway to Christine's bedroom, thinking . . . Actually, he tried not to think at all. Feeling. That was all that mattered. And what he felt right now was a huge ache.

The moment Christine walked into the bedroom, she closed the door behind her. For seconds, the room was plunged into total darkness, then a lamp went on and diffused light fell across the teal carpet, the white furniture, the teal-and-rose-colored furnishings, the rumpled bed that beckoned to lovers. As she walked toward him, she unbelted her robe, slid the garment from her shoulders, and let it fall to the carpet.

Gray's mouth went dry. He could see the dark crests of her breasts beneath the thin cotton of her white gown. Tiny buttons ran down the front of the garment, along with scattered embroidered pink roses. Her hair hung wildly about her shoulders and down her back. And, as she had once before, she took total charge.

Rising on tiptoe, she brushed her lips across his. At the same time, she unzipped his jeans and eased her hand onto his full erection. Gray gasped. Then gasped again as her hand closed around him and began to move in a seductive rhythm. Gray closed his eyes to this exquisite agony. He could feel her lips still nibbling at his, soft, little kisses, but he didn't return them. He was too busy just trying to breathe. He did slide his jeans and briefs farther down his lean hips, but to his dismay her hand ceased its play. He opened his eyes, his intent to plead for more, when he saw her go to her knees. As her mouth closed over him, he made a low guttural sound, reached for something to hold on to, and found only her hair. He tried not to think of how good she was at what she was doing, and from whom she must have learned the technique. All too soon his ecstasy reached a critical point.

"Don't," he whispered frantically, pulling her upward until his lips were only millimeters from hers. He then heard those lips forming the most incredible words. "Did he teach you how to do that?"

The question surprised Christine. She wondered if her answer would surprise Gray. "No," she said, once more brushing her lips across his. "He wanted me to"—she nibbled Gray's lips—"he begged me to"—she bit gently—"but I never would. I couldn't."

Gray closed his eyes, uncertain how he wanted to feel about her response. When her lips moved over his in a ravenous kiss, however, he wasn't in the least uncertain. He kissed her back—fully, completely.

Christine loved his kiss. She equally loved the hard planes of his chest, and slipping her hands beneath the T-shirt, she began to trail her hands over him, but soon the shirt was too restrictive.

"Take it off," she whispered. "Take everything off."

Gray was more than willing to remove his clothing, but, before he could, Christine began to undress him. He let her, sensing that somehow it was important to her. Once he was bare, she looked him over from head to toe, then stepped forward and kissed his lips. As she did so, she cupped his firm buttocks, then slowly drew her hands around to caress his thighs. When she touched the heat of him, he sucked in his breath.

"Lie down," she whispered.

When she led him to the bed, he followed and stretched out on the cool sheets, sheets she'd earlier lain upon, sheets she'd left her scent upon. She sat on the side of the bed, and leaning forward, she brushed

a lock of hair from his eyes, then kissed his lips—
slowly, sensuously.

"Take the gown off," Gray said, reaching for her.

She eluded him, saying, "In time."

Time.

For Gray, it was spent in a place that was part
heaven, part hell. She traced every inch of him, and
that was heaven. She touched an earlobe and kissed the
spot just behind his ear. Then she kissed his chin, and
all along the column of his neck. She paid homage to
his wrist, to the space between his fingers. She lingered over the delicate skin of the inside bend of his
elbow, the tip of her tongue tracing some sensual de-
sign there, then dawdled at his chest before moving
lower to splay her hands across his belly. From time to
time, she returned to kiss his lips and to stroke his
erection. And that was hell, with his ache growing un-
controllably. He had the feeling, however, that this was
somehow a ritual for her. He wondered what she was
thinking.

Did he have any idea how important this time was
to her? Christine thought as she kissed his knee and
threaded her fingers through the dark hair of his legs.
This physical validation of what she so often had
dreamed of. This savoring of what she thought might
never be again. Even so, a part of her could not fully
accept that he was here, that she was touching him.
And so she reconfirmed the fact by touching yet another part of him.

She had just kissed the arch of Gray's foot when he
growled, "Come here! Please."

The plaintive tone of the last word convinced
Christine to hasten along. She reached out to touch
the heat of him one last time, but found a hand
wrapped around her wrist.

"That's not a real good idea," he said.

She understood and began to unbutton her gown. One button, two, then three, and one side of the gown dipped off one shoulder, exposing one perfect breast.

The sight gutted Gray's breath, and he whispered, "Come here."

She moved toward him, raised her gown and boldly straddled him. She felt his hands beneath the gown, felt his fingers touch her intimately, familiarly, in ways she'd thought never to feel them again, felt the tip of him searching for, and finding, her. As he slowly began to enter her, she moaned and slid herself along the fullness of him, wanting, needing, the whole of him. The whole of him was breathtaking, more wonderful than memory. They were two halves of one soul again, each completing the other. Christine glanced up to see if Gray was feeling it too, and saw that he was.

The physical feeling of being buried dep inside her moved Gray. The spiritual joining left him breathless, unsteady, as though the ground had shifted beneath him. What to do? Don't think. Just feel.

Christine made it easy for him because she had begun an urgent rhythm. Gray answered her and she arched her back to meet his every thrust. As she moved, she finished unbuttoning her gown, which dropped around her waist. Gray ran his hands over her bare back, finding the dusting of hair at the base of her curved spine. He brought his hands to cup the fullness of her soft breasts. Suddenly, her breathing grew fast and ragged, and she threw back her head, arching her neck like a swan. Her hair fell madly about her. She looked . . . magnificent. And then, she gasped as tiny little ripples overtook her. And then he was filing her with his seed, crying out as he did so, "Chris-tine!"

•   •   •

Bare except for jeans and moonlight, Gray stood in front of the window, staring not at what was before him, but into his soul. He was troubled, so troubled that he'd slipped from a sleeping Christine's side in the hope that distance would give him perspective. What they had done had changed everything. For ten years, he'd lived with hate. He knew its parameters, its shape, its configuration. It was comfortable. And then he had come back here, to her. And then tonight . . .

Gray sighed. He'd never fit another woman the way he did her, never felt that wholeness he experienced with her. At the moment of climax, as he'd pumped himself into her receptive body, he had felt . . . as though he'd stepped into some white-hot light. The light was Christine. There was nothing else in all the world. She infused his senses. He could feel nothing but her, could taste nothing but her, smell, hear, see nothing but her.

And when he walked out of the light . . . he could no longer feel hate. He felt something else, instead. Something that he was scared to give a name to. Something—

His breath caught as he felt a pair of lips rain tiny kisses on his back. At the same time, Christine's arms banded around him, her hands splaying wide in the hair of his chest, then moving lower onto his belly. She made no attempt to touch him intimately. But then she didn't have to. His body was already responding as though she *had* touched him.

"I love you, Gray," she whispered. "I've always loved you. I always will love you."

"Don't—"

"Just listen to me. You don't have to say anything."

She rubbed her cheek against his back and said, "I want you in my life, in Amanda's life. I used to think that I should pay all the rest of my life for the mistake I made, but surely there should be a reasonable end to my agony." She hesitated, then said in a barely audible voice, "I want you back."

Gray's heart pounded. "I—I don't know what to say."

"Don't say anything. Just think about it. Think about us."

Suddenly, she pulled away from him and moved to stand before him. She had put her gown back on, and in the stream of moonlight, he could make out the buttons and the embroidered roses.

"I want to tell you something," she began. "If we're ever to have a future, you have to know the worst there is to know about me. You have to know why I didn't run away with you." She smiled—uncertainly. "I kept waiting for you to ask, but you never did."

"I, uh, guess I just didn't want to know what had been more important to you than me." At the distress his words caused, he said, "Look, you don't have to tell me. Whatever the reason, it's over and done with."

"Yes, I do have to tell you. I need your forgiveness, if that's possible. Only then can I start to forgive myself."

Gray could see how important this was to her. He could also see her fear. She was afraid of what he'd think of her. "Okay. Tell me."

Suddenly, images flitted across Christine's mind in tortuous slow motion, images of her flinging clothes into a suitcase, images of her father barging into her room, images of . . . "Merritt came in as I was packing and demanded to know what I thought I was doing. Claiborne had told him about the affair, and about the beating. Merritt was livid. I'd never seen him so angry. He asked me if I'd lost my mind. I told him no, that I'd merely fallen in love.

"Merritt proceeded to tell me that I knew nothing about love. I told him it was he who knew nothing of love, that all he was capable of loving was money. I thought for a moment he was going to hit me. I think he thought so too, because he turned away and was silent for a long time. He finally looked back at me and said, calmly, that I was free to do what I wanted. With one stipulation."

Gray waited for her to continue, but when she didn't, he asked, "Which was?"

"He told me that if I went away with you, I could never return to Rosemead. He told me that I would never see him or Adelle again. He told me that he would disown me, disinherit me." To her credit, she looked Gray directly in the eye when she said, "I gave everything up for a home I hated, for money, which I never really cared about, and for parents who had never been there for me."

Gray said nothing.

Tears formed in Christine's eyes. She'd lost him. Even though she knew that her decision had been indefensible, she, nonetheless tried to explain. "I had never been anything but rich. The picture Merritt painted of how we'd have to struggle scared me. He said that we'd only end up hating each other. He asked me what I was going to do when you grew tired of me."

"You believed I would?"

"Until you came into my life, I'd had no one. How could I be sure that you'd always want me?"

That son of a bitch Merritt had played the one card

guaranteed to win him the game: he placed his lonely daughter in the world alone.

Gray cupped Christine's cheek and pulled her forward, saying, "I forgive you." She started to say something, but he stopped her by placing the pad of his thumb across her lip. She leaned into the heat of his palm, allowing his thumb to trace her lower lip. At some point, his thumb slipped inside her mouth. She teethed it gently.

Gray groaned, then lowered his head for a kiss that was slow and sweet and lasted forever.

When the kiss ended, she said, her eyes dark with need, "Tell me that you feel something for me."

"I'm afraid to put a name to it."

"Then don't," she said, rising on tiptoe to place her mouth once more on his. As they kissed, he slowly unbuttoned her gown and let it fall to the carpet. He scooped her bare body into his arms and carried her to the bed. There, he loved her slowly, with tender kisses and soft caresses, and at the end, Christine knew what no spoken words had confirmed. Gray loved her.

Neither knew that a silver BMW kept a silent vigil until almost dawn.

Chapter 20

The ringing of the telephone shattered Christine's sleep. Just as she reached for the shrilling instrument, however, the ringing halted, and she heard Gray's voice in the kitchen. Gray. The night came washing back in waves of memory. He had been such a gentle, yet forceful lover. And untiring. The night would have been perfect had it not been for the dark reason that had brought him there. Hoping that the telephone call was from Agent Carrelli, Christine grabbed her gown and robe, threw them on, and hastened into the kitchen.

She found Gray leaning against the cabinet, with a morning growth of beard and wayward hair. As she entered the room, his eyes, still hungry, found hers and wouldn't turn loose. Beneath the hunger, however, she saw caution. By his own admission, what he was feeling for her frightened him. She had not yet earned back his trust. That would take time.

As she made a pot of coffee, she listened to Gray

relate all that had happened last night. As soon as he hung up, she asked, "Well?"

"He agrees that something serious is going on. He's coming down and we're going to try to make some sense out of all this."

"When?"

"Sometime this week. He's got to wrap up what he's currently involved in. He thinks it would be best if no one knows that he's coming."

Christine nodded. "We can't let anything happen to her."

"We won't," Gray said. "Come here."

When Christine stepped into his arms, the world fell away. She felt only the strength and power of his wide chest, the shelter of his arms, the warmth of his body. She nuzzled her cheek against his shoulder, cherishing the feeling of her body against him.

"I'm sorry about last night."

The words, so at odds with the gentle way he was holding her, wounded Christine. His regret over what had happened between them was the very last thing she wanted. She pulled back and placed her fingers at his lips. "No, please don't say that."

"No, no! I'm not sorry about what happened. I'm only sorry that I didn't think about protecting you. Not that I could have anyway. I didn't have anything with me."

Relief flooded Christine. "I thought you meant—"

"I know what you thought I meant," he said, drawing his knuckles down her cheek. "So, what are the chances?"

Like the Gray of old, he knew that her being pregnant would only complicate things, but also like the Gray of old, he found the idea of her carrying his child a tempting one. He thought of that vine-covered cottage and the rocking chair. The changing of diapers, the softly crooned lullabies, the baby's first steps, the first words—all the things he'd missed with Mandy.

"Not very good," Christine said, wondering if he heard the regret in her voice. Like the Christine of old, she wanted to have his child, but this time with his knowledge. She wanted him to be there to savor a first-heard heartbeat, the sight of their baby on the sonogram, the first kick—all the things he'd missed while she was carrying Amanda.

"Good," he said, wondering if she heard his lack of conviction. He welcomed the distraction of the look in her eyes.

"Ah, Christine," he whispered, "when you look at me that way . . ."

"That's twice you've said my name."

"What?"

"Since you've been back, you haven't called me by name. Until last night. And just then."

"I wasn't aware of that," he said, pondering what, if anything, his not calling her by name meant.

"I was," she said, adding, "Say it."

The tone of her voice suggested that his doing so was important to her. Very important. "Christine," he said. "Christine, Christine, Chris"—his lips brushed hers—"tine." His lips settled over hers—sweetly, but briefly, as if lingering longer meant not being able to say what he did next. "I've got to go. I need to shower and shave and change clothes."

"Will you come back?"

"Yeah."

"Soon?"

He smiled. "I would have already been back if you didn't keep asking so many questions."

She smiled. "Then go."

Reluctantly, he pulled from her and started for the door.

"Gray," she said. When he turned, she asked, "Do you have a woman back in Atlanta?"

Gray thought of the women he'd slept with, women who were a far cry from having a claim on his heart. "No," he said, "I have no woman in Atlanta."

She smiled. "Hurry back."

Gray turned and covered the distance to the door. There, he turned again and said, in a voice that resonated with passion, "I never would have grown tired of you."

Christine said sadly, "I know."

For all intents and purposes, Gray could just as well have moved into Christine's house. During the next few days, he spent much of the day with Mandy, who was now out of school for the summer, and all the night with Christine and Mandy, going back to the motel only to shower, shave, and change clothes. Although Christine had cut back on her hours at Lowell Enterprises, there was no way she could walk away from the job completely, not when she was trying to find someone to replace her. She was afraid that Gray would be critical of her leaving their daughter, especially at this difficult time, but, he hadn't been.

Amanda still called him by his given name, while he had yet to refer to her as his daughter. But there were subtle signs of change: It was he Amanda asked to help her with her curve ball after her shoulder had been unharnessed; she would sometimes slip her hand into his, as though she'd been doing that forever; sometimes he'd slip from bed after making love to Christine—he had assumed the responsibility of protecting her—and simply sit and stare at their daughter; he liked to pore over a photograph album of the child's early years.

The greatest step forward came on Monday afternoon when Gray took Amanda and Christine to the doctor's office for a check-up of the child's shoulder. Matter-of-factly, Christine introduced him as Amanda's real father.

Terry Carrelli arrived early Wednesday afternoon, and Gray, on his way to the meeting at the antique shop, saw a red pickup in the rearview mirror. This was the third time. The sight of the truck nagged at Gray, until it disappeared. Then he chided himself, reminding himself that in a town the size of Natchez, there must be any number of red pickups.

Once in the antique shop, Gray headed into the stockroom, piled high with boxes and furniture from a bygone era. There he saw Nikki, Terry Carrelli and Christine. She smiled. Gray smiled back, but then his attention was diverted elsewhere. To Terry Carrelli, who was extending his hand.

"Thanks for coming," Gray said, thinking that the dark-suited agent looked very much the same as he had the first time they'd met. He even carried the dark-lensed sunglasses in one hand.

"My pleasure. Now let's see if we can make some sense out of what's happening to Amanda."

Gray said, "I'll begin. As far as I'm concerned, Ernie Shaw had an accomplice. Otherwise, what's happening to Mandy makes no sense." He had everyone's attention, and so he continued. "I've asked myself a million times why that voice warned her not to speak about the kidnapping, and I keep coming back to one thing. The accomplice is afraid that she'll say something an adult would recognize as significant."

"Like what?" Nikki asked.

"I don't know," Gray said. "Maybe he's afraid that she saw something she shouldn't have."

"But she was blindfolded in every room but the attic and the bathroom," Christine pointed out.

"Then maybe she saw something in the attic or the bathroom," Gray said. "I asked her to tell me about the kidnapping, and she said something that was interesting. She said Ernie Shaw made what was tantamount to an apology. He said he was sorry he'd ever gotten into this mess—something like that."

"That *is* interesting," Terry said, then added, "I think Gray's right. Shaw's having an accomplice is the only viable conclusion. So let's try to get a handle on who Shaw could have been in league with. Christine, let me throw a name at you. Hal Hoogland. Did you know that he was killed in a hunting accident shortly after you bought out Hoogland Timber?"

"No, I didn't."

"What about his son, Mitchell Hoogland?"

"I didn't even know he had a son. When we purchased the company, we dealt exclusively with Hal. I did know he had a wife who was ill. That was the main reason he wanted to sell the company, to get what he could to settle some medical bills. I gave him a generous price, considering how the business had deteriorated. But then Hal was as close a friend as Merritt had. Over the years, they'd hunted together, although not all that frequently."

"So, is this Mitchell Hoogland important?" Gray asked Carrelli.

"Probably not. But he's dropped off the face of the earth, and it always worries me when I can't account for someone. Although he had no reason to cling to his old life. As I said, his father died shortly after the takeover, and his mother died about eight months ago. And, of course, there was no family business left to inherit."

"How old is he?" Nikki asked.

"I'd say early to mid-thirties."

"What does he look like?" Nikki added.

"I never had a description of him," Terry said. "Why?"

"No reason. He just sounds rather sad."

Gray looked over at Nikki. Had it made any sense, he would have sworn that she'd just lied. But it didn't make any sense, and so he let the thought slip away.

Claiborne was brought up as a possible suspect, but Christine insisted that there was a big difference between wanting the presidency of Lowell Enterprises and kidnapping.

Then Sandy Killian was mentioned. According to Terry, he'd run a background check and found nothing suspicious.

"She's been a very competent nanny," Christine said. "And she had impeccable references. I wouldn't have hired her otherwise. I think she genuinely loves Amanda, and I know Amanda loves her."

"Does she date?" Gray asked.

"Oh, sure," Christine said. "She dates frequently, but I guess she hasn't yet found anyone she wants to settle down with."

"How long has she been with you?" Nikki asked Christine.

"I'd be hard-pressed to say exactly. Five, six years."

"Then why wait until now to kidnap Amanda?" Nikki asked.

That one question pretty much nixed Sandy as a suspect.

Christine sighed, that one sound filled with exasperation. "So, all we really know, or suspect, is that Shaw wasn't working alone and whoever he was working with is threatening Amanda, and all for a reason we don't fully understand, but which might be because she saw something she wasn't meant to see. I don't see a solution anywhere in that."

"What about hypnosis?" Nikki asked.

Silence, as everyone pondered the suggestion. Finally, Terry said, "That's not a bad idea. I could get someone down from the bureau, someone experienced in working with children."

"I don't know," Christine said. "Hypnosis is so traumatic. We're asking Amanda to live through the kidnapping again when we don't even know if she saw anything. We don't even know if there was anything to see. Whoever is threatening her might not want her to talk about the kidnapping for an altogether different reason."

"All that's true," Gray said, "but at least it's worth trying."

"Only if Amanda consents to it," Christine said.

They all agreed with that decision.

Padding barefoot into the kitchen late that night, Nikki turned on the light over the sink and began to heat water for a cup of tea. She kept playing over and over in her mind the information about this Mitchell Hoogland. Was it even remotely possible that he was Jacob Purdy? Was Jacob Shaw's accomplice? But he'd left town. Or had he? Was he just lying low somewhere, threatening Amanda and planning to do God only knew what? Had Gray sensed that she'd been lying? His eyes said that he did.

Suddenly, Nikki had to laugh at herself. Jacob was probably a world away, giving not a single thought to Natchez, or anyone in it. He was probably—

A pair of arms closed around her waist and a voice whispered in her ear, "That shirt looks better on you than it ever did on me."

Nikki leaned fully into Terry, fully enough to know that he wore nothing. Desire waltzed through her. Mercy, how insatiable could she be?

After the meeting, when she'd asked him if he had a place to stay, he'd looked her right in the eye and said yes, at least he hoped so. And he turned out to be the kind of lover Nikki had intuitively known he would be—warm and gentle and considerate. Beneath those tender trappings, however, lay a heated sexuality that had left her breathless and breathless again.

"I haven't been with a woman in a while," he was telling her. "I haven't met anyone I wanted to be this close to. Ah, Nik, it feels like I've known you forever. Making love with you feels so good . . . so right."

"I know. I feel it too." She leaned her head back against his broad shoulder, telling herself that this was enough for now, telling herself that she never wanted him to know about her past relationship with Jacob Purdy.

Terry brushed a kiss to the side of her neck, turned her in his arms, and backed her gently against the cabinet. "I can't get enough of you," he whispered, and she whispered back, "I can't get enough of you." At last, he settled his lips over hers and what followed shattered all thoughts of Mitchell Hoogland, Jacob Purdy, and a cup of tea.

Chapter 21

Amanda consented to the hypnosis sessions, winning Gray's further admiration. As for Christine, she remained uncertain that they were doing the right thing. A psychologist, experienced in working with children and skilled in hypnosis techniques, was flown in, and the first session, so secret not even Sandy knew, was conducted Thursday afternoon at the Eola Hotel. No third party was allowed to be present for the session, although Christine and Gray listened to a recording later. Christine made it through only with Gray's help, although Gray himself was shaken by what he'd heard.

Something was going on behind the scenes with Amanda, Sandy thought. She could only assume that it had something to do with the threats. But what? She only knew that with Gray Bannon around, she was being asked to stay less and less often with the child, and that Amanda had spent a couple of hours at the Eola Hotel that afternoon. Control, Sandy told herself as she brought a hand to her throbbing temple. She must hang on to control. That goal in mind, she straightened a perfectly straight closet, then handwashed every thoroughly clean dish in the thoroughly clean kitchen.

Friday morning, Claiborne awoke in a motel with a strange woman. He vaguely remembered losing at craps the evening before and having a round of consoling drinks. Even more vaguely, he remembered picking up this woman. Or maybe she'd picked him up? Whichever, he'd obviously spent the night with her and, judging by the fact that they were both naked, he could guess how they'd passed the time. It would just be his luck that she was the best lay he'd ever had, and he didn't remember a single second of the event, or events.

Claiborne, both mouth and head feeling like a wad of wool, slipped from the bed and reached for his scattered clothes. He caught a reflection of himself in the mirror. And stopped. The image looking back at him was as much a stranger as the woman he'd awakened beside. His eyes were sunken, and his body had begun to lose its tone. His father wouldn't have approved.

Sometimes, Claiborne thought it was the role of a Southern son to disappoint his father. If that were true, he was one hell of a success.

He sighed. Although he'd never been very lucky, at the gaming table or at life, he was beginning to turn his bad luck around. And before it was over, both Christine and Gray Bannon would have to pay for screwing around with him. It might not be fair, he might be the slightest bit sorry, but the fact remained that Bannon had pushed him one time too often and Christine had something he wanted.

The man watched the mouse. It was the first time he'd seen it in days. It inched forward across the worn linoleum floor, then stopped only inches from the trap.

The man held his breath. Seconds passed. And then, the mouse crossed to the trap. It nibbled at the cheese, and with a mighty thwack, the trap was sprung. The metal caught the mouse just back of its head.

The man grinned. Now, he could execute the plan. After going for broke, after this one final hurrah, he was going to leave Claiborne Lowell holding the bag. He would end up settling the score with the whole Lowell family.

The man made some telephone calls, then went into town for a bottle of champagne. The trip was risky, but he suddenly felt invincible.

Nikki checked her watch. Although it was only ten minutes after three o'clock, she was sorely tempted to close the shop for the day. Only a handful of people had been in. Terry had spent the morning with Gray, Amanda, and the psychologist and had then stopped by the shop to ask for directions to the grocery store. He had promised to make her the best spaghetti and meatballs she'd ever eaten. Her sole contribution to the meal would be a bottle of wine.

Terry.

He could never understand her involvement with a man like Jacob Purdy. But then, there was no need for him to ever know. For that matter, neither had spoken of the future, and Nikki wasn't even sure she wanted to at this point. Everything was just too new.

However, she wouldn't mind spending more time with him—eating spaghetti, drinking wine, and making love. That in mind, she placed the Closed sign at the door, locked up, and headed to the liquor store.

It was doing a brisk business for the middle of the afternoon. She took the first available parking space and had just started to get out when she saw the man, carrying a sack, coming out of the store. The tall, lanky, lithe man, with the overlong hair. Even though she had considered it possible that Jacob Purdy hadn't left town, seeing him shocked her. She kept looking at him, hoping it was merely a case of mistaken identity. But she knew it wasn't. No other man moved with such swaggering arrogance.

What game was he playing?

Although he couldn't see her, she nonetheless closed the car door and eased downward in the seat. She watched. He climbed into a gray Chevy that she remembered all too well, pulled from the parking lot, turned right, and disappeared. Without once questioning what she was doing, Nikki started the car and followed him. She saw him several blocks away, but deliberately kept her distance. That was the sum total of her knowledge about trailing. She'd be lucky not to be spotted.

Fifteen minutes later, the Chevy turned into a gravel drive that led to a small white-frame house. The house, and an unconnected garage, cried out for a fresh coat of paint. A mailbox—no name; just a number—stood at the driveway and had a dented side. In front of the house grew orange daylilies and a neglected blue hydrangea bush. Nikki drove on by, stopped on the side of the highway, and watched through the back window. She observed Jacob get out of the car, sack in hand, and disappear into the house.

Now what should she do?

Wait, came the immediate answer, but she could be talking about hours. Terry would be expecting her, but that couldn't be helped. She might be on the verge of discovering who had kidnapped Amanda, who was still troubling the child with threats. At the very least, she had to eliminate Jacob Purdy—or whoever he was—as a suspect. She settled in for a long wait, but, to her utter amazement, Jacob pulled from the driveway a scant fifteen minutes later and headed back to town.

Nikki waited until he was out of sight, then drove toward the house. There was simply no safe way to do what she had to do, and so she pulled into the drive, got out of the car, and started for the house. It crossed her mind that no one knew where she was, and if Jacob should return and find her, she might easily become one of those disappearances that is never satisfactorily accounted for. Even so, she had no choice.

She tried the side door, but found it locked. So was the front door. And the back. She looked around for something to break out a pane of the glass. A rusted shovel leaning against the house caught her attention. She picked it up and struck the pane nearest the lock. The glass shattered. Carefully reaching her hand inside, she fiddled with the lock until she finally released it. She opened the door and picking her way through the shards of glass, stepped into the kitchen.

Not a breath of air moved in the house, making it stifling hot for this early June day. An unopened bottle of champagne sat on the kitchen cabinet, along with a small television. In the rust-stained sink stood a stack of dirty dishes that leaned recklessly to one side. The trash, which sat on a cracked and dirty floor, was overflowing. Dozens of magazines were piled here, there, everywhere, and to her complete disgust a dead mouse had been caught, but not removed from the trap. She shuddered. And looked around.

Her gaze connected with the snapshot fastened to the refrigerator door with a magnet. She stepped forward. The photograph was of three men, standing in front of a hunting lodge. A rifle was slung over the shoulder of each man. Even though the photograph had to have been several years old, she recognized Merritt Lowell and a younger Jacob Purdy. In the middle stood a man, whose identity she could guess at.

Hal Hoogland.

And if that was Hal Hoogland, the young man must be . . .

Nikki removed the photograph and turned it over. In barely legible handwriting, someone had scrawled, "Hal, Mitch, and Merritt Lowell," and a date some six years before.

"Oh, my God," Nikki whispered.

Was Mitch Hoogland, as Terry suspected, involved in Amanda's kidnapping? She had to find proof, but what would constitute proof? And would he be so stupid as to leave incriminating evidence lying around? Maybe. If he thought it was safe in his house.

Nikki moved quickly through the remaining rooms. Nothing in the bathroom. Nothing in one bedroom. The second bedroom held a single bed and a telephone. Both clothes and a ton of papers were strewn about. She picked up one of the papers, a list of telephone numbers. She began to scan it. A third of the way down, one name jumped out at her: Ernie Shaw.

What to do? The question raced through her mind. Call the police? Christine? Gray? No, she'd call Terry. Reaching for the telephone, she dialed her

number. She could see Terry in the kitchen, his
shirtsleeves rolled up, stirring spaghetti sauce and preparing a salad. He answered on the third ring. She told
him what she'd found. He didn't ask how she'd come
to find it, nor did she volunteer the information. He
simply told her to get out of the house.

At 6:09 that evening, as he was returning home,
Mitchell Hoogland was arrested for the kidnapping of
Amanda Lowell. Less than an hour later, Claiborne
Lowell was brought in for the same crime.

"They claim they're innocent of the kidnapping
charges," Terry said to Gray, Christine, and Nikki,
who had gathered in the living room of Christine's
new home. The clock on the mantel read a few
minutes after midnight. Amanda, who'd had another
rough hypnosis session that afternoon, slept in her
bedroom, with Biddie curled alongside her.

"Do you believe them?" Christine asked. She sat
beside Gray, his thigh running along the length of
hers. His nearness was comforting.

Terry considered how best to answer the question.
"At this point, I neither believe, nor disbelieve, them
in regard to the kidnapping. There's no doubt in my
mind that they were responsible for the theft of the
equipment. They've admitted to it. They really had a
sweet deal going. Actually, the whole scheme was the
brainchild of Mitchell Hoogland. Claiborne, who had
access to the accounts, just stumbled upon it, and insisted on being cut in. He claims he'd ordered Mitchell
to commence the thefts at the time of Amanda's kidnapping, but Mitchell had wanted the FBI out of the
way before beginning. By the way, Claiborne is using
that as proof that he wasn't involved in the kidnapping.

Why would he need money from equipment theft if he was about to come into possession of the ransom payment of two million dollars?"

"That's plausible," Nikki said.

"Until you consider that we have only the word of a thief for that," Terry said. "Furthermore, he couldn't have been sure the kidnapping would go without a hitch, which, of course, it didn't."

"I know about Claiborne's gambling debts, so I can figure out what motivated him," Christine said, "but what was motivating Mitchell Hoogland?"

"It began with Lowell Enterprises buying Hoogland Timber and his father's suicide."

"Suicide?" Gray asked. "You said he was killed in a hunting accident."

"That's what Mitchell had thought until eight months ago when his mother died. She'd confessed that her husband had really killed himself. Apparently, he was depressed—about his wife's illness, about losing the company, about the amount of money he'd gotten, which went only a little way toward paying off the medical bills, and so he killed himself. My guess is that he wanted the insurance money too, so his son could pay off at least part of the debts."

Christine frowned. "But why blame Lowell Enterprises for the death of his father?"

"It was easier to believe that if Lowell Enterprises had paid what he thought the company was worth, well, his father wouldn't have been driven to suicide. And so he decided to make Lowell Enterprises, and you, pay."

"And that's when he came here and got a job with Ernie Shaw's company?" Gray asked.

"Right. Shaw's company provided petroleum products for all of Lowell Enterprise's equipment. Once he was employed in the company, he learned where every piece of equipment was, because he was part of the crew that serviced it. Somewhere along the line, he came up with the idea of shortchanging the amount of fuel. Supply you with less than he should and sell the difference on the black market. It was a risky thing to do and he actually did get caught, except Claiborne saved his ass. As for Ernie Shaw, no one was there to save his."

"Then Ernie Shaw was innocent?" Christine asked.

"Yeah," Terry said. "Which made him determined to get revenge."

"There had to be more people involved than just Claiborne and Hoogland," Gray said.

"There was a whole underground network. Putting it together was what took Mitchell so long. He spent some six months on it. We've got names, addresses, and telephone numbers. The game plan was simple. Choose a site, get the equipment stolen, then transport the stolen goods to New Orleans, where it would leave the U.S. for overseas under falsified papers. Third world countries are paying premium prices for used equipment. They made a killing on the new equipment, which, of course, Claiborne told them when and where to intercept.

"What Claiborne didn't know was that Mitchell was bailing out on him. They had a big score planned tonight, some dozen or so sites, and Mitchell was leaving the country along with the equipment."

"So, where do we go from here?" Gray asked.

"Well, they're unquestionably guilty of theft, for which they're presently being held and for which they'll stand trial. As for being involved in the kidnapping, I've got people going through the magazines in Hoogland's house to see if any were used for the ransom note."

"Just because they were both involved in the theft doesn't mean that both were in on the kidnapping," Gray pointed out.

"That's a possibility," Terry agreed.

"What's your gut instinct telling you?" Gray asked.

Terry considered, then said, "That it could go either way."

In minutes, Nikki and Terry had taken their leave. After Gray closed the door behind them, he leaned back against it and, wordlessly, pulled Christine into his arms. She went willingly, wallowing in the warmth of him. He felt so strong, so sure. Slowly, he pulled back and, cupping her face with his hands, looked deep into her eyes.

"I'm so sorry about Claiborne," he said.

Christine smiled sadly. "Me too." His concern touched her and she whispered, "I love you."

He never repeated the sentiment, but when his lips touched hers, she had no need of words.

Neither Nikki nor Terry had spoken a word since leaving Christine's. Not once had he asked about Mitchell Hoogland. The way she figured it, she had two choices. One, she could never bring up the subject of Hoogland, thereby never risking Terry's disapproval. Or two, she could just jump into the fire and hope she wouldn't get burned. At least not too badly.

"I lied," she said, although she didn't dare look his way.

"I know," he said, never taking his eyes from the highway. Silence, followed by, "Look, Nik, you don't owe me an explanation."

"I was hoping you'd care enough to want one."

This time, he did glance over at her. "You know I

care. But we really have no claim on each other. I've never led you on. I told you right up front that I'm married to my job."

His response irritated Nikki. "And you know what I think? I think that's a crock. Either that or you've told yourself that so often, you think you believe it."

"Dammit, Nik! Drop it!"

Nikki had never heard him raise his voice before, and it was an impressive sound. Yet it didn't scare her. Even as she thought this, Terry pulled the car into her drive. For several seconds, they just sat in the dark.

Finally, Nikki spoke. "I really need to tell you about Jac—Mitchell." At the objection she sensed coming, she said, "I'm not asking you to share anything with me—either past or future." Pause. "Okay?"

"Yeah, okay," Terry said, but grudgingly.

Then Nikki told him everything—about her marriage, about Mitchell Hoogland. She bared her soul to him. He respected that, primarily because it was the one thing he did so badly. He could draw a gun, shoot and kill, with courage to spare, but he couldn't bare his soul.

At the end of her explanation, she paused, then asked pointedly, "Am I going to lose you?"

"Is that what you think? That I'm going to walk because of your relationship with Hoogland?"

Nikki waited for him to answer his own question. And he did but not with words. He took her hand and drew her palm to his mouth. He kissed it, and her wrist, then guided both her arms around his neck.

In the end, they ate cold spaghetti for breakfast and loved it. In the end, Terry knew he was falling in love.

Chapter 22

Saturday morning, Christine awoke angry as hell at Claiborne. How dare he steal from Lowell Enterprises! How dare he punish her! As for what he'd done to Gray, she had never forgiven him, nor would she. By the time she'd finished with her list of grievances, there was nothing she didn't believe him capable of, and that included kidnapping. She had learned earlier that both Claiborne and Mitchell Hoogland, in the face of no real evidence, had made bail.

By early that afternoon, as she was finishing up work at Lowell Enterprises, Christine felt more cautious. She was ready for the ordeal to end but not at the expense of being wrong, which she'd been before.

At two o'clock she was finished with her work. Gray would have left Rosemead half an hour ago to avoid running into Peyton, who should be picking Amanda up at any minute to take her horseback riding. In a hurry to be on her way, Christine reached for her purse, opened it, and pulled out her compact. As she did so, the envelope containing the tape of Amanda's session yesterday fell onto the desk. Only then did she notice that the psychologist had scribbled a note across the front of the envelope.

It read: "Do Amanda's comments about the paper in the bathroom make any sense to you? It's about ten minutes into the tape."

A sense of urgency overcame Christine, that feeling that time was running out, that the clock had almost struck a fateful hour. She pulled a tape player from a drawer and played the cassette.

"Today, I want you to go back to the bathroom," the psychologist said. "I want you to tell me everything that you see there."

"I see a lot of things," came Amanda's slow, relaxed voice.

"That's good."

Christine fast-forwarded the tape.

". . . the bathtub . . . it's dirty . . . the shower curtain is dirty too . . ."

Again, Christine depressed the fast-forward button.

". . . you see the sink?"

"Yes, it's white and has junk around it."

"What kind of junk?" Dr. Douglas asked.

"Toothpaste and a red toothbrush and a jelly glass . . ."

Once again, the machine whirred as it ate up more tape.

". . . the floor is dirty too . . ."

"Is there anything on the floor?"

"The paper."

"What kind of paper?"

"The nervous paper."

"What's a nervous paper?"

"Tied with a knot."

In her head, Christine saw the strips of paper so evenly torn, knots so painstakingly placed in the middle of each. Suddenly, her heart stopped and she whispered, "Jesus God Almighty!"

A part of her screamed that time was of the essence, while another part seemed incapable of motion. She looked at her watch. Ten minutes after two. No, no! She snatched the telephone from its cradle and dialed. It seemed forever before the telephone was answered.

"Hello?" Sandy said.

Christine cried, "Has Peyton picked up Amanda?"

"Yes. About ten minutes ago."

"Oh, God, no!"

"Christine, what's wrong?"

"He was in on the kidnapping."

Silence, then, "You can't be serious. Peyton would never do anything to hurt Amanda. He loves her."

"I thought so too, but, believe me, I know he was involved."

"Oh, God!" Sandy said.

Christine gave no reply. She simply hung up and started dialing again. This time Gray. He answered on the second ring.

"Hello?"

"Listen to me. Peyton is the one who was involved with Ernie Shaw in the kidnapping. He picked Amanda up about ten minutes ago. They're headed for Armstrong's Stable out on Government Fleet Road. Meet me there and call Terry."

She hung up, leaving a dial tone to hum in Gray's ear. For a moment he entertained the notion that he'd only imagined the call. What he thought he'd heard was preposterous. Hadn't he earlier thought about how he trusted Peyton, believed that Peyton cared for Amanda. So, it was preposterous, right? Right. Or was it? Wouldn't the fact that it was an inside job explain a lot? Wasn't there a wound-too-tight quality about Peyton that had never sat quite right with him? Gray shook off the questions, and began a frantic search for the telephone directory. When he couldn't find one, he reached for the telephone and dialed the operator, told her it was an emergency and he needed two telephone numbers, that of Nikki Janowitz's residence and that of her antique shop on Franklin Street. She gave him both, which he immediately dialed. At neither number did he receive an answer, but left a message on the answering machine at Nikki's house.

On a dark oath, he slammed down the telephone, strode quickly across the room, and opened the door. The fist came from out of nowhere, a gigantic thud in the middle of his stomach that left him both breathless and nauseated. The second fist clipped him under the chin. A sea of stars erupted, then began to go out one by one. Blackness was descending. At the edge of that blackness, he saw a red pickup.

It took Christine twenty minutes to reach Armstrong's Stable, which gave Peyton a thirty-minute lead. As Christine simultaneously shut off the engine and slid open her door, a horrible thought crossed her mind. She had no way of knowing if Peyton had indeed brought Amanda here. As she stepped from the van, the heels of her shoes got bogged down in the soil and she fought to free them. When she had, she raced forward.

Armstrong's Stable, located at the end of a quarter-mile dirt road that exited right off Government Fleet Road, consisted of a small office, stables both right and left, with fenced-in lots next to each stable, and a barn

at the rear. Behind the bar were several acres of field
and forest, into which were woven both walking and
riding paths. The buildings, in rough-hewn wood, had
been designed to fit into the environment as unobtrusively as possible. All attention was directed toward the
horses themselves, which Christine knew were Billy
Armstrong's passion. As she hurried toward the office,
she saw any number of those horses, some boarded by
private owners, some belonging to Billy and available
for rent, grazing in the fenced-in lots. A colt, bay in
color and born only weeks before, nuzzled his mother.

When she burst into the office, Billy Armstrong,
lean and tanned by long hours in the sun, looked
up, smiled, and said, "Hi, Christine."

Christine, fighting for breath, said, "Are Peyton and
Amanda here?"

"Yeah, they've been here about thirty to forty minutes. Winchester was sure glad to see—"

Relief flooded Christine. Thank God, they were
there. But just where was there? "Where did they go?"

Billy's smile was fading. "Peyton said that they were
going to ride over to Mistletoe Meadow."

Upon receipt of this news, Christine whirled and
raced back out the door.

Billy's smile disappeared entirely and he stood, calling after Christine, "Hey, is anything wrong?"

Christine gave no reply. She simply made a mad
dash for the path that wound its way through the forest
and eventually to Mistletoe Meadow. She estimated
that the meadow was roughly a half mile away. Even as
she plunged ahead, something told her she should have
asked for a horse. She knew with certainty ten minutes
later. Even though the path was worn, it was still steep
and slow and nearly impossible to negotiate in heels,
yet she dared not take them off, for they afforded her

feet protection. A thick sweat had broken across her brow and perspiration trickled between her breasts. Her breath, rough and ragged, echoed in the woods.

Ten minutes later, the toe of her right shoe caught on a clutch of vines, sending Christine crashing to the forest floor. Even with the cushion of leaves, the fall knocked the breath from her. She tried to get up, but couldn't, and so she turned her cheek to the earth and gasped. The dank smell of dirt filled her nostrils. Seconds passed. Too many seconds, she told herself. She had to get up. Now. Please, God, help her get up. She pushed to a sitting position, then, using a nearby bush, pulled herself upward. She discovered that the heel of her shoe had broken off completely. Both her right knee and right palm stung with cuts and scrapes. There was no time to consider anything except moving on.

Christine had no idea how much time had passed, but suddenly she burst forth from the darkness of the forest and into the light of the meadow. The brightness dazzled her eyes, and she squinted. In the small clearing, she saw two horses grazing. One she recognized as Winchester. She saw no one. No Peyton. No Amanda. The relief she'd felt at discovering they were there disappeared, replaced by grim images that taunted her. She continued to walk, hobble, her feet stepping through the ankle-high grass. Midway across the meadow, she recognized the straw hat with the red ribbon which Amanda had been wearing that morning. It lay upon the grass, as though it had been unlovingly, hastily, yanked from Amanda's head.

Christine froze.

Then she heard her voice calling. "Amanda! Where are you, Amanda?"

Nothing, except distant birdsong and the snorting of two startled horses.

"Amanda! Amanda!"

From the edge of the forest appeared two figures, whom Christine recognized immediately. Peyton and Amanda. Christine's relief was so profound that she collapsed into the grass, sitting, watching, as both figures started toward her at a run. Peyton reached her first.

Kneeling before her, he asked, "My God, Christine, are you all right?" Then, "What's happened? Why are you here?"

Christine, her breath still raspy, her body still smarting from pain, stared into the face of a man she'd never loved, but whom she'd respected, had thought of as a friend. Now she saw him only as a stranger. "Why, Peyton? Why did you do it?"

He appeared genuinely surprised. "What are you talking about?"

"Why did you kidnap her?"

If there had been any doubt in Christine's mind, it vanished the moment the question was posed. Peyton looked as guilty as a child caught with his hand in the cookie jar.

"She wasn't supposed to be hurt. I swear it, Christine. I never would have done it otherwise."

"But why, Peyton?"

Before he could answer, Amanda reached their side. Her face was flushed from running, her small chest heaving from the same exertion. She was carrying a handful of wildflowers. Intuitively, she realized that something was wrong. Very wrong. "Mamma, what is it?"

Christine held out her hand. "Come here, Amanda." At the order, Peyton looked as though she'd struck him. "You don't understand. I'm the one protecting her. Every night I've sat outside the house to make certain that she was safe. I'd never let anyone harm her."

Christine only barely heard what he was saying. She was too interested in getting her daughter closer to her and farther away from Peyton. "Come here, Amanda. Now."

The child looked in confusion from fresh-faced, fresh-dressed Peyton to her bedraggled mother, then back to Peyton.

"Everything's okay, Amanda," Peyton said, nodding toward Christine. "Just go to your mother."

Christine pulled to her feet, unsteady and off balance as a result of the broken heel. Protectively, she edged the child behind her.

Peyton pleaded his case. "Listen to me, Christine, I'm not the threat."

"He's right, you know," someone said.

At the familiar voice, both Christine and Peyton looked up.

The face, too, was familiar.

But the gun was in no way familiar.

Gray saw, and felt, the blackness descending. He fought it, knowing that if he succumbed to it, he wouldn't reach Mandy in time. Shaking his head, he searched for the light . . . and found a fraction of it. It was enough to make out the two men before him. Two men? Yeah. One looked like every Southern town's Bubba. The other one didn't look even that bright. Sort of a Bubba-lite. They were huge, with body weight to equal a freighter and muscles as lethal as weapons. Even as he thought this, a ham-hock fist collided with his cheek, bringing a whole new rain of stars. Gray staggered backward, slamming into his van. Van? He'd obviously been dragged from in front of his room out to the deserted parking lot.

"Mr. Lowell wants you to leave town," Bubba said. "Real peaceful like."

So, that was what this was all about, Gray thought. The gutless wonder was still gutless. Claiborne must have set this whole thing up days before, because that was when he'd first noticed the red truck. He wondered if Claiborne was still so worried about him. Right now, he'd guess that Claiborne was more concerned about his own ass.

"Yeah," Bubba-lite said.

He didn't have time for this, Gray thought. Mandy didn't have time. He was going to have to fight his way out, even if it meant getting the crap beaten out of him.

"C'mon," Gray said, motioning with raised fists.

Bubba-lite smiled, stepped forward, and punched Gray in the nose. Blood began to seep from his left nostril. Bubba-lite's smile broadened. Gray swiped the back of his hand across his nose and motioned Bubba-lite forward again. Bubba moved in. Closer. Closer. Let him get closer. Bubba-lite's fist connected with Gray's chin. Another rain of stars. At the same time, Gray rammed his knee into a pair of unsuspecting testicles. Bubba-lite's smile vanished, replaced by a look of surprise. A wounded-dog howl followed.

Gray took the opportunity to slide his hand into his pocket and produce the knife. He switched open the blade. Bubba smiled, as though he liked the odds. Smiled and raised his ham-hock fist again. This time he was aiming for Gray's gut. As the fist started forward, Gray brought his hand downward and drew the knife across the man's knuckles. Blood spread like a crimson tide. But the fist still dug into his stomach, producing swells of searing pain and dropping Gray to his knees. He gasped. Shook his head. And tried to remember who he was and why he was in such a hurry. Gray. That was his name. Wasn't it? Yeah, that sounded about right, but why was he in a hurry? Mandy, he thought. Yeah, Mandy. Gray watched the man step nearer, ready, no doubt, to deliver one last punch. Gray bided his time, and when Bubba stood right before him, he plunged the knife into the man's thigh. Bubba shrieked and, falling to the parking lot, began to roll around.

Gray pulled to his feet and, with what breath he could muster, said, "You tell Claiborne Lowell . . . Never mind, I'll tell him myself."

Gray left both men writhing in pain. He rushed to his van, started the engine, and with a grinding of gears, backed from the parking slot and then tore out of the motel parking lot. He drove like a madman toward Armstrong's Stable, hoping, praying, that he wasn't too late.

Christine stared at the woman before her, recognizing her, yet not recognizing her. She was the same tall, willowy woman, with butterscotch-colored hair and an air of self-control. Under the circumstances, Christine would have preferred eyes too bright, a voice too loud, and movements nervous and erratic. Instead, she saw dead eyes, heard a calm voice, saw movements steady and sure. They were unnatural, unsettling, frightening.

"Let them go, Sandy," Peyton said.

Sandy smiled in disbelief. "Tell me something,

Peyton, do you want to spend the rest of your life in prison? Do you want to be raped on a regular basis? Because you will be. In fact, you won't last through the first day of incarceration."

"Hurting Amanda, hurting anyone, was never part of the plan," Peyton insisted.

This time Sandy laughed, a soft tinkling of sound that again made Christine's flesh crawl. "This wouldn't have been necessary if you hadn't screwed up everything."

"*I* didn't screw anything up. Ernie Shaw did. If he'd taken her where he was supposed to, Amanda never would have seen the strips of paper." Peyton turned to Christine, his pale blue eyes, now almost colorless, pleading with her to believe him. "It was going to be so simple, and no one was going to get hurt. Just take her, get the money, and release her. I swear to God, I never would have gotten involved if I'd known that it was going to end this way."

If Sandy seemed unnaturally calm, Peyton seemed unnaturally edgy, and that, too, frightened Christine, for it was something she hadn't seen in all their years of marriage. It was as frightening as the long barrel of the gun pointed at her and Amanda.

"Why?" Christine asked. "Why would you get involved in this?"

"I needed money."

"Money? You've got money. More than you could ever hope to spend."

Sandy chuckled. "Had. He had money. It seems that he's been excessively busy embezzling from his company and blaming the losses on poor Jim Lytle."

"Shut up!" Peyton snarled, and this, too, seemed totally out of character. Never once, in all their years of marriage, had Christine heard him raise his voice, even when it would have been justified.

"Don't push me, Peyton," Sandy said smoothly.

Christine, hoping to keep them talking until Gray and Terry could arrive, said, "I don't understand, Peyton. Why embezzle?"

"I didn't set out to. Some of the stocks I invested in cratered, and I was left holding an empty bag. I needed more than half a million to cover the loss. I thought it would be simple to get it back, and so I took a percentage of what my clients gave me to invest and put it on a stock I knew was risky but had been performing well. For six months, I played it. I almost had the half million back, and then practically overnight the company went under. Now, not only had I lost my money, but my clients. I had gone from a half-million to a million-dollar debt. That's all I wanted, Christine. I didn't want a dime more."

Christine thought it seemed some kind of crazy, convoluted point of honor with him that he had kidnapped his supposed daughter only for the exact money he needed.

"Roxie had become suspicious about a special account I'd set up, and so I had to shift the blame onto Jim."

Disbelief crossed Christine's face while a sick feeling settled in her heart. "You would let your good friend take the blame for your actions?"

"I had no choice." At Christine's look of disgust, he said, "I did it for you and Amanda. I couldn't drag you two down with me. You would have had to leave this town if I'd been convicted of embezzling. Surely you can see that I had no choice."

What Christine saw was that she'd never really known this man. Still, she had to ask one more thing.

"But I thought you had millions, Peyton. That's the impression you've always given."

"My family has millions. I'll inherit it, but it wasn't doing me any good now."

"Why not ask for a loan?"

Sandy smiled. "Daddy, could you loan me a million dollars? Your little boy has made some bad investments and has embezzled to boot."

"Will you just shut up!" Peyton cried, then looked away, took a deep, calming breath, and glanced back at Sandy—pleadingly, beseechingly. "Let them go, and you and I can figure out what to do."

"There's only one thing to do." Sandy glanced over at Amanda, who stood at her mother's side. A look of sincere regret crossed her face. "I'm sorry, Amanda. I really do care for you. I kept warning you not to talk about the kidnapping, but you did, didn't you?" Sandy smiled. "I wanted to protect you. God only knows, no one ever did that for me."

"You're bad," Amanda said, her chin upturned in defiance, her gray eyes dark with condemnation.

"Yes, I am, but not every little girl gets to lead the life you do." She motioned the gun toward the horses. "You two mount up."

"What are you doing?" Peyton asked.

"Well, I can't exactly kill them here, can I?"

Kill.

Christine had known what Sandy had in mind, but hearing it expressed so matter-of-factly sent chills down her spine. She instinctively pushed the child behind her.

"No one's going to kill anyone," Peyton said.

"He's right," came a deep, dark, familiar voice.

Christine glanced over to see Gray stepping from the shadows of the forest. She had mixed feelings about his being here. She didn't want his life to be endangered, too, yet, God forgive her, she needed his strength. And if she and Amanda were going to die, she wanted it to be with him.

"Well, well, the gang's all here," Sandy said. "Actually, this will expedite things. I won't have to deal with you later."

Gray stepped past Peyton as though he didn't exist and ignored Sandy, and the gun she held. Instead, he turned his attention to Christine, whose dirty cheek he touched with the back of his hand.

"Are you all right?" he asked in a lover's voice.

"I am now," she whispered, noting his bruised, swelling face. "Are you?"

"Yeah, it's a long story. I'll tell you later."

The word *later* hung in the air like a hopeful promise.

Gray stooped before Amanda and smiled. "I'm going to try real hard to get us out of this. You're going to have to be brave for me. Okay?"

Amanda nodded and stepped closer to him, her hand grabbing a fistful of his shirt, as though she were desperate to adhere herself to him. Gray could feel her fear. It was palpable, swimming through the summer breeze like a dark spirit. It took all the strength he had to tear her hand away. He stood, turned around, and looked from Peyton to Sandy and back to Peyton. Gone was all civility. It was just two males of the species, squaring off over a woman, and in this case a child, leaving sparks of pure hatred to arc between the two of them.

"You son of a bitch," Gray growled. "You were willing to kidnap your own daughter?"

Peyton gave a cold smile. "She isn't my daughter."

"You're damn right. She's *my* daughter—but you didn't know that then."

"Didn't I?" The cold smile turned to a cold sneer. "I suspected that she wasn't my child from the moment she was born." He glanced over at Christine. "Even then, I was willing to give you the benefit of the doubt. But you only confirmed my suspicion every step of the way."

"How?" Christine asked. "I tried so hard."

"Mostly by trying too hard," Peyton said. "You faked every emotion you ever claimed to feel for me. You faked it every time we were intimate." He laughed harshly. "You didn't think I knew, did you? And you didn't think I knew that you often cried yourself to sleep, or that you sometimes sneaked out of bed at night, and went to the nursery, and that you rocked your baby. Sometimes until dawn. Well, dammit, I knew! And it didn't take a rocket scientist to figure out why. I'd heard the rumors about your affair with your gardener, about how Claiborne had run him out of town. It was the only thing that made any sense. And, as if I needed any further confirmation, there was the way you doted on her. She was *his* child. Every time you looked at her, you saw him, remembered him, wanted him. Never once, in all the years we were married, did you want me. All you ever did was tolerate my touch."

Suddenly, Peyton's hostility seemed spent, and his cold smile was replaced by one possessed of warmth.

"I pretended that she was mine, just like I pretended that you cared for me. You taught me how to pretend, Christine, and there were times I couldn't tell reality from pretense. A part of me grew to believe that Amanda was mine. I fell in love with her. How could I not? From the first time her little arms went around my neck, from the first time she called me Daddy, I was hooked." He smiled, sadly, at Christine. "I still love her. I still love you, sometimes so much that I've hated you for not returning my love. If it were possible, I'd take you both back—you as my wife, she as my daughter."

"This is all very touching," Sandy said, "but hardly productive." She motioned toward the horses. "Mount them."

Gray stayed both Christine and Amanda. "No, don't do it." Gray's dark eyes challenged the cool, calm hazel eyes of the woman before him. "If you're going to kill us, you're going to have to do it here, where you'll risk being overheard or overseen. People are walking and riding in these woods. Besides, I don't think you have the guts to pull the trigger on a child that must seem like a daughter to you."

Sandy smiled—serenely. "No one saw me come in, and I saw no one on the trails. The truth is, I can kill you and be away from here before anyone could possibly get here. No one would ever know that I was here. And several people know that someone has been threatening Amanda. Everyone will just assume the threat was carried out. As for Amanda, yes, I care deeply for her and, yes, she's been like a daughter to me, but make no mistake about it, I will kill her. I'll regret having to do so, but I will kill her. Simply because I must."

At Sandy's order to mount the horse, Amanda had stepped away from Gray. He looked at Amanda, at Sandy, then called the latter's bluff. "Then do it."

"Mr. Bannon—"

"Do it!"

The next few seconds played out like a lifetime. Gray saw Sandy's eyes turn dead cold, saw her raise the gun and point it at the child's head, saw her pull the trigger. He had judged the woman wrong. Not only was she capable of taking the child's life, she was going to.

Gray felt his feet moving, his mind racing. He was going to die. He knew this with certainty. A rush of feeling filled him, that nameless feeling, and he thought how appropriate it was that it would be the last thing he felt. Only now he could give it a name. Love. He loved Christine. He always had. He always would. Like Peyton, he'd loved her so much that there had been times that he'd hated her. As for the child, his act would say it all.

Behind him, he heard Christine scream and Peyton shout and then the shattering, stinging report of the gun.

Chapter 23

"He's dead," Terry said.

A sense of disbelief swept through Christine, numbing her to all else. Tears would come later, but now there was only the consoling absence of feeling. There were so many things that she'd wanted to say to him, so many expressions of sorrow and regret. She had wronged him in so many ways that would forever make her indebted to him. In the end, he had paid the supreme price for a child who had never really been his, and that act alone would make her beholden to his memory for the rest of her days.

"C'mon," Nikki said. "Amanda needs you."

Christine looked up into the sad eyes of her friend. She hadn't even known that she was there. She'd seen Terry charging into the meadow with a couple of police officers at almost the precise moment that Sandy had fired the gun. Those officers had carted Sandy away in handcuffs. Sandy had said nothing. She'd simply slipped beneath the protective surface of a cool self-control.

One last look at the still, inert body with the single bullet wound through the heart, and Christine turned away. Tears filled her eyes, not of regret but of gratitude. And for that, she felt no small amount of guilt.

The truth was profoundly simple—she was grateful beyond words that it was Peyton who lay dead and not Gray. For years to come, if not for the whole of her life, she would remember the sight of Gray racing toward their daughter, intent upon exchanging his life for hers. And then, from out of nowhere, running faster than she would have ever thought possible, came Peyton. He had saved Gray.

Christine hobbled forward on her broken heel. As she neared Amanda, who sat between Gray's legs, her back to his chest, Gray glanced up. Their eyes met and merged. She eased to the grass beside him. For long, long minutes, neither spoke.

Gray felt so many emotions that they tumbled one over the other. Foremost, he felt surprise at still being alive. He had unplugged his life, accepted the fact that he was going to die. When he hadn't, a weakness had overtaken him. He had quite literally been unable to stand. In the wake of surprise had come a keen sense of being alive, an intensification of his senses. The sun shone so brightly that it blinded, the birds sang so loudly that they drowned out all other sounds. He was certain that he'd never again take life for granted. And then there was the feeling of love, so strong for this woman, this child, that it consumed him, leaving nothing behind except charred embers of the past.

Gray glanced over at Christine. "Are you okay?"

"Yes. Are you?"

"Yeah."

"What happened to your face?"

"We'll talk about it later," Gray said. He paused, then added, "Is he—"

"Yes."

"I'm sorry," Gray said, wondering at the feelings that must be storming through Christine. Maybe after his death, she had discovered more tender feelings for the man than she'd felt in life. After all, he had been her husband.

Christine saw the question in his eyes. "I'm sorry too. Mostly because all I feel is relieved . . . that it wasn't you."

Gray leaned forward, brushing his lips across Christine's, then trailing kisses across her jaw. He kissed her lightly, then traced a gentle route to her ear, where he placed his mouth and whispered, "I love you."

Later that afternoon, Amanda was told that Peyton had died. She was also told that it was all right to cry. She didn't. Nor did she show any emotion regarding Peyton's or Sandy's involvement in the kidnapping. She merely said that she was glad that it was over.

Gray looked precisely like what he was: a man who'd been in a fight. His bottom lip had doubled in size, and he was seriously working on a black eye. As for his rib cage, it felt as though he'd been tortured on the rack. Christine, who'd been enraged to learn that Claiborne had been responsible, although in his usual cowardly way, urged Gray to see a doctor. He'd told her that he knew something that would make him feel a whole lot better than seeing a doctor.

Seeking out that something, or someone, was precisely what he did after he'd gotten Christine and Mandy settled back at the house. Surely he would be home. His address was easy to find. The house, nestled in the downtown area, was small and the flower beds could have used a weeding, Gray noticed as he leaned on the doorbell.

From inside came a string of curses, then the door was flung wide open. "What the hell—" At the sight of Gray, all the color drained from Claiborne's unshaven face.

Two thoughts crossed Gray's mind: one, Claiborne had been drinking and, two, with his current problems he'd forgotten all about hiring someone to work Gray over.

"I'm not responsible," Claiborne said.

As Gray pushed past him into the house, he said, "Thief, coward, and now a liar. Have you no shame at all?"

"I'm not responsible," Claiborne repeated.

"That's interesting, because the two goons who did this seemed to think that you'd paid them to."

"Look, I've got enough problems—"

"You're right about that. You're up to your sorry neck in them. Do you remember what I said I was going to do if you ever threatened me again?" At the loud gulp that filled the room, Gray smiled. "Ah, you do. Well, a promise is a promise. I'm here to rip off your balls and stuff them down your throat."

Claiborne backed up, but not fast enough to avoid the hard right that landed square on his nose.

When Gray left a few minutes later, Claiborne was sprawled on the floor, his nose bleeding, his left eye swelling, and nausea rising. As for his balls, well, they still hung between his legs, but they sure as hell felt as though they'd been wedged into his throat.

•   •   •

Christine was sure that she would not have made it through the next few days without Esther's help. Mother hen and devoted friend that she was, she'd moved in with her and Amanda and had taken care of the innumerable, and endless, chores that needed to be done. Under the circumstances, Peyton's funeral had been lowkey. Ironically, he was buried on the day their divorce became final. She had tried to feel something as she'd stared at his lifeless body, his golden hair un-ruffled, his tan rich, his suit immaculate, but she couldn't. And all she could think was that he looked very much in death as he had in life—perfect. She would forgive him for what he'd done to Amanda, she knew. She had once made a mistake, and had paid for that mistake with ten years of her life. He, too, had made a mistake and had paid for it with his life. Surely, both debts had been settled.

As for Gray, whose bruises were finally on the mend, necessity had demanded that she see less of him, although he had remained in town to lend a hand and a shoulder to lean on. She clung to his declaration of love. She'd known that he loved her, but hearing it was well worth the wait, as was hearing him call Amanda *his* daughter. The child herself had shed not a single tear, had refused to go to the funeral, and hadn't spo-ken one word about Peyton, or Sandy. It was as though both had ceased to exist. Amanda spent most of her time with Biddie.

Wednesday morning, Esther returned to Rosemead. Wednesday afternoon, Terry called and asked if he and Nikki could come over that evening to bring her up to date on all they'd learned. Christine was eager to have the answers to her many questions. She called Gray and asked him to join them.

At a few minutes before seven o'clock, the doorbell

rang and Christine forced herself not to rush to answer
it. On the way, she fiddled with her hair like a silly
schoolgirl. She took a deep breath, opened the door,
and met a pair of eyes as hungry as hers.

Gray took in the woman before him. He had spent
a lot of time the last few days wondering what their
future held. And missing her. God, how he'd missed
her!

"Hi," she said in a soft voice.

"Hi," he said in a voice barely louder than a whisper.

"Come in," she said, stepping back to allow him to
enter.

He walked into the living room, his eyes still on her.

"Your face looks better," she told him.

"I'll live," he said.

Suddenly, he moaned and, reaching out, placed his
hand at the back of her neck. He drew her to him and
placed his lips on hers. He kissed her hungrily, like a
man in love. She kissed him with the same hunger, the
same love.

"Ah, Gray," she whispered, "I've missed you."

Gray. He loved the sound of his name on her lips.
"I've missed you too."

Christine smile, but the smile faded. "Tell me you
love me."

"I love you," he whispered, brushing his lips across
hers, then settling his mouth back on hers, simply because he couldn't help himself. Reluctantly, he pulled
from her, saying, "How's Mandy?"

"I'm worried about her. She says very little, and
only when asked a direct question. She won't discuss
Peyton or Sandy. I know she's hurting, but I can't
reach her."

Gray thought of all she must be feeling, after learning that those she cared about had betrayed her, after watching one carted off in handcuffs, the other die before her very eyes. That was asking a lot of an adult, much less a child. And yet, he knew that this child was strong. "She'll be all right. I know it."

At that moment, the doorbell rang.

"I'm going to go say a quick hello to Mandy," Gray said as he started from the room.

"Gray?"

He turned.

"I love you."

Sweet seconds passed as the words enfolded him. "I know."

He walked on through the house until he reached his daughter's—*his* daughter's—bedroom. He found the child sitting on the floor drawing. "Hi, pretty lady," he said, squatting beside her.

Amanda glanced up. He was always struck by how much she looked like a young Christine.

"Hi," she said.

"Whatcha doing?"

"Drawing," she responded, but nothing more.

"What are you drawing?"

"Things."

"Things are nice." He paused, then asked, "How about we fertilize your tomato plants tomorrow?"

"Okay."

He waited for her to say something more, but when she didn't, he said, "I've got to go talk to Mr. Carrelli and Aunt Nikki."

Nothing. And so he stood. At the door, he turned and glanced back at her. She was bent over her drawing. Sighing, he walked toward the living room.

"Hi," Nikki said, as he entered the room. "How is she?"

"The same," Gray responded, taking a seat next to Christine on the sofa.

"I was just telling Christine that we have things pretty well wrapped up," Terry said. "Sandy has proven to be remarkably cooperative. If on the strange side. Her jailers tell me that she's a neat freak. She actually gets on her hands and knees and mops the cell floor with a wet handkerchief. She's been charged with kidnapping, murder, and attempted murder."

"Why?" Christine asked. "That's the one question I want an answer to."

"For the money," Terry answered. "But not in the usual sense. To understand Sandy Killian, you have to understand her childhood." And he proceeded to tell them what he'd found out.

"When she came to Rosemead, she saw the kind of total power Merritt Lowell had over others, the total control he had over his life, and she concluded that big money equaled big control."

Christine looked incredulous. "You're saying that from the moment she came to us, she was just biding her time until she could kidnap Amanda?"

"Maybe yes, maybe no," Terry said. "She was looking to make a big score in some way. Frankly, I don't think she was in any hurry. She considered observing Merritt sort of like . . . well, sort of like studying at the feet of the master."

"That he was," Gray admitted, and not nicely.

"After he died, I think she started looking for opportunities to score. About a year ago, she and Peyton became lovers, and she got her first break when Peyton admitted to needing money because of the embezzlement. She wanted money; he needed money. The decision was made the day she found Ernie Shaw here ranting and raving and making threats. She must have thought this was heaven-sent. Here was someone to do the dirty work and to take the fall if things turned sour. Ernie Shaw was just angry enough to do it."

The plan was simple. Sandy was deliberately late that day in order to give Ernie Shaw an opportunity to pick Amanda up. As she left Rosemead, headed for school, she placed the ransom note in the mailbox. Ernie Shaw was supposed to take Amanda to some rented property just outside of town. For a reason Sandy was never certain of—he'd hemmed and hawed about it—Ernie Shaw took Amanda to his house instead and put her in the attic. And gave her bathroom privileges, which proved to be their undoing.

"So, when Peyton walked into Shaw's house that night," Gray said, "he knew that Mandy was there?"

"Yes," Terry said. "He must have been torn in half. Part of him wanted her found, but part of him must have feared what she'd seen or heard. He must have been overwhelmingly relieved when he'd found the knotted paper in the bathroom and was able to flush it. But that relief lasted only until he realized that Amanda had bathroom privileges. From then on, he and Sandy were sitting on a powder keg."

"I asked Mandy if she'd heard anything," Gray said, "and she said that she couldn't with the fan going. I also asked her if she'd seen anything strange, but, of course, she hadn't. She had seen what was perfectly normal, what she'd seen Peyton do innumerable times, what she must have assumed everyone did when nervous."

"I'm sure that's how she saw it," Terry said. "Just as I'm sure that at that point Sandy saw no solution except to warn Amanda not to talk about the kidnapping. I sincerely believe that she didn't want to harm her, that she cared for her. From the inception of the kidnapping, she had made it plain that Amanda wasn't to be hurt, and, of course, that's the only way Peyton would have agreed."

"In the meadow," Christine murmured, "she said she tried to protect Amanda, because there hadn't been anyone to protect her."

"In the end," Terry said, "Amanda had to be protected from her."

"But wasn't she taking a risk just marching into the school bathroom and threatening Amanda?" Nikki asked.

"Not really," Terry said. "If anyone had seen her at school, they would have recognized her as Amanda's nanny and assumed she had legitimate business there."

"I remember the principal saying that she'd asked the teachers if they'd seen a stranger," Christine said.

"Of course, they hadn't," Terry said.

"What about the mirror?" Gray asked.

"She claims she had no part in that, and I believe her. I think it was an accident but," he hastened to add, "she must have secretly delighted in the fact that it could have been interpreted as a threat.

"Somewhere along the line, maybe after the mirror incident, which he was never certain that Sandy hadn't been responsible for, Peyton grew frightened of Sandy and began to keep a nightly vigil. Without question, he kept a vigil after she'd blatantly come to the new house. He wasn't so much worried about the days because Sandy was keeping Amanda less and you two were staying with her more. She knew something was going on when I came to town, and then when that psychologist came to town, but she didn't know exactly what it was. But she sensed that things were closing in on her. I think this is when she really began to lose it. She talked about black headaches and bad dreams and her neat fetish went crazy."

At this, Christine walked to the mantel. She touched the eighteenth-century porcelain figurine and thought how fragile it was, how fragile people were, yet how resilient too, for how else could she explain the longevity of the figurine, of Sandy? Would her daughter prove as resilient?

"I know this sounds crazy," she said, "but a part of me feels sorry for her."

"I think it's fair to acknowledge what she went through," Terry said, "but she isn't the only person who was molested as a child. In the end, she chose her path."

"I don't know that I agree. Some of us choose the paths for others. I set Peyton on a path when I married him, a loveless path that he didn't deserve. I wish you could tell me that he and Sandy were hopelessly, madly, in love with each other, that he'd finally found someone to return the tender feelings that I couldn't."

"I wish I could too, Christine," Terry said. "If it's any consolation, I think that Sandy did care for him."

"And Peyton?" Christine asked.

"Perhaps he got out of it what he most wanted."

"I'd be remiss if I didn't say that he was a nice man," Christine admitted, "that he deserved better than I gave him. He was always so . . ."

"Noble," Nikki said with a smile. "He ended his life on a noble note. And I think—I know—that he would have preferred this ending to life without you and Amanda. He certainly would have preferred it to the ignoble legal repercussions he would have had to face. As hard as it is to say, this ending was far the best for Peyton."

"Yes, it is," Christine said, looking over at Terry. "How can I ever thank you?"

"You just did," Terry said, coming to his feet. "Now Nikki and I need to be on our way."

Thanks were again exchanged, hands were shook, and the hope of seeing each other again was expressed, and then Gray and Christine were left alone in the living room. She did what had always come so naturally. She eased into Gray's arms.

Christine whispered, "Don't leave me tonight."

Silence filled the interior of the car, and Terry was certain Nikki suspected what had to be said at some point that night. Both had gone the long way around to keep from mentioning it, both had worked hard at talking about anything, everything, else. Even as he thought about it, he had no idea what the words would be, or what would be agreed upon. He knew only that an emptiness was already taking hold inside him—an emptiness, a loneliness, that, quite frankly, he hadn't expected to feel. The truth was, he hadn't expected to feel what he was feeling for this woman, things he'd not felt for another, things he didn't want to look at too closely.

"I think they're doing fine," Nikki said. "I mean, considering what they've been through."

"Yeah," Terry said, glad to avoid the subject a little bit longer.

"Amanda will come around," Nikki said. "Kids always survive."

"Without question."

"You were right not to tell Christine about Peyton and Sandy." Nikki said. "She doesn't need any more guilt to carry around."

"And Gray doesn't need to know, either." Terry had learned a long time ago that sexual practices were as varied as the people performing them. And that, oftentimes, they fell under the heading of downright weird. As far as the game Peyton and Sandy played, it was just pathetic. Demanding that she pretend to be Christine, even calling her Christine, was pathetic.

"Pathetic," Nikki said, causing Terry to smile and add, "I was just thinking the same thing."

Silence, then he glanced over at her and said, "You know very well what we're avoiding."

"Yes. So, when do you leave?"

"In the morning." He could feel her disappointment. Hell, he felt it too! "Look, you knew that I was an FBI agent, that I traveled a lot. We both knew this moment was going to come."

"Yes, I knew that. It's okay."

"No it isn't," he growled, his Eastern accent sounding even more pronounced. "I'm going to miss you like hell!"

"Does that mean I'm going to see you again?"

"You want the truth?"

Nikki shuddered at what she knew was coming, but she said, "Yes, I want the truth."

"I came here thinking, hoping, that if we made love, I'd get you out of my system. That maybe we'd even date a while . . . until you started making demands I couldn't meet."

"I see."

"No you don't. That's what I came here thinking, but now . . . now, I'm not sure what I'm thinking. No, that isn't true. I'm thinking that you scare the hell out of me. I'm thinking that I don't know what to think anymore."

But he did know some of what he thought. He

thought, more and more, of blond-haired children, children whose hair he could ruffle, children whom he could hug. He thought, too, of the love that Gray and Christine shared—the way their hands entwined, the way they looked at each other, their complete and absolute happiness. He was no longer certain that he wanted to live without that kind of happiness.

In seconds, he was pulling into the driveway of her house. He shut off the engine. Silence and the dark night descended. Neither moved. He angled his body so that he could see her, but deliberately kept his hands off her. He couldn't think straight otherwise.

"I want you to know that I've been happier these last few days than I can ever remember being."

Nikki hesitated, striving for the right words. They might well be the most important of her life, for, faced with the possibility of losing this man, she knew very well what she wanted for the future. "Am I wrong in thinking that you feel something for me? There's something more than sex going on here, isn't there?"

"Yes, and that's why you scare the hell out of me," he said, seeing images of those blond-haired children again, hearing a voice deep inside him whispering that he wanted to love and be loved, that maybe he was already in love with Nikki, hearing another voice say that life is short and death is long.

She strove for those special words again. "I care for you. Deeply. Passionately. Much more than I was expecting to. But it's all happened so fast, and that's part of the problem. Could we just take things slow and easy and see where they lead? Would you give me enough time to win your trust? You said it took a special woman to be an agent's wife. I'm pretty special, and I already have one failed marriage to my credit. I wouldn't want another."

Terry couldn't help but smile. "I think I could give you some time."

She smiled too. "Well, I figure that we have two choices for the remainder of our brief time together. One, we can sit here looking at each other, or, two, we can go into the house and make love until dawn."

"Hmm, that's a tough one," he said, "but I guess I'll choose two."

In minutes, a trail of clothes led to the bedroom, where Nikki began to show him how truly special she could be.

Gray awoke suddenly.

Straining through the silence, he sought out what had awakened him. He heard the sound of the clock as it dutifully ticked away time. And then there were the soft, even sleep-sighs of the woman nestled in his arms. Occasionally, there was a creak as the house shifted and settled. Beyond that, nothing. No, wait. Something. Faint, but audible. Weeping? Yes, small sobs. That could be coming from only one place.

Gray tried to ease from the bed without waking Christine, but the task proved impossible.

"What is it?" she asked, her voice groggy.

Reaching for his clothes, Gray said, "Mandy. I think she's crying."

Christine turned on the lamp, bathing the bedroom in light and catching the last of Gray's bare body as it disappeared into khakis and a shirt. He'd started from the room before Christine could collect her forgotten gown and robe from the floor.

The hallway proved dark and difficult, but Gray headed toward the dim night-light in Mandy's bedroom. He found Biddie restlessly pacing beside the bed. Even Hamlet, the hamster, spun its wheel in wild agitation. Gray found the child balled in a knot in the middle of the bed—crying in her sleep. Gently, he sat on the side of the bed and, not wanting to startle her, whispered her name. No response. He called again. Still no response. Just heartrending sobs.

Finally, he shook her slightly. Instantly, she came awake, a terrified look filling her tear-moist eyes.

"It's Gray, sweetie. You were having a bad dream."

Amanda's breath, rough and ragged, tore at the room's silence, just as her appearance tore at Gray's heart. She'd cried until wisps of her hair had become plastered to her cheeks. Her chest, concealed beneath a long gown, heaved with fear and exertion. He reached out his hand, intending to brush the hair from her cheek, but an impulsive urge overtook him. Tenderly, he grasped her shoulders and pulled her into his arms, one hand at her back, the other cradling her head. She went to him with the same naturalness with which he'd reached for her. She grasped his shirt in her hand, and laid her cheek against his bare chest. Skin to skin. Warmth to warmth. Father to daughter.

Instead of her tears ceasing, however, they grew in number and intensity. Gray started to try to quiet her, but in the end, he figured that she'd earned a good cry. And so he just held her, imagining all that she was crying for—for the loss of a man she'd loved for nearly ten years, for his betrayal of her, for the betrayal of a woman whom she'd cared so much for. Again, he thought that all this was such a heavy load for a child to bear. At some point, it struck him that she was clinging to his shirt with a near-desperation, as if she feared he might vanish, go away, die, as had Peyton.

"I'm not going away, Mandy," he whispered, as he began to rock her gently.

Christine watched from the foot of the bed. She was happy that Gray was here for Amanda, and relieved that Amanda was having a good cry. It was time to cleanse, to bury the past, to move ahead. For herself as well. No more guilt because she couldn't care for Peyton. No more guilt because his touch didn't move her. She'd never belonged to him. Only to Gray. No more paying for a mistake that had been paid for long ago. Christine walked to the empty side of the bed and crawled in, her gaze going to Gray.

In time, Amanda fell asleep, and Gray gently eased her from his chest and to the middle of the bed. She sighed softly. Biddie had quieted too, as had Hamlet. Gray lay down beside his daughter, but felt compelled to place his hand on her—in a comforting gesture, although it was uncertain whether it was to comfort him or her. When Christine laid hers atop his, a nameless feeling came over him, an emotional contentment that had something to do with the three of them being united. It felt good, almost mystical and magical. And he hoped he felt it a million more times.

Epilogue

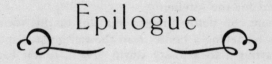

At the sound of crying, Gray awoke and squinted his eyes at the bedside clock, which read 2:15 A.M. At the same time, Christine stirred and, like an automaton, threw off the bedcovers.

"I'll get him," Gray said.

"I'll get him," Christine mumbled, although she made no attempt to rise.

Gray grinned, reached over and drew the bedcovers back over his wife. "Sure you will."

He grappled in the dark for his robe, and padding barefoot down the hallway, he headed for the nursery. A night-light glowed, illuminating the rocking-chair teddy-bear motif. Gray switched on the teddy-bear lamp and looked down at his son. Joshua Grayson Bannon, three months old, looked back——with a little face squinted from crying, little hands balled into fists, and little feet kicking the dickens out of the air.

"Hey, Josh, what's all this racket about?"

At Gray's voice, Joshua quieted.

Gray smiled. "If I didn't know better, I'd say you just wanted your ole man up."

Joshua responded with a couple of cooing sounds that sounded remarkably like, "Would I do that?"

"Yeah, I think you would," Gray said, checking to see if the baby's diaper was wet. It was, and so Gray changed it, then bundled the baby in a blanket and headed for the kitchen.

There, he deftly juggled his son on his shoulder, while retrieving a bottle from the refrigerator and microwaving it to a toasty warm. Then, it was back to the nursery and the rocking chair that he'd insisted upon. He'd also insisted upon a vine-covered cottage, which had sent the Atlanta, Georgia, realtor into a tailspin. One had finally been found on a two-acre tract outside the city limits, which meant that he and Christine had to drive forty-five minutes one way to their jobs, he to the nursery, she to her antique shop, but, hey, it was worth it.

Even now, it sometimes seemed like a dream that he and Christine were married. They had spent the previous summer taking turns visiting each other, Christine and Amanda coming to Atlanta, he returning to Natchez, several trips apiece, until finally, he'd announced emphatically that they were moving to Atlanta, that they'd all wasted enough time, that he missed them far too much when they were gone.

At the end of August, he and Christine had been married in a simple ceremony, with Nikki her only attendant. He'd wanted to buy her a diamond ring, but she'd insisted that she wanted only a gold band. And so they'd bought matching bands, each inscribed with a single word *forever*. Within three months, Christine had been pregnant, a fact that had pleased them both. Mandy had been excited, too, about the prospect of a sibling—as long as it wasn't a pesky brother. Within two weeks of Joshua's birth, however, Thumper mysteriously showed up in the baby's crib, which he and Christine took as the ultimate approval.

Gray stared down at his son, his little cheeks moving in and out in a sucking motion. A baby. A son. A small miracle, with tiny fingers and tiny toes and blue eyes and a head of midnight-black hair that tended to go in a dozen different directions at once. And skin so soft that it had to be touched to be believed. Yeah, Josh was a full-fledged miracle. A very special baby, because this child he'd followed from inception to birth, and he'd follow him well beyond. He'd be there for first steps, first words, first Christmas, hugs, kisses, tricycles, bicycles, scrapes and spills, first day of school, and all else.

In her own way, their daughter was special too. She had been, and always would be, their first child, and the very fact that he'd missed so much with her only made the things he wouldn't miss all that much more special. He'd be there for her teenage years, for high school graduation, and for college, and for dating—if he decided to let her. And he was so very proud of her, the way she'd bounced back after an ordeal that would have left many adults floundering. Not that everything was forgotten. There was still an occasional question that left no doubt the events of the previous summer continued to plague her, but for the most part, she'd gone on with her life. One day, out of the clear blue, she'd called him Daddy, a fact he wasn't at all certain she'd even realized. But he had.

Removing the nipple from the baby's mouth, Gray placed the child on his shoulder and patted the infant's back until he burped. He cradled him in his arms again and replaced the nipple in the baby's mouth. Josh attacked it as though he hadn't eaten in the whole of his life. Gray smiled. And that nice warm feeling washed through him. The feeling he'd once got only when he and Christine and Mandy were together. In part, it was love. Beyond that, it was the soul-deep satisfaction of being part of a family.

When the bottle was empty, when final burps were accomplished, Gray began to rock the baby. And to sing a lullaby that dwelled in the shadows of his mind.

Christine awoke to the warm, friendly rays of the October sun. Still groggy, she stretched out her hand in search of her husband. His side of the bed was empty. She smiled, knowing full well where she'd find father and son. *Father and son.* What an incredible phrase. As incredible as *husband and wife, father and daughter.* Christine sought out the ring on her left hand, as though needing confirmation that this incredible year really had happened. The ring was there, testimony to their marriage, but still she sought proof. Rolling to her side, she glanced up at the crystal vase of lavender roses. Yes, they were there. While she had been busy furnishing their vine-covered cottage with antiques, Gray, with Amanda's help, had been busy out of doors, creating a fairy-tale garden. The first thing he'd planted was half a dozen lavender rosebushes, exactly of the variety that once had grown at Rosemead. Throughout the spring and the fall, they bloomed, lush and full, leaving a sweet honeyed scent to sail around the yard and the house. A scent rich in memories. A scent rich in promises.

Yes, it had been an incredible year. She and Nikki had decided to stay in business together and open another branch of the Natchez store in Atlanta, which meant that she often saw her friend. Occasionally, the two couples—Nikki and Terry had married just that spring; it had been quite a leap of faith for Terry, although Christine knew, with certainty, that the marriage would last—vacationed together. On their first vacation following that momentous summer, Nikki had told her about knowing Mitchell Hoogland in a more than casual way. She thought Nikki felt guilty, as though she'd somehow been responsible for what Mitchell had done. Christine had assured her that that was nonsense.

As for Claiborne and Mitchell Hoogland, they both were serving time in prison. It would have been so easy to write Claiborne out of her life, but, oddly, it was Gray, with his newfound sense of family, who convinced her that she mustn't. She would never forget what Claiborne had done, and a part of her might always be angry—no, hurt—but he was family and blood ties were binding. She'd written Claiborne several times, but didn't receive an answer until a month ago. A letter had arrived, thanking her for the letters and telling her how pleased he was at the birth of her son. It wasn't a whole lot, but it was a beginning.

As for Sandy, she, too, was in prison. Rumor had it that her cell was a showplace of neatness. Christine had returned to Natchez to testify against her trusted employee. Forgiveness was not so easy here. In fact, she hoped never to see Sandy again. As for Rosemead, it had been donated to the historical society, and Esther, free at last of the responsibilities she'd so long and so capably met, was cruising the world. Her last postcard had been mailed from Singapore. Lowell Enterprises had a new head, and Christine's only remaining job was to sit on the board of directors.

Slipping from bed, she headed for the nursery. Sure

enough, she found Gray asleep with the baby in his arms. She had never known happiness like this. She thought of the marriage, the pregnancy, this one so easy, the way Gray had loved every moment of the nine months. He had loved hearing the baby's heart-beat, seeing the sonogram, feeling that first flighty kick. She had loved the way he cradled her stomach, the way he told her that she was beautiful even when she didn't feel it, the way he'd been at her side at the birth of this child. She loved the way he loved her, their children, the way he never took anything for granted. Nor did she. While she didn't dwell on the past, neither did she forget it. Certainly not Peyton's sacrifice. Knowing him as she had, she believed that he would want both her and Amanda to be happy. In some inexplicable way, being happy was her gift to him.

She stepped into the room and gently took the baby from Gray, then laid the sleeping infant in the crib, right next to a worn Thumper. She stared down at her son. He was so perfect, she thought, drawing a knuckle across his cheek. She hoped that he would grow up exactly like his father. She glanced at the nearby clock. Almost seven o'clock. Josh would soon want a bottle and Mandy, Biddie at her side, would want breakfast. If she hurried, she might have time to put a pot of coffee on to perk. She'd just let Gray sleep, she thought, and she stepped quietly by him. In one quick movement, a hand manacled her wrist and pulled her down onto a lap. She stared up into a face framed by a lock of wayward hair and a stubble of beard. He looked like a derelict. He looked completely delicious.

Christine smiled and whispered, "You scared me!"

"Did I, Gypsy Lady?" he whispered back, brushing the hair from her face.

"Yes, you did," she said, placing the palm of her other hand against his scratchy beard.

With a sexy growl, Gray said, "You really should be scared of me. I gobble Gypsy ladies up for breakfast."

"That sounds . . . promising."

Gray grinned. "Fearless, huh?"

"Fearless," Christine repeated, drawing his lips down to hers.

From somewhere came the scent of a satin-soft rose, a scent that neither Christine nor Gray could ever be indifferent to. No more than they could ever be indifferent to their past. Theirs was a love honed and tempered by the fire of pain, a love forged in regret, and because of this, their love was steel-strong, certain, and forever sure.

About the Author

Sandra Canfield, a.k.a. Karen Keast, lives in Shreveport with her husband, Charles, her staunchest supporter. Sandra, a very diverse writer has published mainstream, contemporary, and historical romances. Sandra's fans say they read her books because of their humor, sexual tension, and unusual plots. Sandra's favorite reads are bloody murder mysteries. Her favorite author is Agatha Christie, to whom Sandra wrote her first fan letter.